American Isekai:
Entr~~
The

Curtis Yost

American Isekai: Entrance into Madness

Curtis Yost

Published by Curtis Yost, 2025.

Copyright © 2025 Curtis Yost
All rights reserved, including the right to reproduce this book or portions thereof in form whatsoever.
Edited by Anonymous
Cover Art by Sienna Arts

This is a work of fiction. Similarities to real people, places, or events are entirely coincidental.

AMERICAN ISEKAI: ENTRANCE INTO MADNESS

First edition. February 14, 2025.

Copyright © 2025 Curtis Yost.

ISBN: 979-8230787297

Written by Curtis Yost.

This book is dedicated to the people that want to start over and think it's too late. The feeling of needing to see your vision come true. This book is the start to a new beginning where I won't let anyone dictate what is written. This is for my fellow Indie authors.

If you wish to contact me:

I am Curtis Yost Author on Facebook.

@realcurtisyost on Tik Tok

Email is curtisyostmail@gmail.com

Chapter 1

Death is only the beginning. Throughout history, philosophies from Christianity to Buddhism have tried to figure out what happens after death. Some believe that you will die and come back into the body of a new human. Others believe the only way is to believe in an almighty deity. Unfortunately, there is only one way to know. You must die.

My name was Jacob Smith. I was thirty-three years old and wishing every day the world would end. Please bear with me, I'm trying to remember the first world. A world that you currently know. The city of New York was where I was born, but not where I always lived. I came here because I felt a calling.

I'll start off by saying. When that alarm goes off in the morning, the first words that come out of my mouth are "Fuck." Awakening from a slumber was always the worst part of my days. That morning groan of having to move your muscles. I was in the most relaxed position to sleep and was now being forced to go out into the world.

While I'm remember this, I want you to keep in mind. This is a memory from a dream that I have every night. Once I went to the afterlife, I lost all my memories of the first world. The only way to remember is to dream at night and let a few select nightmares show who I used to be. The way my thoughts are during the dreams. I'm not sure if I was a good guy or a bad guy. The only thing that I know is that justice was the answer to all my problems.

When I opened my eyes, I looked around. The apartment that I lived in was small and had only one bedroom. The walls were covered in wallpaper that was falling. The paper had red roses all over it. The only reason I think the landowner chose the wallpaper was because it was cheap and would cover up the water stains behind.

The water stains could be seen running up the wall and somewhat across the ceiling. The stretched-out stain looked like a man wearing a top hat. I called that one Abraham Lincoln. A little childish to call it that, but who else was going to know. Well, back then nobody would have known. I guess I just told the world.

I sat up to start my boring and mundane life. My day at the office was about to begin, and I didn't have enough time to eat. At least, at work, there was a pot of coffee. I need that little pick me up to get through the day. The smell of it would sometimes be enough to wake me up. Other days, I would need to drink a gallon of coffee just to stay upright.

In front of me, I had a Zbox and a thirty-two-inch television. I used to play all kinds of games on it, but since the games got so damn expensive. I usually rented dvds from the blue box and played it on the Zbox. My goal was to one day have internet to watch tv or to at least get cable. The only way I could do these things was with my phone. Everything was expensive. I could only get something new if my money allowed me to.

My childhood was... It was fucked up. In the beginning, I went to several foster homes. Some of the sights and smells that came from them were...evil. You would not believe what happens in the foster care system. One after another I ended up with people whose only goal was to make money. People in this world always need a motive to do good.

You really don't need to know more than that for now. People don't need to know what my childhood was truly like. The last thing I want people to think is that I'm some kind of victim. There are plenty of victims in the world. I know this because I have met them. I remember faces. I remember the look on their faces. I saw the look of horror and fear of living in this world when I closed my eyes. There must be a reason I remember these things. God only lets me remember what I'm supposed to.

The only reason I brought this up was the families in the foster care system. They were doing illegal things that were unspeakable. I witnessed the horrible monstrosities these people did to the children. The victims needed to see justice. With the help of my adopted family, I managed to save a lot of children.

The University of New York accepted me. I was in for four years and came out of college with a bachelor's degree. My time was put to good use. I immediately came to work for a company that was known for saving children. It paid less than other places were willing, but the reputation attracted me.

Anyway, on with my last day in this world. I was sitting up in bed and looking overtop of my television. There were a set of swords that I got from a collector. I can't remember the reason why I got them. They were exact replicas of the swords Superman had on his back. The shine on the blades came from the window next to me. The bright light might be enough to burn a hole in the wall one day. I needed to be careful.

Next to the swords was a poster of Superman. Behind him was a Red Moon. The Red Moon was a sign that someone was slain that night. A myth that became all to real in the afterlife. The swords were strapped to his back and drops of blood were dripping to the ground. The idea of a man that became a borderline god intrigued me. As a child, I wished my father was a superhero just like him. It turned out. My biological father was more of a villain than a hero.

The blades on Superman's back were made of Sinomian steel. It would vibrate and slice through even the hardest of steels as long as you were fast enough. Superman was faster than light. That was the reason he needed to face the ultimate comic book run, the Demon Saga. They were the only ones that could deflect Superman's blades from attacks.

Superman would stand tall against the forces around him. There was a mask he would always wear. It reminded me of a masked wrestler. There was a star on the forehead of the mask. The color of the mask was golden, and the star was red. The shirt on his costume was blue and made of rippling effect. It looked like fish scales. His pants were green and looked that same as the shirt. His costume was also made of Sinomian steel.

My friends and I always laughed at Superman. It always looked like he had a massive bulge in his pants. It was like putting massive tits on a female superhero. I'm guessing because it is the only logic for overexaggerating a feature like that. It was like staring at porn stars dick at times.

Superman could also fly around the world in less than a second. This led to him saving the world within seconds during one of the storylines. The world needed to be saved, and he had to rewind time to save them all. People called the story corny, but I didn't care. It was one of the greatest things to read as a child.

You're probably asking yourself. Why is this guy telling me about his favorite superhero? In time, you will see. It actually plays a more crucial role in my story than telling you about my time in foster care. The idea of being a superhero would be the driving force for killing the ultimate villain in the next life.

My mornings weren't my proudest moments. I would wake up with a smile. The window would be open. I would look across the street to the building. The building would scare the shit out of me with all the gargoyles that were placed across it. They would distract me during the times when she wasn't there.

Every morning there was a girl that I was deeply attracted to. Her hair was blonde. Between the hours of five and six she would go for a morning jog. She had three pairs of blue pants that would cling to her so tight that there was no for imagination. She wouldn't wear a shirt and only wear a sports bra. I can't believe she got away with running around in a bra every morning, but the cops didn't care.

I would rush to the window and stare out like I was watching the cars. My hands would be behind my back and crossed. It was a stance that my adopted father taught me. I'm not sure why, but it became natural to sit in this position anytime that I needed to stand still. The relaxed position also allowed me to let my freak flag fly.

I watched her open the curtains to her glass door that would lead to her balcony. Every morning, she would stare up at me. My window was always open. I wasn't sure if it was for me or someone upstairs. All I knew was that she appeared to be an exhibitionist. All she really wanted was the attention of anyone that was willing to give it to her.

Beads of sweat would roll down her forehead. The run was long. They were always long. She was fit and could run for the full hour. The bra she would wear would change from a light gray to an almost black color from all the sweat. It was damp and needed a thorough wash. Some days I would think, maybe I should see where she does laundry and try to ask her out. I never did because that seemed stalkerish.

The girl would stand in front of the glass door. She would gaze upon the city while removing her bra. Her breasts looked so supple and sweet. I would give my left nut to have one night with this girl. I would swear it every damn day. She would show off by taking a towel and wiping under her breasts. They would glisten from all the sweat and needed wiping.

I wouldn't blink as she would remove her pants. She would never wear underwear while exercising. I don't know the reason but everyone that walked past her would see the perfect curvature of her ass and nice shape of her camel toe. When she removed the pants, she would reach down and would wipe that down too. It was mostly the thigh area but would rub herself a little too much.

The girl's right hand would be placed against the glass leaving behind a handprint. The sweat and heat from her body would have a sealed steam mark that would be left behind. Her left hand would continue to rub down there. Her eyes looked like they were rolling back into her head. Her teeth would be clenched. I would imagine in my mind her making a moaning sound. Sometimes the show was more than I could bear. That was one of those days.

The girl's arms were shaking from the intensity. She would drop to her knees. The towel she was using would be tossed to the side. She would sit back and spread her legs. I would watch her clean shaven pussy stare back at me. Her arms would be pushed behind her body and kept her up. Her chest would go up and down from exhausting herself. A small jiggle would happen before she would stand up and walk to her bathroom. If you watched long enough, you would see steam coming from the direction she went.

The water she used had to be scalding hot. The steam would fill the house when she opened the door. The glass door would fog up and make it hard to see anything for a while. The water would drip down the door and leave lines. After a few times of seeing this happen, I chose not to stick around for this part. I always enjoyed her shows.

I would be done and leave my room. The door next to my bedroom was a small bathroom. Inside the bathroom was a small sink that barely fit in there. The knobs were thick on the tips and would need to be pulled in a counterclockwise position to turn them on. The sink had a hole in the bottom and was shaped like a bowl. I would have to pull my toothbrush and shaving kit from my dresser every morning because of the lack of space.

The walls were covered in lime green colored tiles. Each square had white and black inside. No matter how many times I tried to scrub the walls. The black would not disappear. The landlord summed it up to old age and wouldn't do anything to replace what was probably black mold. I guess that was what you get for living in the slums.

I sat down on the toilet to do my morning glory. It was hard to sit because my shoulders were placed on the glass shower door and the sink. Both things were hard and cold. When you had a hard time affording heat for your place. It really sucked. It would be like going into an ice storm and putting a cold compress on.

Once done, I would jump into the shower. My time on the toilet was short due to the discomfort. I would look down and noticed my happiness. The show the girl was still taking effect. It couldn't be helped. I was a man after all. Did I put myself in this position? The answer is yes. I would say when it came to things of the flesh. I was a bit of a masochist.

I would never give myself enough time to get around. I would turn on the water and hope that it would warm up quickly. My hands would be placed against the wall. The cold would cause me to arch my back. The water would flow down where my spine was. My back had so much muscle. It created a stream down went down and fell off around where my ass was.

The heat after a while would kick in. My body would stop shaking from being in a constant state of freezing. The heat would kick on to above scalding temperatures. My back would turn red and was on the verge of getting first degree burns. I didn't care and would enjoy each drop like it was massaging my body.

Once I would get comfortable, I would think about two different women. The first you know about. The girl that was constantly filling up my spank bank every morning. The other was the hottest red headed woman I had ever known. She was a childhood friend. I was always afraid of dating her. I didn't want to get attached due to secrets that we were both keeping. I would call her my best friend, but I always got a feeling she was using me.

I think you can figure out the rest. I don't need to get into details about what I do in the shower. You can use your own imagination for that. Also, it just feels weird talking about my sexual part of my life. Even if it is a solo job. That is something that needs to stay private. No pun intended.

When I would get out of the shower, I never seemed to have any towels. I owned one towel, and it was always going missing or put in one of my shirt drawers by mistake. The cold would take over and I would shake my body like a dog. I didn't need to get rid of most of the water in the bathroom. The water on the floor would always evaporate over time. I didn't think it would matter that much. I just had to be careful not to slip and fall. One wrong move and I would break my neck on the damn toilet.

Since the bathroom was always wet when I finished, I would never bring my clothes in. I mean do I really have to explain it. It was my apartment. I had every right to walk around with no clothes on. I would even lift my knees up to open that area between my balls and my legs. The cool area would flow between there. That was a glorious moment. I never understood why.

My body would feel good after the shower. I wasn't ever flexible. I did, however, manage to see the girl in her work clothes about to leave. She would look out her glass door. It wasn't the same when she was clothed but I think she was looking for something. I wanted to take the shot. I put my leg up on the window.

The area between my balls and my leg felt like it was about to rip in two. I was presenting myself to her. I wanted her to see I was game. The slight breeze from the window because it was old as fuck might have killed my size a little. I called this the pay if forward method. I don't know if she was looking at me, but her nose scrunched up in disgust. Now that I think about it, I really hope she wasn't looking at me in disgust. That would really kill my ego. Even though I'm in a different body now.

I looked up and saw a forty something year old woman also looking into my window. She had leopard print pants and was making a heart symbol with her hands. I guess paying it forward wasn't just for her. I was showing the world everything that I had to offer. It was a little embarrassing because there were two sides to me.

The first, I do not speak of. I don't want you to think there is something wrong with me. At least, not yet. The second is the fact that deep down I'm an average guy who wanted to live a long life. Maybe find some love along the way. I also wanted to experience life and most of its pleasures. Did I bang the leopard print cougar? No, I do have standards. I also didn't have enough time to at the end of my life.

I put my leg down and walked over to the other side of my bedroom. There was plastic covering that would go from left to right that acted like a door. I opened it and there were all my suits. I only had three of them. Each one took all the money I had. Two hundred dollars was a lot for a guy in my situation.

My suits were gray and had a material that tickled my skin if I wasn't wearing a long sleeve shirt underneath. I put on my pants that were snug around my waist. I had to wear a belt to look good. The pants were snug everywhere and would have to often adjust my posture to feel comfortable again.

My legs were pressed so hard against the fabric that it was being ironed out just from wear. I had to pray everyday that none of my suits would tear. I never had the money to repair or get a new one. Since I had a desk job, the risk was low. I would still worry about it sometimes getting snagged on the sharp edges of my desk.

I didn't just have my suits in the closet. I was a bit of freak when it came to organization. My regular shirts that I would wear on my off time were ironed and hanging up in my closet. I didn't care that most of them were only twenty dollars and had the logos of some of my favorite superheroes.

Three of the shirts were from the Guardians of Virtue. A rag tag team of angels that would fight against demonic forces. The complex storytelling and look at the afterlife always had me on edge. The problem was that when I died. I wanted something similar to happen and everything was wrong. The outlook on demons, the saving of the humans, the way the angels would fight, it was all wrong. I guess that meant the author didn't die when he wrote it.

I walked over to my dresser that had a mirror. I needed to comb my hair. I didn't have much hair. It was easier to shave it mostly off than to deal with it. It also saved money on shampoo. I still tried to comb it and spike it a little to look good. It never really worked. It was more time to think and contemplate about my life.

After seeing the shirts in the closet, I would think about reading my Superman and Guardians comics. Those comics were what helped me get through some hard times. While in foster care, I managed to get comics that would save me. I would sit in the corners and read the books while holding back the pain. The bruises on my arms and face were chalked up to being a kid. The social workers would never believe that I was being yanked around and slapped for just existing.

My toothbrush was placed into a round blue plastic container. My toothpaste was almost to its end. I had to roll it up everyday to squeeze out the smallest amount of paste. It would barely cover the tip. I left it dry and used my saliva to wet the brush in my mouth. It seems like a gross thing, but as a man. It felt natural.

I would brush my teeth while walking to the bathroom. There was a rhythm to the brushing. I would brush the top area thirty seconds on each side. The bottoms would be the same. I would say in my mind the word Mississippi after every number. After I was done brushing, I would walk into my cramped bathroom and spit in the sink. It would be followed by running water. Sometimes when the water was running, I would lose my ability to hear properly. It was causing a buzzing sound that would put me into a trance. I can't remember what caused it but there appeared to be a level of Post Traumatic Stress the affected me everyday according to my dreams.

I washed out my mouth with water three times. The number three tended to show in many parts of my life. Whenever I knocked on a door, it would be three times. Hell, I had to brush my teeth for exactly thirty seconds to keep me sane. I saw it as a weird tick that became part of my personality.

The phenomenon of people that need to do things in threes was not uncommon. Many people believe that comes from a sense of Holiness. God was a being split into three. The term for people like me comes from a Latin word that means everything that comes in threes is perfect. The phrase was omne trium perfectum. As a person that needed to make sure everything in my life was perfect. This little tick was perfect to calm my nerves and allowed some sort of control in my life.

In the dream, I walked over to the kitchen looking for something to eat. I opened the fridge and there was only a jug of orange juice. The juice looked expired as I sniffed it. The trash can was empty except for a few cans of soup that I had eaten the night before. The cans were washed out and cleaned.

I walked over to the sink and saw a knife with blood on it. The blade was large with a black handle. It didn't appear to be a normal hand for a cooking knife. The grip was perfectly placed to allow for the finger to grip tightly. I took a sponge to the blade and wiped away all the blood. It took longer than it should have because the blood was caked on and dried fast. I placed it in the drawer right after and sat on my couch.

The living room and the kitchen were in the same room. The only thing dividing them was a shag carpet. There was a window at the far end that led to the outside. I called this window the bad window. The one window gave me joy and the other would haunt me. The window would blow in cold air and if someone wanted to. They could pry it open and kill me in my sleep.

My couch was a black pleather couch. There were spots where the black was flaking off. I wish the thing could be replaced but it didn't seem important. It wasn't like I ever had company. People throughout life always appeared to want something from me but never wanted to reciprocate the same thing. Well, most people were that way.

My lack of interest in making friends made the neighbors question me. Some of them were very nice and others didn't work or do anything of value. Their boredom would get the best of them. The women on this floor would make accusation like I was a killer or something. I wasn't a killer, but I was set in my ways.

I would look out the window every morning. There was a reason I called this window the bad window. There was a perfect sight from the window to a gargoyle on the building. Every time I would look at the damn thing, I swore the eyes were moving. It felt like there was a sinister reason they were watching me.

You would probably tell me that gargoyles aren't alive. They can't see you and aren't truly watching over the city. The thing was that my body didn't know this. I would have a deep pain in my chest whenever one was watching me. Sometimes it would get bad enough that tears would run down my face.

Gargoyles were known to be protectors of the people. They were used to protect the church from demons. It was believed that they were demons that would fight the evil forces in this world. It warded off evil that would tempt or harm the people within the church. They were often protectors which means I shouldn't feel afraid. The fear is called Haphephobia.

The gargoyle had bulbous eyes that would stare and never close. It felt like it was always watching me clean and wash the dishes. Its face resembled a frog with cat ears. There were large horns that I felt would stab me in a fight. There were small bat-like wings on its back. The sharp stone looked hard enough to cut me. I'm sure it would rip me to shreds if it ever did attack.

In between the gargoyle's fangs was a small hole. The hole would take some of the water when it rained and acted like a spout. It didn't get far from the face but would siphon it off onto passersby below. They would get soaked and at times the pressure from the water would kill their umbrellas if they weren't paying attention.

I looked at my watch and realized it was time to get to work. I closed my eyes and tilted back. My eyes were rolling into the back of my head. The only thing that I could do at this point was take a deep breath and get up. I opened my eyes and pushed myself off the couch. I got up with a groan. Being thirty-three was the starting age of getting old. My muscles were sore and could barely function most days.

I walked to the door and opened it for one last time. I would never see my apartment again. The door was locked and was about to start my day. I looked down the hallway at my neighbors. They were loud and talking shit about people from the floor below us. There was a guy who would play his music loud into all hours of the night. He didn't care because nobody would do anything to him. It was the slums. The cops didn't want to show up and landlord didn't live there.

Each door was painted red and was flaking off. The wall was white with a weird flower strip close to the base board. It was designed to spruce up the place and instead made most people feel cheap and unwanted. If you don't understand, the landlord would try to make the place look better and would never accomplish anything within the actual apartments.

There was a black and red carpet in the hallway. The carpet was torn up and completely flat in certain parts. There was also a weird smell like someone hadn't cleaned it in years. It was in certain parts a safety hazard. There were children that often ran through the halls. It even made it difficult for the one boy to drive round with his little three-wheeler bike.

. I looked down the hallway and there came the boy that was always riding this three-wheeler. I can't remember his name, but his mother was one of the people gossiping. There was an overly large sized wheel in the front. He would ride that thing for hours. I could hear him riding it all day on my days off.

The boy was black and had hair that was almost completely shaved off. It was curly and had a solid feel to it. It reminded me of a scrub wool that I would use to wash the dishes. He was a good kid. I would rub the top of his head whenever he came by. He seemed to like it and would often respond with a, "Hi Mr. Smith." He was a polite boy.

The boy's mother would often neglect him. She was too busy worrying about her next hookup. The more kids she had. The more money the state would give her to live. The black boy always appeared to look ratty. There was dirt on his face that was noticeable. This was bad that I could notice it easily because he never left the building, and his skin was blacker than a moonless night.

Today, the boy pulled up beside mean and exclaimed, "Morning Mister Smith!"

I knelt and rubbed the top of his head. I looked into his eyes. There was a part of him that looked like he wanted to cry. He wanted a man in his life. I was too busy to hang out with him. The only thing I could do for the poor kid was smile and appear to be a good person. He needed to at least see what a good man looked like.

I responded to him, "Morning Buddy."

The black boy drove off to the end of the hallway. He would do his best to turn around under the window at the end. He would grind the wheels against the floor while he turned. He scooted his butt to help get the momentum necessary to get to the other side of the building. He was always smiling while turning.

I would always worry that the boy would accidentally fall down the stairs. There was a door that would never close all the way. If he lost control around the area, he might go through the door and fall down the steps. I wouldn't know what to do if that ever happened. Luckily, I never had to find out.

The boy's mother ran in my direction. I remember thinking, "Oh great. What does she want now." Her hair was in these locks that allowed me to see her scalp. I don't know if it was because she was losing her hair or the way she braided her hair. I just know that there were scars on the top of her head that grossed me out. The first time I saw her. I thought it was some kind of Sexually Transmitted Disease.

When the mother walked up to me, she put up her hand to stop me. Her right hand almost touched my chest. The feeling of a headache was coming on. I just wanted to go to work. I remember thinking, "This woman better not be trying to fuck me." This seemed to be a common theme with her in the halls. That might be why she was in her mid-twenties and had five kids.

The kid's mom said, "I need a favor from you."

I responded with a grin, "What can I do for you?"

The kid's mom asked, "I wanted to know if you can do some pro-boner work for me."

I replied, "It's pro bono work. I can't make those decisions. I'm not a lawyer. I'm a paralegal."

The kid's mom said, "No, I meant pro-boner work. That is where I suck your dick, and you get me a free lawyer."

My teeth clenched and a shiver went up my spine. Don't get me wrong. I like a good black girl as much as the next guy, but she would need a paper bag to get me off. She was wearing this white shirt that didn't go past her belly. It was strange because the sides were somewhat skinny. The belly was just a giant piece of flab that would go down to her nether region.

I said, "No thanks. You can come into the office and talk to my boss. He might be able to help you."

The kid's mom responded, "What are you gay?"

I replied, "No, I'm not gay. I just don't have sex for favors."

The kid's mom said, "I figured you were a faggot. All the people in the halls think you are. You never have women come by your apartment. You should just come out of the closet instead of teasing us girls."

I responded, "Have a nice day."

I walked around the kid's mom. Her arms were crossed and was tapping her foot on the ground. I got the evil eye from her. It made me feel weird that she even tried. I had to ask myself, "Did people really think that I was gay? I always thought I was just picky about the people I'm fucking."

I went to the steps and walked down. I lived on the third floor and even that distance felt long. I hoped that one day the elevator would be fixed. The landlord didn't want to spend the money to fix it. The cheap bastard said that it wasn't his fault someone let their kind ruin the elevator.

Three months ago, a kid went onto the elevator and smashed the buttons. The door was opening and closing. It went up to the ninth floor and plummeted to the first. This went on for three hours before something went wrong. The elevator was stuck. The mother of the child didn't notice that he wasn't in the apartment.

The fire department was called in to save the child. The kid was stuck between the fifth and sixth floor. Something went wrong with a rotary thing. I'm not a mechanic. I have no idea what I'm talking about. Something got burned up and now the damn thing is broken. The kid was stuck in there for six hours.

The point is that the kid's mother wasn't watching her kid. Now, every time I need to get groceries. I must walk up three floors worth of stairs. I would rarely go to the grocery store because of this. It was easier to go to local diners and sandwich shops that would sell good sandwiches for a low cost. I even befriended the one owner.

While walking down the stairs, I would hold onto a black railing. It was sticky like kids were drinking orange drink and walking down the stairs right after. There were probably enough germs on these railings alone to warrants a hazardous material crew to quarantine off the area. I wanted to clean it some days, but it felt like a pointless venture.

I got down to the bottom of the steps. I was about to walk through the door on the first floor when the kid's mother yelled down, "You'll regret not fucking me faggot."

I stopped and looked up through a hole in the center of the steps. I didn't know what was about to happen. I was just puzzled that it was happening. She was lifting her shirt. I saw her breast from a distance. The nipples were enormous and very dark. The rest of her body wasn't desirable to me but will give credit where it is due. She had a nice set of tits.

I walked through the door and went straight to the sidewalk. I wasn't about to let anything else get in my way. At this rate, I was about to miss the bus to work. The door squealed while opening and refused to close. I had given it an extra push to make sure that the cold air wasn't coming into the building. I'm sure it would be one more thing for the landlord to complain about.

The moment I went out the door. I could smell that New York air. If you don't know what New York air smells like, it smells like bum piss. There was no such thing as fresh air. The homeless were filling the streets. Some days the alleys were filled with at least ten homeless trying to cover themselves with boxes or anything that would protect them from the constant rain that had happened in the last few days.

Most of the stores would kick them out of their buildings. It wasn't out of cruelty It was because many of the homeless people weren't in their right minds and would cause trouble in the stores. They would shit in the streets and in their pants. It was very unpleasant to be around them while they were screaming and seeing things that weren't there. Most of the time I believe it was from drugs. They would rather be high than eat.

I walked down a few blocks to the bus stop. I didn't even have enough time to sit down. The bus pulled up and opened the door. The door slid to the right and the bus driver smiled at me. The bus driver had on a blue and gold cap that he was proud of. He was a man that took pride in this work.

The bus driver said, "I seen you walking. You cut it close today, Jake."

I responded, "No worries. I knew you were driving."

I winked at the bus driver and walked on. He laughed at me. The guy wasn't just on time at every stop. He was usually two or three minutes early. I put my change into that bus and walked to the back of the bus. I wanted to be three rows forward from the back. I needed my three and I needed to stay away from front row crazies.

Chapter 2

The windows were locked. I was sitting alone while staring out the window. It was never cleaned. The smudge marks from a hundred hands made the window so dirty. I could barely see outside of the bus. I leaned my head against it. I realized I could get sick just by being that close to the window. I didn't care. I was still tired. Besides dealing with the filthy bus was a part of living in the city. If I walked to work, it would certainly take me two hours.

A bald man got on the bus from the next stop. He might have had the same idea. The only hair on the top of his head was brown and gray. It came around and looked like a horseshoe. The top was sweaty and reflected a white light from the top of his head. He took his white handkerchief and constantly wiped away his sweat.

The bald man decided to sit right behind me. I wanted to get out of there. The feeling of his hot breath on the back of my neck made me feel gross. My neck was feeling moist and sweaty. I tried to move around. There was no escaping him. That wasn't the worst part. The guy put the handkerchief over his mouth not knowing what hole was about to shoot out a liquid.

The bald man sneezed leaving behind a snot on my neck. I reached back and wiped as much as I could away. I wanted to reach back and kill him. There was a reason I chose to sit in the back of the bus. It wasn't for my own good. It was to stay away from people like him. The problem was it was either sick people in the back or crazy people on drugs in the front.

The bald man said, "I'm sorry. I didn't mean to...cough* cough*"

It's not much of an apology when you cough on the man's neck a few seconds later. I would have moved to the other seat but a woman with her child was sitting in it already. He at least coughed into the handkerchief after that. If I didn't know any better, the way he was wildly coughing and sneezing. The man had a chronic illness that was destined to rid him of this world.

The skin on the bald man was a pale white. There was black around his eyes. He appeared to not only be sick but possibly on the verge of a drug overdose. The smell of his breath had me believing he ate someone's ass right before riding the bus. I tried to ignore him but for some odd reason. The guy kept talking at me.

I looked to the right and there was a little boy. I smiled at him. He just stared at me for a sec. His eyes opened and gave me a smirk. He was a little Asian boy with black hair. His hair was perfectly even around the top of his head. I thought that maybe took a bowl and cut his hair based on the shape of it.

The mother was wearing a white hospital mask. She yelled, "Where is your mask!?"

The little boy held up his mask. His mother was huffing and puffing about him taking off the mask. The city was dirty but that wasn't the problem. Recently a virus had spread through the city and killed a bunch of people. The virus was all but irradicated at this point. That didn't mean that people weren't still paranoid about it. Half the population was ready to move on and didn't care about it. The other half was demonizing the rest of the population. Who ended up being right? I have no idea. I was already dead.

The next stop had a woman come back to sit in front of me. She had a crying child that was in a harness. It was like a backpack with a pouch in front. The baby's legs were dangling and kicking her. I don't think she cared that the baby was crying anymore. Everyone else did including myself.

My teeth were grinding from hearing the baby nonstop cry from stop to stop. I wanted a car so badly. This day wasn't even the worst experience I had on the city bus. I just tried to close my eyes and drown out the world. It's not like I could yell at her for letting the kid cry the whole trip.

A random crazy person up front that was probably on drugs didn't have the same common courtesy that I did. They yelled, "Shut that fucking kid up!"

The woman with the baby yelled back, "I have been trying! He won't stop! I don't know what to do!"

The woman looked back and me and asked, "What can I do? Am I in the wrong for being in public with my child? He has been doing this for days. Look at my eyes!"

I really didn't want to look into her eyes. The outside of the white area was red and covered in veins. Her eyelids were black. It might have been a bad makeup job but wasn't about to say that to the poor girl. She might have been trying to look pretty, and it turned into a disaster. This woman's whole life was probably a disaster.

I held up my hands and looked outside the window. I needed to surrender and hope that my thirty-minute commute was about to end. All I wanted was a peaceful commute to work. I didn't think that was an unreasonable ask. It was good that I looked out because the madness was about to end. My stop was the next one.

The building was right there. The doors opened and I pushed my way to the front of the bus. My legs grazed almost everybody it came across. People would leave their legs in the center aisle to gain some extra room and would refuse to move even at bus stops. I could hear them complaining about me pushing through the aisle like there was a series of double doors.

I finally got out the door and planted my feet on the ground. The city was busy with millions of people trying to get to work. I was one block away from the office. I pushed through the people to the building. I might have gotten a bruise or two from getting slammed a couple of times.

In the front of my office building was a rotating glass door. People would have to push to the right. The center of the door was made up of four sections. The doors were made into a cross shape. When you went through the door, a wind would drop from the ceiling and sealed you off from the building from the rest of the world.

The rotating door always made me laugh. People would refuse to rotate in the right direction. There was even an arrow inside the door to show what direction to go inside. That didn't stop people from going to the left side. The poor janitor would have to clean the glass everyday due to people's incompetence.

I was inside the building now. There was a desk in the center. A hallway was to the left of his desk. The area in the entrance had to be fifteen feet high. There was a deep dip at the hallway that went down to ten feet tall. The elevators were the only thing in the small hallway before it reached the offices on the first floor.

There was a guard at the desk. The best way to describe the guard was that he was a fifty something year old man. The guard's name was Maxwell or Max for short. His hair was combed and always tried to look good for the job. He had done the job for so many years that they gave him a medal for his time in service a few months ago.

I walked to the desk and said, "Hi Max."

Max responded, "Morning Mister Smith. Just to let you know. There is a surprise waiting for you upstairs."

I asked, "What kind of surprise?"

Max replied, "The girly kind."

I was puzzled. What was he talking about? A girly kind was not really the answer to the question. I mean I wouldn't put it past my boss James to bring in a stripper. It was too early in the morning for one of those and Christmas was still a few months away. If you didn't catch onto that, every Christmas party, my boss gets high class strippers into the office. He would always say that it wasn't a real Christmas party until he banged a stripper.

I asked, "Did James get a stripper for the office?"

Max replied, "No, it's not Christmas time yet. I'm talking about that red-haired girl that comes to see you."

Jamie McCalister, she was my friend growing up. I met her in school and kind of reconnected in my early twenties. I can't remember the reason that brought us together. I just remember that there was some kind of sexual tension between us. She was way out of my league, but that didn't stop me from thinking about her all the time. For the longest time, I wanted her to be the mother of my children. Unfortunately, I never got the chance to be a father.

I tried to play dumb. I asked, "What red-haired girl?"

Max replied, "Don't play dumb. The one that gives you the googly eyes."

I said, "Knock it off Max. She isn't into me. We are just old friends that help each other out from time to time."

Max responded, "I bet you do."

I said, "Not like that"

Max responded, "You couldn't indulge in an old man's fantasies. The truth is she reminds me of my wife at her age. The fiery red hair and hot body has me asking only one question."

I asked, "What's that?"

Max responded, "Does the carpet match the drapes?"

I looked down at the counter and shook my head. I loved talking to Max in the morning. He was a happily married man was quite the pervert. Last year during the Christmas part, he dressed up like Santa Clause and did an old man stripper routine. That boy loves his vodka. He would say that drinking excess amounts of vodka was a Right of Passage. A characteristic passed down from generation to generation. I just called it fun alcoholism.

I said, "She likes to help me with some of the cases. Children are constantly coming across her desk. There are a lot of abuse cases where the children need protected from the parents. I can't go looking for them, so she brings them to my desk."

Max responded, "I give up. I'm trying to help point you in a direction get laid and you're denying me. You can deny me but never deny her."

Max crossed his arms and winked at me. He smirked at me and acted like he knew something. I still have no idea what he knew. Maybe she told him something that I wasn't aware of. I never bothered to ask. I just knew that I needed to go up to the office and make the morning coffee. If James Kinegan didn't get his coffee when he got in, he would be a grouch the rest of the day. The other lawyers were dreading whenever I took day off because they didn't know how to make his coffee.

I said, "I better head up there. Jamie is probably waiting for me and needs to head to work after this."

I gave Max the peace sign and said, "You got it, brother."

I walked over to the elevator and pressed the button to go up. The button lit up red. I put my hand behind my back while waiting. It was the same position I had while watching the girl across from my apartment. I closed my eyes while waiting for the elevator to ding at me. I hated getting on this elevator because it felt like the speeds were faster than normal. My stomach would feel like it was being launched into my balls while heading to my floor.

The elevator was making weird noises. It was the sound of steel grinding against each other. With all the elevators that malfunctioned in this city. I didn't want to be the person stuck on one. To make things worse, about thirty people a year die of elevators and seventeen thousand are seriously injured. Tell me that shouldn't worry people every time they get on elevator.

A man walked up and stood next to me. Something felt odd about him. He felt evil in nature. He was wearing a long black hoodie with string tips dangling across his chest. The tips of the hoodie were nibbled on like he was nervous about something. Their right string was shiny from being wet. He clearly nibbled on that one recently.

The man in black had his hands firmly placed in his pockets It was as if he wanted to hide his hands. The pants were large and pressed against his skin tightly. He was clearly a man that liked to work out. The fact that his pants didn't fit right probably meant that the hoodie was hiding his muscles. I wasn't weak, but I wasn't strong either.

The man in black was breathing heavily. It was as if he was about to do something hostile. I just hoped it wasn't on my floor. The last thing that I wanted to do was fight this guy. His right pocket was bulging out. Whatever it was looked huge. It wasn't just his hand. It looked like there might have been a gun. I couldn't be for sure, but Max didn't sense anything. I had to let it go unless he hit my floor.

The elevator made a ding* sound. That was my cue to get on the elevator. The man in black walked ahead first. He didn't act friendly at all. His left shoulder nudged mine while walking onto the elevator. I had two choices. I could wait for the next one which might seem suspicious, or I could ride and watch him up to my floor.

The man in black asked me, "Which floor are you?"

The man in black was trying to cover his voice. The sound of his voice was stressful and sounded deeper than a normal human being. His nose flared out and was breathing heavily. While gritting his teeth, he looked at me and waited for an answer. An answer I wasn't prepared to give. I wasn't sure if I wanted him to know where I work.

I responded, "The sixth floor."

The man in the black hoodie pushed the button for the sixth floor. He didn't press a button for any other floor. I remember thinking, "Shit! This guy might be following me." The sound of the elevator was covering up most of the noises happening inside. I could have sworn that I heard a loud clicking coming from him. My heart was racing. I wanted to get out of that elevator so badly. I didn't want to die that day.

I don't think he knew that I heard the weapon click. He looked at the back of my head and began to whistle. I could feel the moist cool air on the back of my neck from whistling. I watched him move around in a sinister way from the reflection on the elevator door. I must hand it to the janitors in this place. They do good work at night.

The elevator dinged and the doors opened. I got off on the sixth floor. The man in black hit a button to close the door. It appeared the only reason he didn't hit the button earlier was. He didn't want me to know where he was going. He took his right hand out of his pocket for only a moment to wave at me. There was a smile while he waved that appeared eerie.

The top of the man's hoodie was covering most of his face. I don't think I was able to see his eyes once during our interaction. He was cloaking himself from all the cameras and the people around him. I'm glad that I couldn't see into his eyes. They say the eyes are the windows to the soul. I really didn't want to see how dark his soul was.

My office room was three doors down from the elevator. The wall to get into the office was made of glass. The only thing preventing people from seeing inside were these poorly made curtains that were made of plastic. The curtains were three inches wide and looked like extremely long fan blades. A rope made of tiny metal balls was the only way you could open and close them.

There was a door to get inside. It was the only area not made of glass. The door was made of a light-colored wood. A small window was halfway up the door. When you looked through it, all you could see on the other side was blurry images. The same type of images that you would see while looking through cracked ice.

Right below the glass part the number six hundred and sixty-six. Some people quit working for the company because of the door. I was harmless except to those that are superstitious. The sixes literally meant something. It was on the sixth floor, the suite number was six, and the security extension code for emergency calls was six. I knew this because the door next to ours was six hundred and fifty-five.

After dying, the realization of knowing that I was working in a place with that number terrifies me. Especially, when I found out what kind of person I would become. There were a lot of life choices that might have changed. I might have helped more people if I hadn't chosen the life I led. I guess it's too late now.

I twisted the knob. The door was locked. I rooted through my pockets to find the key. The key was attached to a long cloth rope that could dangle around my neck. The keys clanged against one another until I found the right key. When I found it, the knob moved, and I could finally get inside

I was walking right in and saw Jamie standing there at my desk. Two things come to mind about this. How the Hell did she get in my office? A janitor might have let her in, but that could be a fireable offence. The other question was. Why didn't she open the door for me? She clearly knew that I was trying to get into the office. A courtesy opening of the door would have saved me some time.

Jamie was bent over my desk. Her hands were placed on the desk waiting for me to say or do something. At least, that's how I play it out in my mind. My mind was spinning from all the thoughts I wanted to do to that woman. I had to keep telling myself that love wasn't on the table. She was rich and only had the job to do some good in the world. She was way out of my league.

If you're wondering, I'll let you know why I was so fond of Jamie. She was five foot four inches tall. The perfect height for a woman. Not so small that you hate yourself. If someone is too small, it would feel like fucking a child. I would never do that in a million years. She was also small enough to pick up and toss around if at some point she wanted to fuck me. Some days I thought I had with her, but they were only dreams.

Jamie's eyes were the color of emeralds. I could look into her eyes and see. She wasn't just any woman. There was a part of her that was a savage. She wasn't the type to take shit from anyone. With me, it was more a game of tug of war. I would give a little and pull back and she would do the same. It felt like a dance most days. Again, we were only friends, but I wish even to this day we were more.

The sad thing about Jamie was that she would spend every day trying to help children but could never have any children of her own. I don't know the reason. It just came up in a long conversation one night. We got drunk while watching her favorite television show. It was some murder show that she would watch over and over again on dvd. I know it sounds weird, but there was no way she was a murderer. Even though she was a savage at times, she was too sweet and pure for this world.

The freckles on her face were everywhere. The sun during the summer would spread them out. There wasn't a spot on her face that you couldn't find one. It slowed down and disappeared the colder it got outside. I just remember thinking how hot she was when they came out.

I walked over to my desk and was getting ready to sit down. She was wearing a white shirt that was about to bust at the seams. If I didn't know any better, I would have thought her breasts were getting bigger. Her skin was looking a little oily that morning. I think it was oil. The unflattering light just gave her a glow. Especially across her chest, the freckles were forming there. I needed to control myself and fast.

Jamie's bra was sticking out on the top of her shirt. It was red and had these little frilly things coming out of the top. The shape was that of a bouquet of roses. It looked like it was thick on the outside and under the shirt. The bra might have been see-through. I wondered who she was trying to attract.

Even though Jamie was rich, she didn't like to flaunt her money. The skirt she was currently wearing was clearly old and overused. It looked professional enough to work for Social Services, but not good enough for the people that lived in her building with her mother. The two of them I think will live together until the end of time.

The color of the skirt was black, and the golden colored buttons were starting to come off. I didn't know how to sew. The white shirt appeared to be the only reason her skirt was staying up. There was no way for me to help her. I just continued to do what I always did. I would make sure that the children of families would be protected. I think she appreciated that more than anything else.

Before I sat down, I noticed that she was about my height. I looked down and noticed her black high-heeled shoes that probably cost more than my television. It had a steel bottom that made a clacking sound every time she walked. The only time I didn't hear it was when she was gliding on the carpet.

I can't believe she wore those here. Lately, she complained about her ankles hurting and her shoes feeling smaller. She seemed to think it had something to do with her veins and blood flow. Her feet were always in pain, but with a beauty like her. I didn't mind listening to her complain all night.

When I sat down in my chair, Jamie leaned over my desk. Her breasts were about to pop out of her shirt. There were these freckles that were staring me in the face. I did my best not to notice. I tried to put my head down and stare at my desk. She knew better and smiled at me. I don't know why but she loved to tease me.

Teasing me was part of living in New York. I tried to not think anything of it. Most of the women in the city would wear skimpy outfit for the world to see. They would claim it would be for their own benefit as they hiked up their dresses. Some would hike it up so high that you could see the bottom of their asses and weren't wearing any underwear.

Men would whistle at these whorish women. These women would then pull down their skirts because they got the attention. They would get on their phones and film these men. There was a shaming community dedicated to making men feel like shit for being men. The funniest part was that women in their forties would do the exact same thing. The reaction was different. Women in their forties had a sense of humor about it and would walk over to the men flirting with them.

Jamie licked her lips and slammed down a file on my desk. She said, "Last night, this file landed on my desk. He seems to have a violent temper and control issues. The man's wife is filing a Protection From Abuse order against him."

I asked, "What did he do?"

Jamie replied, "In the file are several pictures of when he beat her. There are quite a few scars on her face. According to her account, he took a steak knife and started to cut her face after she flirted with a strange man.

The wife claimed that there was no flirtation, but instead a man asked for directions to the pharmacy. The wounds on her face were deep. He was accusing her of things that he was clearly doing.

The one night the husband came home late. He had his way with a local escort and got every Sexually Transmitted Disease under the sun. After each time, he would come home drunk and force himself upon her. There were severe cuts and bruises on her body from being beaten.

She feared for her life and wouldn't do anything until about three weeks ago when she got the courage to file for divorce. The neighbors filed over seventeen different cases against the family. They were trying to protect the young boy in the house and get her some help."

I asked, "What can we do about it?"

Jamie replied, "I want you to represent the mother. The husband seems to have enough money that the courts will make him pay for the lawyer fees."

I asked, "Is the number in the folder?"

Jamie replied, "Yeah, on page three. She has a burner phone for the time being. He shut off her prior phone out of spite."

I skimmed through the file and looked at the pictures. She summed up the situation. The pictures of her face were awful. Her skin was pale, and her eyes were black from being bruised. The blood was dried below her nose and flaking off. The white spots of her eyes were red and filled with blood. I was surprised that she didn't lose her sight from the incident.

After seeing the pictures, I saw that Kinegan would be willing to take her on. He was known for choosing cases that almost guaranteed wins. His ruthless tactics were feared by many cheap lawyers. The only thing he cared about was slowly making Partner in the firm. Over the last six years, he would fight the fights and let me look for the winnable ones.

I said, "I will take your words under advisement."

Jamie smiled at and bit the bottom of her lip. Those teeth would nibble on her bottom lip that was always glossy from flavored lip balm. Whenever I said that I would take her advice, that meant James would more than likely take on the case. Whenever I would point James in a direction, it would be compared to setting a pit bull on a bunch of school children.

Jamie looked me in the eyes and asked, "Would you be willing to hang out tonight? Some friends of mine are playing Dungeons and Druggs. Would you be willing to join us?"

The weird part about this was. I felt like the playing Dungeons and Druggs meant something different than playing the game. It was like I was waiting for a trigger word to tell me something else. My senses were honing in. I felt my body tense up and my feet planted flat on the floor.

I tried to lean back in my black chair which had to be the only uncomfortable thing that ever existed. It was and office chair with springs in the bottom that would get loose and poke me in the ass. If I wanted to be poked I the ass, I would go see my local proctologist. At least, there would be a reason to be penetrated.

I tried to save for a new chair last year. James told me I wasn't allowed to because I might lose productivity if I did. I thought it was a joke. I held off thinking it was his way to gift me a chair for Christmas. Christmas came and the chair wasn't there. Instead, I got a cheese of the month club. Don't' get me wrong. The cheese was really good, but I wanted the chair even more.

I said, "I have never played that game. I will need to be taught."

Jamie responded, "What time do you get off work?"

I said, "Sometime around six."

James responded, "It's a date."

Jamie grinned at me and dropped her chin. Her eyes turned stone cold and would have frightened a normal person. I wasn't frightened but my heart was beating faster. Her hands slapped together and rubbed back and forth. The blood flow was changing in my body while witnessing her jiggle. I felt so fortunate my legs were under the desk. All three legs were stiff as a board.

My voice was a little uneasy while I said, "I'm more into superheroes than fantasy."

Jamie pushed off the desk and folded her arms. She was looking a little pale in the face. If I didn't know any better, I believe she was about to throw up all over my desk. I was praying that she didn't. I was a sympathetic puker. Whenever someone would throw up, it would cause and affect that make me have to join it. Between the smell and the sight of it. I didn't stand a chance.

Against all odds, Jamie managed to finish whatever code was between us. She said the line, "You mean like Superman? The man who is immortal and has every superpower imaginable."

I felt something in the pit of my stomach. There were butterflies forming. I was getting excited, and I still don't know why. My heart was pounding hard. I could feel the pain as if it was about to fly out of my chest. The pounding was sharp enough to cause pressure on my spine. I needed to figure out how to calm myself down

I said the last line to confirm whatever deal was being made. I said, "He has about every power except shooting lightning from his eyes and fire from his ass."

I could tell there was something fake about her interaction. She giggled at the joke and pretended that it was funnier than it was. It was all a show for the cameras in the office. Everything was monitored for the protection of the employees and the clients. The only room that had the footage was on the first floor down the hall from Max.

Jamie batted her eyes at me and said, "Well, if you come tonight. You'll be my hero."

I feel like I was such a chump. The batting of a beautiful girl's eyes and I melted. I could never say no to her. I just wish that my memory would allow me to remember what the message was supposed to be. If it was about sex, I will be really angry with myself for not living to the end of the day.

I said, "Okay, well, what am I supposed to be."

Jamie smiled and said, "Anything you want."

Jamie was done with me and walked toward the door to the office. The other paralegals were coming into the office. They didn't have the same tyrannical rule of Kinegan. I loved to see her come and I loved to watch her walk away even more. Her butt swayed back and forth. I didn't just watch. All the other paralegals liked to watch. Even the women were caught looking at her walk away.

That interaction was intense. My eyes were starting to water. I just wanted this day to end. I wanted to enjoy whatever she wanted to do. I just wish I knew what she wanted to do.

Chapter 3

I leaned back into my black chair. Another spring got loose and stabbed me in the back. My suit luckily acted as a buffer. I leaned forward and stretched out a little bit. I closed my eyes and tried to breathe. Jamie would always try to remind me to breathe. My nose flared out and my nostrils got cold. While exhaling, I opened my eyes and was temporarily blind from the light in the office.

When I got my sight back, I looked to my left and looked through Kinegan's office window. I was at this precise desk to be closer to him. I didn't mind being closer to him, but what was on the other side of the windows would haunt me. If you don't remember, I have a large fear of gargoyles.

I hated gargoyles. There wasn't just one on the other side of the window. There was three of those rat bastards. Their dark color went from gray to black as the rain began to shower across the city once again. Their eyes would form with the rain and appear dark as night. I swear they would blink and move in the rain.

The first gargoyle had the head of a serpent. When the rain bounced across the top of its head, it looked like it was slithering back and forth. It watched me work. I know that I sound delusional. Listen to my story a little longer, I'm still not sure what is reality and what is faux bouncing between the afterlife and the first world.

The second had the face of a lion. Its ears were sharp like that of a bat. The fangs on the beast were going over its lower lip. If it was flesh and bone, I'm positive that it would have bitten its own lip and caused it to gush out blood. Instead, there was just a funnel in the back of its head that shot water through its mouth to the ground.

The third and final gargoyle was like a fat hunchback with elf ears and sharp teeth. This was an odd choice in design. The back protruded while giving him a gut to keep his form. His eyes were bulging and looked like they were about to fall out of his skull. The fact that there were no testicles on the gargoyle. I made up a story one day about getting him getting kicked in the balls. I would say that he was hit so hard that they went up into his belly. There were a lot of boring days in the office.

I looked over at the clock and realized. It was only eight-thirty in the morning. The coffee was almost ready for Kinegan. At this point in the day, I didn't want coffee. I wanted something a little harder. Whiskey seemed like a good choice. There was whiskey in the office, but anyone that touched it would be instantly fired. There was only one thing left to do. I needed to slam my head against my desk and hope things would get better. I didn't but that was how I felt.

The coffee maker made a sound. There was a ding* that came from the maker whenever it was done. I walked over because I knew in within the next thirty minutes. Kinegan was about to walk through that door. He would be on the verge of being late for court. That was why I would have a thermos ready for him.

I would start by pouring the coffee into the thermos. He needed to have three tablespoons of French Vanilla creamer, three packets of fake sugar, and one teaspoon of cinnamon. The perfect concoction for the man that will destroy lives. Nobody knew the recipe but me. I wonder what happened after I died. He must have brought Hell upon all the paralegals.

Max had his own mix of what to drink. On the days that the building was closed, he would tell me not to say a word. There was a brand of liquor he would call hooch. He would watch a sports game on his phone and would be hammered by the end of his shift. Nobody spoke up against it, and nobody cared.

During the days that Max needed to be alert, he would huff and ask if I could hold the bottle for him. I didn't mind holding the bottle in my desk drawer. I wanted to make sure he would have his drink at the end of the day and see that he kept his job. The only real downside was that the bottle smelled of bum piss. When I opened the drawer, it stank so bad.

There was nothing else left on my desk except for the file Jamie gave me and ten-year-old computer. The photos were hard to look at. I was hesitant to look at the file. I was the type to do anything to protect the innocent. When I had to look at some of these files, it made my blood boil. I wanted to kill every last one of them.

I opened the file and gave it a good read. According to the file, which was over sixty pages long, the wife ended up in a battered women's shelter. She took the boy with him in hopes of saving him from the abusive dad. The Protection From Abuse hadn't taken effect yet. She is still in hiding before the court date.

The next few pages had pictures of the little boy. The little boy's face was punched in. That was apparently the final straw. She ran away and was homeless for a day or two before getting help. The nose on the boy was broken and his right eye was bloodshot. The father had punched him aggressively three times in the face before the mother got him off.

His name was...I recognized the name. I looked at my itinerary. It was the same name of the man who was coming in today at four o'clock. We were about to represent this animal. I had to put a stop to this. Unfortunately, there was no photo of the husband in the file. That was disappointing because I felt the need to track him down and punish him. I'm sure it was all legal. I wasn't a bad guy.

While going through the file, I wasn't paying attention to what was happening around me. My heart was sinking while thinking sick thoughts about what I was about to do to the guy when he showed up at four. All I knew was that there was no way James could represent this piece of shit.

A shadow loomed across my desk. Someone was staring over my shoulder. I looked up and there was Kinegan towering over me. I swallowed my spit hard and waited for him to say something. He did this thing where he would watch you and not say a word for an awkward amount of time. It was weird when it happened to you, but to him. It was a power move.

Kinegan asked, "What do you got there?"

I replied, "A social worker file for a case that might be coming up. Jamie brought it to me."

Kinegan said, "I like that girl. She is a golden child. Everything she brings us lately has led to us to victory."

I responded, "Well, luckily, she gave this to us today. We have an appointment with the opposition tonight at four."

Kinegan said, "The woman's a client already."

I responded, "No, the woman's husband is looking to be a client. He wants us to represent him."

Kinegan said, "I trust your judgement. You do you. I have to leave for the courthouse. Where is my coffee?"

I responded, "It's on your desk."

Kinegan said, "Good man. I'll see you at the end of the day. Just makes sure payroll is done. Just remember, you are my Ying to my Yang."

Kinegan acted like he was about to karate chop something. He was doing martial arts moves with little kicks while stepping backward into his office to pick up his suitcase and coffee. He took one sip of the coffee and cried out, "AAHHH, Perfection." He looked at his watch and stormed out of the office to the courthouse.

Kinegan knew our goals were always similar. He trusted me to not waste his time. I was his shield, and he was the sword designed to kill. There was only one thing left to do at this point. I had to call the child's mother. She had to accept our services. The rest could be set up later.

I had the number in my file. The phone was this weird looking old-style phone that had several extensions attached to it. The buttons were red and white. I would have to push one of those to call out. The number was put in the phone. The phone rang. When it got to the third ring, it went to voicemail. I called the number three times. She didn't respond to the number until the third because she didn't recognize it.

I was on the phone talking to the woman. I won't bore you with the details. The important thing was a man walked into the office and came straight to my desk. His shadow covered my desk. I tried to ignore him until I was finished with the phone call. I couldn't hear her properly at times due to his heavy breathing. Once I finished the phone call, I hung up and looked up at the figure.

The man in the black hoodie was standing over me. The hood was still covering half of his face. His hands were in his jeans. His presence was quite intimidating. I felt rage coming toward my direction. His nose flared up. I saw his mouth move like it was grinding. The bullpen got louder because more people were coming into the office and starting their shifts.

The man in black asked, "Are you done?"

I replied, "I am done with the call. What can I do for you?"

The man in black said, "I'm here to acquire your services. The master told me to come to you."

I asked, "Master?

The man in black replied, "Your father. He sent me to see you."

I said, "That is impossible. My father died when I was three. He was gunned down by some thugs on a corner."

The man in black responded, "The Boogeyman can't fool me. I know your father and I know you. I'm not a threat. I just have a problem. My whore of an ex-wife is taking me to court. I'm making sure that my services can be met."

I asked, "Well, what is your name? I might be able to fit you in."

The man in black replied, "You don't need my name. You don't need anything from me."

The man in black pulled back his hood. The left eye was white with a little blue in it. A scar came across the eye down passed the corner of his left lip. The cut was deep like someone took a knife and slashed him. He had the wound sewn up at some point. It wasn't sewn up by the hospital. The healing was too crude.

The hair on the top of his head was slicked back and shaved on the sides. The man used a lot of gel on the top of his head to make sure not a single hair was out of place. Even under the hoodie, he managed to keep all the hairs on his head in an organized row. The light shined on his hair and created a bright reflection that was shinier than a polished table.

There was a tattoo on the left of his neck. I could only see part of the tattoo. It looked like a symbol for a pentagram. The tattoo rippled and looked like it was spinning around. The more he paced back and forth. The more movement came from the design. I thought it was a cool concept until it felt like a sinister force was connected to it.

I said, "If you refuse to give me your name, I can't help you."

The man in black smirked at me. He responded, "I'm not sure if this place is a good fit yet. I have a few questions of my own."

I asked, "Like what?"

The man in black replied, "Like, what do you think evil is?"

I said, "Evil is nothing more than a value system that goes against one's values."

The man in black responded, "Tell me. How does a person determine what is a value? Your father's value system is clearly not the same as your own."

I flared out my nose and needed to calm down. I said, "My father was a drug addict. If you think we believe in the same things, you are sadly mistaken."

The man in black replied, "This is turning into the same old song and dance. You are lying to me, and we aren't getting anywhere."

I asked in a frustrated voice, "Fine, how would you determine evil?!"

The man in black replied, "Most people look at the world around them. They can easily spot what the world says is evil. Murder, theft, rape, and paying taxes to name a few. You, however, can't name one of those. Stop hiding who you really are."

I asked, "Who do you think I am?"

The man in black replied, "You are the son of death himself. The ripper of souls and the darkest being to ever walk this world. The only beings darker than him lives in the next world. You should ask your brothers. They know a thing or two."

I said, "I guess you know something about me. Fine, I will give you the real answer of what I determine evil is. Evil is the people pretending to be good while doing terrible things to hurt everyone around them. They see a child on the street. They hand him a dollar only to lure him into a trap."

The man in black responded, "That's better. This game is getting good. Are you telling me that you are evil. A man that during the day protects men, women, and children from the bad people out there. At night...you become you."

I said, "Again, you are mistaken."

I could feel my heart pounding. This man was a freak. I tried to explain to him that he had the wrong guy. He wasn't acting like a normal client. Hell, he wouldn't even tell me what he needed protection from. All I could get off this guy was that he had nothing but evil intension behind that evil smile. He flashed that evil smile every chance he had. He wanted me to claim we were both evil, but I wouldn't bite. The altercations just felt really weird.

The man in black said, "I'll see you around, hero. Don't let the demons control you like they do me."

The man in black turned around and walked out of the office. I had no idea what that was all about. The only thing I can tell is that he needed to be on an FBI watch list. The man definitely had a few screws loose. He kept insisting that he knew my father, but that would be impossible. My father died while trying to steal from a drug dealer.

I scratched my head and tried to get back to work. I needed to send out all the bills from the work James and I performed this week. It didn't take much time to do. Fridays were usually boring. I would usually pull out my phone and watch a television show on it unless someone came in.

The guy in front of me looked back at me. If you want a name, tough, I don't remember it. He said, "Dude, that guy was kind of scary. I didn't know you dad died when you were young."

I responded, "Mind your business. Just keep an eye out for that guy. I don't know him, and he was giving me bad vibes. I couldn't tell if he had a gun in his pocket."

The guy said, "That guy didn't have a gun. Right. He didn't have a gun right!"

The guy's eyes looked like they were about pop out of his skull. People are always afraid of the death. The people fear it the most are the ones that experienced it once before. The question you are probably asking yourself is, "Is he afraid of death?" The answer is. I fear death more than you will ever know. It's not the actual death that I'm afraid of. It's what happens after death that scares the fuck out me.

Chapter 4

There was literally nothing that happened between nine and three o'clock. I mailed out bills and watched a show on my phone. Jamie turned me onto a show that she loved. It was about some girl that had an urge to kill people. It was kind of gross but had me on the edge of my seat every episode.

The wife and son that I had called earlier walked into the building. The boy's face was still bruised, and his nose was crooked. His black hair was a mess. It looked like his hair hadn't been combed or even taken care of in a long time. The oil in his hair shined. He might have been protected from the father, but the mother didn't seem to know how to take care of the boy.

The woman looked around the office not knowing where to go. I put away my phone and stood up. I walked to her. She was shaking the closer I got to her. My presence startled her. I thought it was because I was semi-tall man and might be approaching her too fast. I grabbed her right hand gently and held on.

I asked, "Did we speak on the phone earlier?"

The woman replied, "I believe so. I'm sorry you startled me. I saw those eyes and thought…"

I asked, "You thought what?"

The woman replied, "Your eyes reminded me of a man that I once knew."

I asked, "Is that a good thing?"

The woman replied, "The only way that would be ever a good thing is if you dragged him to Hell."

My time in the office was weird. People usually found me to be nice and friendly. I was always willing to lend an ear and listen to their problems. I would console the grieving and help them get the help they needed. If I couldn't, I would send them to Jamie or Kinegan to do the rest. They were the true warriors in the name of justice.

I took my right hand and gestured toward my desk. I said, "Please have a seat."

The woman was trying to hold back her tears. Life was rough on her. The scars on her face and the bruises from her last fight were still showing. It was more than that. She was trying to be brave for her son. Her son needed to know that everything was going to be alright.

Once she sat down, I said, "I got a file from the case worker. She is a friend and asked that I have you come in for a consultation."

I opened a drawer and pulled out a box of tissues. I pushed the tissues in her direction. I had them just in case someone decided to cry. I did my best to be nurturing. I wasn't the nurturing type. I was more the defending type of person. I was the type of person that wanted to see justice come to the victims. I wanted them to live. I wanted them to know they could live their lives in peace.

The woman said aggressively, "Cut the shit! I have no money. He had all the money. I'm barely getting by. I just need to get out of this damn city."

I asked, "Why haven't you?"

The woman replied, "Because the law will take my son away from me. They would say that I kidnapped him. I was about to get a free lawyer from the state. What do you have to offer that is better?"

I said, "For starters, we can get him to pay for our services. If he isn't contributing anything to you and the Protection From Abuse goes through. The state of New York will have no issues demanding that he pay for our services. We just have to get a judge to sign off on it."

I looked over at the door and Kinegan was walking through the door. As usual he was late to the party. He was looking at his watch. His steps were long and fast. The briefcase was swinging and almost hit the water cooler. He looked up and saw the wife and son were waiting for him.

Kinegan walked into his office and sat his briefcase down next to his desk. His hands smacked together like when an Olympian puts chalk on their hands before an event. He walked over and wiped the sweat of is right hand on his shirt. He smiled at the woman and stared into her eyes for a second.

Kinegan said, "I hope you weren't waiting long. The hearing went longer than anticipated."

The woman responded, "Not at all. I was just discussing payment options."

Kinegan asked, "What did he tell you?"

The woman replied, "He said that the bill will probably go to my soon to be ex."

Kinegan said, "If he said it, the chances are it's true. I've trusted this man for over half a decade, and he is rarely wrong. Let's go to my office."

The woman stood up and walked to the office. Kinegan lightly touched her back to help get her into the office. When she sat down, he walked over to the door. While getting ready to close the door, he asked, "Did you get lunch today, Jake?"

I replied, "Not yet."

Kinegan said, "Go get lunch. I wish you would leave the office during lunchtime."

Three o'clock was my lunchtime because he always wanted someone at the office. When the office was unmanned, we couldn't bring in new clients or have me look up things for the current clients.

Those would be lost billable hours and that was considered unacceptable. He needed to have high billable hours for the company to make Partner.

Kinegan felt bad about it one day and wanted to buy me lunch. He wanted to get fancy. There was a place called Franco's down the street that would be fifty dollars a plate. I wasn't into that fancy shit. All I wanted was a sandwich from the guy down the street. Since I'm a cheap date, he would give me money for a sandwich every Monday to start off the week right.

I grabbed my coat and walked out of the bullpen. The elevator was close by. I hit the button to hear that same high-pitched noise that drove me crazy every damn day. I knew that one of these days the elevator would fall. I got onto the elevator when the doors opened. I needed to be back by four thirty to answer the phones. Man, I was hungry.

Hunger always hits you the hardest when you are having a slow day. The time goes at a crawling speed. You can almost hear the clock ticking over the sound of all the paralegals talking on their phones. The rumbling of your stomach was being heard in the office. Mine turned a few heads. They thought I was starving myself to death.

I got to the bottom floor of the building. The doors opened to the bottom floor. I looked over and saw Max smiling and waving at someone coming through the doors. I looked over and realized the man Max was smiling at was him. It was the man in the black hoodie. His eyes looked like they were out for blood.

The man in the hoodie walked aggressively in my direction. He was a weird guy that should never have been allowed into the building. His eyes locked with mine. His right shoulder charged me like a linebacker. My left arm was feeling numb from the blow. I think he hit some kind of nerve.

The man in black whipped his head around and winked at me. He smiled while rushing to the elevator. He kept hitting the numbers on the elevator before hitting the button to close the door. As the doors were closing, he took his right arm and waved at me. Something bad was about to happen. I could feel it. I was just glad to get out of there.

I walked over to Max and said, "Did you see that?"

Max responded, "Him. He is quite the guy. He has been here about seven times today to meet up with his wife. They just got married a few weeks ago. She fell in love with his charm. She looked past the scars on his face. He messed with me at first. Why do you ask?"

I said, "I just got a bad feeling."

Max asked, "So how did things go with the little lady?"

Max lifted his eyebrows at me. He might have drunk a few spirits already. If I was right about the man in black, his night was going to get a lot worse. I had to choose whether to warn him and put him in danger or leave it alone and deal with the aftermath. I chose the aftermath because he was a dear friend. That last thing he needed was to put his life on the line for strangers. Especially, while he was drunk.

Max hiccupped and said, "I see the sparkle in her eye. I have been married for twenty-six years. I'll tell you. The sparkle my wife gave me is the same sparkle she gives you. Also, I checked she is twenty-nine and single. You go for it, kiddo."

I responded, "Good to know Max. I'll take it into consideration. I have to go. Kinegan will be expecting me to come back with a sandwich."

I walked over to the rotating door. My left hand was waving bye to Max while my right was reaching out to touch the door. I pushed to the right and the door was jammed. The wind was blowing above me, and I couldn't hear anything happening. I looked up and there was my ultimate enemy. The neanderthal.

The guy was pushing the door to the left instead of the right. The door can only go one way. The design of the door is to go one way. There was a fucking sign pointing for the door to go one way. I was pushing the door in the direction of all these signs around us. The thing about the neanderthal is this. He doesn't believe in being wrong. He believes that if you push on something enough times. You will get a different result. Even if you break it.

I used the rotating door to get out. The guy had a red shirt and jeans. His hair was basically a combed mullet. Never trust a man in a mullet. That haircut is God's gift to let us know how stupid that person is at first sight. If you don't believe me, find a man with a mullet. I now want you to talk to that person for five minutes. If you get a coherent thought, you found a damn unicorn.

The guy pushed in my direction. He was swearing at me and calling me names. This was the type of man that would rather kill me than admit he was wrong. I was pushing against him, but I couldn't overpower him. The guy had retard strength. Everyone knows you should never fight a retard.

I backed away from the door and put my arms into the air. He kept pushing on the door in the wrong direction. His face was pressed against the glass like somehow it would help him get through the door. All the man did was leave an oily imprint of his face on the door. There was steam on the glass and tongue marks from where he tried to lick it.

I yelled through the glass, "Hey dumbass, you go right."

The guy took his middle finger and flicked me off. He slowly walked to the right and pushed on the door a little. It was like looking at a rotating fuck you. I finally got outside. The opening to the door freed me from that idiot. I looked back. He grabbed his balls with his left hand while flicking me off with the right. What can I say? That is New York in one moment.

The rain was pouring down. I could barely hear anything over the loud sounds of water falling from the sky. The front of the building was covered with a tarp that acted as a tent over the entrance. The color of the tarp was red. It wasn't flashy with like the name of the building on it. It just acted as a buffer between the people trying to get into the building.

While the rain was slamming down onto the tarp above, I was thinking of the delicious sandwich that was about to come my way. The sandwich shop was called Sinful Sandwiches. I met the guy at a colleague's funeral. When he started the business, we talked a little about the deceased. This led to us asking about each other's work.

The man was a cook for a high-class restaurant. There was a falling out between him and the owner of the restaurant. He promised himself that if he worked food again. He would be his own boss. After going to his third year of Alcoholics Anonymous, he felt and urge to dedicate his store to God. He called the place Sinful Sandwiches.

I'm a simple man that didn't want a whole lot. That said. He had the best sandwiches in town. Each slice of meat felt blessed. The best part was that the store was only three blocks away. In days like today, it sucked. At least, I knew a seat would be waiting for me. The owner would make sure of it. Even if it was in the back of the store.

When the rain dropped to the ground, I could smell and feel the water mist coming at me. I wasn't quite ready for the frigid water to slam against my skin. I could hear how hard it was splashing against the tarp. Nobody in the street was dry, and they had umbrellas. I forgot my umbrella. When I realized that there was no umbrella to at least protect me a little, all I could think about was that damn sandwich and exclaimed, "Fuck!"

I took one step out onto the sidewalk. The collection of water bent the side of the tarp and fell on me like a waterfall. I was soaked to the bone. My clothes were cold. I folded my arms and just stood there while people walked around me. The rain didn't stop, and I was wetter by the second.

I shivered and continued to walk. My eyes were closed while the water was streaming down my forehead. I curled in a bit while walking. I hoped to warm myself up a little. The cold made it harder to move. My heart was beating faster in hopes that I would warm up from the excessive blood flow.

While walking down the busy street, the people with umbrellas weren't mindful of their surroundings. The side of the umbrellas bent and washed onto other people like the tarp did. The water was bouncing off and pouring onto my already frail body. I knew that I was about to get sick. There went my weekend. I thought. I was about to spend my weekend with cold meds and maybe watching movies on my phone if I didn't get a chance to rent one.

At that moment, my eyes averted to my right. I could see nothing but a woman in the red dress. The water was making it hard to see her fully. My heart took one hard beat. It was like time stood still. The sound around me became deaf and I was now being shown what to do. A task that I felt deep within me. I could not escape.

The umbrella she was using was blue. The water was bending it almost in half. I felt like she was trying to cover the child at first. Her focus was never on the child. She was looking down in front of her because her phone was in her right hand. The child was a distance thought to this woman.

I watched as the daughter who had fairly dark skin wasn't looking where she was going either. She was wearing a blue dress. I'm guessing by her height that she was about seven years old. She kept looking around while her mother was charging forward. The rain was making it harder to see for me. I don't know if she would be able to find her mother if she went too far ahead.

The little girl pulled out a red ball from her pocket. When she stood still with the red ball, I stopped. The mother left her daughter behind. I was getting ready to run over and help the little girl. She didn't see me coming. Instead, she jumped in a puddle. The puddle splashed and soaked her black shoes. The shoes were dress shoes with black buckles on top instead of having shoe lasses.

The little girl wasn't watching her surroundings, and I couldn't get to her in time. She tried to bounce the red ball on the sidewalk. The water on the ground made the balls splash in the water. The water carried the ball into the street. There was a drain close by. The red ball was rolling with the water.

I was pushing through the crowd. A public transit bus was coming to a stop. It would have been damn near impossible to see the little girl in the street. I pushed everyone out of the way when I saw her leave the curb. Nobody noticed or cared about the little girl and just watched everything happen.

My wet clothes wouldn't allow me to run. It was the reason that I wasn't fast enough to get to her before stepping down into the street. This was my only chance in life to be a true hero. I was about to save the life of a little girl. The girl didn't notice me and bent down to grab the red ball.

I grabbed the little girl with my left arm. Her arms were swinging to fight me off. Her feet almost hit me in the face. Time was slowing down. There was only left for me to do. I tossed the little girl toward the sidewalk. Her right shoe flew off her foot. Her body was flying. I gulped and waited for the bus to hit me.

Time around me stood perfectly still. The raindrops were still. I was no longer being rained on. I was trying to move. My body would not move. Everything around me just froze for no reason at all. At least, that's what I thought.

The bus was black with a shiny silver grill on it. I looked at my soon to be deformed body and wondered what was taking so long. That was when I heard whispers around me. The whisper around me got louder before I finally noticed a dark figure standing on top of the bus. It was sitting on the sign that would tell you the next destination.

The figure growled at me. It moved and came out of whatever shadowy form it was in. It was the gargoyle across the street from my apartment. Three more gargoyles moved forward and stood on the top of bus. They were the same gargoyles that were across the street from my boss's office.

I yelled, "You freaks of nature! What do you want?!"

The gargoyles in the back opened their mouths. No sound came out until the one across the street from my house started to speak. When he spoke, The three behind were echoing his words. The sound was deep and at times sounded like gargled water was in their mouths. I could not be more terrified if I tried.

The gargoyle said, "Hello, demon."

I responded, "I'm not a demon."

The gargoyle said, "Don't fuck with us demon. You can't fool our sight. We see everything."

I asked, "Why do you think I'm a demon?"

The gargoyle replied, "Your soul is tainted with demonic energy. If we didn't know any better, your demonic energy is the reason most of us believe we can be friends. Do you want to be our friend."

I asked, "If I become your friend, will you save me?"

The gargoyle replied, "I can't save what is already dead. I can only watch you in the next world, Son of the King."

I asked, "Why do you need to watch me?"

The gargoyle replied, "I have been tasked by my master to watch over you. I have seen everything that you have done, demon. To be honest, I was told to be your friend. The truth is. I am getting great satisfaction from watching you die. I can't wait to see if you burn in Hell."

The three gargoyles in the back were singing, "BURN IN HELL! BURN IN HELL! BURN IN HELL!"

The gargoyle opened his mouth like the others. His skin turned black. A liquid black ooze surrounded his body. It was bubbling and looked like a tar substance. The darkness grabbed all four of them and they all disappeared. The rain was moving again. It was slow. They were right. At that point, my body was already dead.

I blinked. At the end of your life, the brain tries to catch up to death. My body was mangled and dragged under the bus. My head dragged across a pipe that seared into my skull. I'm not sure what it was but it was hot and might have been what truly killed me. It caved in the right side of my skull.

The good news is that I could no longer feel a thing. My body was fighting to stay alive and wouldn't let me feel anything at all. My mouth was filling up with blood while I was trying to look around. While trying to move my head, a full inch felt like I was doing a full sit up to see what was happening.

I looked at my legs or lack thereof. My right leg was completely ripped off. I couldn't see it anywhere. If I hadn't seen the leg missing, I would believe that it was still there. The same went for my left arm. It was ripped off from the elbow down. I wasn't sure whether dying would be a good thing because of the scary warning the gargoyles left, but like all things. Death was inevitable.

My left leg was shattered into a million pieces. I know it's a bit of an exaggeration, but the bones were sticking out and shards were poking out the top of my leg. It was freaking out some of the people that witnessed me being hit. There were high pitched screams everywhere. I just wanted to see if the little girl was alright after that.

The good news was. The little girl seemed be alive and well. She was being held by someone. It was hard to see. My eyes were blurry, but I knew that body anywhere. I had no idea why she was coming back to the office, but she was there. The girl of my dreams. Jamie was holding the little girl I saved. She was taking care of the little girl, but her mother was nowhere to be found.

My eyes were watering while taking my last few breaths. After seeing the little girl in Jamie's arms. I knew one thing. She was in good hands.

Chapter 5

There were always tales told to me about seeing a bright light You would see angels or God. I didn't see any of that. The last thing I saw was Jamie before I closed my eyes one last time. The feeling of nothing was gone. I knew that I transferred to the afterlife. Instead of seeing bright lights. I saw nothing but darkness.

I was lying on my back in a place devoid of light. There was no light, no sound, and nobody around me. When I opened my eyes and realized there was nothing in this world, I asked myself. Is this Hell? Did I not make it into Heaven? The answer to that question was far more complicated than a simple yes or no.

I was trying to sit up, but the pain from the last life was still in my muscles. The pain was disappearing, but I needed time before getting up. Since the only thing I could do was think, I tried to sort out what was happening around me. I thought to myself. "I see no screams or fire. This couldn't possibly be Hell."

It was a large step to realize that my soul wasn't Hellbound. At least, not yet. I would at least have some sort of relief before the torture began. The only thing that was wrong now was I didn't know what my next steps were about to be. How would I find not just companions but a way into Heaven.

The pain was leaving my body. The area where my missing leg and arm were feeling itchy. I reached over to check my left arm with my right. My fingers caressed my flesh. My arm grew back. I kept stroking my arm and felt a little tickle. I started to laugh. It was an uncontrollable laugh. I thought I lost everything, but this world gave it back to me.

I grunted while sitting up. The pain was still in my back, but not enough to prevent me from standing. I stood up and put my right hand on my back. I bent backwards My spine was cracking. It hurt me so good. There was a pinch that hurt bad. Right after the pinch, there was an unbelievable feeling of relief.

My knees bent. I needed to stretch out a bit. I'm not sure why but I had a feeling that running was my next step. I would always stretch my arms before a run. I would grab the elbow and pull the arms toward me aggressively. I could feel the tendons and muscles ripping from my shoulder. There was always a satisfied look on my face when my shoulders didn't pop out of their sockets.

Once I stretched out a bit, I looked around and realized there was nothing but darkness. I had to figure out a way to run. It wasn't just about running. I needed to find a location to see. What was the point of running if there was no destination! I raised my knees up and slammed them down. The world around me became even more confusing when I realized what happened.

My feet hit the ground and lit up from the step. When my foot hit the ground, a bunch of colors shined off the floor. I could see images on the floor. Even if it was only for a few seconds, I saw parts of my life within the footsteps. Around the images were the colors of a rainbow, the colors would shine for six seconds before fading away.

While the colors and images were fading away, they were rippling like water. If I were to stay still, the darkness would engulf the area again. I had to run to see. I had to charge in one direction hoping that it would be the right place to be. I needed to have faith that I was able to find my way where there was nothing but darkness.

My first few steps were hard. The lack of light made it easy to hesitate. Once the first few steps lit up the area, I had no issues looking ahead and trying to find a path. The faster I ran. The more images would pop up and eventually. I could hear the images come to life. I could hear my sisters' laughter. I could hear Jamie giggling at me while eating a pizza. I could hear the last time I laughed in the last world. It was a world that I would never get back no matter how much I tried.

While running I focused on the sound of the images and didn't hear what was happening around me. I kept running until the sound of feet smashing against the ground was getting too loud to ignore. The sound was hard and heavy. Whatever it was. I couldn't ignore it anymore. It was charging at me like a rhino.

I stopped running and kept tapping my right foot against the ground. I wanted to make sure no matter what. I could see what was charging me. The sound was getting closer to me I could hear it charging until it got within ten feet of me. I stopped tapping my foot onto the ground. I had to make sure. I could hear whatever beast was in the darkness. The sound stopped and the area was filled with a deafening silence.

I was breathing hard through my nose. My eyes shifted hoping that whatever charged me would also light up the floor. I didn't move and closed my eyes. The fact that it didn't charge me yet had to mean something. Maybe it was attracted to the light that I was putting on the floor. I had just wished it would talk to me.

A deep voice from the darkness said, "Nice try."

The last thing I remember was getting hit in the chest. My body flew backwards and hit the ground. My head hit hard enough that the floor lit up with a memory. The floor lit up and I saw a black figure with a tar substance covering its body. Its hand was holding onto my ears and repeatedly slamming my head against the floor.

The memory under my head kept yelling the words, "Kill him, KILL HIM!"

The colors of blue and red were flashing across the face of the monster. Every tooth within its mouth was sharp like a fang. It was drooling a thick black substance onto my face. My face was covered in the substance and went into my mouth while dripping around my neck. The taste was salty. It didn't taste like tar. Instead, it tasted like saltwater.

The deep voice was snarling at me before it said, "I told you that our meeting wasn't over."

I looked closer at the beast. I realized it was the damn gargoyle that sat across from my apartment. I knew there was a reason for hating that damn thing. The liquid shit in my mouth formed a rope that was getting longer. I could hardly move or breathe. I reached up and tried to pull it out of my mouth.

While trying to remove it from my mouth, the gargoyle jumped up and slammed himself against my chest. I couldn't breathe. My eyes looked like they were about to pop out of my skull. The floor around me lit up into a large image. It had the sound of a woman screaming right before she shot off a gun.

The gargoyle grabbed the little bit of black substance and stretched it out. The black substance on his arms and body were making the black rope longer. He pulled on the rope spinning my body a hundred and eighty degrees. A couple more pulls ripped the black substance out of my mouth. It fell onto my neck and created a noose.

The entire landscape was changing. I could see more than darkness. The land was going to be his own little place of happiness. The land around us was black with a lone stream running through the place. The sky was filled with black clouds. Each cloud was shooting off a red bolt of lightning.

The red lightning was crashing to the ground creating high level explosions. The stone was shooting into the sky and fall slowly over the valley that seemed to be devoid of anything living. There were red streaks in the sky. The white clouds were literally being blown in between the red light beyond the black clouds.

I was trying to rip off the black substance rope around my neck. I couldn't seem to get it off. I looked up, and there was the gargoyle smiling and ripping more substance on the ground. He kept chomping his teeth. The sound was making me feel a little nauseated. He turned around and skipped off knowing that the rope was too thick and too sticky to get off.

The gargoyle whistled into the distance. I could hear the ground shaking. Whatever he was ushering over was causing the ground to shake. The loose rock around was bouncing around and floating off the ground. I couldn't see where the being was coming from. The areas still looked devoid of life.

The gargoyle slammed his foot onto the ground. Below his foot popped out a horse. The rocks around the horse burst. I was pummeled by a few of the rocks in the face. The dust from the ground filled the air. I was choking on the dust. It felt like I had eaten enough dirt that my body was forming a rock inside.

The horse was made of the same black substance as the gargoyle. Its front hooves raised into the air. It was standing on the back hooves while the front was spraying the black substance all over the ground. It was slowly moving toward my body. I needed to get out of there before it reached me.

I hopped up off the ground and ran with the black substance around my neck. I needed to at least try to escape. While running forward, the gargoyle wrapped the black substance rope around his right arm. He gave me a little extra rope before he ripped it back. My entire body flew backward onto the ground.

The gargoyle asked, "Where do you think you're going? We got places to be."

The black substance the horse flung to the ground reached my body. The substance wrapped around my legs and hardened. I was now unable to move my legs. There was literally no way for me to run away. I tried to rip off the black substance around my legs and failed. Instead, my arms got stuck in it.

The black substance seemed to have a life of its own. It didn't just harden around my hands trying to rip it off. It began to travel up my arms. The substance was warm while it creeped up my body. I hadn't realized it until that point, but my body was bare. The skin to substance contact was feeling extremely weird. It felt like sticking your dick in that green slime stuff from television.

That gargoyle was staring into the sky. He was waiting for something. The lightning in the sky was striking faster and harder. I was thinking, "Fuck me! This guy is about to drag me through that storm isn't he. I mean why wouldn't he. He was a fucking rock in the last world. He probably lives here and is used to get hit by lightning."

I finally saw what the gargoyle was after. A star was shooting across the red sky. The star was the only thing in this damn place that wasn't red and black. The horse made a noise when it streaked across the sky. It knew that we were to follow it. It turned around in the direction of the lightning storm. The gargoyle jumped onto the horse. His right hand was holding onto the black substance rope. His left hand grappled onto the horse.

The gargoyle looked back at me and said, "This is going to hurt you more than it's going to hurt me."

The horse raised up its front hooves again. This time, the black substance on the horse was being set on fire. The flames were scorching across the body of the for horse. The flames were vibrantly colored with oranges and yellows. I was curious about what was happening until I saw the gargoyle catch fire.

The gargoyle's legs were on fire. That meant everything was catching fire. Even the black substance rope around my neck. The flames were getting larger on the gargoyle's body. I slowly reached in the direction of the rope. I did my best to pull it off by wiggling my neck around in a circle. I couldn't do it. I didn't have enough strength in my neck. All I could do was watch the flames. They were slowly working their way down the black substance rope like a fuse on a bomb.

The flames finally reached my neck. There was a burning sensation that wouldn't go away. My body was healing from the damage, but the pain wasn't going away. At this point in the story, I thought that maybe I was wrong. Maybe, just maybe, I really was in Hell. I was being tortured by my greatest fear, a fucking sadist gargoyle.

The gargoyle slapped the ass of the black horse. It ran toward the storm. The rope went up my neck and started to choke me. If I was alive, I'm one hundred percent sure that it would have broken my neck. My head was bashing against every rock along the way. My body kept hitting things and rolling while smashing into larger rocks.

The star was showing the gargoyle the way. It rode down the stream, and now the flaming horse was walking on the water. Steam was coming off the water while it was trotting. My body was laying there beside the water. I could only close my eyes and hope for relief from the scorching rope.

The flaming horse was making noise while trotting around in a circle. It was looking for the star. The star was in the sky and remaining still. The steam coming off the water made it harder to see around me. Eventually, I was getting confused. At least the gargoyle seemed to know where to go.

I felt the noose around my neck start to get tighter. I thought, "Oh Shit!" The rope pulled and dragged me into the water. I apparently didn't have the gift of staying above water. My body went under the water and dragged to the bottom. I couldn't breathe underwater. The air bubbles coming out of my mouth were leaving my body rapidly.

I was hoping that I would be knocked out from the lack of air. Not in this place, this place seemed to enjoy never-ending suffering without relief. The pain got worse with each blow to my body. The only thing that made any of hit better was the fact that the water put the flames out on the black substance rope.

The gargoyle was riding in the center of the red storm. The lightning was within feet of hitting the water. The water was pure for the most part. The only thing tainting it was the blood being washed away from my body. I looked through the top of the water for a while being tossed. Things looked more dangerous than I ever imagined. On each side of the water were tornados.

The tornados were tossing around rocks that were flying into each other. I would guess the tornados were over six miles long. I don't know what kind of force was preventing it from coming closer to the gargoyle and me. The only thing I could say was. The tornados appeared to be afraid of the water. They would ease closer to the water and then back off.

I closed my eyes and took on all the blunt forces under the water. My body was in a state of pain from drowning but not able to die. I waited while listening to the muffled howling winds from up above. The red lights were flashing through my eyelids. I was becoming blind with my eyes closed. I had no idea what kind of madness this was.

The black substance rope on my neck was getting tighter. The gargoyle was pulling on it. I flew up above the water. My body was tossed between the tornadoes. This was a path that the tornadoes couldn't follow. There was a chasm that my body was thrown into. The reason the tornadoes couldn't follow me was because of the rock formations around me. A small street of water less than three inches thick was below me.

I flew headfirst into the center. With the water being so shallow, I hit my head very hard. My head caved in a little and blood poured into the water. My head ached and could barely move. I knew the gargoyle wouldn't let me take a break. He looked at me with a smirk on his face. The horse turned around and made noises.

I slowly nudged myself with my left arm. The slow movements pushed me around and onto my back. I didn't wish to keep drowning in three inches of water. The sound of the stream was fading as the water was clogging my ears. I was tired, sore, and just wanted to be back to the old world.

The gargoyle said, "Get up pussy. We haven't found the star yet."

I asked, "What is so special about this star?"

The gargoyle replied, "As a demon, you should be afraid of the star. I don't think you are. I think something is driving you in that direction. An ungodly urge to push yourself beyond what you're currently capable of. If you choose the star, you will suffer. You will suffer in a way that you could never imagine. If you choose to stay with me, you will feel pain, but it will be nothing like what your guide will put you through."

I did my best to sit up. I was leaning on my right side and used my left hand to push me over. My hands were under the water while getting myself up. I spit up a little thinking it was water at first. It was blood flowing into the stream and being washed aways. My knees were digging into the stones below. They were being scraped.

I continued to cough up blood. It took me a moment to realize that the black substance that bound my body was missing. I was just a naked fool playing in the stream at this point. I stood up and walked in the direction of the gargoyle. His size was half mine, but his body was stronger and firmer than my own. A real scrapper if I ever saw one.

The gargoyle pulled on the black substance rope a little. I was falling forward a little. Since I wasn't fighting him anymore, I didn't fall on my face. I was accepting my fate. My spirit was losing. I was becoming the gargoyle's slave in this dangerous wasteland. With the red light shining down on us, I couldn't tell if anything around me was bloody.

The gargoyle and I reached the end of the chasm. The walls felt like they were closing in. the horse was going way too slow. Something might have been spooking the horse. It could sense something in the distance. The sounds of my feet and the horse's hooves splashing in the water were echoing throughout the chasm.

The horse stopped moving. The fire was extinguishing from its flesh. It looked black once more. When the horse was extinguished, so was the gargoyle. I was getting the feeling that this was the end of the journey. He was no longer gripping on the black substance rope anymore. I might have been able to run away but something in my mind was preventing me from doing it. I don't know why, but I felt an urge to be at that place at that very moment.

Chapter 6

The gargoyle got off the horse and yelled, "Hisaw!"

The horse ran off back the way we came. A trail of fire was following behind it. Every bit of black substance hit the ground and ignited shortly after. The flames stayed lit because of how shallow the water was. The flames spread out across the water causing steam to fill and block any chance of escape.

The walls looked like they were sweating. The black and red rocks were dripping water down it into the stream. It wasn't just the fire. The heat alone scorched the land and made it impossible to go back the way we came. I would probably get third degree burns from the heat alone. I couldn't help but stare at the steam at least.

The steam was making hissing noises and loud stomps. Something was hiding in the steam. I witnessed a red glow coming from the steam. The eyes of many creatures that absorbed the heat around them. My blood was pumping and forcing me to sweat. I wasn't sure if the gargoyle knew of the other creatures. Not that it mattered. The gargoyle would do whatever he wanted anyway.

The gargoyle yanked on the black substance rope again. I flew forward. It was keeping me away from whatever was in the steamed-up chasm. I turned around and saw that there was an opening to the chasm. An open area where there was a lake in the middle of nowhere. The journey was about taking us to this place.

I hastened my walk. My legs were longer than the gargoyles. When we got to the exit, I looked into the sky. The sky was filled with the largest Red Moon I had ever seen. It looked full and shined brightly. There was not a single spot that the red light didn't touch. My eyes were glowing from the red. I felt at peace for the first time since coming here.

The surrounding area was a crater. The large crater created walls that sealed me into this lake. In the back was a white waterfall, it poured all the water into the lake and the leftovers were in the stream. It almost looked like two separate mountains with no trees surrounding where the waterfall was dropping from.

I walked forward to see where the water was leading me. I didn't get the chance. The star above the gargoyle and I flew through the sky and slammed into the middle of the lake. The impact splashed upward and created a tidal effect. The waves went high and mostly splashed the rocks. All that was left of the wave when it got to us was water going up to my knees.

The gargoyle walked forward and released the rope. I was finally free. The strange thing was that I didn't know what to do with that freedom. The gargoyle was clearly against me. It had to have some kind of motive for letting me go. I walked toward the lake. The lake was open and didn't show any signs of hostility.

The gargoyle said, "This is the moment of truth. I either let him deal with you or I do. Giving you to him is like unleashing a horrible plague against the world. My conscience is telling me that my duty is to kill you."

I reached up and rubbed my neck. The black substance rope was tight and created scars on my neck that were hard to heal. I kept rubbing it until blood was dripping from my neck. My blood smearing against my hand. The longer I rubbed. The more I noticed a change in the texture and color. It was looking less red and more purple. The purple blood was drying up and filling the hole where my scabs were. The blood was drying to my skin and giving a scale like look to it.

The gargoyle leaped up and dropped on the lake. He was literally walking on the water. His eyes turned red, and the black liquid was pouring out of his pores. The lake was turning black before my very eyes. The Red Moon shined upon his back. The black substance reflected and shined against the area the star fell.

The gargoyle said, "I am now standing between you and your guide. You will have to defeat me to get there."

I responded, "You must be joking. How am I supposed to beat you?"

The gargoyle said, "That's not my problem. You have two choices right now. You move forward and fight me or stand there for all eternity. The entrance behind you is closed off by the steam. To make things worse, there are things far more violent and bloodthirsty than myself."

The gargoyle was grinning while watching me. His eyes were staring into mine. It was pacing across the water. Each step was making ripples. I looked down to see its reflection but there was no reflection. The only thing that could be seen on the water was a red light. The red light kept rapidly flashing across the water. I could barely see was being put into a trance. I was losing my ability to tell what was real and what was my own mind playing tricks on me.

I saw beyond the gargoyle. The location where the star fell from the sky. It created a brightly lit white building with a door on the front. It reminded me of the shack my adopted father would take me to go fishing. The ice would be frozen, and we would fish in the middle where there was a hole. The building was always cold. I hated and loved it at the same time.

The gargoyle said it. I had to beat him. He wasn't giving me any choices. I took my first step onto the lake. The liquid below me wasn't normal. It might have been the same material that I walked on when I came here. There was a solid warm density to it. The thickness of the water was denser than my body. I was incapable of sinking.

My feet ran out onto the water. The game appeared to be simple. I had to get past the gargoyle and enter the building. I crept closer. The gargoyle was watching me closely but didn't move an inch. It was possible that he was bluffing and wanted to see if I would challenge him. I smiled and walked closer until I was within three feet of him.

The gargoyle asked, "You ready to challenge me?"

I replied, "I do not wish to challenge you. I will just walk around you. Have a good day."

I walked around the gargoyle. This appeared to be painless. I think it was more shocked than anything. It couldn't believe I just walked around it without a fuss. My back was turned to it. The gargoyle continued to stand like a statue. I decided to ignore it and get to the door slowly and calmly. So, what did I learn from this incident? The world is cruel, and I was a fool.

A large pinch was felt in my chest. A fluid was coming up the back of my throat. It was purple blood. I was suffocating because my lungs were damaged. My head was shaking violently while trying to look down. My eyes didn't want to see what was happening, but I had no choice. I had to know what was causing my body to be petrified.

A large stone claw had pushed its way through my chest. In its hand, my heart that still had life in it. The pumping of purple blood was leaking into the lake water. The color of the water was changing and forming symbols that I could not identify nor read. The claw pulled back through the same hole in my chest. I fell forward.

The hole in my chest was leaking into the water a Hell of a lot more since the gargoyle's hand was clogging the hole in my chest. I was on my hands and knees trying to stay up. The purple blood was flowing out of both my nose and mouth. I was having a hard time keeping my mind straight from all the pain.

I looked back at the gargoyle. The heart was still beating in his hand. His teeth looked to getting longer and sharper. It squeezed the heart and grinded his stony hands across the outside. The blood was pouring out until it was bled dry. It held onto its flattened form. Something came over it. It bit into the heart and ripped it in half.

The half of the heart in his mouth was still bloody a little. Its drool was mixed with the black substance. It didn't notice or even be bothered by the liquid's mixing. It just kept chewing on the heart until it was all swallowed. A few pieces of my heart were caught in his teeth. He took a nail on his claw to rip it out.

The gargoyle walked over to me/ It took its right foot and placed it on my butt. It took all of its weight and pushed forward. The force dropped my body onto my stomach. I tried to crawl toward the light shelter but couldn't move fast. The gargoyle seeing I was trying to escape grabbed my right arm and flipped me on my back.

The gargoyle stood over me and said, "Not so fast. This is the Void. There is not release. There is only suffering. Death is an act of mercy that God gave the world. You, however, aren't in the world. You are in the Void. A place where demons, angels, and world beings can torture one another without consequences. It is the ultimate savage land for sadists.

You were unlucky enough to be caught and brought to this part of the Demon Void. In here, people don't know what is worse sometimes. Of course, it's Hell, but those humans that suffer here don't know that until it's too late. By the way, I don't think you will be needing this."

The gargoyle grabbed ahold of my right arm and yanked on it hard. I slid half a foot away. I didn't have the strength to fight it. It put its right foot on my armpit and pulled up some more. My shoulder was pulled out of its socket. I screamed because my body was already numbing the chest and focused on that. That sharp pain helped me spit up more blood by forcing it out of my airways.

The gargoyle said, "Whew, that's on their good isn't it."

The gargoyle pressed into my armpit even harder. His claws were digging into my arm and cutting deep. He grunted while pulling. My flesh was stretching and slowly tearing. The layer of skin that was over my muscles was ripping to shreds. He readjusted himself to get another good pull going.

My arm couldn't handle the immense amount of force the gargoyle had. The muscles were showing and being torn. The blood was acting like a lube against the gargoyles rough stone surface. It wasn't enough to stop him. He took one last pull and ripped my arm clean off. He stumbled a few feet and managed to get the part of the bone that connected to my shoulder.

My muscles were wiggling around like little worms. There was no bone to connect. They could only sit there and try to react the way they normally did. I screamed and freaked out from the loss of my limb. My eyes widened hoping that this was all just a dream, and I would wake up in my bedroom at any moment.

A high-pitched squealing was happening in my ear. I could taste pennies for some odd reason. My sight was a little blurry. The gargoyle was getting closer to me. My right arm was in his hands. His feet stepped up on my stomach one at a time. The hole in my chest was closing. It wasn't wrong about one thing. I couldn't die in the Void.

The nails on the gargoyle's feet dug into my stomach. It was sitting erect as much as it could. The arm was raised into the air. My vision while watching it was like driving a road with ice on the windshield. You get what is happening around you, but it's not totally clear until you hit something.

In this case, it was totally clear. The bone on my ripped off arm was hitting my forehead. I could feel the swelling on my head instantly appear. He didn't stop after one blow with my own arm. He repeatedly tried to bash my skull in. The blood was being flung everywhere. It was rolling down my chest. The blood was drying around the wrinkles in my neck. I couldn't see out of my eyes because my sockets acted like little pools for the blood to flow into. I couldn't see. I could only suffer.

The sky above us was lighting up. The clouds were turning purple. Little bolts of lightning were flashing within them. I took my left arm and wiped away the blood on my face. The gargoyle was laughing at me. It was hurting me and that's all he could see. It was so focused on hurting me. It missed the big picture.

The chasm was still filled with blistering hot steam. The steam didn't seem to bother the other gargoyles that lived in these lands. One by one they formed a line around the lake. The grouping appeared to be never-ending. Something was drawing them to the lake. Were they there to watch me suffer or was there something more sinister happening?

The gargoyle on top of me dug in even deeper. His weight was too much for me to get up. I couldn't move. All I could do was watch the sky slowly fill up with purple clouds. I couldn't figure out why they weren't red like all the others. Something was about to happen. I could feel it. I could smell it.

I could smell blood in the air. The air was filled with my purple blood flying everywhere. The gargoyle on top of me was covered in so much of my blood. Its body had purple stripes spread throughout the black substance. It swung my arm into the air rotating it around. The blood was splashing off it onto my face and chest.

The purple cloud located what appeared to be my flesh. It was coming after me. The Void was trying to attack me. The lightning came down and struck my arm. It acted as a lightning rod. The body of the gargoyle turned into a conduit. The force of the lightning shot across its body and created many small arcs across my body.

The purple lighting tickled while it aimed for my mouth. I could feel the lightning enter the corners of my mouth and try to fill me from the inside with its power. The hole in my chest was starting to close. The blood was filling up inside my body. I was being healed. I was beginning to feel good again.

The gargoyle on top of me looked around and saw all his brothers and sisters. He yelled, "What the fuck is going on?!"

The gargoyle looked down and saw his feet sinking into my body. It threw my arm off to the right. His arms were pulling on his right leg to escape. No matter how much it struggled. It couldn't pull itself up even an inch. It looked at everyone around. All the other gargoyles were watching. The gargoyle on top of me realized what was happening. A look of dread came over its face. Its body was slowly sinking in and was being absorbed by my mind.

The gargoyle on top of me yelled, "You knew didn't you! You had me watch him for years! This demon needs to be sent to HELL! HE...IS...HELLBOUND!"

When the gargoyle realized that nobody was going to pull it out, it looked to me and said, "You fucking little shit. If you absorb me, I will spend the rest of my existence making sure that you will never know peace. You will only know despair. Let me go."

I responded softly with blood coming out of my mouth, "I'm not sure where or what is happening. What makes you think that I know how to stop? I don't know how to let go. I'm just trying to get home."

The gargoyles eyes were lit up. I really didn't know anything about the world. I didn't know that there was no way back to the first world. It was a one-way trip to the afterlife. The only way to escape the void was through one of the three gates. Only through those three gates are you able to reach the other gates God put in existence.

The gargoyle put his hands on my chest. Its eyes were wide. He said, "Welcome to Hell mother fucker."

The gargoyle's body slowly melted into my own. The black substance was falling off his face. It was no longer in solid form. Everything that once was about him was now flowing into the small left-over hole in my chest. A bright purple light shined out of my chest. I was now healed and didn't have to deal with the gargoyle anymore.

I still only had my left arm. Turning over onto my stomach was a chore. With each nudge, I got there and pushed myself up. I was on my knees and with one hand. I lifted my head and looked around. There were so many red eyes staring at me. I had just absorbed their friend. My nerves were shot. The only thing left for me to do was get to the room the star built.

I pushed myself up on my feet. My left leg didn't want to work and was dragging against the water. My foot rolled over one of the symbols. The symbols that my blood made earlier were washing away into the chasm. My blood was pouring into the water more but this time. It was lying on the surface.

I got to the door of the building. The rest of the gargoyles left me alone. They just wanted to witness me getting to my destination. Little growls and high-pitched screams were coming from the gargoyles. A few ran on top of the water but when they got close. They retreated to their original spot.

When I got to the door, I took my left hand and tapped on the door. There appeared to be no knob. I wasn't sure how to open the door. The gargoyles surrounded the brightly lit building. I looked closely at the door. There was an outline of where the door opens but not large enough to fit my sausage fingers in.

I said, "Well this is disappointing."

I had a weird thought. Blood was coming out of my stub where my right arm used to be. What would happen if I spread my blood all over the door? I used my right side to knock on the door. Blood was spreading against the door. The purple blood stained the building at first. The door after a few seconds absorbed the blood.

Above the door were the words, "Drink from this cup. For this is the blood of the covenant. This blood is shed for the remission of sin."

I had no idea what these words meant. I looked to my right and there was a golden table with a bronze chalice sitting on it. I walked over to the chalice and there was red blood sitting inside the cup. The door was telling me to drink from the cup. This was gross not knowing whose blood was inside. It wasn't like it mattered whose blood it was. I needed to do it to enter my final destination.

I picked up the chalice and drank from the cup. There was so much blood in the cup. The corners of my mouth dripping from inhaling the blood so fast. My teeth were now dyed red, and my arm was beginning to heal. I could feel the tingle and watched the muscles no longer just wiggle. They were forming new muscle tissue.

I looked back and saw the gargoyles getting closer to me. I drank from the cup what was taking so long. The door opened. I ran around to the door to get inside quickly. There was white light that was blocking the way. I had two options. I could either run in blindly or wait for the herd of gargoyles to catch me.

I ran into the light faster than an atheist from the truth. My body entered the light and was dissolving. I felt nothing but warmth and healing rushing over my body. Each cell was being ripped off me and coming back together on the other side of the door. The bright light blinded me for a second, but when I opened my eyes. I knew this was where I was meant to be.

Chapter 7

The ground below me was white. The room was over twenty feet long and twenty wide. There were ten perfectly shaped tiles on the floor in each direction. The texture of the tile was like a soft gymnastics mat. My feet were leaving prints on the floor. The warmth on the floor felt like Heaven.

I looked ten feet in front of me. There was a mystery being sitting on the floor. My eyes were still adjusting to the bright light from teleporting into the room. The blurs just looked like a black blur on the right side and a white blur on the left side. I rubbed my eyes hoping that I could see what was in front of me.

The rubbing helped a little. I could at least see where I was going. I kept taking steps forward until a loud booming voice said, "Stop."

I asked, "Can you tell me what is happening?"

The being replied, "Stay silent demon."

I said, "I'm not a demon."

The being said, "You are a demon. Your father, your blood father, was the King of Shadows. He helped build your soul and now. You are here with the markers of a demon."

I said, "That doesn't seem fair. I'm being judged for a man that I never knew."

The being said, "You may not have known him, but you embraced his ways. I know more about you than you know about yourself."

The truth was. I'm sure he knew more about me than I did. When I died, my mind was knocked hard. My memory even in the afterlife wasn't that good. I tried my best to remember my old life, but most things just didn't click. The only way that I would ever remember my whole prior life would be by God himself.

I looked down and saw that my whole body wasn't healed yet. My right hand was still forming the tissue around my fingers. They were dripping blood onto the ground until my skin wrapped around. I took my right foot and tried to wipe the blood away. All it did was smear the blood all over the perfectly white ground.

The being huffed at me. He said, "Come sit down boy."

I walked toward the being. I'm not sure why but there was something intimidating about him. He spoke his mind and didn't give a damn about anything else I usually saw honesty as a virtue. Unfortunately, with the being, the truth tended to be more terrifying than any lie I could think of.

When I got closer, I saw who this being really was. The right wing was black. The feathers were dropping and creating burn marks on the floor. The stem of all the feathers had a glowing golden color to them. I was afraid to get near him. I didn't want to get burned by the feathers. I didn't want to piss off the being before me that appeared to have endless power.

On the left side of the being was a large white wing that also had feathers fall. The feathers that were falling from that wing were floating through the air. They would twist and turn to stay up. The feathers were glowing. It appeared to have healing powers. I knew this because the feathers flew to me and surrounded my left leg. The leg was instantly healed when the feather lit up right before disappearing.

I walked closer to the being. I was slow and steady. My mind was telling me to stay back. I did everything in my power not to spook him. I sat down five feet from him and asked, "What is your name?"

The being replied, "I am Gabriel. The angel of death and a man after God's heart."

Gabriel was holding a Lily in his right hand. The flower looked to be wilting. He appeared to be doing everything in this power to keep it alive. The flower appeared to be wet. Since there was no water in here, I could only assume his tears were watering the Lily. The color was pure white and matched the room.

Gabrielle asked, "Have you figured out why you are here?"

I replied, "I'm here to be judged. I am here to figure out if I'm going to Heaven or Hell."

Gabriel said, "I am here to evaluate some thing about you. Your destination was already planned out. God has chosen me to bless you with power. Even being a demon, you have a mission that God has bestowed upon you."

I asked, "What is that?"

Gabriel replied, "You are destined to fight Lucifer, the Morningstar."

I asked, "What happens if I refuse to fight the Morningstar."

Gabriel replied, "That is not for me to decide. Even if you refuse, the battle will find you. It is the way of God."

I asked, "How do I accomplish this goal?"

Gabriel replied, "I will guide you."

Gabriel raised his head up. There was a scar across his right eye. The eye was pure white with a little blue in the center. I don't think he was able to see out of it. The scar went from right above him eye down to his nose, over the lips, and barely touched his chin. It was thick and deep. I don't know what caused this much damage to his face, but one thing was for sure. He was a man of war.

There was a scare over Gabriel chest. The scar was deep and appeared to be a puncture wound. He should have been able to recover without scars. The weapon used on his appeared to be designed to kill him. Someone used it to stab right through his chest. Not once, but twice was he stabbed.

The way Gabriel was sitting on the ground. He was hiding away his junk. It was tucked away while sitting on his feet. His hands were lying across his lap and touching his knees. He seemed like such a soft guy. I wasn't sure why he was so intimidating to me. It had to be the deep voice that if raised could destroy glass ceilings.

Gabriel said, "I sense you were a father. Tell me about your boy."

I responded, "I'm afraid you are mistaken. I was never a father."

Gabriel said, "This I know to be false. I have met your child."

I responded, "My child? Who was my child?"

Gabriel stood up. He walked over to me. His dick was swinging back and forth and almost hit me in the face. His right hand put his pointer finger on my forehead. A memory was coming to the surface. He couldn't give me all my memories because Gabriel was nothing more than a messenger, a conduit for God.

I raised my head and looked at the ceiling. My eyes turned white. I could see a memory. A faint memory but it was still a memory. My mouth opened and a bright light shined out. The color of the light was a bright red. In the deeper part of my soul, my blood was affected by the event.

The Life I Wish Lived

When a memory appears, we see things only in the lens of what once was. I walked up to a large red door. I hated the color of the door. It brought back feelings of former trauma. The color was the same as oxidized blood. I can't remember why, but the look and smell of blood bothered me.

I had a bouquet of blue roses in my hand. Blue was the girl I was coming to see favorite color. We had been dating for a few years at this point. I was happy to see her. I was in the city earlier that week. She had called me to tell me that she was pregnant. I was overjoyed and waited until school was done. I couldn't miss any classes while I was in college. I think it was my fourth year of college.

I wasn't wearing anything fancy. It had on a Guardians of Virtue shirt and a pair of jeans. I actually combed my hair for this meeting. I wanted her to know that I was happy and couldn't wait to be a father. I never had a father and there was nothing in this world that would stop me from being one.

I knocked on the door three times. I was holding the flowers with both hands. The door opened and there was her dad standing. He was a few inches taller than me and had a beer belly. He shaved his head ball because most of the hair was missing at this point. He was wearing a white shirt with a pair of jean shorts.

I asked, "Is Vivian here?"

Her father replied, "She is probably in her room. You seem to be handling things ...differently."

I asked, "What do you mean?"

Her father replied, "Well after the you know what. I figured you would be an emotional wreck."

I said, "I'm willing to step up."

Her father responded, "I better keep my mouth shut. I thought she told you."

The stairs were to the right of me. I walked in. There was an opening to the kitchen and to the left was an open space with a fireplace. The living room had a high ceiling. The only thing stopping people from falling to their deaths was the banisters in front of each door upstairs. I smiled realizing that this would be the start of our lives.

I took off my shoes at the door. It was always a demand of her mother and father. They had known me long enough that I thought things were okay. We had sex occasionally and they seemed okay with it. I was a good guy and respected not just her but her family as well. I realized while going upstairs. Something appeared to be wrong.

I went upstairs and went straight to her room. Her room was pink and filled with boy band posters. I might have been the more mature one in our relationship. I knocked on the door and slowly opened it. I could see inside that she was lying in bed with a pair of headphones on. I knocked again. She still couldn't hear me.

I sat down next to her and touched her hand. She jumped from being scared. I looked into her eyes and asked, "How are you feeling?"

Vivian replied, "About what?"

I said, "About the baby, we are about to be parents."

Vivian responded, "Yeah about that. I was talking it over with my dad. He seemed to believe that I'm too young to have a kid."

I said, "We are in our twenties. I'm about to graduate soon. The timing couldn't be more perfect."

Vivian responded, "It's too late. I already got rid of it."

I asked, "What do you mean you got rid of it?"

Vivian replied, "I mean that I went to Planned Parenthood and got that damn thing removed."

I asked, "Why didn't you talk to me at all? I might have put you at ease."

Vivian replied, "Because it was none of your business. I'm the one that would have to put up with it. Do you really think that YOU. A damn orphan that was raised by those people. Would make a great father!"

I asked, "Is that how you really see me? I was prepared to do everything for that kid. It would have strengthened our bond. We could have formed a family together. Do you have zero faith in my abilities?"

Vivian said, "There will be other chances. I'm sure of it."

I was a little brash when I said these next few words. I responded, "No we won't. You didn't talk to me about it. You showed me no respect for the decision. I'm not sure if you even see me as an equal in this relationship."

Vivian said, "Yeah well, my body, my choice. You don't get to say anything about it. Any part of that child is now flushed away. If you don't like it, then you can go eat a bag of dicks!"

I threw the flowers on the bed. My heart was sinking into my chest. I spent those last few days thinking about nothing but how much being a father would mean to me. In just a few days, all my hopes and dreams were washed away. I was losing my meaning for living. I had to think of another way to find meaning in my life. It certainly wasn't her. I could barely stand the sight of her at that moment.

I walked out of the room and looked back at her. I said, "We are through."

Vivian responded in the most hostile way possible, "Good! I didn't need you anyway!"

I thought Vivian would dive into a pillow or something. I thought she would be at least sad. She wasn't sad at all. She was angry. I knew that something wasn't right while walking out. As far as I can remember, we lost our virginities together. Again, my mind is a little fuzzy about things. I say this because people in my life were often blurry while I try to remember.

While going down the steps, I looked over to the living room. Her father had his feet propped in his chair. He was watching the news with a beer in his hand. He took a sip of the beer and made that awful slurping sound. I was already on edge from being mad and that didn't help at all.

Her father said, "From that commotion, it sounds like she finally told you. Good riddance. We didn't need a bastard around here anyway."

I responded, "I was prepared to marry her."

Her father said, "Trust me son. You don't want to marry her. That would be a whole world of suffering. She wasn't ready and I guarantee you aren't either."

I responded while sliding my hand against the railing going downstairs, "My child was murdered. Did you have anything to do with it."

Her father asked, "Are you getting ready to threaten me? If you are, this won't turn out the way you think. You don't have the guts or the instincts to take me on. The kid is dead, and she is gone. If I were you, I would just move on and forget the last few years."

I didn't want to forget the last few years. She was my life that last few years. I didn't want to bear it anymore. I stormed out the door. The people that lived in that house were pure evil. I should have been glad. I was able to escape the family. They showed their true colors. For some odd reason, I didn't feel that way

I walked to my car that was on the other side of the street. I tried to put my key in the lock. My nerves were jittery, and I couldn't seem to put it in the hole. My keys were scratching the paint on the outside of the car. When I got the key in, it didn't go in far enough. I kept turning right and it remained locked. I took the palm of my hand and slammed the key in. The key was set and finally got in the car.

My fingers had a hard time pulling the handle outward. I was on the verge of having an anxiety attack. I sat down in the car. I looked out the window and saw a tree that was blocking out most of the moon and stars above. The sky looked clear and would have been a wonderful night to lie on the deck and watch the stars with Vivian.

My hands gripped the steering wheel. I squeezed hard enough that my knuckles were turning white. I took my hands off the wheel just to slam my palms against it. I screamed loud enough that the neighbors could have heard me. I kept screaming,

"FUUUUCCCCCCKKKKK, FUCK, FUCK, FUCK FFFFFUUUUUUUUCCCCKKK!"

I wasn't quite sure how to deal with grief. It always came out in frustration and anger. There was a weird feeling like a golf ball was caught in the back of my throat. I was losing my voice from all the screaming. My eyes were getting watery, but I couldn't cry. I couldn't find any relief for my pain. The only thing I had was…I had a person in my life. I don't remember who. My memories showed them as a black blur.

I drove home across New York City Bridge. Half the light on the bridge appeared to be out. Most people didn't want to walk across at this time of day anyway. Most of the thugs and gangsters were using it for business. The only good citizens that were out at this time were the drivers.

The reason so many of them were doing business on the bridge was not to be spotted by the locals. A group of citizens in the city were hunting down and killing criminals. The number of criminals out numbered the people fighting, but there was so much death. It became known as the great vigilante crisis.

I got home and went straight to bed. It might have been the next day or a few days later. It was a long time ago. I drove over to her house again. I wanted to apologize for what I said. I wasn't ready to let her go yet. I guess you can say like the younger generation would say. I was simping for her.

My head was pounding. My heart was running a mile a minute. I couldn't seem to do it. I had spoken to someone, and they warned me not to do it. I looked in my rear-view mirror. I think the person who told me not to was following me. All I could see was a black blur walking down the street. Whatever the black blur was, they were looking out for me. It was probably a colleague from school.

Seeing that person was all the motivation I needed. I drove off from the house. I didn't look back. It felt liberating to know that I overcame this part of my life. At least, I thought I would overcome this part of my life. I spent years trying to get over her. There was nothing I could do about it.

The day I went to Vivian's house. That night, she went to take a bath and cut her wrists. The father was out of the house and went to the bar. When he came home, the bathroom door was open. There was blood filling the tub. He was in shock and tried to get her help. The police ruled it as a suicide. I couldn't help but wonder if it was my fault. I wondered if she couldn't handle what happened to us. I might have read the situation wrong. I felt like her blood was on my hands.

That Saturday was the funeral. The church had a giant steeple in the center of the building. The glass on the windows was very colorful. They had images like Jesus sitting with children and a sheep. The church was white, and the paint was flaking off. The paint was sharp enough to cut someone's finger.

I walked into the church and sat down. The pews were made of oak and were painted black. I sat in the back hoping that her father wouldn't notice me. Apparently, he was blaming me for everything. The preacher said his words to the crowd. It was a heartbreaking sermon about how life was a treasure.

I waited for my time to walk up to the casket after the sermon. The person that might have been there for me was sitting next to me and would periodically hold my hand. The hands were soft and gentle. It was either a feminine man or a woman. The fact that it might have been a woman explains a little about what happened next.

I got up the courage and walked to the casket. Vivian looked beautiful. Her wrists were covered in makeup. Her lips were red as blood. Her eyes were covered in blue and black. She looked so peaceful. In all the days that we were together, I never saw her look so much at peace. Her father might have been right. I wasn't good for her.

Her father saw me looking at her in admiration. My eyes were watering and had a hard time seeing. I don't know to this day why I couldn't shed a single tear. The water stayed in my eyes. It wasn't like I tried to be a tough guy. It might have been that while I was a child. I cried so much that there were no tears left to shed.

Her father walked over to me and grabbed the back of my neck. His hands were huge. I felt him squeeze hard. His nails dug in and punctured my skin. A few drops of blood were dripping down the side of my neck. His fingerprints were being engraved into my neck. I could feel the bruises starting to form.

Her father said, "You should not be here boy."

I replied, "She was the love of my life. I need to be here. I need closure."

Her father said, "You don't deserve closure. This is all your fault."

Her father pulled on my neck and yanked me to the entrance of the church. With his left hand he opened the door, and with his right hand he tossed me around like a rage doll. He threw me forward. I flew down three steps that lead up to the church. My pride was hurt more than anything. I stood up immediately. I was ready to fight.

The door to the church slammed shut. Her father walked down the stairs. He was getting ready to beat me down. Instead of being violent, he tried saying everything that he felt. He needed his own closure knowing that he was the person who insisted on the abortion. He also wanted to put all his rage toward me for getting her pregnant in the first place. I couldn't see that then. I can now.

Her father yelled, "It's all your fault! You're the reason she is dead! I want my little girl back!"

I said, "Me? You were the one that pushed her into things. I was ready to step up. I wanted to be a father. I wanted to...I wanted to marry her. Because of you, not just one life was lost. I lost my child and her. Because of you, you lost a grandchild and your daughter. Both of them were your own flesh and blood. Your ego is getting in the way of the truth.

When this is over, I get to go home. I will probably cry for a few days, but I know that this wasn't my fault. I know that I would have given my life for her. You need to acknowledge that the events evolve around you. She killed herself because of you!"

The argument shifted rather quickly. Her father didn't like being blamed for his daughter's death. His face was bright as a tomato. His hand was pulled back. His fist was clenched. The spots on his fingers were red but the knuckles were white. His anger was there but wasn't sure if hitting me was a good idea.

The church door opened, and the black blur walked out of it. The person watched the fist be pulled back. I closed my eyes and waited for the hit. If I fought back, he would have killed me I just hoped that he wouldn't hit me multiple times. My chest was hurting from anxiety. I couldn't breathe. The blurred person ran at her father. They didn't make it there in time.

The fist flew at my face. My nose made a crunching sound. I thought he broke my nose. My nose was turning black and blue while I was flying backwards into the grass. My butt hit the ground and skid. The grass left stains on my clothes. It was the only suit that I bought for this occasion. I stress that because I didn't have the money for another. I needed others for work.

I held my nose while it bled out. I put my hands up to catch the blood. The blood was soaking my white shirt. The blurred person came over and picked me up. While trying to pick me up, her father lunged forward. I wasn't sure if he was about to hit me again. Instead, he pulled back.

Her father said, "There is no way that my little girl would kill herself. You had to of done something. She would not KILL HERSELF!"

Her father walked back into the church. The door was slammed shut. The man was dealing with so much. The blur brought me back to my car. We got in after my nose stopped bleeding. When I got in the car, I was driven by rage and slammed the steering wheel. I didn't want to believe that it was my fault, but my guilt was taking over.

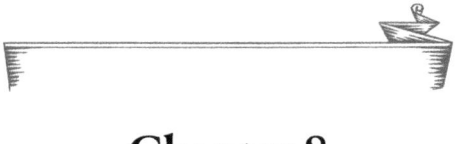

Chapter 8

Gabriel took his finger and removed it from my head. Sparks were flying off his fingertips. There were burn marks on my forehead. My eyes were turning from white to purple. I could see perfectly. The only reason I knew they were glowing purple was the flickering of purple light shining on his chest.

Gabriel asked, "What did you see? Did you witness your son?"

I replied, "Although he was never born. Despite the travesty that followed. I believe I had a son."

Gabriel had a strange look on his face and asked, "How did he die?"

I replied, "He died because his mother got rid of him."

Gabriel asked, "What was his mother's name?"

I replied, "Vivian."

Gabriel said, "Interesting, you had a memory of a child. That memory isn't the same as my boy I met. I wonder."

I asked, "Why is knowing my son so important? I didn't raise him, nor did I have anything to do with him. If I were to become a father, I wouldn't know what to do."

Gabriel replied, "Most men never know what it means to be a father until they become one. I was once a father. My child, my son, is destined to cross paths with you."

I asked, "Who is your son?"

Gabriel replied, "You do not need to know that now. Just know this. If you don't treat my son the way he deserves to be treated. I will bestow my wrath upon you."

I said, "You mean God."

Gabriel responded, "No, I mean me."

Gabriel's blind eyes flickered with a golden spark. I looked deep within it not seeing the full picture. In an instant, Gabriel was within inches of my face. He dropped his Lily to the ground. His nose flared up while reaching out for my neck. Things were changing course real quick. I didn't know what he was doing.

Gabriel said in a very deep voice, "You will coexist with my son."

Gabriel was drooling a black liquid out the right side of his mouth. It was thick and curved down to the tip of his chin before falling to the ground. His right eye was turning a purple color. I stared into the eye sharply while trembling in fear. All I wanted to know was who his son was. It wasn't that hard.

Gabriel said, "DEMON, you are flawed. I want you to know that I am the guide. Your conduit that will bless you with power. Do not betray me! Do not betray God!"

Gabriel's nails were digging deep into my neck. When he stood up straight, I realized how large and powerful he truly was. The angel had to be over ten feet tall. His hand could have completely wrapped around my neck if he wanted to. The grip was getting stronger. The only hope I had of not dying was the words of the gargoyle. You cannot die in the Void.

I swung my arms. I had to come up with the strength to fight. I couldn't even make a scratch on his body. When he saw me fighting, he hoisted me into the air. I was choking. My airways felt like they were closing. My hands grabbed his wrist hoping to gain a little control. There was no way to escape. There was only suffering.

My legs were kicking at Gabriel. The teeth on the right side of his face were growing. The teeth looked sharper. They reminded me of the gargoyle's teeth. He chomped down three times away from my face. If I was in the first world, I would have pissed my pants by now. Instead, I did the only thing that I could think of in this world. I climbed his arms like a tree.

Gabriel's arm was sticking straight out. He shook it up and down. I held on for my life. The ceiling was about fourteen feet high. This was the part where my idea wasn't so great. He raised his arm and slammed my head against the ceiling. White sparks were flying off the ceiling.

The sparks burnt my face and caused minor lacerations. He raised his arm up three more times. I refused to let go of the arm. Even though I was bashed against the ceiling, I'm positive worse things would happen if I let go. The cuts on my face were healing rapidly. I just hoped there would be no scars.

Gabriel let go of my throat. He trusted downward. I slid off his arm a little. He took his nails and dug into my chest. My chest looked like a werewolf had just attacked it. The scratches were deep, and an endless supply of purple blood was coming out. With a flick of his arm, I flew into the wall where it zapped me with white lightning.

My back arched from hitting the wall. Gabriel's face was changing back into an angel again. He took his foot and pressed it against my chest. The foot was so large. It hit part of my groin, and his toes were in my face. He put more pressure on my body making the walls shock me some more.

My teeth were glowing white. My chest was flashing lights through it. You could see my bones. The color of my insides was purple. I screamed in pain. I tried to push the foot off, but he weighed so damn much. I couldn't breathe any longer. I could hear my ribs breaking under the pressure.

When Gabriel saw me spitting up purple blood, he asked, "If this is all you got, how are you able to fight Lucifer?"

Gabriel loosened the grip a bit to let me speak. My body slowly slid down the wall. I could barely speak but had enough energy to say a few words. I replied, "I don't know. I know nothing right now. So far, I have come here and gotten my ass kicked almost immediately. I just wish I was him."

Gabriel asked, "Who do you wish to be?"

I replied, "Superman."

Gabriel asked, "Explain this Superman to me."

I replied, "Superman has been my hero since I was kid."

I coughed up blood and continued, "He was filled with endless world breaking strength. He could fly anywhere and move faster than the speed of light. With the blades of his home world, he is able to slice down any adversary and punish anyone that deserves it."

Gabriel said, "Interesting, that sounds a lot like a... The pieces are coming together. You boy are going to be fun to watch."

Gabriel grabbed me by the neck. He lifted me up and gently put me on my own two feet. He let go of my neck and smiled. He put both of his hands onto my arms. My body was yanked it while whispered into my ear, "I will see you soon"

Gabriel took three steps back and lunged at me with his right foot. The kick knocked me into the wall. The white lightning shocked me again. He kicked me again and cracks were forming in the wall. He gave me a smile right before kicking me one last time. My body bashed through the wall. In the end, I fell through what appeared to be an abyss.

I flew through the darkness. The sky was filled with millions of stars. Not one star was lighting up the way. The pit of my stomach felt like it was going into the back of my throat. I wanted to scream but my throat was filled with blood from that last kick. Like everything else in my life, the pain from this fall was inevitable.

My back was the first thing to slam into the ground. My body bounced and dropped again. My back was arched and couldn't go flat. Purple blood was streaming out my nose. My mouth was filled with blood. I kept coughing. All I could do was groan. The pain was slowly subsiding. All I could think was. There had to be a better way to guide me.

I slowly sat up. I was making noises that didn't sound human. My left arm pushed off and got me onto my two feet. I couldn't see where I was going. The angel should have at least explained what was happening. I had never been more lost in my life. That was why I needed to walk forward.

I took three steps forward. A star in the sky shot across. I thought, "Oh shit, not again."

The light blew up and formed an opening. Below my feet was a golden brick road. I looked around and nobody came to me. I was actually alone this time. The Void was showing me where I needed to go. I felt so lucky. Luck wasn't something that I was used to. I became hypervigilant.

While walking forward, the smoke was clearing from the dropped star. The road was leading me to an area between three doors. I walked to the center of the doors. The doors decided to move on their own. They were spinning around me in a circle. The rapid movement was spinning around and making images.

I didn't recognize any of the images. It seemed like a world that I never knew. A place of giant snakes, dragons, warriors with superhuman strength, and a kingdom of evil. The memories of this place would be seared into my mind, but it would take time for all the memories to open and show me my destiny.

The doors were slowing down. When they came to a stop, smoke was blowing from underneath the doors. There appeared to be three doors. The first was a golden door that had roses and thorns around the edges. The street leading from the center to the door was made of gold. I could see my reflection in the door.

On the golden door read the words, "Blessed is those who enter me. I am the Gate of Light. Anyone who enters me had receive eternal life and live prosperously."

The golden door had the sweetest melody coming from it. The beings behind the door were singing hymns. I might not fit in. I'm pretty much tone deaf when it comes to singing. I just liked the idea of being in a home where everything is peaceful. I can't remember the last time I had peace. I don't think I ever knew true peace.

I looked to the next door. It was made of iron, and the frame was made of spikes. The sound coming from it was different. It had endless howling and screaming. The beings behind it were suffering. Purple flames were flashing from under the bottom of the door. The flames were hot enough that I could get close to it.

The walkway to the iron door was made of stones with red blood filling the cracks. The blood was boiling and leaving behind a stench that would make the strongest of stomachs throw up. The stones were moving up and down. It was coming upward with the intent of trying to escape from underneath. Steam was coming from the blood when the stones popped up a little.

I tried to look closer. The door was trying to push forward. Flesh was burning and trying to come through the center and bottom of the door. Beings were fighting to escape. The souls of the beings behind the wall pulled away from the door. I could hear a loud growl followed by the sound of eating. The screams went away. The souls had been devoured by something large and sinister.

The sign on the door read, "To all you enter this place, you have chosen the path of self. This is the Gate of Fire and Brimstone. There is no relief. There is only anguish. Pray for the poor souls that enter here."

The gates were clearly for Heaven and Hell. The stories I grew up with were true. All those times I went to church with Vivian. When I came to know God after being almost killed by those thugs. It was all true. I still had this feeling like I wasn't good enough for Heaven. Let's face it. I know why but I'm not getting into that.

The last gate, the Third Gate was different than all the other gates. The left side was made of human ashes. The smell was horrendous. The ashes were flaking off and floating into the darkness. The right door was made of burnt wood. The world behind that door was clearly not a good place to be.

The walkway to the gate was made of sharp rubies and emeralds. It wasn't as good as gold but something that seemed valuable. I was about to walk to the door to check it out when I realized. My feet were bare, and the rubies would cut up my feet good. The best way to describe it would be. When you are bare foot, and a kid leaves out the tiny plastic block piece. You never want to kill a child more than that moment. It brings you to your knees. That's what the rubies would do.

The sign above the door said, "This is the Gate of Redemption. This is the home of the Devil. Enter this place with the intent to fight for your master."

I was tired of fighting. I couldn't think of anything that I needed to redeem myself about. The truth was that redemption wasn't just for your deed. It was the deeds of your ancestors as well. In my case though, I really did need to redeem myself. I just didn't know it yet, but I really needed redemption for my own life.

None of the doors were opening. I just stood in the middle of all the doors. Two of the doors looked like the stuff of nightmares. The one door had screaming and torture, one had melodies and appeared to be a Paradiso, and the last one was dead silent. It created a mystery of the unknown that I wasn't prepared for.

The choice for me was simple. I walked over to the Gate of Light. There were no handles on any of the doors. I knocked on the door three times. I had a smile on my face thinking that choosing the right door was the goal. I was being given a choice. The thing about God is. He gives people the gift of free will. He never once said that you have the gift of free outcome.

When the door didn't open, I tried to fit my fingers in the cracks of the door. My fingers were too big to fit in the narrow crack. My nails were digging into the door. It wouldn't budge an inch. I felt exhausted and took a minute to evaluate the door. There had to be more to opening the door than I could grasp.

I saw the roses and thorns surrounding the door frame. I drank from a blood cup earlier. I was thinking of grabbing the thorns. There was a moment of hesitation. I didn't want to feel pain anymore but thought this would be the only way. My heart was racing wondering is there was poison in the thorns. This just felt too easy.

My eyes closed and I reached out for the rose's thorns. It felt like a series of bee stings on my hand. I gritted my teeth. My hand slid down the stems. My hand was being cut, and blood was dripping down the flowers. The rose stems were soaking up the blood. The color of the roses went from red to purple.

The stems on the roses were becoming petrified and became white as snow. The petals went from purple to black. A glow of fire appeared in the center of each petal and burned outward. The black petals were flaking apart and turning into ashes. It was as if my blood caused decay and burned the petals. The stems appeared to be changing as if a fuse was lit.

The stems were showing their souls to the world. A golden light in the center of the stem was flashing. They were singing a high-pitched sound. The flicker was getting faster until it became a solid gold color. The light was allowing the stems to move around. They wrapped tighter around one another. I just thought that if my neck was in there. It surely would have decapitated me.

The petals on the flowers were gone. I swallowed hard not knowing what was happening. My hands were covered in blood still. I decided to wipe my blood all over the golden door. The door whispered to me, "It is not your time." The ashes from the petals surrounded my arms and hands.

I looked up and saw the ashes flying above me. The screams from the Gate of Fire and Brimstone came back. The knocks on the door were loud. Beings were fighting for their very souls. After a loud screeching scream, the doors blew off the gate. Behind the door was purple fire that ripped the flesh off the people and staining their bones purple.

The entrance to Hell disappeared. All I could see was darkness. The frame of the door and stones to the entrance turned to ashes. The ashes were floating above and sucking in the gate. With that gate off the table, I felt a little relieved. That just meant the Gate of Light was still available and I didn't need to prepare for suffering.

The Gate of Light was glowing. My heart was filled with pride. I was about to enter the Kingdom of Heaven. The door was opening A bright white light shined through the door. I could feel the warm glow. I felt all my pain slowly dissolving. My skin was being healed in its presence. I could see figures in the distance. I don't know if they were angels but there was laughter.

I tried to step inside. The gate didn't allow me access. When I walked toward the portal, it disappeared. I was now standing in the darkness of the Void. What a cruel joke to think that I deserved Heaven. I looked back and the frame was turning into ashes. The ashes flew in a circle like a cyclone.

The ashes of the gate went into the sky. The only gate that was left would seal my fate. The Gate of Redemption would be my life, my doom, and my redemption. I looked at the gate with water in my eyes. I wasn't prepared to go in. the only thing it could do was walk back to the center. The door wasn't open yet.

The voice in my head said, "You are going to suffer. Nothing you will do will ever amount to anything. This gate is not the Gate of Fire, but there will be times when you will wish it was."

I responded, "Who is saying that?"

The voice was laughing. All I could hear was its eerie laughter. My heart was feeling like it weighed a thousand pounds. I dropped to my knees. The rubies on the ground were lighting up. My head was throbbing. I could see a white light in front of me. The voice said, "Your soul is mine."

I could see the darkness again. All the energy left my body. I fell forward. My head slammed into the ground. The only sound I could make was groaning. There was drool coming from the corner of my mouth. I opened my eyes wide to see what was happening at the gate. All I could feel at that moment was despair.

My arms were getting heavy. I couldn't move a muscle. The ashes on the door were floating away. The burnt door was breaking apart and splintering. My body was trying to lift off the ground. My chest and legs were floating off the ground. My hands were the only thing clinging to the ground.

I raised my head. The cheeks on my face were rippling. My teeth were baring and flickering a purple tint. Purple lightning was surrounding my body. My hair was flying backward and almost falling out of my head. I looked up and the ashes were coming down to my body. The ashes flew around my body like a cyclone.

Little pieces of the ashes were coming together. It started at the base of my shoulder blade. Each ash was forming abnormal shapes. After the ashes were growing and spreading out like a set of black angel wings. The feathers on my back were falling off. The cyclone around me was taking control and tearing up the wings.

The weight on my arms was lessening. The cyclone around me lifted me up and tossed me into the direction of the Gate of Redemption. My body was getting ripped apart by the rubies. My arms, legs, and chest had hundreds of lacerations while bouncing off the rubies. The blood was being soaked up by all the emeralds.

The Gate of Redemption was acting as a black hole. I took my hands and stabbed them into two large rubies. My hands were pierced through. I clenched my fists hoping not to be sucked into the black hole. My fingers were digging into the rubies. These two rubies were the only thing keeping me in the Void.

While holding onto the rubies, the blood was splattering all over the emeralds. The more it soaked up the blood. The larger each emerald had become. The emeralds were rising straight up and looking more like swords. The blood eventually raised them up to touch my flesh. The cuts from the emeralds were making them grow faster. I just remember thinking, "Oh Shit!"

The emeralds pieced through my arms, chest and legs. I couldn't breathe with five emeralds piercing my lungs. I was spitting blood onto more emeralds. The emerald below rose up and stabbed me right through the bottom of my chin. It pierced through my skull and came out the other side.

The pain wasn't the worst part. The emeralds were sucking every last drop of blood out of my body. My skin was turning pale, and my eyes couldn't blink. The emeralds were slowly breaking. I could hear them crackling of the emeralds with the suction of the black hole in the gate.

I could barely think or even know what was happening. The emeralds shattered into a million pieces. The wings on my back reached out and held onto the sides of the door frame. I was completely running on instinct. My wings couldn't hold on and cut into the gate's frame. When the gate was sliced, I flew into the black hole.

The darkness around me sealed me into a dark shell. It was made of a squishy material. I couldn't see, hear, or smell anything. The place I was stuck in was the perfect deprivation chamber.

Chapter 9

The darkness around me was closing in. There was a rubber shell keeping me inside. I thought nothing of it at first. Except as time went on, my wings were dissolving. They didn't turn to ashes. They just disappeared. Everything about me was changing, but it was hard to see because there was nothing but darkness.

My skin was healing from all the damage. The places where I had scars were no longer there. I could feel my skin in the dark. It was getting smoother. My head was getting larger than the rest of me. I was confused as to why my soul was warping this way. I felt so fragile compared to what I used to be.

The area around me was closing in. I didn't know if the dark orb that I was living in was closing in or I was getting bigger. I didn't have anyone to talk to. I didn't have anyway to evaluate my situation. The only thing that I knew was the place was warm. I spent most of the time sleeping. I was losing track of my time in the orb.

As time progressed, my memories were disappearing. From day to day, I forgot the people in my past life. I didn't know who Jamie was, my mom, my adopted parents, and all the friends that I met through Jamie. I forgot so much that I needed to remember. My lack of knowledge pushed me in a direction that made it hard to understand why I instinctually do what I do.

After about six months in what appeared to be the Void, I finally heard my first voice. It was a mix of several dialects that I didn't recognize. The words were muffled. I could barely hear what was said, but the voices were vibrant and cheerful. I could hear three voices. I learned to recognize the mysterious tones. Their voices seemed soothing in a way. I felt a sense of protection.

I would kick and punch to escape. The longer I was in the orb. The more it closed in and created a tighter area. If you're thinking that I was in a pregnant woman's belly. You would be right. I wasn't just being put into a new place. I was being part of the Circle of Life in the new world. The best part about this scenario. I wasn't the only one this happened too.

After hearing the first three voices, I started to hear a fourth voice. A being that was connected to my very mind. An inner voice that would plague me for a long time. It waited until my memories were gone before it showed himself to me. This was his way of gaining power before I could defend myself.

The voice said, "Hello, little one."

I could not speak yet. The only thing that I knew was the darkness. My memories were completely wiped and couldn't truly understand what was happening. Its voice was like the other three I had been listening to too. The only difference was that the voice inside my head wasn't muffled.

The voice said, "You and I are connected. I am here to make sure that you will not just fail. You will be a failure in every aspect of your life. I am your inner voice. I am the only being that will make you whole in the fucking world. Over time, you will obey my every command."

The voice would go on for days. I don't know why it tried. I never understood a damn word it said. I just kept looking outward for a long time. I was waiting to be unleashed upon the world. Only then, would I learn what it means to be human in this new world. Only then, would I find my place and become one of the strongest beings that ever lived.

The day had come, I was born in the fall months. At least to our calendar years. The people in this world went by years and days. Three hundred and sixty-six days in a year. I couldn't argue because the world feels primitive compared to the last world. My companions and I would still use the first world's way of using a calendar. We just couldn't do it around the normal townsfolk.

I was born to two people that wanted a child. This was a first for me. My mother accepted me but didn't really want me. As for my father, I never met my real father. My real mother said that my father had disappeared after a one-night stand. He was very dark and very mysterious. That was part of his allure.

My new parents went by the names James and Ann Marie Damieno. I was fortunate to be born into a family with a last name. Only the prestigious were given last names. The only reason for that was my grandfather. The great Marcus Damieno. It had been said that he was the fastest man alive and could tell the future. A gift that nobody else in the world could achieve. That was why King Alexander allowed him to own a last name.

When I was born, I was put into my mother Ann Marie's arms. She held me in close against her warm body. I was frightened by how large she was, but the moment she spoke. I started to calm down. She was one of the three voices that I heard. Even though I was so young, I felt safety in the three voices.

My mother had long beautiful brown hair. Her eyes were brown and was gentle in a way only a mother could be. I fell right to sleep in her arms right after my first feeding. My mother was worn out but refused to let me go at first. Apparently, while I was sleeping, I was removed from her chest by a slave that my father owned.

The slave's name was Talya. She was my caretaker. Talya for the next nine years was the most attentive and protective person in my life. She basically raised me. The weird thing about Talya wasn't the fact she wasn't my mother. It wasn't even the fact she could track me down from hundreds of yards away. It was that she wasn't human.

While my mother was sleeping, Talya would hold me to keep me warm. She had the softest light gray and bluish fur around. I would nestle in her chest. The warmth would put me back to sleep. The sound of her heartbeat was always calm. My ear would be placed on her chest to hear every beat.

At the time, she was about fourteen years old. There was a dark gray spot on her nose that always made it easy to spot her in a crowd of wolves. It was hard to figure out which wolf was when they got together in pack formation. The other way was by her scent. The rest of the wolves smelled her natural aroma, but I smelled her shampoo that my father would give her. A rare commodity that she gained because of her loyalty to keeping me safe.

My father was quite the guy. He would hang out with his friend Draco Simpson. A royal that dedicated his life to being some kind of warrior. I would learn much later in my life what kind of job he had. I just knew that he is some kind of royal that was close to the throne. The two of them would often get shit faced and come home.

The most unique feature of my father was that he had one arm. He went to the Priests in town one time to see if they could recover his left arm. Whatever they told him. freaked him out. He said the price of healing his arm was too great and refused their services. He now only had a prosthetic that comes out in times of trouble.

In my time in the world, grew a little and started to understand the language a bit. Some of it was from Talya and the other was from the voice inside my head. I understood certain words like weak and incompetent from the voice. Most days it felt like the voice was too harsh on me. Other days, I felt like the voice was right. It never had a positive thing to say to me. Despite that, I did my best to remain what my father would call, a happy warrior.

When I turned two years old, Talya asked my mother if I could go out and play with the pups. I needed to be more acquainted with them since my father had homes for over one thousand wolf slaves. I didn't know what a slave truly was. This was identified quickly when I met my first gathering.

I had on a pair of brown shorts and a white shirt. These were referred to as the commoner's clothes. My father wanted me to learn how to be a commoner and yet have a last name that distinguishes me. I would have the capabilities to be respected while being able to live a normal humble life.

My father had hopes for me but didn't want to put the pressure on like his father did. He even named me after the Archangel Michael. I just realized that I got this far and didn't tell you my new name. My name is now Michael Damieno. The third generation to obtain the Damieno name and the heir to a bunch of farmland and wolf people.

Michael was one of the greatest angels to ever walk through Heaven. His warrior spirit was said to be unmatched and was one of the greatest leaders to fight in the War for Heaven. My father saw me as a warrior for Heaven. He didn't want to believe that I had demon in my blood like his father Marcus Damieno.

There was a myth told about my grandfather. It was said that he was the son of one of the strongest generals in Lucifer's army. The demon's name was Mephisto. With his super-fast speeds, Mephisto could never been seen during battle. Those same speeds were seen in my grandfather. That seems to be the only correlation.

When I was three years old, that was when my life truly began. My father had just come from the city. The horses looked worn out. With the three of us living in the country, it was always quiet. The sound of him coming home was loud enough to wake me up from my slumber. My mother had also woken up.

My father came through the front door and slammed it hard. My mom came running to the front of the house. She put on a robe and tied it. My father walked past my mother. His right shoulder checked her and pushed her back toward the sink. My father was almost never aggressive toward her. There was fear in his eyes like something was about to happen. His eyes turned red and was preparing for war.

My father walked over to his prosthetic that was hanging on the wall. There was a strap that wrapped around his right arm to help keep it straight. The strap would go across his back and down his left stub. The rest was a metal triggered forearm with hand on the end. It was made with Holy Steel.

The Holy Steel prosthetic was placed on my father's specialty made shield. His shield was designed just to be held up with one hand instead of a full forearm. He grappled around the handle and flipped a switch in the forearm that would close the hand. Once the hand closed, the only way to remove the shield would be to flip the switch in the opposite direction or remove the prosthetic all together.

My father ran upstairs to check on me. He saw me standing at the steps. He yelled, "Michael, get your ass down here with your mother! The two you need to find some kind of shelter in the home! Don't forget the safe room!"

My mother was scared. She asked, "James what is going on."

My father ignored her and tried to put on the rest of his armor with his right arm. He was struggling and often needed my mother to help him. Seeing that my mother was too busy trying to get me down the stairs. My father huffed and tried to get the armor on all by himself. There was an intensity that could only be seen in high-ranking warriors.

My mother walked over and picked me up seeing that I was scared. She kept rubbing my head and telling me to shush. Her intention was to calm down, but it wasn't working. My bottom lip was quivering, and I couldn't say a word. I could only cry. I was still innocent in this world and had no sense of preservation.

My mom kept screaming, "James, James, James, JAMES! You know what Darren!"

My father turned around and said in an angry tone, "Now is not the time Kiesha."

My parents stared at each other. It was a stalemate. That was the first and only time that I heard my parents' first world names. That was the level of seriousness in the situation. My mother looked at him and pursed her lips. My father closed his eyes and wasn't sure if there was enough time to explain.

My father flung open the door and looked outside. He didn't see anyone coming and took a minute to breathe. He looked into my mother's eyes and said, "Fine, he is dead."

My mother asked, "Who is dead? Is it Draco?"

My father replied, "No, Alexander is dead. Draco witnessed Norman kill him."

My mother asked, "How? Why? When?"

My father replied, "Not now because it appeared Draco's dad is next on the chopping block and if we aren't careful. We will be too."

My mother asked, "When was the last time you got rest?"

My father replied, "It doesn't matter. I'll sleep when I know the threat is dead."

My father was fearful of what would happen to our family. Norman knew how close Draco and him were. Norman was now the king and had all the power he wanted at his disposal. Nobody would put it past him to kill everyone that Draco has ever known or cared about just to prove a point.

My father went outside and stood in the yard. I don't think he moved a muscle. It was called a Sentinel Stance. His arms would drop to his side, and he could sense everything happening in the area. This move was well known among the Protection Warriors. They would use it to defend against targets trying to do a sneak attack.

My mother held me closely and walked me up the steps. She pretended not to be scared. I felt her arms trembling. When you are that young, it is easier to sense the emotions of others. I was crying and sobbing on her shoulder. Snot was running down my nose and was wiped all over my mother's clothes. She didn't seem to mind but now that I'm old or older. I recognize that I was a gross little snot monster.

I was set in my bed slowly. The Red Moon was shining through the window. I felt weird when the Red Moon shined on me. I swore it was following me around some nights. I knew it wasn't true but there was a feeling like I was being fed energy. Whenever, the Red Moon would show itself to me. I would also have very bad dreams that I would later recognize as visions of my past life.

I couldn't sleep at all. I don't think my mother could either. She sat in a rocking chair in the corner of my room. All she did was stare at me. I didn't know who this Norman fellow was, but I recognized through their actions that he was a scary guy. I wished for the whole time. He didn't make my mother cry the way she did.

The sun came up. I didn't get a wink of sleep. I stood up on my tippy toes and looked out the window. My father was in the same position all night. Along side him were some of the young wolf men. They stood guard to not just protect us but to protect all the female wolves and cubs within the village.

When the day started, my father came inside. He knew this was about to be his time to rest. The execution of Marius Simpson was about to commence. He just needed to make sure there was no assault on him and his family out of spite. The wolves stood outside and continued to watch.

My father came into the house. The door was slammed shut. He walked past the steps to my parents' bedroom. He flopped on the bed. I don't think he had the energy to take off his prosthetic. I ran down the steps to see him and there he lie. He looked half dead and refused to move. The only reason I knew he was alive was my father could snore loud enough to wake the neighbors.

The night ended, but the day was beginning. He needed to relax. My father was trying to figure out how. It occurred to him. I had never heard the story of how he lost his arm. To a young boy it was exciting and scary.

Chapter 10

My father went out into the woods and grabbed some wood. There were two things he would do with the wood. One would be to keep the house heated. The other was to make furniture. There was something gratifying about making something with your own hands. Except in his case, he made it with his own hand.

My father made wood benches and chairs. He would spend hours with his hobby making...pieces of furniture. I would never call them well crafted or even strong enough to sit down on. Almost every piece he ever made would fall apart the moment you sat on it. I was three and my mother refused to let me sit on one alone.

My father put the logs on the fire. The heat blazed. He wanted to make sure my mother and I were warm. The crackling of the wood was calming. The small pops every once in a while, would scare me, but I loved to sit on the bear rug in front of the fireplace. The sparks were flying out of the wood and almost hit me.

My father pulled me back before I could get hit with ashes. He raised me above his head and smiled. I looked at him with bugged out eyes. I couldn't blink. Every fiber of my being didn't want to fall. He only used his right arm. He bounced me up and down. It was like he was performing a balancing act. I was tossed up and caught with his arm.

My father sat down on a bench that he built the week before. My father plopped me down on his knee and bounced me a few times. He was getting me into a mood. He was about to tell me a story about how he lost his arm. He stared into the fire and took a deep breath. He needed a minute to get past the trauma.

My father said, "Have I ever told you the story of how I lost my arm."

My mother responded, "No, no you're not. He doesn't be getting nightmares so you can relive your glory days."

My father looked back at my mother and said, "He needs to learn a little bit about the world. To completely keep him away from the world won't do him any good. If he becomes a hero in six years, he will have a hard time surviving. People will demand things from him."

My mother responded, "They don't demand things of you."

My father said, "Yeah, that is because they see a one-armed man and mistaken me for weak."

My mother responded, "Fine, but if he has nightmares. You're the one staying up with him."

The Serpent and the Broken Man

NINE YEARS AGO, MY father was making his way through the kingdom. He appeared to be an advisor of sorts to King Alexander. He had another advisor, but your grandfather had the ability to see the future. He was able to see a looming threat to the kingdom. A threat that would destroy a large part of the kingdom.

About thirty miles out, there was a cave with some of the most horrifying beasts that the world had known. People stayed clear of the cave because of all the noises that came from it. That would never stop your grandfather. He was too fast for the beasts inside the cave. There was only one problem. He didn't know if he would have enough strength to kill all the snakes. The snakes that resided in the cave were large enough to fill their bodies through the tunnels.

Your grandfather, the great Marcus Damieno, walked into the chambers of King Alexander. He was decked out in his bio armor that was made of Hellfire and Brimstone. He is believed to have enough control to internalize the flames. It is believed that the flames of Hell are what keep him alive. The fire would be stoked by his emotions. The more heat was irradiating from the inside of his body. The more emotional your grandfather would get. These moments would often scare everyone in his vicinity.

Your grandfather said, "My lord, I have come to talk to you about a threat."

King Alexander responded, "A threat, toward the kingdom or toward me."

Your grandfather said, "Toward the kingdom my lord. I have seen the future and know that a great snake will attack our city walls. It is believed to be from the caves to the south-west."

King Alexander responded, "Those caves haven't been disturbed in years. The Basilisks inside mind their own business and eat those overgrown rodents that would normally spread disease to the locals. What makes you think they will leave their home now?"

Your grandfather said, "I have seen it. In two days, a lone Basilisk will attack the city wall. It will be the size of Kaiju. There might be some losses in the process of taking it down. I want to take a team to the caves and wipe the Basilisks out before they harm the people of the kingdom."

King Alexander responded, "How do you know that your vision isn't caused by you attacking the Basilisks in the first place?"

Your grandfather said, "I don't know this. The problem I have is if we wait. The Basilisks may come at us like an army and cause more damage. I see an isolated incident versus and an all-out war."

King Alexander responded, "On day, you will tell me how see these things. I will not grant you my Paladins, but I will grant you the funds to grab heroes from the guilds. Will this suffice your request."

Your grandfather said, "That should be good enough."

Your grandfather put his arm across his chest and bowed to the King. The spot where his eyes should have been. There were two holes where a lava substance glowed purple. The lava never seems to drip off his body. It is almost like blood that flows through his circular system. The people around him could clearly see. The Hellfire in the lava was clearly a driving for keeping him alive.

The King wasn't sure if your grandfather was a friend or foe. He always feared that one of his tactics would disarm the kingdom. The day that would happen. The kingdom would go to Hell in a hand basket. This decision was designed to lose a bunch of hired hands and not the kingdom's protection.

Your grandfather had purple lightning surrounding his body. In an instant, he sped off. The man was faster enough to head to all the guilds in a mater of minutes to say he needed a group dispatched by that night. Those that were ready would meet him at the gate in three hours. He was ready to fight.

I wasn't invited to the fight. Your grandfather believed that I was too weak for the battle that was coming. I was a level ninety-eight protection warrior. I mean a real ninety-eight. Not the fake one we tell people to prevent battles. There have been times over the years that people tried to kill me because of my level. They saw killing me as a victory to brag about. It would be used to get better jobs and prestige. In the end, I'm still standing, and their deaths were taking a toll on me.

Once upon a time, I believed that your grandfather knew that I was strong. He would constantly put me through Hell daily. As I got older and stronger, I noticed something about him. He wasn't allowing me to team up with him and would often choose less qualified individuals. My mind would make excuses for his actions. I would say things like "He loves me and that is why I can't go. The truth was worse. The truth is your grandfather doesn't care about anyone but himself.

I stood at the gate waiting to be taken with him. I found out that there was a mission that would pay well. For me, it was more about prestige than money. Your grandfather was always being paid for missions. The King would often hire him as a mercenary. The strange thing was. He never cared about the money and would give it to me to keep. Between his money and my own from missions. He had a few vaults filled to the brim with gold. We are worth more than half the city.

I only tell you this because I want you to know in case something goes down. The money is held in my guild's vault. If at any point, I pass. I need you to know how to take care of your mom and the slaves. Farming doesn't pay enough to take care of everyone. Also, with money, there is power that can save your life one day.

When I stood at the gate, your grandfather spotted me. He walked over to me and grabbed me by the back of the head. The heat from his hands were searing into the back of my skull. He placed his forehead against mine and snarled. His armor was creating searing lines across my forehead.

Your grandfather asked, "What are you doing here boy?"

I responded, "I have come here to help the cause."

Your grandfather said, "To help the cause. You must be mad boy. Someone as weak and pathetic as you don't deserve to be on this team. Leave this up to the professionals."

I responded, "My level is higher than half the guys out here."

Your grandfather said, "They aren't weak ass tanks like you. A level forty-three heavy weapon warrior is more valuable than a guy who is only good behind a shield. You stay here and watch the wall. These pathetic Paladins in the castle won't save you and most of the good tanks won't even try without a price tag on the job."

Your grandfather removed his forehead from mine. The smell of burnt flesh filled the air. Some of my skin came off and grilled on his armor until it burned. The skin turned black and shriveled up. It fell shortly after. The skin was now ashes and flew away before hitting the ground.

Your grandfather said, "Move out boys. We got some hunting to do."

I was still young back then. I had been training as a warrior since I was nine years old. The only reason for my level was because your grandfather made a point to beat my ass every day. I have spilled more blood on his account than any child should. As much as I hate what he did, I can at least acknowledge. He made me stronger.

I went back to the city. The night was young, and the guild was lively. Most of the people in the guild were drunk off their asses. They had just come back from a successful mission. The church had tasked them with retrieving a special sword. I don't know what was special about the sword, but rumor had it would kill demons.

I drank heavily that night. I danced and sang with the others. We all danced and sang because the booze was flowing, and the money was good. It was a great night to celebrate even though I wasn't part of the party that got the sword. To them, I had saved their lives a hundred times before and deserved to be noticed.

While celebrating, a young man who was a year younger than myself walked into the room. He had dark hair that looked dyed to me. It was like he took ink and smothered it over his hair. The color of this hair was strange to me, and I wanted to know who he was. I walked over to the young man and put out my hand.

I said, "I'm James, and you are?

The man with the dyed hair responded, "You don't need to know my name. I am just a person looking for a job."

I looked at the man and pointed toward Henry. Henry was the guild leader. He was a Master Creationist. A hero class that could warp and manipulate everything around. It was different from an Illusionist because he was literally manipulating the entire building while we were speaking.

I walked toward Henry and said, "This mysterious son of a bitch is looking for a job."

Henry responded to the dyed hair man, "Hello, Draco. It's nice to see you again."

The man's name was Draco. The only Draco I knew of was the one that Marius the Legionnaire spoke of. He was training his son to be the next Legionnaire. The guy was supposedly fast but had no real battle experience. He would battle with the Paladins in the kingdom and was only a level forty-six.

I said, "So, your Draco...Simpson I'm guessing."

Draco responded, "What's it to you large and dumb?"

I said, "Looks like we got a diva here. Just so you know. You should be nice to the people around you. They may one day save your life."

Draco responded, "Like I would need someone as pathetic as you. I see the shield on your back. You're either a Protection Paladin or Warrior. Since you look a little rough in the face, I would say that you're a warrior. I walked by a hundred of you just coming here. They live by the shield and die by the shield. Getting to know you would never matter. You'll probably die next week."

I said, "Let me guess, daddy issues. Just so you know. I'm one of the top Protection Warriors in the kingdom. By looking at your knives. I would say you are either a Fury Warrior or a Rogue. Since you are wearing more leather than a dominatrix. I would say Fury Warrior.

Draco responded, "You know a lot for a peasant."

I said, "Listen, there might be a job coming up. A big one. If you want to show daddy what your made of, I suggest you stick around the kingdom for a few days."

Draco responded, "What kind of job are you talking about?"

I stuck out my hand to shake and said, "The big kind. You judged me too soon. I am James Damieno. The son of Marcus Damieno."

Draco responded, "The son of Marcus is a common warrior. You must have been a letdown."

I said, "You have no idea."

Draco smiled at me. That was the day he decided not to look down on me. He bought me a few brews and cheered on the group. I think he asked some of the patrons in the guild about me. He wanted to make sure that I wasn't lying. The funny thing is that everyone knew that I was the son of the great fortune teller himself, the great Marcus Damieno.

A full day had passed, and the next day was forming. I don't remember much from the day prior because I was so fucking drunk. All I know is that I woke up drunk with a woman in each arm. Man, Draco really knew how to hook a guy up. He was scrawny and weak compared to me. The fact that I'm six foot four really worked to my advantage. Aww, those were the days.

Here is a spot where I'll stop my father's telling of the story. My mother was getting pissed at him for bringing up the women in the story. There was about ten minutes of her verbally abusing him for trying to teach their three-year-old boy about his one-night stand with two other women at the same time. Apparently, that was uncalled for. I won't get into the details, but I figured that I would note it. I wanted you to know why we skipped part of the story. My father really got into some details about…It was a three-way. You're an adult. You can use your imagination on what happened. It creeps me out thinking of my father as a, in his terms, sexual beast.

Anyway, on with the rest of his telling of the story.

An alarm was ringing. The castle was becoming under siege. I hesitated a little at first. I didn't wish to leave the bed. There were more interesting things there. The bells of the church and the three corners of the city were going off at the same time. That meant only one thing. The people of the city needed to be prepared for an impending attack.

I put on my legs piece and chest piece. My short sword had a leather strap that was wrapped around my waist. Something was calling me back to bed, but I knew that I needed to protect the kingdom. I put on my helmet and picked up my shield. The straps were designed to allow the shield to be strapped to my back. I looked into the room and told the bed that I would be back and to wait for me.

I didn't come back. I was a changed man after that day.

Chapter 11

I went down the hall and came downstairs. Henry was at the bar handing out the merit slips. Merit slips or also known as defender slips; were payment slips where the castle guards would watch. They would see if you deserved payments from the kingdom. It can range from thirty copper to thousands of golds depending on your bravery and necessity in the battle.

I picked up my slip and slid it into my right pocket. My right hand was on my sword. I walked out of the guild. My heart was pounding. This was going to be a good day. I was going to earn so much money from this. There was no better tank than me. At least, that's what I believed at the time.

The peasants were walking to their homes and hiding. I was walking to the gate. All the other guild members were trying to get a good spot on the field. They were so busy trying to get to the battle that none of them seemed to understand what the threat was. I tried to listen to the members of the king's army. The word they used was snake.

My immediate reaction was to run. It appeared that my father failed with the group. The group of soldiers that were at the gate didn't kill all the snakes, and they came at the city in reTalyation. I was positive none of the snakes would have made it to the city if I had joined him. My nose was flaring up while I began to charge at the wall.

The doors were closing. I was too slow. I wasn't going to make it through the gate. There was a loud slamming sound and the locking of the doors. The walls of the city were ten thousand feet tall. It was some of the highest walls of any kingdom. It was too high for any snake to come over but that didn't mean it couldn't be broken through.

When I got there, I took my hands and slammed against the door. I wanted to fight. I needed to fight. I needed to prove to your grandfather that I was a great warrior. I don't know why I needed to prove anything to that piece of shit, but I was young and naïve at the time. My hands kept pounding on the door.

I heard a voice behind me say, "You were right about the attack. How did you know?"

I responded, "My father mentioned it might happen."

I looked back and saw a well-armed warrior named Draco standing behind me. He was a little better armed than before, holding two knives in his hands. There were large knives one side in holster. The leather straps braced to his side. Each handle on the knives had a different color liquid that could be almost seen through the ball at the bottom of the blades.

I said, "We can't battle if we can't get out."

Draco responded, "How fast are you?"

I said, "I'm slower than a racing snail."

Draco responded, "How high can you jump and fall from?"

I said, "I don't know. My legs have never failed me, and I've fallen hundreds of feet. Why?"

Draco smile at me and yelled, "Follow me!"

Draco was moving fast toward and tower. There were many towers along the wall. The towers were steep and had thousands of steps in them. The Hunters and Archers would watch from the top of the wall. These towers were used as ways for them to get up to the top of the wall.

I yelled, "Are you fucking kidding me?! You want me to jump off a ten-thousand-foot wall!"

Draco responded, "Yeah, tough guy. The kingdom needs us."

I was thinking about what he said. It made sense to me. That was the problem. It shouldn't have made sense to me. Falling from that height is no joke. To make things worse, I was running up some of the narrowest steps imaginable. My shield was grinding on the walls. Sparks were flying in my face from the shield, but I kept going.

Darco was almost to the top when he yelled down, "You not able to keep up fat boy."

I stopped for a moment to look up. What an asshole? In fact, as I'm telling you this story. I wonder why he is my friend. Anyway, I ran up to the top of the tower. I finally saw some sunlight. That was when I heard a blast hitting the side of the wall. I fell backward and almost went down the steps.

Draco pointed down at the Basilisk. The length of the snake had to be over a thousand feet long. The snake was surrounded by three Rogues. The Hunter next to us was smiling. He thought that the Rogues were about to take down the Basilisk. Rogues were always the best choice in large animal fights.

I'll tell you what Rogues do. They have a spiritual energy within them that allows them to turn bigger than a tree or smaller than an atom. They use spiritual energy to commune with other spirits and can go invisible. This power is often used amongst the sneakiest or thieves. Most of the Rogues that are good spend their lives power themselves up to be a Kaiju Force. They are needed the most against large beasts and demons. Even though they can't kill a demon, they can control them.

The Basilisk was looking at the three rogues. I was looking around to see if there were more snakes. I couldn't see any. My father might not have known, I thought. This might be that last snake from the cave. Even though I hate your grandfather, there is still a part of me that cares if he's alive.

The Rogue in the front reached for the mouth. It was strong enough to hold the mouth shut while the other two grabbed the tail. They were trying to stretch the tail out and pin it to the ground. By stretching it out and controlling the beast. Other classes could come in and easily kill the snake.

The Basilisk was stretched out. Its tail was being held and couldn't harm the castle wall anymore. I watched thinking that this would be the end. I wouldn't need to fight. I at least had a voucher to get paid a simple thirty copper coins for my trouble. It was a disappointment but at least nobody would get hurt.

My arms were folded while making sure the snake was killed. An Ice Mage was at the top of the tower. I jumped down and created a slide under its feet. The white hood on the Mage's head was flapping with the rest of its blue robe. The Ice Mage didn't have shoes. The feet were covered in ice instead.

The Ice Mage leaped into the air and yelled, "Arctic Blast!"

A giant blast of frigid cold temperatures drafted downward onto the middle of the Basilisk's tail. The ice was surrounding the snake and freezing it in place. The cold temperatures were the snake's biggest weakness. They were cold-blooded creatures that often looked for warm locations to stay alive.

The Ice Mage landed on the back of the Basilisk. He wasn't physically in the best shape but managed to stay on the red scales using the ice around him. He kept spraying ice everywhere. The Basilisk was calming down and the fight appeared to be almost over. After seeing the Basilisk falling asleep from the ice. Other Ice Mages were getting ready to jump off the wall to take it down.

The eyes on the Basilisk were closing I stared into the left eye on the snake. Something didn't feel right. The snake was faking. He was trying to get everyone to drop their guard. My heart was skipping. I was feeling fear. A tank will always feel fear, but it is an uphill battle to overcome the fear when in battle. I guess you can say that goes for all the classes.

I looked over at the Hunter and said, "Stop the Mages from attacking."

The Hunter responded, "Why? This kill is in the bag. They are just keeping it calm so we can grab the materials off the creature."

I said, "The Basilisk is playing you all for fools. Can't you see the eyes."

Right after saying that. The Rogue in the front loosened his grip. He was suffering from being over five hundred feet tall. They could be enormous in size, but it would take a large toll on their stamina. That was why they depended on other classes to help take down the Basilisk. A price that sometimes ended their lives.

The Rogue in the front lost control of the Basilisk's head. It pulled back rapidly and shot itself forward. The poor Rogue was bitten on his right shoulder. He dropped to his knees and looked at the snake. The snake lunged forward and bit the head of the Rogue off. It swallowed the head whole.

The rest of the Rogue's body was shooting an enormous amount of blood out the top. It remained still for a few seconds before falling on its left side. The sound of the body falling could be heard throughout the kingdom. The dust flew upward and left a hole in the ground. Upon his death, the body started to shrink back to its original size.

The Basilisk's head was no longer under control. It swerved around and looked at its back. A long-forked tongue came out of its mouth. It was looking at the Ice Mage standing on its back. Its eyes were turning a yellow and black color that shifted from left to right. It reminded me of tiger stripes that flowed to the center of the snake's eyes.

The Ice Mage pursed his lips before saying, "Oh FUCK!"

The Ice Mage raised his arms. He shot off more Artic Blast at the Basilisk. The snake wasn't affected by the cold as he thought. It blinded the snake just for a second before the head shook it off. The snake hissed at the Ice Mage making him damn near shit his pants. The Mage tried to jump off the left side of the snake but failed.

While the Ice Mage was jumping off, the Basilisk swooped down and bit the Mage. He The body was cut in half. The body went into the center of the fangs. The top set of teeth moved back and forth sawing the body in half. The legs flew to the ground. The snake raised its chin up and let the top part of the body slide down its throat.

The Rogue on the left side of the Basilisk went in to control the mouth. He thought that he could gain control once again. He just needed to act fast. Unfortunately for the Rogue, the snake was quicker. He reached out to grab the neck and managed to succeed. The snake's neck was now under control. His goal was met, but the snake didn't give a shit.

The Basilisks tail whipped around the back of the legs on the Rogue. He fell backwards onto the ground. His large size didn't give him much room and slammed his head at the base of the wall. He was knocked out by the immense force of the fall. The only real action he should have done was shrink. It was too late.

The Rogue was being wrapped up. The Basilisk was moving around the body of the Rogue. It squeezed the body with all its strength. The red color of the scales was covering the body while the snake was moving. The clenching of the snake's tail was tightening the more it wrapped around the body.

The Basilisk squeezed harder with each second. The bones within the Rogue's body were crackling under the pressure. I could feel the crunching in my bones, and it wasn't even happening to me. I watched as his eyes were turning red from being filled with blood. Death was the only option for the Rogue.

The Basilisk's head came up and hissed at the Rogue's body. The tip of its forked tongue was tasting the face. It opened its mouth and unhinged its jaw. It swooped down and bit the head off the Rogue. The teeth were grinding the skull. The flesh from the face was getting stuck between parts of its teeth. It swallowed what was left whole and turned around looking at the last Rogue.

The Rogue wasn't ready for a one-on-one battle. The idea of the team was to take down the powerful snakes using tactics to control it. He grabbed the knives out of their sheaths. I say knives, but their powers made them grow twice the size of my body. He tilted the blades; the dull end was firmly placed on his forearms.

The Rogue straddled from left to right. The Basilisk was getting ready to strike. Its tongue was sticking out and trying to appear intimidating. The truth was it didn't just appear intimidating. It could do everything it sought out to achieve. The speed was too much for the Rogue and it knew that.

The Basilisk lunged at the Rogue. With his size and the fact that he used up way too much energy, he couldn't dodge the strike. The large five-foot fangs bit into his chest. The Rogue looked down and knew he was dead. The venom was already going through his system. He tried to stab the knives through the head. It was unsuccessful. The scales on the head were too solid. Sparks were flying off the snake's head, but no damage was done.

The Rogue's flesh had green and black veins coming to the surface. It looked like lightning slowly flowing through his body. It slowly went up to his face and turned his eyes black. He couldn't move. He was trying to breathe. The venom had affected his lungs, and black blood was dripping out of his mouth.

The Basilisk removed its fang from the Rogue's chest. It came back and waited for the Rogue to attack again. The Rogue dropped to his knees and held onto his chest. There was a river of blood coming out. He couldn't hold himself up anymore and fell forward onto the ground. His body was shrinking back to its original size. All three Rogues were down for the count.

The tension was getting worse. The people were afraid. People were screaming. Everyone knew there was no hope. Those were the strongest Rogues in Tryanon. Panic was setting in for all the people at the gate. When one of the archers yelled that the Rogues were dead. People realized that the merit slips might force them to actually fight. Many of them ran away. Especially the tanks, I was literally the only tank willing to stay at the wall.

I asked the Hunter on the wall, "What happens now?"

The Hunter replied, "Isn't it obvious. The Ground Mages keep the wall up as long as possible. The people retreat from the city and hope that a strong person comes along that can kill the Basilisk."

I said, "We can't give up. We need to find some strong sparkies and melee savants to kill this thing."

The Hunter asked, "What is a sparky?"

I replied, "You know. The arrows that fly though the air and shoot through shit."

The Hunter said, "You mean Star Piercers."

I responded, "See you knew."

The Hunter said, "There is not a Hunter or Mage in the world that will attack the Basilisk right now. They don't want to risk their lives for a possibility of saving the kingdom."

I responded, "I'm a tank. I need some others to join me. I'm not sure if I can do it alone."

The Hunter looked around and noticed the Archers and Hunters were trying to flee to safety. The Basilisk was hitting against the wall. Each hit was pushing the wall over a little more. The only reason it was still up was the fortification provided by the Ground Mages. The Ground Mages were strong and focused. They aren't just good for growing plants. They are great at building things on the ground and keeping things together.

Draco looked at me and said, "How crazy are you feeling today?"

Chapter 12

Draco said, "That is a big bitch. All the other tanks have run off. If you're as powerful as you claim, this might be your ultimate fight. After today, you will either die a hero or live long enough to see yourself become a coward."

I responded, "I love your faith in me. You are a fucking prick."

Draco laughed at me. He was more of a guy who liked to pull strings. I had no idea. He knew who I used to be in the first life. The two of us being united again was a godsend. I didn't know it at the time, but we were family. I won't get more into that. I'll let him tell you who he is if he wants to be known.

My feet were having a harder time standing up. Each hit from the Basilisk was tossing everyone on the wall around. I closed my eyes and took a deep breath. I was about to do the most insane thing a man could do. I was getting ready to solo a damn god tier snake.

My mind was racing. I tried to think of every reason not to attack the Basilisk. In the end, the killing of the snake wasn't just about defending the city. My father told me that I wouldn't be any use. I needed to prove his ass wrong. I wanted to prove my resolve to my father. I needed to prove to him. I was superior to him in every way. He needed to know. I was ready for the mission to the cave.

I said to Draco, "You better not let me down brother."

I ran over to the edge of the wall and leaped off. It seemed like a good idea at the time. When you're falling and gravity is taking over, you question your life decisions. You start thinking things like what the fuck have I done. The Basilisk is bigger enough to eat me whole. He was fast enough to easily snatch me out of the air. I needed to swerve or something.

My shield was still on my back. I curled up into a ball and dropped backward. The Basilisk came up to snap at me. There was glare on the shield that shined in the snake's eyes. He had snapped at me and missed. With my weight, size, and the fact I was dropping ten thousand feet to the damn ground. The snake couldn't catch me, and the shield hit the tip of his nose.

When I bounced off the top the Basilisks left nostril, I flew past a few tree branches and landed on my feet. My shield was still ringing from hitting the nose. My knees were bent, and I looked like I was sitting on a horse. My sword was keeping me upright by digging into the dirt. My knees were shocked bad enough that I couldn't move a muscle.

I fell to the left of me and let the dirt cover me until I could get my bearings. The Basilisk stopped hitting the wall for a little bit. It was trying to find me. I pushed myself up with every muscle in my aching body. Pain wasn't a new concept to me, but it didn't let me be in full form. I took the shield off my back and unsheathed my sword.

I yelled up to Draco, "You coming!"

Draco yelled out, "I might be crazy, but I'm not stupid. I'll use the front door. They will open it now that you're tanking the beast."

I thought to myself. What a fucking pussy! I jumped off the damn wall like he insinuated, and I got no help. I leaped high into the air and went out far into the field. My feet slammed into the ground causing a dust up. The sound of the slam got the Basilisk's attention. He heard me moving around and charged me.

The dirt shot out from its sides. I couldn't believe how fast a damn Kaiju could be. It lunged at me, and I jumped to the left. The Basilisk's nose went into the dirt. It lifted its head and snot out what dirt it could. When it sneezed, the snot hit the ground and began to sizzle. I had no idea that the nose was filled with acid. This fight was about to be tougher than I thought.

I looked over at the wall. It was filling up with Mages ranging from fire to ice. They were charging what power they could. Mages could do a lot of instant magic, but to charge an attack. It took time. I didn't feel like there was time. The longer this fight carried on. The more of a chance the Basilisk could catch me.

The Gates of Tryanon opened. There was a fighting force coming this way. With a tank at the helm, their courage came back. It wasn't just the men that came to the battle. Their pets joined them on the battlefield. The Hunters with Beast Tamers classes were able to send out their pet companions. The strong ones could even use Kaiju as an attack if necessary.

I was feeling better about the battle. They all sat back and waited for instructions from the Commander. The Legionnaire Marius Simpson was standing on the wall waiting for the perfect opportunity to attack. He had faith in me knowing who my father or your grandfather was. We had a good name that was upheld.

I believed Marius was waiting for me to gain full control of the battle. As long as I had Aggro, which is a fancy way of saying I had his full attention, the assault team could run in and kill the Basilisk without any casualties. When I looked at him, he nodded his head to let me go full on berserk.

I yelled, "Warrior's Roar!"

I banged my sword against the shield. I use chi energy to do most of my attacks. I kept banging on the shield causing the Basilisk to remain in a trance state. I was swaying back and forth and could only see me on the field. The noise shook the snake and caused pain in its head. It would do anything to end the noises haunting its mind.

All eyes were on me. The Basilisk hissed while trying to attack me. The tongue was sticking out and going up and down. I shifted from left to right. As long as I kept moving, there was no chance of me beating the snake. I just needed to keep moving and messing with its head. I was a ninety-eight warrior. I had to show the world what I was made of.

While dodging, the assault squad was getting ready to attack. Draco got impatient or something and didn't wait for his father's signal. Instead, he ran out the gate faster than a bat out of Hell. A trail of dust was left behind. He made to much of a commotion. I was losing Aggro from the Basilisk.

I yelled, "Draco, get off the field."

The Basilisk was charging in his direction. He could have easily left the battlefield. He had to be the fastest man I ever saw besides you grandfather. The snake was ready to eat. He was about to run but something was wrong. Fear took over his body. He had never seen a creature that large before. He felt pain in the back of his throat. He couldn't move a muscle.

Marius looked down upon his son and shook his head in disappointment. He walked over to the other side of the wall. He didn't guide the assault squad to help at all. He left his son there to die. I had just made a new companion. There was only one way to save the guy's life. I needed to take the Basilisk head on.

While running at the Basilisk, my sword was banging on my shield. It was slowing down significantly but still dove at Darco. When the nose got within a few feet of Draco, it stopped and sniffed him. I didn't want to eat him. I couldn't figure out why, but the hesitation gave me enough time to take my shield and slam the snake on the right side of his face.

I yelled, "Someone get him out of here."

Draco's body disappeared a few seconds later. Here is the thing son. Never underestimate the power of people. Each person can have a role to play in a battle. There is a group of people called Time Mages. Your mother is one of them. These people can slow down or stop time around them. They can't wield heavy weapons or armor usually, but they can easily move the pieces in a battle. A Time Mages main goal in a fight is to act as a support. Sometimes that means pulling people out of a battle or replacing someone in battle. A Time Mage pulled Draco from the fight. Your mother said it wasn't her, but she knew the woman that pulled him.

The Basilisk growled. I knew at that moment. I was about to get fucked up. The tongue came out and hissed in my direction. It was literally a foot away from my face. I had never been so glad to be wearing a helmet in my life. I breathed in its stinky breath, but at least the saliva didn't hit me.

I leaped backward and hit my shield some more. The Mages were getting ready to attack. There were enormous fireballs formed on the wall. The heat was killing the grass below and fires were forming on the other side of the wall. I just needed to buy the Mages one more minute. They needed to focus distracting the Basilisk and prevent it from hitting the wall. A disruption on the wall might screw up their spells.

The Basilisk hissed at me and lunged again. This time, when it came at me, it stopped and raised its head high into the sky. It was waiting for me to move. I stayed perfectly still waiting for it to attack first. I might not be able to dodge the attack, but I could sure as Hell try to defend against it.

I took my right hand and tightened my left gauntlet. My left arm pushed further into the shield's strap. The shield was almost up to my shoulder. I looked into the Basilisk's eyes and stopped beating on the shield. I had its attention, and it was pissed. The Basilisk lunged at me for one last time.

The mouth went at me fast and fiercely. The teeth in the center between the fangs were trying to bite me in half. When it got close enough, I lunged into the Basilisk's mouth. My left hand grabbed the tooth right next to the fang. With my gauntlet acting as a buffer, I wasn't getting poisoned. I could, however, hear the sizzling on my armor.

The Basilisk was trying to close its mouth. It couldn't close the mouth with my boots on its teeth. I was forcing the snake's mouth open. My legs were stiff. It was a matter of time until they gave out. I fought my best to keep its mouth open. The snake decided to raise its head up. I was now over three hundred feet in the air. It kept fighting to close it on me.

The Basilisk's jaw was unhinging to open. The tilting of the jaw made it harder for me to keep it open. This was the moment of truth. I took the sword in my right hand and jammed it up through the inside of the snake's mouth. A violent acid was coming out the mouth and spraying the insides. I leaped outward to avoid the spray. While leaping outward, the Basilisk's fang went through my shield and stabbed me in the arm.

The venom from the Basilisk went into my arm and caused it to go black. It was stabbed in the forearm so I had time before it would work its way to my heart. I leaped off the Basilisk's mouth and tried to land gracefully to the ground. The fang cut through my arm and scrapped down to my hand. It nearly sliced that part of my arm in half. My bones were stronger than normal. The gash was only bone deep.

I didn't fall gracefully. Instead, I landed on my right side. My shield was destroyed, and my sword was still stuck in the mouth of the Basilisk. The poison that could melt armor was spraying everywhere. I didn't think anyone could get near me. I accepted my fate. I felt that my duty was to the kingdom complete. I could finally die in peace.

I closed my eyes waiting for the Basilisk to eat me. There was no hope for someone like me. I didn't believe a Time Mage could be strong enough to carry someone of my size. The weight of my armor alone had to be over a hundred and fifty pounds. The entrance had to be at least six hundred feet. That distance would be too far for even the most experienced Time Mages. I took one last breath and waited for my demise.

I heard a voice yell, "NOW!"

I was stripped of all my armor. A Time Mage had retrieved me. She was strong enough to remove all my armor and bring me back behind the wall. I wasn't just behind the wall. I was at the top of the wall. She wanted me to see what I had accomplished. I have all the Mages time to charge what was necessary to kill the creature.

There were three large wolves that charged in and bit the tail. The Basilisk couldn't seem to locate or do anything to the wolves. Some animals were preventing it from being able to move its mouth or see where it was. Its head was moving around with its jaw open. The teeth on the wolves were sharp but not sharp enough to cut through the scales on the tail.

The Fire Mages dropped their arm. The fire was focused and full of vengeance coming from the Mages. The fire flew closer to the head. Each blast was hot enough to burst the scales. Watching the scales was interesting because it reminded me of popcorn going off. The fires were coming together in one giant fireball. I believe parts of it were purple. Purple is the ultimate color for fire. It is referred to as Hellfire.

The Hunters and Archer were shooting arrows into the weakened spots where the scales popped off. The Hunters that could use Star Piercing arrows were making sure it drilled in their hard. The meat from the Basilisk could feed the kingdom for a few days. Nobody wanted to poison it.

The Ice Mages slid down their ice trails and landed on the end of the Basilisk's tail. They blasted the front the end of the tail with what could only be described as an ice storm. The ice kept the snake from being able to move. Each one of the Ice Mages kept shouting "Artic

Blast." I felt all I needed to do was make sure the snake died. I needed to know that my life wasn't given up for nothing.

The Basilisk's head dropped to the ground shortly after the warrior ran out there and climbed on its back. They kept stabbing at the opened-up flesh areas like neanderthals. Warriors aren't the smartest class, but they do get a lot of jobs done through blind brute force and pure determination.

Being a Protection Warrior, I had a skill called Ignore Pain. I was using it at this time. The skill is great during battle but when you leave battle. The pain comes back to you in full force. I felt the venom working its way up my arm. I needed to have someone heal me fast. Unfortunately, no Priests or Paladins had come to the wall that day.

Your mother was sitting next to me and holding my right hand. She was so strong that it shocked me. The squeeze of my right hand would normally break their hand. Your mother was too tough for that. She held onto me and watched over me. She just kept saying for me to stay with her. I took those words to heart.

A Warrior Captain came to my aid. He brought out his sword. The end was enormous. He called the blade his Executioner's Blade. Executioner Blades were known to be the largest, heaviest, and sharpest blades that existed in the kingdom. Their design was to create a solid swing downward decapitating a foe. The only way it couldn't carve though flesh is if the being carrying the blade was weaker than the being swung at.

Often for a greater effect and more wind resistance, there would be holes in the blades. Inside the holes would be rings that would distract while being swung. The blade would be two inches thick. The tip would be curved upward and three teeth on the end. The teeth were the same as a saw not a human tooth. One side was sharp while the other side remained thick and dull. If a Warrior wanted to keep a person alive, they would guard with the opposite side and mercilessly beat their opponent.

The Warrior Captain swung down on my arm. The blade didn't make a scratch. Sparks flew off the blade while hitting my skin. The blade shook and made a vibrating sound. That never happened to him before. He wouldn't stop. He swung down again hoping this time he would save my life. Once again, my level and defense were too high to be saved.

The venom was creeping up through my veins. I could see it almost touching my elbow. It was a slow death in my eyes, but a valiant death, nonetheless. Your mother stroked the hair on my head stared into my eyes. I'm not sure if it was just the fact I was dying, but to me she was the most beautiful woman to ever walk the planet.

I smiled at her and said, "In a world filled with despair, I'm glad I could spend my last moments looking at someone as beautiful as you."

Your mother responded, "You're no dying today. We will save you. I need to save you."

Your mother was crying. Her eyes were covered in water. She had on some kind of makeup that was running down her face. Women in this world don't usually wear makeup. So, it stunned me. All that beauty, and she wanted to cover it up. I wanted to look away, but couldn't I didn't want to waste a moment looking at her beautiful face.

Chapter 13

The Priests and Paladins felt they were needed elsewhere instead of the castle. The High Priest didn't think it was worth it to risk the lives of his fellow Priests. That decision would cost him future Priests. A Guild was formed shortly after for the sole purpose of having healers for the battlefield.

I did everything in my power to save myself. The pain was getting worse. The hole in my arm where the Basilisk's tooth cut me was swelling up and closing shut. My blood was no longer siphoning the venom out. It began to go up my arm faster. The elbow was now black as night. I just hoped for a quick death once it reached my heart.

I lay back and closed my eyes. My teeth were gnashing so hard. They were chipping off. I let out a loud scream. If you know anything about Protection Warriors, we have the loudest screams of any other classes. It's how we get the attention of beasts and prey. I say that but that doesn't include certain violent species like Draco's kid.

A Fire Mage heard my cries and ran over to see what was wrong. He was an older man with white hair. His beard was perfectly groomed with black tips. He looked like a man that singed the hairs every day. His robe was black with golden buttons running down the center. There was a crest above his left pocket. I didn't recognize the crest. All I knew was that he appeared to be friendly.

The Fire Mage asked, "What is going on here?"

The Warrior Captain replied, "This is the young man that took on Basilisk alone."

The Fire Mage said, "I see. You are a brave man for doing what you did. Very Stupid, but also brave. What is it that we are trying to do?"

The Warrior Captain responded, "I tried to cut off his arm to save him. My blade can't make it through his flesh."

The Fire Mage said, "That Executioner Blade is sharp. Too bad the owner isn't. Let me see what I can do. Stand back."

The Fire Mage took his right hand and placed it on your mother's shoulder. He pulled her back gently and got on his knees. He slapped his hands together and rubbed them fast. There were smoke and red sparks flickering off his hands. He wrapped both hands around the arm. The heat from his hands were searing my flesh. The smell of burnt flesh filled the wall. When he was done, he left behind handprints.

I was in a lot of pain from the Fire Mage burning me. It was worth it because he was able to temporarily stop the spread of the venom. He closed his eyes and felt around the burn spots on my arm. I wasn't quite sure what he was trying to accomplish but knelt to see something within the burn marks.

The Fire Mage said, "If you have enough energy for Ignore Pain. Now would be the time to use it."

I didn't have much Chi left. I had just enough to help negate half the pain he was about to inflict on me. I opened my eyes when I saw what was about to happen. The Fire Mage was blowing on his hand. His hand was flickering blue sparks Blue is the third hottest area of a flame only second to Hellfire.

The Fire Mage yelled, "Devil's Spark!"

The Fire Mage's right hand turned into a flame. The shape of the flames looked like a dagger. The Warrior Captain took a piece of leather that would normally be used to hold a knife and shoved it in my mouth. He grabbed ahold of my arm and held me down. The fire blade touched my arm and didn't just cut my flesh. It cauterized any area that was being cut.

The Fire Mage cut my arm right above the elbow. The smell of burnt flesh was getting worse. While cutting, the blood wasn't coming out. The wound was getting cauterized immediately. Things were looking good. The light was shining through my arm. I could see my bones by looking. I wanted to scream so bad. With the leather inside my mouth. It made it hard to show any form of expression.

The Fire Mage finally finished cutting. There was no blood coming out of my forearm, but venom was. He was amazed at how I managed to keep it under control. The arm was dissolving at my feet, and the venom was causing the arm to boil. The venom was strong enough to burn holes in the ground of the wall closest to the entrance. He had to set the arm on fire to prevent it from causing more damage.

The Warrior Captain yelled, "Get this man to a hospital. Hopefully a healer will come by."

I couldn't hear much more of what happened after that. My body felt so weak. I was slowly fainting. Your mother ran over to me and caressed my face. She was still crying while watching over me. The last thing I saw was her giving me a kiss on the forehead. I felt it. I loved it. I was exhausted.

The next thing I knew. I was waiting in a hospital bed. There were no Priests around, but Paladins were in the healing area doing their best to heal the patients. It sucked because Paladins were more about healing themselves. There is something in their blood that creates healing radiation, but it is nowhere near as strong. Not a single Priest was in the area.

I looked around and at the foot of my bed was Draco and your mother. Draco said, "You crazy son of bitch. You did it. Without your efforts, the Basilisk would have destroyed the wall and killed thousands of people. I'm almost certain that the king will give you the King's bounty."

I responded in a groggy voice, "Why would I get the King's bounty? I didn't kill it. I didn't even make it to the end of the battle."

Draco said, "I might have put in a good word. Also, my father, the Legionnaire witnessed a single man go up against one of the mightiest creatures and come out alive. Just trust me on this. You need the money. A tank without his shield arm won't be much of a tank."

I responded, "If you think my days as a hero are over, you are sadly mistaken."

Draco said, "Please don't do this to yourself. I'm sure there is something out that can interest you."

I responded, "I'm a Damieno. We are the strongest bloodline to exist. It is foretold that I am the direct descendant of demons."

Draco said, "You saved lives. Don't make this into a personal thing. I'm sure your father would understand."

I responded, "You obviously don't know my father. When I turned nine and my father found out I was a Warrior instead of a Hell Spawn. He killed my mother out of rage."

Draco said, "Well, nobody's father is perfect."

Draco looked deep into my eyes. He looked like he was trying to find something. I lay there waiting to see what he was doing. After a few seconds I swung my left arm at him. The end of my sawed-off arm was covered in a tan cloth. I had drops of blood throughout. My arm was shaking. That was when it hit me. I could no longer be apart of the guild. I needed to start a new chapter in my life.

Draco said, "Easy pal. I thought I saw something. I know you. I knew you from the first world. You were my cousin. Isn't that right, but you knew that already."

The truth was that I had no idea who he was, but Draco guessed my name. Whenever someone knows your name from the first world, you better pay attention every time. They might know a weakness of yours. Over the years, I have paid attention to everything he ever said. I can't think of a single time. I ever thought of him as a threat. Instead, he became an asset that I will one day hand off my most valuable commodity. YOU!

Your mother was sitting at the end of the bed. That day, she found out from Draco what my first world name was. It turned out. I knew her from High School. Nothing about the two of us clicked in the first world, but this was a new world.

I kept an eye on your mother. She was never a fool. I didn't mind watching her. I found her to have the beauty of a million suns and the smell of flowers. Both of those things if not careful could kill you. Your mother loves me, and I know this. I also piss her off a lot. If this old man isn't careful, one of these days, I'm afraid she will poison my soup.

After a few days of recovery, I was asked to come to the Throne Room. The room is located in the castle directly in the middle of the city. The whole city was wrapped around in a circle. The poorest to the outside and slowly worked its way to the center where the King lives. Draco lived in the area closest to the castle. A large plot of land provided by the King for his Sister, Draco's mother.

I walked up to the castle gate and was escorted inside. I never saw so many Paladins in my life. My entire life was around the Warriors. Since Warriors died more often than any other class. It was getting scarce to find them at times. That made me more special than the people in these other classes. I would be the inspiration for so many children. They didn't understand the death aspect but understood that we were the class that saw the most action within the Kingdom.

I walked up what had to be the longest set of steps that I had ever seen. There was nothing to hold onto and every floor to the top of the castle had a door leading across and below the Throne Room.

When I got to the top of the steps, there were these enormous doors with the Varguss family crest on them.

Two Paladins opened the doors, and a large red carpet was in front of me. There were sets of Paladins on each side of the carpet leading up to the Throne where the King was sitting. I was nervous because I had never visited the King before. Your grandfather had on many occasions but never brought me along. He claimed that I was too weak and would end up being nothing more than an embarrassment while visiting the King.

I walked forward and stood before the King Alexander Varguss. I didn't know how to bow and just tried to remember what the Japanese did in the television shows. I held my head up and kept my arms to my side while bowing. I had no idea that I was supposed to drop to my one knee while bowing.

Marius was standing to the left of the King. He was wearing a bright white robe with gold symbols engraved within it. His hands were behind his back while shaking his head. His eyes were closed. I do believe he was trying not to laugh. I realized that I probably embarrassed my father by doing that.

A man in a black robe was to the right of the King. He had a fully grown beard and appeared to be the father of a being that would be later known as the Warlock of the Tower. He seemed well mannered despite being referred to as the Lord of the Dark Arts. His eyes were white and didn't appear to have any pupils or color to them. That didn't stop him from having a smile.

The Warlock of the Tower, however, turned into one of the evilest beings to live in this world. The man was so evil that his flesh was naturally rotting on its own. The son's name was Gandriel. I was terrified whenever looking into his eyes. Eventually, he too would be an advisor to Prince Norman.

King Alexander asked, "Do you know why I have summoned you?"

I rose up from the bow and replied, "I was told that I would be receiving a reward from the King. Was I mistaken?"

King Alexander said, "You aren't just receiving any reward. You are receiving the King's bounty. A reward that carried with it thirty thousand gold and a wish of your choosing."

I responded, "That is very generous my Lord, but I'm afraid I don't deserve this. The words of Draco might be a little too much. I'm afraid there were better men that day."

King Alexander said, "You don't have an ego like your father. That is quite fascinating. By the way, I wouldn't go by the words of Draco Simpson. That kid is still learning and would probably find favor with a man offered up their red-haired daughter. No, NO, no, it was Marius that brought you to my attention. He boastfully claimed without you. The fight might have been lost, and thousands would have died."

I responded, "I have faith that the men would have prevailed."

King Alexander said, "Thirteen men died from the Basilisk. Do you know what that means?"

I responded, "I do not."

King Alexander said, "Six decades ago, the Basilisks attacked the Kingdom of Tryanon. The walls were too short, and the damn snake crawled over. That's why we now have ten-thousand-foot walls. When the Basilisks came into the kingdom, there were over sixty-two thousand people that died. There wasn't a white knight or a savior.

After studying the Basilisks, we learned their weakness and have hunted them on several occasions. The venom is good for combat, the skin is good for armor, and the meat will fill up the bellies of people. We must be careful and have everything planned out in advance. We need to make sure the species fear us.

It looks like the one that fought us was a rogue Basilisk. The others didn't come, but that might have been because of your father.

To think, if you went on the mission with him. We wouldn't have had a savior. A titan to give the Mages on the wall time to charge their attacks. To slowly get troops out the gate to line up and bring courage to the troops. Without you, we wouldn't have had the opportunity to see a victory. There wouldn't have been one unified attack. You sir have saved the kingdom. I am indebted to you. I don't know of a single person that doesn't acknowledge their family is safe because of you. Do you disagree with me."

I responded, "I'm flattered and will take your reward."

King Alexander said, "Good, now tell me your wish."

I responded, "Honestly, I don't know what to do. I have one arm now. I might want to have it healed."

King Alexander said, "I can't force the Priests to do heals to that extent. As you saw, I couldn't get them to the front to heal the wounded. They are defenders against the demons of the land unfortunately. You would have to go to them and hope all they want is money. I can however offer you women, a position in my cabinet, or land."

I responded, "Land, that seems interesting. Some farmlands would be nice. Being in the government isn't my style. I'm not smart enough. As for women, I just want one at the moment."

Just when I thought everything was about to be settled. Purple lightning filled the room. It was like a large gust of wind. Everyone felt the need to cover their faces. I knew that lightning anywhere. It didn't want him to show up at all. Instead, I hoped that the Basilisks killed him, but he would never be killed so easily.

A voice came from smoke that appeared in the room. His body was covered in Brimstone Armor. The bright purple light shined from his face armor. It always looked like he had a sinister grin and two bulging eyes where the purple lava would move around in. The armor would go from head to toe. He would never show his body after killing your grandmother.

Your grandfather said, "Did I miss something? A royal gathering with my son attending. I do believe. I should have been invited."

King Alexander responded, "You are always welcome to attend. You know we have no way of contacting you. Your inability to stay in one place makes it impossible to track you down."

Your grandfather said, "You are always wise in your words, but let's face it. We all know the truth. I show up whenever I want and do whatever I want. I also knew about this meeting long before you even knew it would exist."

King Alexander asked, "Did any of your men survive your assault?"

Your grandfather didn't say a word. He just laughed in the face of the king. The laughter echoed throughout the Throne Room. Everyone knew that your grandfather was the only survivor. It was almost always a constant. I do believe one man survived an assault with him. He eventually went crazy and took his own life.

Chapter 14

King Alexander didn't appear to be amused by the deaths as much. Those were still citizens of the kingdom. His duties were to protect the people of the kingdom against foreign and domestic threats. He basically sent those men to their doom. The upside was. If they failed the mission, the kingdom didn't have to pay. They failed the mission.

Money didn't matter to King Alexander. He found value in the people of Tryanon. The people were what made the kingdom. It wasn't about the buildings or the statues. It was about keeping good citizens alive. He would give every dime in the kingdom if it meant keeping everyone safe. In a world of magic, that was always a possibility. That was why keeping Marcus happy was essential.

Your grandfather said, "I'm assuming the boy has already told you about wanting land."

King Alexander asked, "Is this a scam?"

I replied, "No, I haven't spoken to him since he tried to go on the mission."

Your grandfather said, "Relax. I just know things. I'm just trying to point you in the right direction. There is some land about ten miles out from here. A dirt road will direct them. He will just have to find people to help his weak ass farm. He will find them at the slave trade center. There is huge shipment of demi-humans that came in."

King Alexander asked, "Do you hate your son that much? You would put him in a situation with violent demi-humans."

Your grandfather replied, "He is a Damieno. I assure you. They will listen. He might be weaker than me by a lot, but he is still stronger than many of you puny humans. Even if he has one hand behind his back."

The brimstone was breaking on his face. The grin was getting bigger, and lava was dripping out onto the floor. The lava touched the red carpet and burned holes in it. It would take weeks before they got a new carpet. The room was filling up with smoke and making it harder to see. He stomped out the fire just walking forward.

King Alexander said, "Find out who owns the land that he is speaking of."

Marius responded, "There is no need to find out. I know the owners."

King Alexander asked, "Whom?"

Marius replied, "My wife and son own the land. In a way, you can say I do too, but that is royal land. I would never give away royal land."

Your grandfather said, "Just ask Draco. The boy is inching for this opportunity. I guarantee it. I'm sure you know of his admiration for James. A lifelong bond that won't be outdone. Well, for a while, that is."

Marius responded, "What does that mean?"

Your grandfather said, "Everything in life eventually comes to an end. It will be the children that will resolve the future."

King Alexander said, "Convince your son to give up the land. If he says no, I will force the issue. It was the boy's request and keeping peace with Marcus is important. Having his only flesh in blood being a permanent member of the community will certainly keep us in his good graces."

Your grandfather said, "Right you are sir, but more importantly. I believe in his heir."

Your grandfather came in and vanished just as fast. He would often drop hints at the future. I never understood how he did it. He always appeared to be right about things. He even knew about me losing my arm. Like everyone else, I disdained the fact that he existed, but he is what we call a necessary evil.

With your grandfather gone, I asked, "Where do I pick up my gold?"

King Alexander replied, "It has already been placed in your guild bank. You can retrieve it at a moment notice. If you're listening to your father, you will need much of it."

I bowed and walked out of the room. I walked to the guild and pulled out enough gold to fill a pouch. I would say one hundred pieces of gold was all that could be filled. The coins jingled while walking to the slave area of town. I felt like everyone was watching me while I walked to the cages.

When I walked into the slave trade center, I looked around and saw twenty floors. The stairs were the only thing that separated the cages. There was howling and chirping. I couldn't believe how many demi-humans were in the place. The place reminded me of an evil colosseum where everyone had their rights taken away.

A man came over to me and asked, "What can we do for you? We are about the auction some new goods that just came in."

I replied, "I'm just a simple farmer looking for slaves. What can you show me?"

The man took me over a cage on the first floor. He said, "We just got a whole community of these in. They are wolf demi-humans. Their ability to work at night is probably of value to you. This little one with a few nights will be quite subservient. I promise you that."

I knelt to see a little female cub. The way the trader spoke of nights made me feel sick to my stomach. She was so small and adorable. Not really the type of animal that could do heavy lifting or building. She was the type that might be good for taking care of some of the younglings when they are born.

I asked, "How much?"

The man replied, "For her, I can probably do four silvers."

I said, "No, I'm asking how much for all the wolf people."

The man responded, "Well I would say about ninety gold."

I asked, "Is that for all three hundred and seventeen of them?"

The man said, "Yes for that many of them. For an extra five gold we can even collar them for you."

I responded, "If you have them collars and ready by nightfall. I'll give you a flat one hundred gold."

The man asked, "Can we see the gold first?"

I showed him the gold and the man said, "Once the gold hits my hand, they are all yours."

I gave him the gold and his team went right to work. The man I had been talking to asked for me to cut my hand and spill the blood into a wooden cup. The cup was probably the cleanest thing in the slave trade. I put out my hand and let him cut. Apparently, to make sure that ownership is done. A small drop goes into each collar. If the master dies, the collars explode or go to the next of kin. The slaves have three days to find the next of kin. Most are lucky and the next of kin live at home. Some are unlucky and there are no heirs. The unlucky slaves wait and countdown the days until the collar explode.

When they were done with me, I walked over to the cage with the little pup. She was so adorable. I stuck my fingers in the cage, and she growled. It was the most adorable thing ever. When she realized that I couldn't be frightened, she ran to the other side of the cage. She was now the frightened one. I couldn't blame her.

I said to her, "I will reunite you with your family soon. This nightmare is almost over."

The little pup was crying. It didn't look like the tears of someone that was joyful. It was the tears of someone that lost everything. Now that I thought about it. A community of wolves usually ranged to at least over three thousand. This appeared to be only a small amount of what should have been. I wondered if I was late.

I walked over to a random guy and asked, "Is this all of them? I figured there would be more wolf demi-humans."

The guy replied, "This is all that was sold to us. The poachers are known for stealing what they think would make the most money for the least amount of hassle. Most people want guy slaves to be docile. They don't want ones that are feral and might kill them without a care of their own safety. Those wolves are killed immediately and made examples of. They skin the body for meat, clothing, and bones for medicines. We get the subservient ones. Don't worry, you still get the best that wolves have to offer. Spending that much though. That is buying a high-ranking hero money. I hope you find one in the group."

The guy ran off. He just saw this as another day. The slave trade was filled with some of the evilest people imaginable. They just saw a dollar to the bodies of the people. I couldn't save everyone. I just knew that I could save them. I walked over and sat down in front of the cage with the little cup.

I asked the pup, "What is your name?"

She replied, "Talya."

I said, "Well Talya. I'm hoping to give you a good home. Since I only have one arm, I need help with many tasks. This includes farm work."

Talya asked, "You have a farm?"

I said, "I just got some land and will need help to start the farm. Will you help me?"

Talya was frightened of all the humans but was warming up to me. She climbed all over the cage and would tell me about the people in the village. Most of the knowledge she had was more than enough to tell me what I was dealing with. If I was evil, a lot of the stuff could have been used against her people. That's the thing about being good. I tried to take her advice and help them because they were about to help me.

A familiar voice came up behind me. It said, "So, you're taking my land. After all we have been through. Well, the land already has a house on it. It's old and needs some work. Just to let you know. I'm hoping to start building a house right next to your land. I'll need my father's help. He said I will get it when I start a family. I was hoping sooner. I believe I need to help me stretch out and learn to go solo. I can't live with my dad forever."

I looked back and saw Draco standing over me. I looked up and stood next to him. I still towered over him in height. He punched me in the chest knowing that it wouldn't affect me at all and pointed over toward the street. There was a carriage ready for me. He wasn't just happy to give me the land. He wanted the two of us to be neighbors. I hated the idea at first, but Draco has a way of growing on you.

Nightfall came and the slaves were all collared up. Apparently, the traders weren't sure if they would sell any of them that night. Due to their feral history, people were weary of wolf demi-humans. Some have been known to eat their masters in the middle of the night without caring if they died.

The wolf people were following the carriage. I didn't like the idea of being inside the carriage. It had this see through glass that would get steamy with a little breathing. I sat on top of the carriage to gain full perspective of what was happening around us. I even let little Talya sit in the front of the carriage next to the driver.

The animals around us were calling out to the wolves. I didn't understand anything happening. The wolves stayed silent and walked the dirt road to the house. When we got to the house. I got off the carriage and walked over to the house. The door looked a little bit off the hinges and many things looked rusted.

I looked back at the wolves and said, "This is the start of our new life. Everyone will need to work together. As long as I'm alive. There will be peace. I am but one man. Over time, I hope to be as much a member of your family as your parents and children. I need someone to start the fire, and all the children will be staying in the home tonight."

These were easy orders. Many of the wolves would want these demands. They are very maternal. The pups are always the priority in their society. That was how everything began. Talya never left our home. She has been living here since. It was weird for you mom when she stopped by. Over time they became best friends.

I would head into town at least once a week and court your mother. She was taking less missions to make sure that we could have our dates. I would do my best to bring her the best fruits and vegetables that could be grown. She loved my vegetables and immediately came by the house more often to cook them. That became her personal project. She wanted to feed everyone.

Starting a farm wasn't easy at first. To compensate for the lack of food, the wolves were given permission to hunt the ground for meat. It made up for all the food I couldn't provide at first. I also couldn't go into the city and buy large amounts of vegetables from the stands. It would make me appear to be a failure.

On several occasions, I would buy the services of a Ground Mage. They would help the food grow. As time progressed, I realized that the food wasn't as good when the magic was involved. I don't think it was the Ground Mage's fault. It's just when something is artificially grown. It doesn't taste nearly as good.

As time progressed, I realized your mother was the one for me. We got married by the tree right outside the house. It was technically a large wedding. The wolves were all there to watch us. Draco was there to be the witness. The Priest who married us was scared half to death. He had no idea a bunch of wolves would be there.

I started to take up working on things like furniture. I'm not the greatest, but I'm getting better. I can feel it. I will make my masterpiece real soon. I did my best to make your crib. Draco ended up buying a crib for you. The one I made fell apart before we put you in it. I still think Draco sabotaged the thing.

If anything is to be learned from our experiences, it is this. I did my part. Everything that you are is why I'm fighting in this world. I hope that one day. You will live in peace. As of right now, there will be no peace in the kingdom. This will be the dark times in our lives. We have to keep our chins up and pray to live another day.

Everyday the family is growing. There are now thousands of wolves living on the land. Each one raising pups for the future generation. With you alive, as long as you do not die. The community will survive. Above all things, do not lose yourself in the noise. Never let power take over you. You can't control things all the time. You will need to fall back on your community.

Never become the being who patiently endures injustice and silently bears insults. The person who does these things soon becomes unjust themselves or becomes unable to discern right from wrong. When you lose your focus and just accept what is happening, you become complicit in the actions of the world and will no longer be able to lead those around you.

Whatever you do, do not become your grandfather. He is an evil shrewd man that lost faith in humanity a long time ago. I tend to have a hunger for justice against him. I instead realize most days that my yearning for justice is not that at all. I yearn for revenge. In time, I want you to learn to lead, fight, and protect.

As we sit in front of this fire, I want you to remember me. I want you to look back on me in fondness. There are greater forces out there than I. All I can do until then. Is be the best man that I can and live by example.

Those were the last words of my father. I didn't remember the words said that day until recently. The story however hits me hard.

Chapter 15

My father sat me down after telling the story. While trying to stand up, he pushed on the bench to hard and broke it beneath his feet. He looked at the wood and tossed it into the fireplace. He would say waste not what can still have use. He didn't get discouraged and carved up another bench the next day.

Not much happened over the next five months, I was just a little guy, and the voice was getting worse. I was being taunted some days to the point where I couldn't hear anyone around .me. All I wanted was absolute silence. The voice would constantly let me know that I was worthless. When I would ask who they were, they would go silent for a moment only to mock me harder.

The day had started, and the slaves were already working on the farm. I woke up and walked down the steps to the kitchen. My mother was feeding some of the local pups and Talya was waiting for me. She had on her flower dress with a white apron overtop. Her arms were crossed and waiting for me. A lone tooth was on top of the bottom lip and her left foot was tapping the floor.

Talya said, "You were supposed to be awake and ready to go by now."

I asked, "Why?"

Talya replied, "The pups are waiting for you. Today was the day you imprint on the next generation. I'm sure their families are wondering where you are."

Mom said, "I'm sure they understand. It's not like they can do anything about it. He is a growing boy and needs his sleep."

Talya responded, "It's more the principal than anything."

At this point in my life, I didn't remember any humans besides my parents. Draco would come by often to see my father. The last time I saw him. It was over a year ago and not many people remember that part of their lives. There are a few races that do because they grow faster than others, but humans never do.

The voice in my head said, "You failed again. You failed to wake up on time. Did that little dream of yours cause you to lose sleep again. Boo Hoo...This time you disappointed Talya and the pups who are looking forward to seeing you. If you show up now, they probably won't care about you at all."

I mumbled under my breath, "Shut up...shut up, shut up, shut up, SHUT UP!"

Talya asked, "You say something Michael?"

I replied, "No!"

The nights were getting worse. I had the same dream over and over again. I couldn't sleep well most nights and woke up in a heated sweat. The dream would be more of a nightmare. Every night I remembered the last day of my death in the first world. Since I didn't recognize myself or even the world. I didn't know how to describe anything that I was witnessing.

Talya turned me around and walked up the steps behind me. We got to my room, and she pulled my shirt up. The shirt was still drenched from the night before. I had to put on fresh clothes so the pups would recognize my scent better. The clothes were washed in only water to get rid of most of the grime.

I was used to Talya taking care of everything in my life. That's why. When she dropped my trousers, I didn't think twice about it. I didn't quite have the concept of modesty. She had a bucket with water in it. On the seventh day, she would put soaps into the bucket to kill some of the bacteria on my body.

The water she was using was freezing cold. She got the bath and had it heated an hour ago. It was my own fault. The window was open by my bed and some small breezes were making me shiver. When the water was warm, I loved baths. The sponges would act like little massages against my skin. I didn't realize it at the time, but I was fortunate to even have a bath.

Talya put a pair of brown shorts and a white shirt on me. My clothes were close to the same as commoners. My father didn't want to raise me like a royal. He wanted me to blend into my surroundings. He didn't want me to be a hero and instead wanted me to become a farmer. He wanted me to live a peaceful life. A life where I wouldn't suffer. That problem with God and prophecy is. We don't have a choice, the plan is always followed, and in the end. Those who go against him suffer a horrible fate.

While dressed, I walked down the steps. I didn't wear any shoes and ran to the back of the house. Behind the house were about ten slaves tilling the land. Their sweat was dripping off the tips of their fur. Their natural coats must have been awful. Apparently, with them opening their mouths and letting their tongue stick out. It would cool their insides.

I ran across the field to reach the lake. There was a clean lake where we would go fishing all the time. The water wasn't very deep where I would go. It would go up past my waist. I was almost three feet at the time. I was a runt. I didn't grow large for a while. The day I did grow. People noticed.

Talya yelled, "Wait!"

I looked back. There was nothing scarier than seeing that woman run. Talya would go down on all fours and chase me. My heart would sink and run faster. The wolves were fast people. It took her a few seconds before catching up. Her right arm reached out and grabbed me. My shirt lifted a little bit, and her fur tickled my skin.

Talya said, "Your too slow. They are waiting for us."

The field Talya ran across was large. The lake was about half a mile away. The farmland was vast. The area around the lake was covered in pine trees. I could see them moving. When they moved, that usually meant that they were filled with wolf pups. You didn't know for sure until you heard their little growls at one another.

Talya took us to the trees. She sat me down and put out her right hand. I walked in and felt the pinecones and needles under my feet. In the first world, I would have been in severe pain from stepping on them. In this world, I felt nothing. My skin felt harder and could withstand the wild a little better. It was as if something was hardening my feet.

Talya and I walked through about a hundred feet worth of forestry. The lake was right on the other side. When we got to the lake, the sun was beating down on me. The heat was making me sweat. It was either that or the anxious feeling of being around new beings. I was a little antisocial since my father wouldn't let me go to the city.

I saw a group of young pup girls in the water. They were splashing and howling. There were three of them. Their fur was drenched. One of the pups came out of the water. She went down on all fours and shook her coat. Some of the water sprayed my clothes. She walked over and put out her paw.

The pup said, "Nice to meet you."

The pup wasn't shy at all. She smiled at me. The water was dripping from the top of her nose into her mouth. I was hesitant to give her my hand. Her nails were sticking out far. I didn't want to get scratched. When she smiled, the teeth had me worried I would be bitten. My hands stayed by my side. That didn't stop her. She picked up my hand held with both her paws. She shook my hand.

My eyes were bulging out of my head. I swallowed hard in fear. I forced myself to smile. Talya had her paw on the small of my back. She was pushing me to socialize, but it was so hard for me. I wanted to cry. The only beings I truly knew were Talya, my mom, and my dad. Meeting these new pups and trying to form a relationship didn't come naturally.

The voice said to me, "You fucking pussy! How pathetic are you? This is a female pup. She isn't even the same race as you. What kind of freak gets nervous around a different race? It must be the fur. You must be into some real kinky shit. I know from being with you. You are at least a peeping tom and an exhibitionist. You sick fuck."

The voice would always pick the most inopportune times to talk. I wanted the voice to stop. I didn't know what the voice was talking about half the time but always came across as aggressive. The constant sense of fear and intimidation would be tough for an adult. It was tougher on a three-year-old kid that was about to turn four.

Talya said, "Go swimming with them. The boys will come out of the tree soon. They need to bathe in the water to get all the sap out of their fur."

I walked slowly to the water. Talya pushed me because I was taking too long to get there. The dirt under my feet was making me sink. It felt like quicksand. The dirt seeping between my toes gave me a squeamish feeling. A cold chill went up my spine while walking into the water. I was clearly being overdramatic.

The water touched my feet. It was freezing. I looked back at Talya to see if she would let me not go in. Her arms were crossed and tapping her foot. I couldn't get out of this. The only thing I could do was dive into the water and hope for the best. My body felt like I had already jumped into a bath of ice cubes.

The pup that shook my hand jumped into the water. She was happy to see me playing. Her eyes kept blinking at me while taking her whole arm and swaying it at me. At one point, I thought that I was drowning. The waves kept crashing up to my face. The taste of the non- decontaminated water had a taste of seaweed and fish.

The male pups were jumping around in the trees still. All I saw was the shaking of the trees getting closer to the top. The trees at the top were shaking more violently letting the needles fall to the ground. The male pups got to the top of the trees and howled across the lake. They held onto the top until they were ready.

A lone pup jumped off the top of the trees and dove as close to the center of the lake. He had height, distance, and flexibility while falling to the water. When he hit the water, it looked like he had done it a thousand times before. His body went under the water and didn't seem to come back up.

I looked over at the water waiting for the male pup to come back up. He wasn't. I looked at Talya to see if she could do something. She didn't want to move from her spot. It was a constant look of motherliness. The arms crossed and her right foot was tapping. I wished she would smile more. She always appeared to be so unhappy.

The male pup hopped up behind the girl that shook my hand. He was playing around and pulled her back to the center of the lake. Her paws were swinging and trying to attack the male pup. Eventually, she swung around and took her claws against his nose. It was a deep cut. He held onto his nose and whimpered like the pup he was.

The female pup said, "Serves you right."

The male pup responded, "I was just playing. Why did you do that? You crazy or something."

The male pup kept putting his nose under the water. The blood from the scratch was floating away. When he was done trying to wash it away, he walked out of the lake. When he sat down, a school of small fish went over to the blood that was sitting on top of the lake. The fish were eating it faster than when they eat worms.

The female pup swam over to me and tossed her head up. The hair soaked in a lot of water. The water hit me in the face and strands of soaking hair were dropping like bricks upon the surface of the water. I tried to keep my eyes open but couldn't because there was too much water coming at me. My eyes felt like they were burning.

The female pup smiled at me. She reached around me and gave me a hug. She stuck her head on my right shoulder and acted like we should dance in the water. I didn't know what was going on. I closed my eyes and hoped that Talya would say something. She did nothing since there was no danger.

The female pup asked, "Why are you squirming? I'm just holding onto you."

I didn't like the feeling. The hug gave me a feeling of being trapped. My mom, dad, and Talya were the only ones that would give me hugs. A stranger giving me a hug to me put me on the defensive. This was part of the reason that Talya wanted me to meet the pups. She knew that I was lacking that social connection.

The voice in my head said, "You can't even escape a little pup. That's right. Let a vicious animal take control over you. You truly are pathetic. If I had control, she would be drowning in the fucking water. Nobody puts their hands on us. NOBODY!"

I felt the voice was right. Why would I let this pup hold me? She wasn't a family member or a close friend. I took both my hands and pressed them against her chest. I violently pushed her into the water. She was trying to catch herself before falling into the water. The nails on her paws dug deep into my back and scratched across.

The female pup's claws dug deep and caused damage that would probably scar. My back felt like it was on fire. The burning was not a sensation that I was used to. The blood was dripping fast into the water and the fish were coming up to me. I didn't realize why the male pup got out of the water until this moment.

The fish were eating the blood on the top of the water. They couldn't tell where all the blood was coming from and started to nibble on my legs. They were chewing on my flesh and hurting me even more. I didn't have the common sense to run out of the water. I did what all three-year-old children would do in this situation. I screamed at the top of my lungs.

Talya looked over the water. She saw the scratches on my back. I watched her jump into the water and ruin her flower dress to pull me out. The fish were scared and ran away out of fear. The blood was still dripping off my back. With her right arm, she picked me up above the water and walked to the land.

Talya sat me down and spun me around. I felt heat coming from her body. She yelled, "Which one of you did this to the master? WHICH ONE?!"

The female pup started to cry. She said, "I'm sorry. I tried to hug him, and he pushed me. I didn't mean to. I swear."

Talya looked at me. The wounds were deep. She ran over to the water and tried to rinse off my back. The smell of blood was strong. The blood was covering my shirt. She kept looking around the area. I could see her stressing. I thought that she might be scared, because I got hurt by the pups and it was her fault. My mom and dad can be tough sometimes.

I was wrong. I heard a growl coming from our left. It was a deep growl that didn't sound like any of the wolves. A creature was coming to attack us. I looked to the left and saw a giant brown bear. The creatures were meat eaters and needed a few wolves to take down. Their pack mentality worked in this type of situation.

The bears had an incredible sense of smell. They could smell the blood from a mile away. The sound of the bear running at me caused my heart to race. There was no way for me to run away. I would have to depend on Talya, and she wasn't faster than a bear. She stood in front of me and spread her arms around.

Talya yelled to the pups, "Go get some help!"

Chapter 16

The pups ran away to get help from their families. Each one was making squealing noise while running away. The further out they got. The more their howls were getting deeper. They were begging for someone to hear and save Talya and me. Unfortunately, their voices weren't strong yet and needed to get closer to be heard.

The bear ran up to Talya and growled in her face. Saliva was dripping off its jaw. The lower lip was quivering while drooling all over the ground. There were a few more whimpered with the growl until it backed up a few feet. It noticed that Talya wasn't moving a muscle. It just wanted to get to the blood that smelled young and sweet.

I took three steps back and fell on my butt. My entire body was trembling at the sight of this horrid creature. My eyes were wide and couldn't blink. I gulped and tried to use my hands to push back further. I needed to find a way to escape. My only way of escaping was Talya, and she was keeping the bear's attention.

Talya was howling at the bear. She hoped that it would scare the bear or at least gain its attention. She couldn't get its attention because it wasn't drawn to my body. It was drawn to my blood. There was something special about my blood that I didn't know about until later in life. It had special abilities, and most living creatures were drawn to it when exposed.

The bear got up on two legs. It had to be about ten feet tall. That was three times my size horizontally and vertically it was six times my size. It snorted air out its nose. The bear's nose was clogged a little and shot snot onto the ground. I'm still impressed considering how strong Talya was. She didn't try to run. She didn't experience fear. She just did what had to be done.

A loud noise erupted in the distance. I looked over and saw nothing but dust clouds coming from the house. A large, strange figure was leaping through the air and dropping into the fields. It was powerful enough to shake the ground and scare the bear. The sound could only be coming from one being. It was my dad.

The bear dropped down onto all fours and backed away. It kept looking around while only seeing the trees and water. It let off a few whimpers before turning around. It was trying to run away. My father would never let that happen. He leaped over all the trees and smashed down to the ground. It was trapped between Talya and my father.

My father reached back with his right arm and grabbed the bear by its left ear. He slammed the bear into the ground. The ear on the bear was almost completely ripped off. The blood was soaking his hand, and the left side of the bear's skull was crushed inward. To my father, this was nothing more than food for the community and a nice fur coat for himself.

The bear whimpered and let out one last scream. The sound echoed bouncing off the trees in the forest. The lake was rippling from the sound. It was crying out for help but died almost instantly after. The sound of the bear's scream reached out and got something else. I couldn't see what was coming but the sound of two more bears were off in the distance.

My father removed his hand from the bear's head. A white and red goo was sticking to his hand. It looked like some kind of spider webbing that he was trying to get off. He whipped his right hand toward the direction of the water. It wasn't coming off and he didn't have time to clean it knowing that another threat was looming.

There were loud growls coming from the other side of the lake. The trees were rustling. The trees were bending to the will of something charging through them. My father squinted his eyes while watching not one, but two bears come out of the woods. It was hard to tell at first, but both the bears were three times the size of the one my father killed.

I looked down at the dead bear and realized that it was just a cub. My father didn't care that it was a cup. To him, it was about protecting his cub at any cost. That didn't go for just the bears. My father would give up his life if it meant making sure that I was safe. A thought process that his own father didn't seem to have.

As the bears were charging at us, the sky was changing colors. The clouds were getting darker. It happened so fast that I had no idea what was happening. The lake was now dark, and purple lightning was shooting from the sky. This anomaly only happened when one thing was happening. My grandfather was showing up.

My father said, "Fuck me. Not now."

In an instant, the tree's needles were falling off the trees and floating into the lake. A bright purple light flashed in front of me and flowed around my father. The lake became electrified and every fish within it was floating to the surface. I tried to look more but the light was too bright to keep my eyes open.

My father said, "Now is not the time dad."

My grandfather came in with his Brimstone Armor. There were cuts in this smile on the Brimstone face helmet. The purple lava was forming within the helmet and looked like a jack o lantern. The light from the armor was flashing and shining across the lake. The smile got bigger as he was getting ready to speak.

The chest area on the Brimstone Armor had a purple glow like some kind of nuclear reactor. The Brimstone was separated at parts and had the lava flowing through it to the fingertips. The fingertips where the nails would normally be. They were purple and sizzling.

The heat was intense and would burn anyone that tried to touch it. The lava flowed down to his feet and not a single spot could be penetrated by a normal weapon.

My grandfather responded, "When I show up is always the time, I come precisely when I want to. Looks like you have your hands full with those bears."

My father asked, "How did you find out about the bears? I just found out."

My grandfather replied, "I see all remember. I know you never believed it."

My father asked, "Are you here to kill them then? We need to keep the boy safe."

My grandfather replied, "Honestly, I came to send a message. You are way too weak to be my heir. If you don't get stronger soon instead of playing farm., you will die."

My father said, "I just killed a bear with one hand. I think we will be fine."

My grandfather responded, "You stupid fuck. A bear isn't a real challenge. Maybe I should show you a real challenge?"

My grandfather ran to the left of my father. He would change positions knowing that my father couldn't keep up. He went from the rear to the front in an instant. My father closed his eyes and tried to relax. He tried to block out anything that my grandfather was doing. Luckily for my father, the bears stopped running in our direction for a moment to watch.

I blinked for a second. When I opened my eyes, my grandfather was holding onto my father's neck about thirty feet in the air. My grandfather held on and burned his neck. It looked like he was about to break it. My father was using his right hand to grab the arm. The red sticky substance smelled bad while being cooked.

My father beat my grandfather's arm harder and harder. Eventually, the lack of air got to him. He couldn't hit hard anymore.

His arm was still gripping the arm, but it had no strength. A bolt of purple lightning flashed across the sky and dropped down on my grandfather's body. The purple lava eyes were getting wider and brighter. He was ready to finish what he started and with a large smile at that.

My grandfather slammed my father to the ground harder than anything I had seen before. The power so incredible that the wind broke a few trees and broke up the ground. The water from the lake was slowly draining into the hole that my grandfather just made with my father's body. They had to have dug out a three-foot hole from just a single attack.

The dust came up from the attack but settled faster with all the water that was flowing into the hole. The water looked muddy and covered my father. He was grunting and trying to get up. It wasn't easy to accomplish. I couldn't find my grandfather anywhere. The attack only stunned my father.

My grandfather asked, "You had enough?"

My father responded, "Yes, I need to defeat the bears."

My grandfather looked back at the bears and laughed manically. He said, "Well, since you're still conscious. I think you need a few more lessons before I'll let you fight the bears."

My grandfather jumped up and slammed his knees into my father's ribs. The sound of ribs breaking was heard from the echoes in the trees. That loud crunching sound was terrifying. I couldn't move. There was no way to move. My grandfather was too dangerous to run from. I was scared of death, but Talya wasn't. She held her arms high and closed her eyes hoping to take any attack before I would.

My grandfather grabbed ahold of his face and pushed him into the water. The hole had sunk deeper, and his face was now under. My father was drowning before my very eyes. I thought that I might lose him. The air bubbles were forming. His arm was failing until it reached up one last time and went limp. It splashed the water onto my grandfather and just sizzled.

My grandfather got off his body and stood in the water. The area sizzled and all the water turned into steam. Nothing could be seen. My grandfather was sparking off purple lightning from his body while walking to me. He kept laughing while walking over to me. He walked up the Talya's left side and breathed hard enough smoke came out of the helmet.

My grandfather said, "You truly are a good bitch aren't you. I like your loyalty. You would give up everything to protecting the boy. You and I know that there is nothing you can do. There was never a way for you to survive an attack from me or even the bears. I can't believe how pathetic you were and yet so strong."

My grandfather had a tendency to talk in the past tense since he would see the future. It confused me at first. After asking my father, he explained to me Hell Spawns were that way. They have a tendency of seeing the future and sometimes partaking in the future. I have no idea how it worked but the way he treated my father about death. It was eerie. It was like he saw my father's death and was trying to strengthen him for the final battle against Lucifer.

My grandfather just walked past Talya. She was trying to move but was too petrified to save me. Her body was moving slowly but what could she do. A single touch would have set her on fire. Especially, with all the hair on her body. She started to cry. This was never supposed to happen. My father was convinced to let me have a day to discover life and was destroyed.

My grandfather got close to me and said, "See you around kid. Try not to get cut again."

In the blink of an eye, purple lightning surrounded his body and shot off. The electric currents touched me and caused my long black hair to stick straight up. The slight jolt caused my heart to race a little faster. There were little purple arcs crawling across the top of my skin. I felt dead and alive at the same time.

The steam was slowly disappearing. I saw my father sitting up in the water. His face was covered in blood from all the attacks my grandfather gave him. He used his arm to push himself up. I had never seen so many bruises, swelling, and scratches on him before. In fact, I once was a sword fly at my father, and it shattered when touching his chest.

The water was streaming down his head and running down his shoulders. His eyes were closed while the blood was mixing into the enormous puddle that might now be an extension of the lake. He burped up some water and drooled it down his lower lip. His chest appeared to be weighted.

The sky was moving. The black clouds brought by my grandfather were disappearing into the distance. The lightning stopped, and the bears didn't appear to be afraid anymore. They were slowly walking toward us. When the sky was blue again, a bright light shined off the water. It looked like a crazy storm had hit the area with needles floating all over the surface. Branches were broken off the trees. The water was still calming down.

My father said, "I hate that mother fucker. Well, I best get to doing what I do."

My father stood up using the side of the puddle. He leaped up onto the edge and walked forward. I could tell that something wasn't right. He was limping with his right foot. The wounds weren't closing fast and the whole body was covered in blood. There was even a small hole in the front of his chest.

My father's right arm looked like it might be broken. The problem was that there were no wolf heroes in the area. He was the only one that could defend me. The good news was that he was a hero. The bad news was that he needed time to heal. Time was not on his side as the bears were charging him.

Talya walked over to me. She was getting ready to take me away when she noticed something odd. The deep scratches that set the original bear off were missing. To make things even more interesting, I didn't have any scars from the female pup's scratches. She felt around my back with her paws and saw nothing. She was confused but decided not to question it. It was better to let it go than to deal with my father.

Talya picked me up. My legs were dangling over her left arm and propped my back up with the right. I looked up into her nose and saw her as a hero. She was breathing heavily while getting ready to run. There was a small snorting with her long nose. She looked down at me and turned around. She was ready to charge in my father's direction

The steam covered the area so I couldn't see what was happening. My father was yelling and screaming. The steam was turning red from blood. I couldn't tell if it was my father's blood or the bear's blood. I just knew that someone was dying in that mist. I looked back hoping to get a glimpse of my father fighting but didn't have much luck.

Talya was running through the fields faster than she had earlier. We had gotten away from the fight. The sound of her paws hitting the ground sounded like a stampede. When she got closer to the house, she slowed down and looked back at the lake. There was a huge crash, louder than anything a bear could do. That was when she knew my father was safe.

Talya sat me down and was looking through my hair. It was a little harder to look through since I was stuck up from the lightning shock. There appeared to be no bruises or cuts on my body. I came out of everything unscathed. It was fascinating to her. She knew that I shed blood. It didn't really matter to saying anything yet, but she kept a close eye on me.

I got into the house and my mother was waiting there with her large soup scooping spoon. I can't remember what it was called. It was shiny and held a bowl of soup with it. That's all I can tell you. Her arms were crossed and was tapping her foot just like Talya would do. I kept forgetting. I technically had two mothers, and they were both ready to punish me.

My mom asked, "What happened?"

Talya replied, "There was a bear attack. James is down there taking care of it."

My mom asked, "If it's just a bear, why isn't he home already. He is missing soup time."

Talya replied, "You'll have to ask him."

There were so many uncertain things. What could she say? It wasn't her place to speak of the master's father. She didn't want to let them know how bad things got because she would never let me out of the house again. Even when my father got home, he said that he was just hunting for some meat and some of the slaves were skinning the bears as we spoke.

I would say it was a happy ending for the most part, but she wasn't fooled at all. She saw the blood and rips on my shirt from getting cut, and my father was covered in blood from head to toe. This was not a happy ending for her at all. I knew this because I wasn't allowed to leave her sight for a long time despite being safe.

Chapter 17

My father was a strong man, but that day where I almost perished by the water was a wake-up call. My mother demanded. If I was outside at all, I had to be watched over. Between the awful nature of my grandfather, the new king, and the church, I was always in a state of danger.

I became a prisoner in my own home and never left the farmland. The only socializing I managed to have. It was with slaves. The slaves were often too scared to talk to me. To make things worse, the pup were told not to get near me because the families heard of the incident. Nobody wanted to get near me in case I were to get scratched. They all knew it was an accident, but there was always that fear of having the master's son. My father was good in nature, but hurting his little boy might bring out his wrath.

The days turned to years; I did not leave the farm for six long years. The field in the backyard was the only place I was allowed to plow and that was with my father present. I was becoming a man, and my family didn't want to let me go. I think part of it had to do with the fact that I was a weak runt.

Talya noticed changes in me that weren't normal for a human. Apparently, it wasn't normal for me to hear voices. She told me to only speak to the voice while she was around. The voice was something that my grandfather had trouble with. People didn't know if he was crazy, or the voice was genuinely telling him the future. The truth was it was probably a little bit of both.

The other change was two things that would randomly happen to me. The first thing was my skin would get hard and become increasingly difficult to harm. This didn't happen often, but it did happen. I didn't know how to control it. My mind was somehow connected to the skin and the voice took credit for making my skin hard. Since my father had a great hatred of my grandfather who had similar capabilities. Talya said that it was best to keep a secret.

The second thing was that my body was healing from all injuries like it was nothing. Yes, I was small and was bruised easily but whenever a scratch opened a wound. It would close almost immediately if caused by someone else. The only being that could cut me, and let it bleed out properly was my father. It didn't make any sense.

I mention this now because you will see later that things in my life are about to get really weird. My father was abnormal for a human. He could leap through the air and drop down harder than anything I have ever seen. He would mention stories about warriors and being with magic at their fingertips. I just had no idea that the stories were just a small part of world and that it was an endless rabbit hole filled with evil, magic, and abilities that could wipe out entire civilizations.

The day started with Talya storming up the steps. She had a wooden spoon and a pot lid. The lid would chime because it was made of Holy Steel. She hammered away at the lid while running up the steps. The slamming of her paws against the stairs didn't make things any better. I just wanted her to go away.

Talya said, "Wakey, Wakey, rise and shiny. Get your hiney out of bed."

I responded, "It's too early. The sun is barely out. I just want few more minutes."

Talya said, "Nope, today is the day you go to the city and…"

My mother came into the room. She stopped Talya from saying more by yelling, "Hey!"

Talya said, "Shouldn't he know that today is…"

My mother responded, "James wants him to be surprised. If Marcus was right, his life is about to change forever."

Talya said, "If that happens, I won't be needed anymore."

My mother responded, "You will always have a place in our home. We know the sacrifices you made. I'm sure a wolf companion has been out there waiting for this day."

I asked, "What are you talking about?"

My mother replied, "Don't worry about it. Just get on your damn clothes. Did you get a soap bath last night like I told you?"

I replied, "Yes."

I lied. I hadn't bathed in a few days. Since I was older now, I was able to bathe myself in the bucket. Now, whether or not I actually did it was another story. I just didn't enjoy bathing because the water was warm, but the rest of my body was cold. I didn't see the point in bathing more than once a week.

My mother came over and sniffed me. A mother knows when her kid is lying. She said, "You smell like ass. It's your funeral. Your dad might not notice but the girls you are about to meet will."

I asked, "What girls? Are some pups coming with us?"

I was so out of the loop that I didn't realize there were more girls in the world that were human than my mom. The only education I got was learning to read and write. My father would often tell stories and try to acclimate me the best he could. He did his best to teach me common sense which was lacking in the world. Everything I learned felt pointless. The best teacher is life experience. By the end of the day, I would have two life experiences to work from.

I whipped the covers off my body and jumped out of bed. I was standing there in the nude and Talya looked away. My mother had a frown on her face. She wasn't happy with the fact that I didn't wear pajamas to bed. I just liked the feeling of being free in my own room. To be naked in one's room was a right of passage. That's what dad said anyway.

My mother said, "Put some pants on. Your pale white ass needs it."

I responded, "Why are you looking?"

My mother said, "I gave birth to that ass. I can look whenever I want. Put on some damn pants and meet your father outside."

I responded, "But..."

My mother said, "Pants. Now! NO arguing."

I grumbled and crossed my arms. This was supposed to be a day off from doing chores. I shrugged it off and walked over the wooden rocking chair in the corner. It had my clothes for the day on it. I have ten pairs of the same pants and shirts. A white shirt that was snug to my body and a pair of brown pants that were just large enough to hold my balls in place.

I walked down the stairs. My mom put some eggs and toast on a plate. I ran over and stood there eating. She would scramble the eggs because I would try to eat them with my fingers in the morning. Forks were available but I didn't care. God gave me fingers for a reason. Also, I enjoy licking my fingers off. It was like having a second meal.

My mom saw me walking out the door and she ran over to me. Her arms reached around my head and pressed me against her boobs. Even though they were nice and soft, a boy doesn't like that and I was grossed out by the prospect. She kissed the top of my head and pulled me in even tighter. I could barely breathe and was straining to escape this woman's will

I pushed her stomach to escape and eventually she let go. This day was hard on my mother. I didn't know why. It felt like a normal day to me. The tears were streaming down her face while waving goodbye to me. I looked back at her one last time with a confused look on my face. Everyone knew something that I didn't.

I walked over to my father. He was still loading up the cart with the crops we pulled over the last two days. There were large wooden buckets that he used to transport them in. There was a metal ring around the buckets to keep them together. The crops were considered the best because he made the crops the old fashion way instead of using Ground Mages.

My father looked at me with my white shirt and brown pants. His face changed the closer I got to him. His nose wrinkled up. His face looked like he had eaten something sour. He reached out and grabbed my right arm. He lifted me high up. My feet weren't touching the ground. He went in for a good sniff.

My father said, "You didn't bathe like I told you."

I responded, "Yes I did."

My father, knowing that I was lying, got close to my face. His breath wasn't the greatest. He said, "I don't believe you. You swell worse than the ass end of the horses."

My father sat me down. My toes were the first things to touch the ground. I took three steps back. My hair blew into my face. I couldn't see. I puckered up my lips and tried to blow it out of my face. My hair was long and hadn't been cut in a long time. I took my hand and pushed it back. I hated having long hair, but my mother seemed to like it. Even if it was greasy all the damn time.

My father asked, "You ready to get in the cart. You are my little buddy."

I nodded my head yes. My father grabbed me by the back of my pants and hoisted me into the air. I was only forty-seven inches tall. Even as a human, that was small in comparison. It didn't mean that I couldn't farm and be strong. It just meant that I had to work twice as hard because I was literally under four feet tall.

My feet touched the seat, and I walked over to the other side. I was used to sitting on the cart because we would ride around the farm at times, but this was the first long journey I had been on. I didn't realize the journey was about to be long until my father finished packing the crops and closing the lid in the back.

My father walked over to the cart and said, "Do you remember my friend, Draco?"

I responded, "The coward from your stories."

My father said, "Whoa, DO NOT tell him that. I repeat. DO NOT tell him that. His ego is quite fragile and since there is only one story I told you about him. He has grown a lot. In fact, he might be one of the bravest men I have ever met."

I asked, "Can you tell me some of those stories?"

My father replied, "Those aren't my stories to tell. To be honest, if one of us is a coward, it's probably me. I'm the one that has been hiding myself and you guys for all these years. If not for the ceremony, I would probably still keep you locked up in the house."

I asked, "Why don't you?"

My father replied, "There are two things preventing me from doing it. The first thing is your destiny is set. Marcus has foreseen you doing great things."

I asked, "What is the other?"

My father replied, "Marcus."

My father grabbed ahold of the seat and pulled himself up. He was such a large and heavy guy the wheels on his side were slouching. The only thing keeping the cart upward was the left horse. My father grabbed the reins. He closed his eyes and took a deep breath. Right before swinging the reins. He would say a few words.

My father would say, "One, two, three. Breathe slow, gentle, soft, and silent. Know your worth and be at peace."

My father opened his eyes and swung the reins. The horses lunged forward and caused a large jolt. I held out my hand to catch myself from falling off the seat. My little hands could barely grab anything. If I had to depend on bracing myself, I would have probably broken my arms in the process.

My father wrapped the reins around his left nub. There was a strange way he learned to knot it. It gave him control and allowed his right arm to be open for other things like eating. In this case, he didn't want to eat. He just wanted to put his arm up on the bench and pull me in closely. He didn't show it, but this was an emotional day for him too.

The ride appeared to be peaceful. I closed my eyes and let the wind run through my hair. The leaves were falling from the trees and flowing past us. I looked down the side of the cart and noticed a single leaf rotating in a constant three-hundred-and-sixty-degree spin. I looked back and saw the leaf get crushed by the passenger side rear wheel.

When I looked back, I noticed something was shaking the trees a little. The leaves were falling in certain spots more heavily. The leaves were covering up whatever was shaking it. I looked over at my father and grabbed ahold of his sleeve. I tugged on it to gain his attention, but he was looking ahead and ignoring me.

I said, "Dad, there is something in the trees."

My father responded, "Don't look in the trees. Just enjoy the ride."

I said, "But…"

My father responded, "No buts. Just enjoy the ride. One, two, three breathe."

I said, "Slow, gentle, soft, and silent. Know your worth and be at peace."

My father responded, "That's right. As long as you remember that. Everything will be okay. What you are seeing in the trees are friendlies watching over us."

I asked, "How do you know?"

My father replied, "Because I know the beings in the trees."

The beings in the trees were definitely not from the wolf clan. The fact that my father was so cavalier bothered me. All I could do was trust him. I didn't understand how he knew who was in the trees when we couldn't see them. I did what all kids in my position would do. I sat back in my seat, crossed my arms, slouched deeply, and pouted like a baby.

The sound of the horses trotting was starting to slow down. My father looked over at me and rustled my hair. He pulled up on the reins to slow it down even more. I looked to the left and there was the start of one of largest walls I had ever seen. It had to be twenty feet tall and stretched out a quarter of a mile long.

The dirt road was leading to the road in the center of the wall. The Holy Steel gate was shining brightly from the sun. There were parts in the wall where it looked like the gate was ripped out a few times. The sun was coming from the other side of the gate. The trees to our right would block out the sun if coming from that direction. The closer we got to the gate. The more I noticed the designs on it.

The designs looked like a pair of bird wings. I couldn't recognize the bird it came from since it wasn't colored, but it appeared to be like some kind of crest. My father rolled up to the gate. He didn't say a word. He just looked forward waiting to enter. I grabbed my dad's sleave. He pushed me away and said, "Keep your eyes forward. The less you know right now. The better you are off."

I gulped. My dad having a serious look on his face was causing my heart to race. He mentioned how Draco had changed. He was no coward. It made me wonder. What kind of place was I entering? I looked ahead to see something coming from the left side of the gate. It was shrouded in darkness until the light flashing from the gate brightened the being up.

The being had black and white fur. It had the face of a cat. There was white on the inside of the ear and stripes throughout. It took the locks off the gate. The chain slid off onto the ground. The cat person moved to the left gate first and walked over to the right. The gate was screeching while it moved. The cat person bowed while my father flicked the rein.

The cat person said, "Welcome back, James."

Chapter 18

The cart went forward a few feet before the road turned into a complete circle. In the center of the circle were some of the largest bushes I have ever witnessed. My jaw dropped and my eyes widened. My father looked over at me and smiled. He took his pointer finger and put it under my chin. He pushed his finger up to close my mouth.

I asked, "Can I get off the cart to touch them?"

My father replied, "I wouldn't. Those are Draco's ancestorial bushes. I did that once and he attacked me."

I asked, "Did he win?"

My father replied, "No, but the only reason was that my skin is too durable, and he didn't use any weapons. He explained the bushes to me, and we went in for gin and a smoke."

I said, "I didn't know you smoked like the wolves."

My father responded, "I don't." He looked down on me realizing he slipped up. He continued, "Don't tell your mother. It's just on occasions to help relieve some pain."

The reins were pulled back when we got in front of the house. My father got off, and the cart jumped on its own. Some of the vegetables flew out of the cart and onto the bed. I went over to the step. It would take me a minute because of how far it was down. I swung my arms and dropped to the ground.

The jolt from dropping had me falling backwards. When I fell, my head looked up at the roof. I gulped seeing the countless numbers of cat people watching us from above. I stood up getting ready to run. I looked over at the wall and saw thousands of them perched on the wall. My father and I were completely surrounded.

My heart sank thinking that we were about to be attacked. I was petrified. My arms were shaking, and a few tears were coming down my face. It became increasingly harder to breathe. This felt like the end of my life. The way the wolf people spoke of the cat people, I thought that they would rip out our heart and devour them for fun.

My father grabbed me by the back of the neck and lifted me up. He said, "Go to the door. I think some people are waiting for you."

I slowly walked to the door. My feet were dragging. I didn't know what would be on the other side of that door but with my father behind me. I knew that he would protect me. Well, most children do see their father's as strong and mighty. They see these things through their accomplishments.

I knocked on the door and a bunch of screaming was happening. The high-pitched sounds were a little bit much. I was getting ready to walk back to the cart. My father put his hand on his waist and shook his head. I was shaking violently when the door opened. I slowly turned my head to who was there.

I raised my right hand slowly and said, "Hello."

There were three girls standing there. The littlest one had to be about five years of age. She had a blonde hair and a glow in cheeks. The hair was past her shoulders. Her dress was pink and looked old. It looked to either be roughly worn by her or previously worn by one of the older sisters.

The middle height girl had red hair. She had dirt all over her face that smeared. A person might think she was camouflaging herself. She might have succeeded if not for the severe body odor. She was wearing brown leather pants and a green cotton shirt. There were scratched all over her arms and calluses all over her hands. The twigs in her hair gave her that extra… gen a se qua.

The tallest of the sisters was a red-haired girl. Wow! Did she have a chest on her. There was something alluring about her. She was wearing a black shirt and black baggy pants. She smiled at me and had almost fangs in her teeth. They were longer but not long enough to call her a vampire.

The tallest girl stared into my eyes and said, "You! What the fuck are you doing here."

My father responded, "Matilda, that wasn't very nice."

Matilda was looking at me closer. She couldn't help but stare into my eyes even deeper. It was freaking me out and exciting me at the exact same time. My heart was racing but for a good reason this time. She was so beautiful to me. I was so nervous that I couldn't speak. I just stood there and stared back at her.

My father said, "This is Matilda, Isabella, and Ruth Ann."

The smallest daughter cleared her throat and responded, "It's Rue."

My father said, "Sorry, she is my little kangaroo."

Rue smiled and ran over to my father. She jumped at him and reached out her arms to give him a big hug. It looked like these girls had a better relationship with my father than I did. She wouldn't let go of him and slid down to my father's right leg. She held on while my father was walking forward.

My father asked, "May we come in?"

Matilda replied, "Yes, please come in."

Matilda and Isabella left the door open and walked to the center of the room. The house was enormous. The entrance was three times the size of our house. I looked ahead and right on the other side of the hallway was an open kitchen with quite a few cat people in maid outfits. It felt like a fairy tale.

Matilda stormed off to the right. She went down the hallway. She seemed a little nervous about meeting me. Before she walked down the hallway, she was breathing heavily. It was like she was having an anxiety attack. You would think that this type of reaction would mean she likes me. Strangely enough, she never had any romantic feelings toward me. I unfortunately can't say the same.

I walked inside and a strange smell flooded the room. It seemed unnatural. My nose wrinkled from the smell. My eyes were watering. I looked around to see if there were some types of candles. My mother would often fill our home with different smelling candles. She claimed that it would calm her down.

I asked, "What is that smell?"

Rue replied, "It's probably Isabella. She always smells like she crawled up a cow's ass."

Isabella said, "Dad said that one time. You don't have to repeat it."

Isabella was slightly taller than me. I would say about fifty-two inches. Her arms were crossed. She seemed to have the same attitude as my mother and Talya. Her right foot was dropping rapidly. She didn't appear to like me which was a big difference. She would scowl at me when looking in my direction.

When Isabella wasn't scowling at me, she was looking around the room. I tried to look away. I didn't want to be noticed by here. To be honest, I still didn't know why my father brought me to this place. The people were rude and seemed to have a vendetta against me. I just wanted to go home.

While waiting, I noticed two more little girls walking by. They looked just like Rue. I looked in the kitchen and there were two babies there. I couldn't figure out what was happening. It was like this place was an orphanage and each child looked different except for what appeared to be a set of triplets.

After a few seconds, a man with black hair came out of the room Matilda went into. His hair was a deep dark color. He wore a black suit that had three buttons with a cotton white shirt underneath. The pants were black and had a crease on the front of the pants. While walking to my father and I, he buttoned up his sleeves.

My father said, "What took you so long?"

The man responded, "I was relaxing before we left. I didn't expect you for another hour or two."

My father said, "You were smoking."

The man responded, "I'm spending the next two days going through what is possibly the most important moment of our children's lives. Why would you think I'm smoking?"

My father said, "You were smoking."

The man responded, "Of course, I was smoking. I'm about to be with our kids for the next two days."

The man looked at me and said, "Hey Michael, I haven't seen you in a while. I would say you've grown, but its barely noticeable."

My father responded, "It's seven years since you saw him. You could be nice about this."

The man said, "Fine. I'm Draco. Your father's best and only friend."

My father responded, "I have friends."

Draco said, "Name one and your wife doesn't count."

My father was silent. He didn't really have friends other than Draco. I had heard one story of the man. I honestly thought that Draco would be this big joke. The only story my father talked about him was from when they first met. This guy didn't appear to be weak at all. In fact, while looking into his eyes, there was something deeply terrifying about them.

Draco looked at me and said, "Boy, you smell like bad sex."

My father responded, "They both do. Do you want me to pitch in on *Wong's*?"

Draco said, "No I practically own the joint. It couldn't hurt to let the little ones experience the baths there. I'm sure the only way he had a bath the last few years was water and a bucket. It will be a good experience for the kids."

My father responded, "There is nothing wrong with water and a bucket. I used that method on every trip I ever took."

Draco said, "Those were missions. Just living life isn't supposed to be that hard."

Draco walked over to me and lifted my top eyelids. He was looking deeply into my eyes. He pinched my cheeks and wiggled them about. I couldn't fight it. The guy was almost twice my size. His hands were enormous, and his arms were large enough to break a tree with a simple bear hug.

Draco said, "His eyes are brown, and his hair is black. His size is way too short for a Warrior or Hell Spawn. I'm a believer in Marcus. You know this, but the boy will need a miracle if he is to be blessed tonight."

My father responded, "You're a fucking idiot."

Draco smiled at my father. When he breathed, I smelled the weird smell from when I entered. It was him. It wasn't the smell of weed but it had a distinct aroma the tickled my nostrils and made me want to…eat maybe. I'm not sure. It just gave me a feeling all over my body. I didn't want to walk, stand, or even breathe while smelling it.

Draco went over to a coat rack by the left side of the entrance. It had a black top hat and a cane with a demon on the handle. He walked out the door while smashing the bottom of the cane on the ground. Each hit harder than the last. I didn't know if he was being aggressive or pissed about something.

I walked out the door and there was a large cat man sitting in the front seat. His fur was fluffy and had orange and white stripes. He had these white colors around his eyes like some kind of bandit. His ears were perked up and listening to everything happening around us. He quickly whipped his head in my direction. It startled me.

My father pointed at the cat man driver and said, "That is Reginald. He has one of the most important jobs of all the cat people."

I asked, "What is that?"

My father replied, "He drives the important people around. His priority is to make sure the horses, you kids, Draco and all the people that live in the house are taken care of. The only being above him is Draco and his kids."

I asked, "What happens if all the people he needs to take care of die."

My father replied, "That is a dark scenario. Just like the wolves at home. They are wearing collars. The collar will explode and kill all the cat people. Nobody would be safe. That's why its important to do what they say. They don't just have your best interest at heart. They have all the children, elderly, and females' interest at heart."

I said, "That is barbaric."

My father responded, "The collars also protect the cat people. Just like the wolf people."

I asked, "How?"

My father replied, "In this world, there are people out to kill, rape, and destroy any species. These beings are called poachers. That collar on their neck keeps them away because the trouble that would follow would be far worse. Not only that, but if the slaves are being resold with the collar. The merchandise would be damaged from the collars. Nobody wants to buy a headless slave."

Reginald said, "It's okay kid. The way Draco seems to procreate. That will never happen. The truth is things were much worse when we weren't slaves. Working for Draco, we are guaranteed food, water, shelter, and protection.

Draco also has status as a Legionnaire which means if anyone touches us without permission. The death penalty follows."

My father asked, "You ready to get in."

I nodded yes. The door was open from Draco already going inside. There were no windows to the outside. I was being put into a cage where no light could get in. The black color on the outside seemed to shine brightly. I couldn't tell what it was but there was a protective layer to the carriage.

My father lifted me up by the back of my pants. It gave me a huge wedgie. I didn't want to sit down after that. I wished that I didn't have to be helped up but being so small was working against me. My little legs could reach up high enough to the steps. This was an ongoing thing for a while, well sort of.

I sat down on the left side of the black carriage. There was a lantern above our heads. It turned itself on. The heat from it was abnormal. I stared at it while it flickered. There were moments when I could have sworn it went completely out. It would immediately come back like a small explosion.

Isabella jumped up like it was nothing and sat down next to her father. The girl appeared to be some kind of freak. I don't know of anyone that could jump like that. Even the wolf pups had some good jumping, but nothing that high. Her toes touched the edge of the carriage, and she slid into the seat right next to her father.

Draco closed the door and opened a small door behind him. He said to Reginald, "We are ready to go. I just need to make a quick stop to *Wong's*. The kids are filthy and probably need a quick change of clothes."

The carriage jolted hard. It was moving. I realized my father wasn't in the carriage. I had to ask, "Where is my father?"

Draco replied, "Your father isn't coming. We will meet him later. He has...business to attend too."

Chapter 19

The carriage was dark enough to tell campfire stories in. The flickering of the light appeared creepy. The lantern swayed with the movement of the carriage. The longer we sat in the carriage. The creepier Draco got with his smile. I couldn't tell if he was trying to get me in his good graces or plotting something against me. My father did describe him as a rival on more than one occasion.

Draco said, "So, it appears that you will marry one of my daughters."

I responded, "What?!"

Draco said, "I spoke to Marcus, and he saw you marrying one of my daughters. He also said you will be one Hell of a sword wielder. I'm not so sure looking at you but he hasn't been wrong yet."

I responded, "I'm not ready for marriage."

Draco said, "Well, he didn't give a time frame. All I know is that you will marry one of my daughters."

Isabella responded, "That is so gross. He is weak, stupid, and smells."

I scowled at her and said, "Looks who's talking ugly. What did your sister say? You smell like a cow's ass."

Draco shook his head and yelled, "That is enough you two!"

I said, "She started it."

I folded my arms and grumbled under my breath. It was definitely not her. I would never marry someone so obnoxious. If I was about to marry any of the girls. It would have been Matilda. The rest of the girls appeared to be too young. I looked away at the black wall and tried not to even see her.

Draco said, "I'm going to need a Hell of a lot more Jun Jun to make it through this shit."

Isabella responded, "What are you looking at me for? I'm not the freak who isn't even four feet tall. I don't even know why someone who is clearly not capable of fighting is trying to get Blessed."

Draco said, "Well thanks a lot. You just let the cat out of the bag."

A loud knock came from Reginald. Draco exclaimed, "Sorry Reginald! Old habit!"

Draco asked me, "What do you know about this day?"

I looked back at him and replied, "My father has told me nothing. So far all I know is people are crying like I'm about to die or something."

Draco said, "Not exactly."

I yelled, "What?! I'm about to die!"

Draco said, "No! Nothing like that. You are just entering a new life."

I asked, "Will your plans for me freak me out? Am I about to lose my virginity?"

Draco replied, "No you won't be freaked out. As for the second, do you want too? I can make that happen. You just say the word. I know a few girls that would for the right price."

Isabella yelled, "DAD! James said..."

Draco said, "Right, right. James said no hookers. He never said anything about escorts. I mean he is nine and about to change his whole life. Blowing off a little steam before this couldn't hurt."

Isabella hit her father. She folded her arms for a second before repeatedly hitting him again and again. She hit so much that her hand was hurting and stopped. She flung her hand around. It moved like it was filled with jelly. Whatever she was thinking, I think it worked because Draco stopped talking about whores right after.

I asked, "So, what is this *Wong's* place?"

Darco replied, "Your father never told you about Wong? Wong is probably the coolest pacifist in the world. He is a Creationist class hero. Instead of trying to kill and make tons of money He had chosen to open a shop and sell his goods. Wong helped me build my house, build the cat people's homes, a little fancy work with things from the last world, and he creates portals to other worlds he created. Want a little taste of the past world, see Wong. The man is a god in this world but has one major flaw. He can't defend himself."

I asked, "What happens if someone attacks him?"

Draco replied, "Already happened. People tried to extort him for years knowing his inability to fight back. I realized his worth and put together a security team for him."

I asked, "Does he pay you for it?"

Draco replied, "He pays me in ways that you couldn't put a price on."

I said, "Okay, I understand."

Draco asked, "What is that supposed to mean?"

I replied, "You just got done telling a nine-year-old that you knew how to hook him up with whores. You have like seven kids. I'm not judging. I'm just pointing out what I see."

Draco laughed. His eyes were watering from laughing so hard. He was trying to wipe it away and stop. It was hard for him to stop with all the coughing. It took a while, but he eventually calmed down. He looked into my eyes and smiled. It was creepy seeing him just stare at me.

Draco said, "You missed a kid. I have eight kids in that house right now. You are quite observant considering Isabella's sister, who is about two years younger, wasn't at the house. I can't help but laugh because you seem observant and yet put all the pieces in the wrong place. If you were wondering, he keeps my deep secrets and gets what

I need done in secret. If you ever saw his face, you might realize. There is definitely a reason why I would never fuck that man."

Isabella responded, "These conversations keep getting weirder. Can we be silent until we get there?"

Darco said, "Come on! The kid is gold. You might learn to like him if you gave him a chance."

Isabella responded, "I doubt it."

Draco licked his lower lip. He looked a little thirsty. You could tell he was deep in thought but couldn't say a word. I think it was difficult to get her to come with us. My father was deep in thought driving to Draco's house. I don't know what this ceremony was, but it seemed to make both our parents sad.

Isabella didn't seem to be enjoying herself. I couldn't tell if it was me or her father that was the problem. For all I knew, she knew something about this day that I didn't. It was a look of fear. After today, she would be demanded to grow up. I guess anyone would fear that.

Draco started to speak but Isabella cut him off. She said, "No. I just wanted to spend my days in the trees. There is no reason just because I'm nine to drag me into your religious shit."

Draco responded, "I was just about to say. You two need a new wardrobe. There is no reason my daughter and godson need to walk into the church looking like you do."

I puzzling asked, "What?!"

Draco replied, "What? The new clothes? It's a small thing really."

I said, "No, the other thing."

Draco responded, "The going into church looking ugly."

I said, "For fuck sake, the godson thing."

Draco responded, "Your dad didn't tell you. If anything happens to your mother and father, you come to live with me. It's really not a big deal. Your father will outlive all of us. The guy is constantly getting his ass handed to him by the strongest guy in the kingdom. I don't think anything can kill him."

I said, "What your saying is that I am like a son to you already."

Draco responded, "Kind of, but I try not to think about it that way. Marcus said you will marry one of my kids. Thinking of you as a son would just be icky."

The horse came to a stop. My body flew forward from the abrupt stop. If things could get worse, I wouldn't want to be alive anymore. I flew right into Isabella's lap. She appeared to be grossed out by my presence. I was breathing heavily in the lap. My face was right where were crotch was. She was trying to push me away but instead. She was pushing me right into the crotch harder. I couldn't breathe at all.

Isabella kept yelling, "Get him off me! Get off you pervert!"

I rolled my body onto the floor. I lay on the ground limp from not being able to breathe. My lips were puckered while coughing. There wasn't a whole lot I could do about it. When I inhaled, Isabella was so sweet. She repeatedly kicked me in the stomach to make sure I could continue to exhale.

The door to the carriage opened. A bright light shined in. A man in full armor was standing at the door watching Isabella kick the shit out of me. The armored soldier looked confused. I think there was a small chuckle that came from him. I had a feeling this guy knew Draco and Isabella. This was clearly assault and he didn't want to save me.

The armored guard said, "Nice to see you again Lord Simpson."

Draco responded, "Good to see you too."

The armored guard asked, "Do you folks need more time?"

Draco replied, "We're okay. These two are the best of friends."

The armored guard said, "I need to ask you folks to get out. We need to do a security che... Holy Fuck! It smells in here. What is that?"

Draco responded, "That is the smell of children. Do you want them?"

The armored guard tried to close the holes in his helmet. He acted like the smell was eating away at his armor. It wasn't that bad. There are a lot of peasants that roam the kingdom that smell far worse than us. I don't know what his problem was. He kept stepping back and swatting around his helmet like a swarm of bees were attacking him.

Darco asked, "Are you embarrassed yet?"

I replied, "Look what you did Isabella."

Isabella's jaw dropped. She couldn't believe that I put all the blame on her. She folded her arms and jumped out of the carriage onto the ground. Draco got out right after her. He turned around and put his arms out to catch me. He knew that with my small size. It would be difficult to jump off and might injure myself.

I looked up at the wall. My father wasn't playing around. The sun was brightly shining from above and made it harder to see the top. I'm not sure what was at the top. My father mentioned Archers and Hunters before. I just saw shadowy figures moving around the wall. Ten thousand feet high was a bit much, but not too monsters.

The armored guard went into the carriage to look around. He had to check for possible hidden bandits in the thing. It became a problem that spies, bandits, and thieves were sneaking in through royal carriages. It's less common now. They don't feel the need to sneak in. The church and king just let them into the city.

The armored guard came out and asked, "Where are you folks headed?

Draco replied, "We are heading to *Wong's* before the Enlightenment Ceremony."

The armored guard said, "Wow, Isabella is nine already. She will probably be a savage like her old man. Good luck."

Draco laughed while responding, "I'm not that old."

I looked around at all the people having their carriages, carts, and whatever the guards were checking. They were checking the bags of the people as well. A lot of people walked into the city today. I had never visited the city before. I didn't know if the number of people coming in today was normal or not.

People were trying to walk by our carriage with all their gear. They were looking at Isabella and I funny. I didn't realize people had expectations of a carriage like ours. People were usually clean and refined. They were members of royalty. I was neither. I was just an average farm kid whose father was friends with a royal. Not sure what was up with Isabella but that was my excuse.

The armored guard said, "You're welcome to get back into the carriage. I'll walk you through sir."

Draco responded, "It's always a pleasure to be searched."

Draco picked me up and tossed me into the carriage. It wasn't an easy throw. It was a get the fuck in there. We need to get out of here throw. My knees scrapped across the floor and ripped my pants. I know it didn't matter since he was about to buy me some clothes, but my knees were also skinned. I wasn't happy.

Draco came in and Isabella hopped in right after him. They both sat down, and the armored guard closed the door. I'm not sure why but the carriage felt twice as hot now. It could be that the trees weren't blocking the sun anymore and we felt all the suns rays while waiting in line.

Draco said, "You look like you hurt yourself. Sorry, I wasn't thinking."

Isabella responded, "What? Big man can't handle a little scrape. Is he going to cry about it?"

Draco said, "That's enough. He didn't mention it. I did."

The carriage was moving forward. The road below us appeared to be poorly made. Every couple of seconds, we managed to hit a ditch. The carriage kept bouncing hard from hitting each pothole. I was feeling sick to my stomach just traveling to *Wong's*. It might have been safer just to walk there.

The bouncing wasn't just affecting me. It was affecting Isabella. Draco was used to it and didn't budge an inch. Isabella at one point bounced so high that she hit her head off the roof of the carriage. She managed to dodge the lamp by a few inches. She kept rubbing her head with the right hand and holding on for her life with the left.

After Reginald drove for about ten minutes, the carriage came to a stop. We appeared to be at *Wong's*. I could hear Reginald getting off the Carriage. I closed my eyes and waited for the light to shine in the carriage. I was about to be prepared for the bright light this time. Going from dark to light really hurt last time.

Darco asked, "What are you doing?"

I replied, "I'm not going blind again."

Draco said, "We're in the city. The buildings are blocking out the sun."

I opened my eyes and there was Reginald staring at me. He was dumbfounded that I was trying to protect my eyes in the city. I sighed and waited for Isabella to get out. Draco got out next and helped me onto the ground. I looked to my left and saw a large man in black robes, a woman in white robes, and a small child about my age staring at me.

I didn't like the way the man was staring at me. There was something very dark in his eyes. I couldn't tell if they were just trying to buy apples or start something with me. I looked away and followed Draco to the door. This was not the only interaction I would have with those people.

Chapter 20

There were sirens going off into the distance. The street on the other side city was filled to the max with people trying to get to the church. This wasn't just a big day for me. It was a big day for so many people. On average, one in a hundred people managed to be Blessed at the Enlightenment Ceremony.

The strength of the person Blessed would escalate and transform some into almost different species of human. The longer a person lived and fought. The stronger they would be. Some people would become almost godlike in their power, but never enough to kill the Demon Lord. This would happen from generation to generation until finally a group of people would go to war with the Demon Lords army and win.

I'll tell you more later. Right now. Draco is heading over to the door in front of what looked to be a log cabin. The outside would sparkle when the light hit it just right. I could see a wall around the cabin made of rainbows. This was clearly no ordinary build. I watched Draco move around. He appeared to be doing some kind of dance to open the door.

Draco took three steps forward. He knocked on the door with his right hand and took three steps back. A high-pitched squeal was charging it. It created small flickers of light that sparked in random spots on the wall. He looked at the door and appeared to be waiting for something. The guy was intense about the door.

A strange high-pitched voice yelled at the door saying, "I have been expecting you, Draco. Come in."

The door to the cabin opened and Draco didn't hesitate to walk in. I don't think Isabella had ever been here before. She seemed scared just like me but wasn't positive yet. She looked back at me and used her hand to summon me over. I think she wanted me to go first. I knew at that moment. She was undoubtably afraid. Her eyes were shaking and looked glossy. She did her best to remain still and look calm. Unfortunately for her, she didn't have a good poker face. The eyes gave away too much. In my time in this world, the eyes would always tell you more than any other part of the body.

When I walked into the cabin, I looked up and the ceiling was five times higher than the cabin should have been. The ceiling was well lit with a chandelier. The chandelier had eight black candles what flickered a little. Since the candles worked together, there was never a second that the room wasn't lit up.

The room appeared to have no furniture at all. The only door was the entrance to the place. The floor was wooden and perfectly stained to prevent it from getting splinters. I wasn't used to a building like this having lived in a run-down house in the middle of nowhere. The walls looked like the logs on the outside. I was in awe just looking at all the space.

A cane was tapping on the floor. I looked over and there was a strange looking man. His ears were large and pointed like a bat. There were weird whiskers under his pointed nose. He looked to have enormous teeth in his mouth. I figured this because the teeth were pushing on his cheeks.

There was a hardened shell on his back. It appeared to be black with tan colors within the cracks. The best way to describe him was that his back looked like that of an armadillo. A long lion's tail was wrapped around his waist. The hand on the cane looked almost human. The hand was purple with sharp black nails long enough to pierce through flesh. It was like seeing someone with ten knives on their hands.

The being asked, "What can I do you Draco?"

Draco replied, "Good to see you Wong. I'm just here to get these kids a wardrobe change and a bath."

Wong was the name of the beast. He looked over at me with those lopsided eyes. He was eyeing me up in a peculiar way. It was like he saw something within my soul. His mouth opened a little bit. His teeth were all fangs. I felt like he was about to eat me, but when I looked closer. I noticed that he was giving me a large smile. He was trying to be friendly, but it didn't come across that way.

Wong said, "You have something wrong with you boy. I see your future and it isn't bright. You and that thing within you have vast potential. Well at least you do, the entity that lives in you. He will destroy you if you give him the chance. Watch yourself boy."

Draco looked at me and asked, "What is he talking about boy?"

I replied, "I don't know."

Wong said, "You know boy. I'm sure he has been whispering in your ear or years. A darkness that you will eventually have to overcome. It's not my place to tell you who or what it is. I'm just saying this transformation will change you. The darkness within you will flourish. Your heart will race and the people around you will suffer."

I responded, "You know nothing about me."

Wong said, "You might be right, but I recognize that signature anywhere."

I asked, "What do you mean?"

Wong replied, "Your signature reminds me of a man I once knew. I still think of him as a friend, but the darkness took over. There was trauma in his eyes. I wish I could help him still."

I asked, "Who was he?"

Wong replied, "He was a nobody that grew strong. If he was alive today, I know that this would be a wonderful world."

Wong backed up toward Draco. There was almost a tear coming from his eyes. Whoever was is friend. The man seemed to have a deep impact on him. All wasn't lost. He still had Draco and gained a family with them. At least, that's the way Draco made it sound. He did say there was something special about this man. I just couldn't see it yet.

Wong walked over to Isabella. The air from his nose was blowing her twig infested hair. She turned her face away. The feeling of his breath on her made her flinch. A moist layer was forming on her right cheek. He looked down at her chest and then her legs. He made a weird clicking sound with his tongue.

Wong said, "Your ego will get the better of you. I can see it already. You will have to submit in battle and let others be your strength. If you don't allow others to guide, you in life. You won't just be lonely. It might be the key factor that kills you. Learn your lessons while young. The spirits in your life will guide you, but the demons will protect you."

I asked, "How do you know these things?"

Wong replied, "That is my little secret. They are fully analyzed. The clothes should be done within a few hours. Just go get baths and enjoy your last day as children."

I was puzzled. What did you mean by last day as children? No matter what happens. Isabella and I would still be children. We were only nine years old. At least, that's what I thought. In a person's life, there is almost always that immediate change. It was something that Isabella and I never saw coming.

Draco said, "Just bring us the clothes when they are done."

Wong nodded to confirm that he would do that. He raised his hand. On the other side of the room, the boards below were shifting. The floor was cracking and snapping. I was having a difficult time standing on my feet. It felt like a quake. I bent myself forward and held my arms out like an airplane.

Isabella looked back at me and asked, "What are you doing?"

Isabella spent most of her childhood in the trees. She was like a monkey swinging around. Her fingers were a little longer to properly grapple things. Her ears were slightly larger than normal. It even had a tip on the top like she was a bat like Wong. I could never figure out who or what she was until later in life. To me, at that moment, she was just a stinky girl with weird abilities.

Draco said, "Alright kids. Go down the stairs."

I walked over to the steps. I wanted to be the first one to go down them. When I saw how steep the steps were, I decided to pass. The stairs lead to hallway the was slender and only had enough room for one person. Two if the people were small enough. I looked back and started to walk toward the entrance.

I hated being small. Draco reached out and grabbed me by the back of the shirt. He pulled me in close and said, "You either walk down those stairs or I will push you down the stairs. It is your choice."

So, I was walking down the stairs. My feet were dragging. It sounded like sandpaper on wood while walking those narrow steps. My legs were stiff and could barely lift them up. The movement was slow as my whole body was trembling not knowing what was down here. While I shuffled down, I felt a cold wind blowing through the hallway. I closed my eyes and tried not to see what was down here.

Once I got to the bottom of the steps, Isabella pulled a dick move on me. She ran past me and slammed into my left shoulder. She said, "For once in your life, be a fucking man."

The jolt from the hit forced me to take a few steps. I saw what was at the end of the hallway. It was a oval shaped portal with rainbows on the outside. In the center of the portal was white lightning in a black space. The crashing sound of the lightning sent shivers down my spine. I wanted to go home.

I turned around to walk out and Draco was standing there. I couldn't escape. His whole body was covering the hallway. He said, "You can either go through that portal or I will shove my size fifteen shoe up your ass. It's your choice. You can't go through life not overcoming a single fear."

I walked to the portal. Isabella had yet to go through. She looked over at me. I think she wanted to see me go first. I closed my eyes. I was getting ready to go inside. It became increasingly difficult to go in the more time I waited. The wind from the portal was blowing hard. My cheeks were rippling. My eyes were drying out. I didn't want my ass to have a shoe shoved up it. Something told me that this guy might be literal.

Draco said, "For fuck sake."

Draco kicked Isabella in the back and pushed her into the portal. Her eyes were wide, and she was trying to look back at her father. The portal had taken her. She was spinning around in a circle. I thought I was about to be sick just looking at her. After seeing that violent display, I realized. He might be a bad father.

My body was shaking. I looked back at Draco and noticed that he had left an opening. I dove to the spot that looked open. I didn't even see him move. He grabbed me and put my body under his arm. My ass was pointed toward the portal. He squeezed me tighter. He squeezed so hard that I couldn't breathe.

Draco said, "Buckle up boy."

Draco didn't walk into the portal. He leaped in and did a full-on cannonball. When his knees came up, his left knee hit me in the stomach and knocked the air out of me. I looked around and everything was looking colorful. The whole place looked like the nineteen seventies threw up everywhere. I wanted the portal to slow down. It was like being a turd getting flushed down the toilet.

I screamed loudly. Eventually, Draco and I flew out of a hole and onto a large gathering of pillows. When we hit the pillow, a bunch of white feathers flew upward. My face pushed into the pillows and my ass was up. I couldn't breathe. I tried to move but couldn't because he wouldn't let go of me.

Draco finally let me go and said, "See wasn't that fun."

I responded, "Rar a rar wo rar."

Those words meant nothing. My face was still pushed into the pillows. I turned over and spit a few feathers out onto the ground. I got up and looked around. It was just a hallway with two doors on the side. I jumped off the pillows and looked up at the signs above the doors. The sign to the left said "Girls" and on the right in blue was the "Boys." It was very self-explanatory.

I looked over to my left and there was Isabella. Her arms were folded. She said, "It's about time you showed up. I thought I would be doing this alone."

Isabella walked over to us and was getting ready to walk into the boy's room. Draco said, "You're not coming in with us."

Isabella responded, "Great, so I will be alone."

Draco said, "Not exactly."

I heard a thumping coming from the girl's bathroom. I looked over and a being that looked like a rabbit or bunny came out of the girl's bathroom. She was wearing nothing but a towel to cover her boobies and her nether region. I was a little excited to see whoever this being was. She walked out like a...adventurous woman.

My jaw dropped while I watched her come out. She asked, "How have you been Izzy?"

Isabella didn't miss a beat. She ran over to the bunny girl. We will just call her a bunny girl. Her arms couldn't fully wrap around her hips while squeezing. The towel was starting to fall off. I couldn't keep my eyes off her. Her gray ears were twitching. I think she was excited to see Isabella.

Draco said, "That is Jasmine. She works for me. I have had her here for years."

I responded, "Okay, I didn't see any other rabbit people. Are there..."

Draco interrupted me and said, "We will not talk about her family."

I asked, "Why?"

Draco responded, "Because its none of your fucking business, that is why!"

I couldn't argue with that logic. I didn't know what got into him. The longer the day was going. The more aggressive he seemed. It was like he planned out the whole day, but didn't plan out the questions I would be asking. He knew where and how I grew up. This shouldn't have been a shock.

Jasmine looked over at me and said, "Aren't you a cute one. You seem to have your father's eyes. A little small for a man. I'm assuming your James's son."

I gulped and responded, "Yes ma'am."

Jasmine said, "Just to let you know. I give the best baths. Just ask Draco."

Draco responded, "That's enough. I need you to make sure that she is clean for the Enlightenment Ceremony."

Jasmine said, "As you wish, just remember our deal. I need that taken care of tonight."

Draco responded, "I'm your master."

Jasmine said, "I don't give a fuck about that. You will live up to what we talked about tonight. I want it done."

Draco responded, "Don't worry your pretty little head. We have our agreements. I appreciate what you do here."

I had no idea what they were talking about. It became clear in the later years. Draco had something that belonged to her. Something that she needed a lot and if she didn't have it. She would rather die.

Chapter 21

Jasmine took Isabella into the bathroom with her. Her butt was waddling, and her tail was moving. The towel was shifting to entice Draco. He looked aways and tried to focus on getting me into the bath. It was kind of funny because she looked back at him, and he couldn't help but take a peek.

Draco's right hand pushed me through the doorway. In front of us, there was a wall made of bamboo. The green parts of the bamboo were shining. There was a light shining from the ceiling, but I couldn't find the source. The light was all evenly spaced out. I looked back at Draco to see where to go.

Draco said, "Come on my dude. Can't wash ourselves until we get in."

Draco pointed in the right direction. There were two sides to entering, but apparently it didn't even matter when we walked in. I noticed all it did was take me to the other side of the room. There were two benches in the center of the room. A series of holes were on the wall to put our clothes into. Below were spots to put our clothes. There were holes where baskets filled with soaps, oils, and shampoos lay there to be used.

Draco was quick to take his clothes off. Before I got the chance to ask what to do with the clothes, he was already naked, his clothes were in the hole, and he was stretching his arms. He stretched three times by reaching across and pulling on each arm before putting his leg on the closest bench.

Draco said, "Hurry up, we need to get in. Time is running out before we get to the church."

I was taking my clothes off. I slowed down when I realized he was strutting his stuff. It was old man balls just dangling there. His wrinkled dick drooped down further than I could get my forearm. It had to be the grossest thing I have ever seen, and I spent my childhood shitting in an outhouse.

I asked, "Can you put that away?"

Draco replied, "Are you serious? Alright kid. Nudity amongst men is nothing to be ashamed of. When I battle, it isn't uncommon for clothes to get shredded and tits to pop out of a uniform."

Draco looked at me with my grossed-out face. He made this weird squinting face. His eyes closed and walked over to a six-foot-tall bamboo rack that had white towels on it. He grabbed one quickly and wrapped it around his waist. It was loosely tied down. I just hoped it wouldn't fall and I would be forced to see his ugly junk again.

I walked over and grabbed a towel to cover up. The towel was white when I put it on, but because I was so dirty. There were black and brown spots from the dirt that was covering my skin. The towel was wrapped so tightly that it was leaving an imprint on my stomach. I didn't care. I just didn't want to be seen naked.

Draco took his right arm and made the gesture to walk behind him. There was a door to the bath that was covered in what looked to be large popsicle sticks that were being held up by wires. Draco walked through with no problem. The wood was making a chiming sound after he went through. I followed him and all the wood pieces were attacking me from the side. The wood kept moving. I put up my arms to protect my face. I couldn't see a damn thing. My right shoulder got lambasted a few times, and I was now bruised.

Once on the other side of the wood, I looked and saw a pool with black tiles around the outside. The inside of the pool was made of large stones and gray materials that I had never seen before. I gulped before trying to get near the water. The steam coming off it was blinding. I heard the rushing of water into the bath. The smell of pure water filled the air. I wasn't used to such a magnificent smell. There was something beyond the steam.

Draco said, "Isn't this place magical. The water is fantastic."

I walked over and dipped my toe in the water. It was extremely hot. Draco was getting sick of my hesitation. He picked me up and threw me to the other side of the bath. I wasn't good at swimming. I was losing my mind from the shock of hitting the water. I went underwater. My equilibrium was out of wack. My body was fighting to reach the surface. The longer I was under. The harder it was too come to the top. This happened because I was drowning.

My toes touched the bottom of the bath. I scrapped my toes across the bottom until my full foot was placed across the ground. I managed to stand up. When I stood up in the bath, only my head was able to reach. Water was raining from the sky on me. A hot waterfall was flowing into the bath. I was gasping for air and couldn't see a thing. My eyes were closed while trying to feel around and find my way out.

A large arm came over and pulled me out from under the waterfall. It was Draco getting me out. He sat me on a seated area built in the bath. He swam over to the other side of the bath. The steam was simmering, and I could finally see what was happening around us. My sight inside came to soon and saw his asshole and bottom of his sack. I wanted to throw up.

The water was clear. My legs were looking clean already. There were small sparkles on my legs. I wasn't sure what was happening, but my flesh was tingling. The dirt that was on there was disappearing. The water was dissolving everything that was dirty. I sunk down into the water. Only my head was poking out of the water.

My muscles were slowly being massaged by the heat. I didn't want to admit it. This was probably the most relaxing moment in my life. My lips went below the water's surface. I closed my eyes and blew a few bubbles only to sit up right after. I cupped my hands and filled them with water. I pushed the water into my hair. I felt a tingling flowing through my scalp. This was the cleanest I had ever felt.

Draco looked at me with a disappointed look on his face. He asked, "Where is your soap boy?"

I replied, "What soap?"

Draco said, "There was soap in a basket under your cabinet. It doesn't matter. Howlers is coming."

I responded, "Howlers?"

Draco said, "Yeah, she's one of your dad's slaves. She became a hero, and the wolf people didn't want her to grow as a warrior. I can't pronounce her real name. I just call her Howlers."

I responded, "Why do you call her that?"

Draco said, "Because she is so cute, it makes humans want to howl at the moon."

A sound came from the doorway. My head whipped over to see who it was. A wolf woman walked into the male spring area. She looked a lot like Talya. The gray around her eyes gave me a somewhat panic attack. My heart was beating watching her come toward me. I became attracted to some of the wolf woman over the years. Up until recently, I had never seen another human woman besides my mom.

Howlers, as Draco said her name, was wore a red robe that tied off. The fur looked fluffy like she bathed in here every day. Her hands were still paws but looked more human than the other wolf People. She had gray, long, furry fingers. Her feet appeared to be borderline human. She just casually walked in with a basket full of soaps and sponges.

Draco looked at the wolf woman and said, "Can you give the boy a good scrub? It's his Enlightenment Ceremony tonight."

Draco looked at me and gave me a wink. The wink was of a man that was perverted. I'm not sure how he knew that I liked some of the wolf woman. I just know. He made sure to make my time here the best. I thought to myself that I could wash myself, but apparently not or we wouldn't have to be here in the first place.

Howler walked over to the side of the bath. She dipped her toes into the water to test it. The water appeared to be to her liking. She stripped off the robe and set it to the side. I watched her fluffy white and gray tail wag. Her belly was pure white and made my jaw drop. I couldn't breathe.

Draco said, "With her being a hero, he is more human like than the other wolves. It doesn't surprise me to see you like this."

I responded, "Shut up!"

Howler giggled while she came over to the bath. She climbed in and dunked herself under the water. When she came up, she was literally inches from my face. My heart was beating harder while the water coming off her fur hit me. Her hot breath from her nose was making me feel weird. It turns out that breathing on my neck was always a way to get riled up.

Howler grabbed the basket filled with soap and set it in the water. The baskets could float. She turned over and sat down next to me. Her right arm reached out and pulled me in. She gave me a kiss on the top of my head. I wasn't sure what was happening. The water was still falling from her fur and drenching my head.

Howler picked me up and sat me on her lap. The basket was pulled over. She pulled out a bar of soap and a washcloth. She dunked the cloth in the water and covered it with soap. I was thoroughly being scrubbed by her. I was enjoying this a little too much. Even though I was small, my body still reacted like a man. There were certain parts of me that were getting bigger. I was a little embarrassed.

I was perfectly still hoping that she didn't notice my arousal. She used her breasts to keep my neck still while grabbing the shampoo in the baskets. She scrubbed my head deeply. It felt like a massage. I closed my eyes while she dug deep and got all the mud that had been caked in for probably weeks.

A small bucket was pulled out of the basket Howler took a scoop and poured it over my head. The water seemed never-ending. I was choking and gagging the longer the water was poured. I spit up some of the water that went into my mouth and blew out. It was a weird natural reaction to prevent more water from going in.

Howler looked down at me and said, "That wasn't too bad was it."

I responded, "I guess not."

Howler said, "It was good seeing you again."

I asked, "Have we met before?"

Howler replied, "Quite a few years ago we met. I was a pup who swam with you. I might have accidentally scratched your back."

I looked closely. Wow, she grew into a full wolf woman. I had a huge crush on her back then, but now. There is no denying that she was beautiful. She sat me on the seating area next to her and grabbed the basket. She didn't bother to grab her clothes and walked out of the bathroom area.

Draco asked, "What the fuck was that?"

I replied, "We knew each other when she was a pup."

Draco lit a brown cigar looking thing in his right hand. He took a nice big puff and said, "Okay, wolf people do grow faster than humans."

Draco had a glass and a bottle of Scotch sitting on the side of the bath. He poured himself enough Scotch to fill to the top of the glass. He brought his head down to the glass and sipped off the top hoping to not lose a single drop. Once he felt comfortable enough to move with the glass, he looked at me with a smile on his face.

Draco pointed his cigar looking thing at me and said, "Right now is the time to talk like men. There are no women around so any grievances or thoughts will not leave this bath."

I asked, "Why now?"

Draco replied, "I have Jun Jun in my right hand and Scotch in my left. All my stress is melting away. I might be able to answer some of the millions of questions that you have in this state."

I asked, "If that's the case, why is it so important to marry one of your daughters? I obviously have no real value."

Draco replied, "The answer to this question is quite complicated. The quick answer is that Marcus said it will happen, but that is not all. I mean making sure we follow the Sacred Timeline is important, but there is a matter of your father and I friendship. He is the best man that I could ever ask for. The idea of making us family would be amazing."

I said, "There is more isn't there."

Draco responded, "There is more. My father hated King Alexander for giving away part of the land that was owed to him. Your father took a huge chunk of land when he was given a wish after the Basilisk attack. By having you marry one of my daughters, the land will come right back into the family. I mean no ill will toward you about it. It's just a sore subject."

I said, "You feel owed the land."

Draco responded, "I feel my children are owed the land. I feel that I owe my father what he was owed. Even if he is dead already."

I said, "I wish I could help, but I don't love any of your daughters."

Draco responded, "Not even Matilda."

I said, "I barely spoke to her. She ran off and doesn't want anything to do with me it seems."

Draco responded, "Matilda is complicated. Most people don't know anything about her. You are probably right. Her eyes are set on another."

Draco took a deep puff of the cigar looking thing. It was followed by a sip of the Scotch. He closed his eyes and appeared to be trying to remember something. Something that was deep within his mind. He took another sip and leaned forward. He swirled the Scotch in his glass and looked into my eyes.

Draco said, "I think I know where you are going with the next question."

I asked, "Have you ever been married?"

Draco replied, "I was once. I remember her so vividly."

I asked, "Was it Isabella's mother?"

Draco replied, "No, it was Matilda's mother. Matilda was the only daughter we had together. The rest of my daughters I love so much but their mothers couldn't compare."

I asked, "What happened to all the mothers?"

Draco replied, "Many are dead. Some are alive and have issues preventing them from seeing the girls. That just makes me the only person capable of raising them. A part of me loved all my daughter's mothers."

I asked, "What happened to Matilda's mother?"

Draco swirled the Scotch in his glass more. He stared at the glass and yelled, "It was my fault!"

I said, "You killed her. Didn't you."

Draco responded, "I would never kill my angel. I just said it was my fault."

I asked, "Can you tell me how you knew that she was the one to marry?"

Draco replied, "That I can do."

Chapter 22

Love and Demons

It was the summer right after your father and I met. I was in the guild looking for work. He helped me with a few jobs. It was more an advisory role and a backup to make sure that I didn't get killed on C rank missions. His ability to lure away the enemy and take a million hits was crucial in my early years.

If you didn't know, each mission has a ranking system to guarantee that weaker heroes don't get the hardest missions. However, your father and I were part of the guild called the Reaper guild. The guild was by far the strongest in the kingdom. They still are. Only the strongest heroes get into it. That was why a C rank mission for the Reaper guild was an A rank mission for other guilds.

There was a board to the right. It was a simple security mission that was C rank. It required a total of five people. I couldn't do it alone. The lack of intel made it a C rank. They thought wild animals were attacking the locals and needed to be exterminated. Apparently, the animals were killing the kids from a local village.

I walked up to Henry. He was running the guild at the time. He was a Creationist class that had a gift for portal and material manipulation. For years, he was one of the greatest support classes. He was building camps and fortifications that saved thousands of lives. After a few years of defending, the former Guild Master asked him to run as the new Guild Master.

The former Guild Master was getting older. Humans only live to be about seventy to a hundred years old, and he was eighty-two. Henry was the perfect choice because he wasn't just a strategist but could manage the guild hall. Due to his Blessing, the inside of the guildhall becomes a labyrinth at times. Even to this day, I have a hard time navigating through the place.

Anyway, I walked up to Henry and asked if anyone was taking the job. I wanted to see if they needed a warrior. Being a warrior didn't help me to find work. Most warriors would die from missions due to their lack of healing while being a front confrontational class. Most people looking at us just saw a sacrificial pawn in a game of chess.

Henry looked at me and said, "I'm not sure if they will take you, but there are four guys about to take on the mission. They are at that table over there."

Henry took a moment away from cleaning a beer glass to point at a table with four guys. The guys were chugging their ales and laughing. I was a bit of a dick back then. Being a royal that was being groomed to be the next Legionnaire, I thought that I was the cock of the walk. These guys gave me a wakeup call. I walked over to the group and slammed my hands on the table.

The group looked at me with a shocked look on their faces. They didn't know who I was because the Legionnaire was my father at the time. I was nothing more than an observer. There were people that knew who I was, but my name wasn't recognized nearly what it is today. All I got was a look of "We're going to fuck you up boy. You just ruined the mood."

I said, "I heard you guys are doing the protection mission in Tacoma Grove. I want in."

A Barbarian on the other side of the table stood up. He had to be over eight feet tall. There were veins popping out of his head and his muscles had their own muscles. There was a leather strap that held his axe scrapped across his chest. The axe was taken out and leaning against the table they were leaning on.

The Barbarian said, "Is that so? My name is Bardock. I have to know. What makes you special for this mission."

I responded, "My name is Draco and I'm one of the greatest Warriors to ever live."

Bardock laughed and said, "Is that so? Is this your way of saying that you have been sacrificed more than any other Warrior. From experience, the only Warriors that seem to survive are the cowards. They run away and never return until it comes time to collect the bounty."

I responded, "I don't need the bounty. I'm just after the experience."

Bardock said, "That is different. So, you are telling me that you are willing to waive your bounty. That is quite intriguing."

Bardock tilted his head and stroked his beard. He looked at me. He was trying to figure out what the catch was. When someone in this world offers something that is too good to be true. It almost always is. In my case, I just wanted to level myself up. Money wasn't important because of my status in royalty.

The mission required five people according to the listing. If there is less than the required number of people that attend, the person who made the mission can turn the group away and wait for the next. It was a gamble because if they waited too long. A random group of five people could steal away the job.

Bardock said, "Why don't you want the bounty?"

I responded, "I don't need it. I come from a rich family."

Bardock said, "Who is your family?"

I responded, "Last name is Simpson. I am the Legionnaire's son."

Bardock was laughing. He said, "The Legionnaire's son. The same man that got pulled from the Basilisk fight for being a fucking retard. You just ran out there and thought you could solo a Basilisk even after several Rogues couldn't take it down."

I responded, "Well I told you that I need the experience."

Bardock said, "Fuck it. That just means you got balls kid and luck is on your side. The four of us are B rank heroes. We'll bring you along. Just don't think for a second that we will save your ass. You do something stupid like that with us. You're on your own. Is that clear?"

I nodded my head, yes. I looked at the other three guys. They were smirking and laughing at me. They felt strong enough to take on this mission without my help. I didn't care that they felt that way. I just wanted to get some experience from a real group. I was tired of having James save me when things were getting out of hand.

Bardock said, "This is Spark, Flea, and his Assholiness."

The guy Bardock referred to as Assholiness said, "Names Aoi. They just came up with the name to mock me."

Aoi was a Priest. He was referred to as a Discipline Priest. He wore a white room with black stitching into the collar. The belt was black and was strange to me because most Priest robe belts were cotton. His belt was made of leather. There was a golden staff leaning on the table next to him. At the top of the staff was a circle caught in a larger round circle. The outside of the circle was where the sun was. It had six triangles connected to it. The triangle gave it structure.

Fleas was the Rogue in the group. He had a black shirt on and a pair of black leather pants. He had black boots on that looked brand new. When he walked in the boots, the squeaking sound would draw attention to himself. There were two brown leather straps on both sides. Each side held three knives on it.

The last was Sparky. A name given to him because he was a Fire Mage. Fire Mages were also called the Mages of Destruction. All they knew how to do was blow shit up. The Robes on him were pure black. Even the belt on the robe was pure black. The material of the robe was blander and had something that prevented him from burning his flesh.

Sparky had a crooked staff that he would carry with him. The stave had a round topper that reminded me of a snail's shell. The staff looked black in certain spots and in the center. It thought that it had a living fire inside. When you got close to the staff, you could hear a rumbling. The staff appeared to be speaking to Sparky at times.

Bardock said, "Gentlemen, let's get a good night's sleep. We meet at the gate in the morning. I'll grab the quest from Henry."

Bardock went over and got the quest. The other three finished their ales and left for their beds. I thought at the time I could trust them and have them come to the house for some rest. I thought a little kindness might have gotten me in good standing with the group. I was about to invite them when Henry shook his head, not too. He knew something that I didn't.

I left the guild hall and walked home alone. It didn't take me long due to my abilities. I ran home and grabbed a quick meal. I ran upstairs and went to bed. I didn't get a good night's sleep because of my anxiousness. The sun came up and I barely got a wink of sleep. I went downstairs and ate a quick meal.

I walked to the gate with my eyes feeling sore. I figured that one of them was driving the cart to the next location. They wouldn't trust a new guy to drive their horses and cart. I could easily try to steal all their things. That would have been the rational thing to assume. It turned out the trip was far worse than I thought.

I got to the gate. My bag had to be over a hundred pounds filled with camping gear, food, clothes, and hygiene stuff. I had a strap with a long knife on each side. The knives were easier for me to use Manipulation on. They require less Chi and would always penetrate any normal adversary. I was just not good against large monsters.

When I got to the gate, the other guys were sitting there waiting for me. They didn't give me a time when we were leaving. All I figured was we needed to meet at sunup. The moon was still in the distance. I thought. I was plenty early. I walked over with this huge pack on my back. I was ready to go.

Bardock said, "You're a braver man than me. I would never walk to Tacoma Grove with that much gear."

I responded in a puzzled voice, "Walk?"

Bardock said, "Yeah walk. We thought you might have changed your mind since you weren't here yet. It turns out that you're a prissy man baby that needs his whole house for a fucking mission. I'm sure you will regret taking all that."

I asked, "Where is all your gear?"

Bardock replied, "Flea shrinks things. It's in his pocket."

I asked, "Can he shrink my stuff?"

Bardock replied, "You'll have to ask him."

I looked at Flea and without skipping he said, "NO! It takes Spirit to do this. I'm not using up my Spirits energy because you want to be pampered. You want experience. This will be how you get it. Is that a cast iron pan?"

I responded, "Yeah to cook with."

Sparky said, "Let me guess. You need to build a fire as well. You want to sleep in a tent and turn this into a camping trip."

I asked, "Should I just leave the bag? You seem offended by me having it."

Bardock replied, "We don't want to waste any more time. Let's just go. It will be part of your learning experience. Don't fall behind!"

I wasn't sure why they were being jerks to me. It could have been because I was new or that I was the youngest member of the group. All I knew was that they resented me for some reason. It was turning into a long trip. I wasn't sure if I should continue but if I cancelled on them. It might have caused trouble for all future missions.

The road to Tacoma Grove was long. It was a small village in the middle of a forest. They would come into town once a week to hopefully get food for the village. That was the only reason that we even knew the people existed. I guess when they came in on their last run. The people gave us the mission.

I walked out of the gate and followed the group. The guards left us alone and were only taking care of the people trying to get into the city. It was a time of pride for them. Some of the gate guards would spend hours every night polishing their armor before bed. They wanted to look nice since they were the first people you would see when coming in. I wish that I could get them motivated like during the times of Alexander. After Norman took over, there didn't seem to be any pride.

The group got to the end of the road. There were five roads going in different directions. The road to the far right is our land. The road I went down that day was the second road from the left. It took us northwest of Tryanon. The road was a little bumpy, but I managed to walk around when I felt a dip.

Bardock walked next to me. He wanted to make sure I was prepared for any battle. He noticed something strange about me. I didn't have a sword. Warriors were always known for having swords. I remember the look on his face. His forehead was wrinkled, and his top teeth were showing.

Bardock asked, "Where is your sword? I don't see it connected to the pack."

I replied, "I don't use swords. They are too heavy for what I do. I'm sure I can someday."

Bardock looked frustrated. He said, "You have no sword. What kind of Warrior doesn't use a sword? There are two things they use in battle, swords and shields. If you aren't using either, what are you using?"

I had a strap around my arms that looked like suspenders. There was a knife on each side. The knives sank in a bit because of the large bag on my back. It was hard for Bardock to see. He looked at me and thought that I didn't know anything about my class. The truth was that they didn't know anything about my class. I was a speedster Warrior which is rare. I was confused by the statement, not realizing Fury Warriors were rare at the time.

Bardock said, "You fight with knives. The knives look to be twelve inches long, but that isn't the way a Warrior fights. What kind of Warrior are you? I saw no shield. That means you're not a Protection. You're clearly not a Sword Master or an Arms Warrior."

I responded, "I am a..."

I wasn't paying attention and my right foot felt squishy. I have never felt so good about not being barefoot like Bardock. I stepped in a steaming pile of shit. It wasn't just any shit. It was horse shit. The entire front of my boot was covered in it, part of the side, and the bottom squished into it. I left my mark not only with the poo, but the group as well.

Bardock broke out into laughter. He stopped for a second to say, "Well this is a shitty situation. Watch where you walk."

Bardock's laughter was contagious, and the others looked back. They stopped walking and noticed that I was still standing in the shit. I could have just stepped out, but I was ashamed of myself. I had been talking a big game, and the guys learned what kind of person I really was.

My foot was difficult to retrieve. The shit was thick and wouldn't let me go. When I raised my foot up, it was moist and dripping from the boot. I stretched my right leg out and attempted to shake it off. Bardock jumped back to avoid getting hit with shit on my boot. He continued to laugh at me.

Bardock said, "You're supposed to dodge those. I tell you what. You are something kid. It's a shame you will probably die on this trip."

Aoi said, "Great! Now we will have to smell you the whole trip."

I had a difficult time walking for the first three miles. Bardock left me to join the other three. He was up ahead by quite a bit and tried to lead the group through safely. I was falling behind from the weight. My back was sore, and I wanted to go home. I wanted to put myself in a position where I could make a name for myself. Things were not going as planned.

While walking with these guys, I was guaranteed to be mocked when coming home. I could still hear them mocking me for stepping in shit. Every chance I had, I would try to wipe more of it off into the grass along the way. That's the thing about beginnings. They are just beginnings. I would spend every moment trying to learn from every situation. I would see how the people around me fought. I tested my abilities against the people around me. The lows would eventually become highs and the only thing that could teach me was experience. As time progressed, I was eventually feared by not just men, but countries. Over the next year, I would eventually make my father proud.

The walk took all day. The sun was going down, and I thought that we were about to build a campsite. I looked up at the White Moon and saw the Red Moon chasing it. I had an eerie feeling about this trip. My heart was racing from hearing something coming toward us in the wild. Chances are, it was an animal that was more scared of us than them.

The group ignored the sounds around us and ran forward. The town called Tacoma Grove was only a quarter mile away. They started to run and so did I. The sound of whatever the wild beasts were, scared me. I wanted to go faster but was exhausted by the long journey and weight on my back. It's why you never see me wearing heavy armor.

The group reached the village. The villagers had bright red fire in their lanterns that lit up the streets. There wasn't a single person on the street. We walked through the town in hopes of finding an inn for the night. We were all tired and wanted to sleep before we killed whoever was stealing the kids from the village.

Bardock yelled, "Can anyone help us?! I want to fucking sleep."

Chapter 23

An old man opened the door to his home and walked out cautiously. His back was arched and shook to the point where the glass on the lantern he was carrying rattled. He looked over at the group and shined a bright white light at us. It was creepy because the guy kept raising his lantern at us until his arm was fully erect. After wiggling the lantern a few times, he thought that we were safe and raised his hand to usher us closer.

The building right next to the one was the inn. He walked over to the door and knocked on it with the palm of his hand. When the owner didn't open the door, he made a fist and hit it six more times. The door creeped open. The person inside looked out the door and saw the five of us standing in the street. The person nodded their head and walked back into the inn.

The old man said, "Come in. It's nice inside."

The group walked in without hesitation. I was the last to walk through the door. I was being cautious because something seemed strange about the town. The people here reminded me of an inbred community. A group of mutants likes from an old eighties' movie back in the day. I loved watching them with my boy Ben. I just wish they didn't freak me out so much.

I just realized you don't know what an eighties movie is. You will by the end of the day. I promise you that. The Blessing should start your awakening process. Everyone gains their memories from the old world. The memories are quite a shock at first. It's a common occurrence we all go through. I just hope that yours isn't worse than mine. Mine made me damn near comatose for almost a full day. HA, those were some good times.

When we walked in the old man asked, "What brings you to Tacoma Grove?"

Bardock replied, "We accepted a mission to rid the forests of the beasts that are taking your families. We were under the impression it was children."

The old man said, "Good to see you. I will compliment your rooms for you."

Bardock responded, "Can you tell us what is happening? We need details to help us locate the missing people."

The old man said, "There isn't much to go on. A few people have said that northeast of where the people are being dragged away. We hear the voices of people being carried off but there is usually a fog that follows. We have no idea what kind of beast is capable of doing these things."

Bardock responded, "Something is missing. What aren't you telling me old man?"

The old man was shaking, and his voice was cracking when he said, "You are the eleventh group to try. The rest seemed to disappear into the fog."

Bardock went over to the table on the side of the room and exclaimed, "What are your specials?"

The group hadn't eaten all day. He needed to make sure we were well fed for the mission. We all sat down at the table while Bardock ordered the meal. The inn owner appeared to be very intimidated by Bardock. She didn't know what to expect from a Barbarian. Barbarians had a reputation we aren't about to discuss.

Bardock huddled down and said, "Eleven people have disappeared from a C class mission. Something feels wrong about this."

Aoi asked, "What are you thinking?"

Bardock replied, "I don't know. You and Sparky are the smart ones."

Sparky said, "Eleven failures tells me that they are feeding something. The rank of the mission was C which means they wanted weak people to feed whatever is out there. They were counting on four B class Heroes to take this on."

Flea responded, "What if the beast is S class?"

Aoi said, "If there was an S class beast out here, the town would be destroyed. As it is, whatever we are against. They seem to cause little destruction."

I tried to chime in. I responded, "What is with the red lights?"

Flea asked, "What about the red lights? The flames are red. It happens with certain oils."

Sparky replied, "The kid is new, but he might be right on this one. It couldn't be the oil the town uses normally because the old man had a white flame. Good job kid."

Bardock said, "Don't give the kid an ego. We still don't know what the red lights do."

Sparky responded, "What kind of creatures are deterred by red lights? I am having a hard time thinking about this one."

The food came. everyone forgot what they were talking about. The food made us tired. There is something called a food coma. After you eat, you get relaxed to the point where everything else happening doesn't matter. Especially, on days when you don't eat and immediately engorge yourself.

I went up to my room and dropped my bag inside. I realized while in the room that I didn't need over half the stuff. I had a place to sleep on the trip. The pots and pans would be for cooking, and I had food, but it wasn't necessary. I should have known this before going from E rank to C, but all the missions your father did were close to the city.

The bed was wooden and had a thin mattress on it. The bed I usually slept on was a hundred times better than this. I got on the mattress and stared at the ceiling. My back was stiff from carrying all those supplies. I moved to the right and my entire spine was cracking.

I couldn't move from the cracking. My eyes got wide and couldn't close them. My neck was stiff and forced me to look at the ceiling closer. The moon was bright and flashing on the ceiling. There was something strange on the ceiling. I tried to look a little closer. I overcame my pain and stood up on the bed. I needed to see what was up there.

I placed my hand on the ceiling and noticed there were pieces of dried-up flesh and blood. My finger was covered in black and red substances from the ceiling. I just wanted to leave. There had to be a reason why the blood was there. I didn't waste time. My first reaction was to take the large dresser on the other side of the room and place it in front of the door.

I crawled into bed and shut my eyes. I didn't sleep well that night. Part of it had to do with the shitty mattress. The other part had to do with the fear of being killed in my sleep. I slept a little. It just wasn't solid enough sleep to be fully out. That night, I could not dream. All I could do was let the voice in my head take over. It constantly made me second guess everything.

The light from the sun sort of shined through the window to my right. The trees were blocking out most of the sun. My eyes were open and might have been bloodshot. I sat up with my back crackling from sleeping on such an uncomfortable mattress. I tossed my legs over the side of the bed and rubbed my eyes.

A loud noise came knocking at the door. Bardock yelled, "Wake up. We eat. We leave."

I walked over to the door and pushed the dresser away. The sound of the dresser scrapping against the floor. It made enough noise that all the guys in the hallway could hear it. I knew they could hear it because of the abrupt laughter coming from them. It was like their only goal was to mock me.

I opened the door and Aoi said, "You afraid of the dark boy."

I responded, "I just didn't feel safe. I found blood on the ceiling."

Bardock asked, "Was it fresh?"

I replied, "No, it was dark and dry."

Bardock said, "Don't worry about it then. Let me explain. Places like this are always covered in blood. Quite often men trying to hide or escape something. Bandits, thieves, and Assassins come to these places trying to find people that are running from the law and want to make a quick coin."

I responded, "What you're saying is. Someone died in my bed."

Bardock said, "Probably at least a dozen. Don't sweat the small stuff. Your father certainly did pamper you didn't he. In these areas, you need know what is happening before it happens. Even if you aren't sleeping, they will still find a way to kill you. You might as well get some rest while you got the chance."

I responded, "That sounds comforting."

Bardock said, "It wasn't supposed to. It was supposed to get you to stop being paranoid and get over whatever is in your head. The last thing we need is your running away when things get tough. You want to learn how to finish a mission. You must first overcome the fear that all adversaries give."

Bardock reached out and wrapped his enormous left arm around my head. He pulled out and walked me down the steps to the table. We need to eat before we set out on the mission. He kept flexing his muscles to show me how tough he was. All it ended up doing was make me smell like hoagies. Even my hair smelled terrible from his armpit. I thought I was about to throw up.

I was let go. His stomach hit pushed me away. I almost fell on my ass while trying to stabilize myself. My mind was a little fuzzy while trying to walk back to the table. I'm still unsure if it was the stink of his pits or the hit in the head. All I know is that I struggled to get to the table.

I sat down. We all got eggs and every meat imaginable. These people tried to fatten us up. I looked at the Bardock and asked, "Are you paying for this much food?"

Bardock replied, "No, its all complimentary. These people really want us to feel at home here."

I asked, "Isn't that weird?"

Bardock replied, "Stop being so damn paranoid. These are good people. I have seen my fair share of scummy people. To make things better, they are afraid of us. People don't betray who they are afraid of. Death is a powerful motivator."

I looked down at my plate. The food looked good, and I was very hungry. I wanted to eat but couldn't bring myself to eat the food. Something felt off. Especially after last night, I had never felt so tired after a meal like that before. It could have been my stomach was always full. I always had plenty of food to eat due to my status, and my belly wasn't used to it. The other option would be that something was making me feel tired from the food.

Sparky said, "If you don't want your food, we will eat it."

I pushed the plate to the center. Without missing a beat, the four of them were taking the food off my plate and putting it on theirs. The sound of them smacking their lips together was grotesque. The juices falling down their lips and falling onto the table seemed unsanitary. I had to look away.

Aoi finished eating and asked, "Where is your bag?"

I replied, "I left it in the room. I'll pick it up on the way back. All we need for the mission right now is our weapons."

Bardock said, "See. You're catching on. Except a little food wouldn't hurt. Something dry that can be nibbled on like a cracker."

Bardock stood up from the table and threw his chair against the back wall. He was just trying to pull it away and it slipped out of his fingers. He looked up at the inn owner. She ignored him and was wiping down the counter. I think he was more worried about offending the owners than anything. His eyes were wide, and his mouth was open.

When Bardock saw no reaction, he said, "Let's go boys."

Everyone stood up and walked out of the inn. The red lights were still on and burning. It was strange because most people would have turned them off by now. The lanterns were wasting oil and red flame oil was a highly valued commodity. Why would a small town like this be wasting fuel? Red vipers' blood isn't even rural to these parts. I thought.

I took out my blades to examine them. I sharpened them from the last time. It just felt like something was missing. I looked over at the Rogue and realized. He had more blades than me. That was the moment I realized. I needed to have backup blades. After that, I realized that I needed a blade for every occasion. If you want to know more about that, I'll tell you later.

The group walked to the end of the town. I was wondering if anyone would see us off. Most of the people in the town appeared to be afraid to leave their homes. This was the downside of not living in the city. Without proper protection, people tend to stay in their homes and never come out unless necessary.

The sound of birds was flying through the trees. I looked up and saw ravens flocking toward our direction. The black birds were making whistling noises. The birds were too small to carry bodies out of the village. However, ravens were referred to as the bringers of death. Whenever someone sees a raven, it's best to watch your surroundings because they know something that you don't.

I was thinking of saying something about the birds, but every time I said something. The guys would say I was just being paranoid. I was told to lighten up. My inexperience was a flaw in their eyes.

It turned out. My observations were often needed to complete a mission. I love being right most of the time.

There was a different type of experience I had access to thousands of books. My reading from the library and attention to detail was one of my greatest assets. I just didn't know how to convince them that this was the case.

According to them, Sparky was the smart one. It just sucked I was following a group of fools into the forest. That was where I learned most of my lessons. I learned how to navigate and react to fools. As a leader of Tryanon's army. I needed to learn who to trust with information and who to ignore. I guess you can say. My greatest lesson was to never underestimate the power of fools in large numbers.

Chapter 24

The woods around the village weren't very long. The group made our way through and saw a giant cliff. It was steep and about three hundred feet high. Water was dripping down the side of cliff but wasn't strong enough to form a waterfall. The only explanation for it being so wet was. A possible water stream was above. If the area above was cut out, the stream could flow into the ground below and drown the trees.

The green moss on the outside made it too difficult to climb. We walked toward the cliff anyway. The closer we got the more fog was forming around us. My boots were sinking into the wet dirt below. While walking, the boot was acting like a suction cup and making noises. Everyone's feet were making noises. That's why they didn't growl.

Flea said, "To the right, there is a cave."

Flea had the ability to not just notice traps, but he could see hidden locations. It had something to do with his sight. Apparently, he could also see how many kills a person had. The part he didn't realize was most of my kills weren't low level beasts. The reason I got rank C so fast was with the help of James who only killed high level beasts as a principle.

The cave was found. Bardock was the first to go inside. It was getting darker the further we went in. Our footsteps were making a splashing sound. The walls were dripping. We believed it to be water.

Water could be the only explanation for what we were standing in until Bardock got a little further down the cave.

Bardock said, "I don't smell anything flammable. Light it up Sparky."

Sparky put out his right hand and a yellow flame came out. He was bigger and brighter than any torch. The light flickered violently when he realized what we were standing in. There were bones, blood, and flesh. He turned the flame closer to the right side and looked down. His left hand reached out to the face of a dead child.

The child's face was chewed on. The skull was broken and smashed a hundred times. The brains were sucked out the top of its head. The left side of the kid's face was eaten to the bone. The weird part about the biting was the bite marks. A single bite had layers of teeth. Nobody in the group had met a beast like that before.

Sparky said, "This is unnatural. What kind of beast lines up corpses and eats at them slowly. It's like the creatures don't care if the meat is fresh. In fact, I think they prefer the rotten flesh."

Aoi responded, "There are rumors that demonic creatures have been known to do this."

Bardock said, "Knock that off. We don't need to be scaring the Warrior with your nonsense. Every time we are on a mission you claim demons and every time it's usually bandits, thieves, or animals."

Aoi responded, "I think we should fall back until we find out what kind of beast this is."

Bardock said, "Don't be a fool. We stay the course. If the beast is in there, we need to see it anyway. Just be cautious."

Bardock kept walking forward. He took his axe off his back and held it tightly against his chest. He wasn't scared because most Barbarians were able to take hits and use Chi to heal themselves. Their rapid healing helped them to be balanced tanks and attackers. Their skin wouldn't harden like a Warrior's.

The cave led to a dark round room. The roof looked like it was over a hundred feet high. It was round and covered in water. The water surrounded a small island in the center of the room. We walked slowly trying to make a little noise. The splashing was echoing through the cave but didn't appear to be waking anything up.

Sparky walked up beside Bardock. He knew that Bardock would defend him because he was our only light source. All we could see was darkness on the wall and a small figure in the center of the room. They crept up to the island to see who the small figure was. The shadow from it spread against the wall.

The figure was a woman. A red-haired woman that was captured by the beast or beasts. She appeared to be sleeping. Her body lay limp as if someone or something had paralyzed her. The only reason we knew she was alive. She was breathing and we could see the water puddle in front of her moving.

Bardock walked toward the body. He put his axe in his left hand and walked slowly. His foot slammed down. He smashed a bone under his feet. The crackling sound of the bone echoed throughout the cave. The echoes came from all directions. There appeared to be many tunnels in the cave.

The red-haired woman woke up. She was wearing a black robe like Sparky's. Her eyes were green and glowing. The flickering light from Sparky grew and spread further throughout the cave. She appeared to be sleeping in ashes. It appeared she covered herself in the ashes so the beast in the cave wouldn't notice her.

Flea, Aoi, and I walked to the center. We were seeing if the woman needed assistance. After all, Aoi was a healer. She might have been injured and needed us to help with any wounds the beast might have inflicted. The bloodied water disgusted Aoi while walking through. He liked to keep his robes clean.

When we got to the woman, Aoi said, "We have come to save you. Do you have anyone wounds that need healing?"

The red-haired woman looked around and stared blankly into my face. She was shaking her head and uttered the words, "You need to leave. You stand no chance against them."

Flea said, "She is warning us. We need to leave."

Aoi responded, "Come on. Let's get out of here."

The red-haired woman said, "It's too late. You're all going to die down here."

The sound echoed through the cave. It was like a million insects coming to our location I looked over at the red-haired girl. She curled up in the ashes and covered her head. The cave was shaking all around us. Rocks were falling from the ceiling. The cave appeared to be collapsing. A hole broke through the ceiling and water started to come down north of the cave.

Flea said, "Fuck you guys. I'm leaving."

Flea turned invisible and ran toward the direction we came. We could see where he was going because his footsteps in the water were still showing. The splashing seemed to attract the other creatures in the cave. We couldn't see them yet but could hear them coming through the cracks in the wall.

Flea made it to the rooms opening, but that was it. We couldn't see what attacked him. All we could see was a hole in his chest where his heart used to be. Something else was invisible. The heart appeared and had what looked to be a long tongue grasped around it. The heart was pulled through the back of the body and was being consumed by a creature.

The creature left its invisibility. The skin was red with a long slender head. It appeared to be hairless. The top of the head was shaped like a banana. I think it needed room to store its extremely long tongue. There were three sets of sharp teeth in its mouth. The eyes were black and seemed to reflect the light around it. The bones on its chest were sticking out making it look starved. The arms were short with three fingers on each side and thick legs with three large toes.

The creature that killed Flea would be known as a Licatung. They are stealthy sons of bitches. A bane on humanity. They see through all stealth and counter it with their own. While moving, they don't make a sound until after they strike and come out only to devour their prey. People usually die from them, and they don't worry about being attacked. Demons require the three elements to kill them, Demonic Energy, Holy, and Arcane.

The Licatung wrapped its tongue around Flea's body. It turned him upside down and bit his head off first. When the head was bitten off, it spun him upward. The strap with his knives flew off and slammed against the wall. It unhinged its jaw like a snake and dropped Flea's legs into its mouth.

The knives dropped into the water. It would take forever to find the knives. I thought they would be lost forever. It was a shame. They were nice knives. I could have done so much killing with them. HAHA! Anyway, give me a second. I need to drink a little. Glug glug* Ahh. Okay, so where was I. Ah, yes.

Everyone in the group was freaking out. Even Bardock, the brave leader, who was an absolute fool was looking a little frantic. It was up to Aoi and Sparky to come up with a plan. The two of them knew each other's skills in magic from prior missions. They looked at each other and gave a quick nod to show they knew what to do.

Aoi stood in the middle of the island. He crouched down like he was sitting on something. White sparks were flying off his fingertips. He pressed his palms together to form a ball of light. The white ball expanded. His fingertips could no longer touch. The force was getting stronger and whiter with each passing second. He yelled, "Mega-Dome!"

Mega-Dome was a shield that was large enough to surround the whole island. It prevented anything from getting inside. The shield was large and strong but needed to be sustained by the Priest. Unfortunately, it was the only way to keep the Licatung and whatever was out there away.

Sparky raised his arms into the air. His eyes closed. The light disappeared from his right hand and the whole cave went dark except for the dim light provided by the Mega-dome. The sounds of splashing and footsteps across the walls were all we could hear. It was so loud that we couldn't hear one another while all the creatures were flooding into the room.

Sparky yelled, "Flamma Procella!"

A brightly lit fire burst at the ceiling of the cave. A ball of fire was in the center and what looked like fire eradiation patterns were coming off the ball. The fire surrounded the Mega-dome and burned everything in its path. We heard a hundred screeching creatures being burned on the outside of the shield.

The water around the group was steaming upward. The outside of the Mega-dome was filled up with steam hot enough to cook every crustacean in the world. The fire was wiping around. It made the steam move around our shield. The heat was intensifying and making everyone sweat. The shield around us was giving way a bit. Aoi was getting tired.

Sparky was done using his spell and dropped to his knees. He gave I everything he had. The sweat was dripping from his forehead. He clenched his chest because his heart was beating so hard. The pain in his chest was mainly from his lungs straining to keep up with his heart. His eyes were squinting hard. He looked up and all the fire left the room.

The steam was still rising so we couldn't figure out how much damage he did. The fire was red and yellow. At the time, I thought the only way to gain blue or purple fire was to combine fire with other mages. I was proven wrong years later. You would never believe me if I told you who taught me that.

The steam was making a hissing sound. It was trying to find a way out. The holes in the walls were small and it whistled while trying to escape through the cracks. I looked around to see if I could get a glimpse of any creatures. I could only pray that they weren't all Licatung. We needed to be able to see them to be able to escape.

The steam around the group was moving. A tiny red blur was leaping through the steam like it was their natural environment. The heat seemed to draw more of them in. It was as if they were born in some sort of volcano. We still had to wait for the steam to simmer before we could even think about it.

The red-haired girl took her hand and ushered me over. She said, "The only person here that can kill these things is the Priest. Holy magic can kill the Imps."

I stood up and exclaimed, "IMPS!"

Bardock said, "Imps in these parts are a myth to scare travelers. The only place Imps exist is I the Dark Kingdom."

Aoi responded, "I don't give a shit where these are supposed to be. All I know is they appear to be here."

Imps are Demonic creatures with a long slender tail. On average, they are a little over three feet tall. They have long pointed ears and have can very round heads. They have three fingers and a thumb. The fingers have an extra joint and the nails are five inches long. They don't appear to be strong but manage to be very fast and work together in groups. Of all the demons, they are the easiest to kill but that doesn't say much. You still must be a certain race or class to kill them.

Sparky stood once he got his bearings. He said, "Imps, it had to be Imps."

Bardock responded, "We don't know that yet."

Sparky said, "I know Barbarians are dumb, but you can't be that dumb. It's literally the only possibility that explains why my fire didn't affect them. They need Hellfire to be sent back to Hell."

I asked, "Can you make Hellfire?"

Sparky replied, "Fuck no! I can't even make blue flames. What the fuck makes you think I can do purple?"

Bardock said, "What you're telling me is that you are just as useless as the boy this mission."

Sparky responded, "Cram it up your ass. You're just as useless as me. The only person here that can fight these things is the damn Priest."

Bardock said, "Good to know."

Bardock didn't waste a second. He grabbed Sparky by the robe and picked him up off the ground. He raised him over his head and smiled. He was a survivalist. It didn't matter what he needed to do. He was going to be in charge to guarantee his survival. His muscles were flexing and gripping hard slowly tearing the robe.

Aoi yelled, "What the fuck are you doing?"

Bardock said in a gruff voice, "I'm giving the rest of us an escape route."

I responded, "Let him go."

Bardock said, "You with me or against me kid."

I backed off. I didn't want to take on a higher-level Barbarian at the time. Sparky was dangling there. He was absorbing all the heat within the room. His skin was turning red and glowing. A dark skeleton was shining through his body. The steam on the outside disappeared. We would finally see what was around the group.

There were hundreds of Imps crawling over top of each other. Each Imp made a small screeching sound followed by clicking. The Imps were scratching at the Mega-dome. I looked over at Aoi. I didn't think he could hold the barrier much longer. A small drop of blood was falling down his nose.

Sparky said, "See you in Hell."

Bardock smiled and threw him to the edge of the Mega-dome. His legs and torso were the only parts left inside the barrier. The head and hands were poking out of the barrier. The Imps saw his head. It began to drool through their three rows of teeth. I wanted to look away but couldn't. This was our only chance to escape.

Chapter 25

The Imps took their claws and stabbed their nails through the upper part of Sparky's throat. They rapidly pulled him backwards toward the entrance. Sparky screamed loudly. The heat from his body kept repairing him. The heat in his body only made things worse. It kept cauterizing all his wounds. The intense heat drew in the Imps.

Before the group knew it, Sparky was covered in Imps. They were gnawing away at his face and body. He kept screaming while blood was blocking his airway. His robes and skin were being ripped off. Blood was splattering the outside of the Mega-dome. There were bones crushed and launched at the barrier.

I asked, "What was the purpose of this?"

Bardock replied, "Just watch. It was better to do this now instead of later."

The Imps were done eating the flesh on Sparky. They saw the three of us as the next target. Their nails were grinding into the Mega-dome. Purple blood was covering the outside of the barrier. It dripped slowly and sizzled on the barrier. The Imps were mad and didn't care about their own safety. Their heads continuously bashed against the outside. The barrier was flickering a bit.

The screeching was getting louder from the Imps. They had a bloodlust that couldn't be quenched. The smell of our flesh was the only thing driving their insatiable appetite. They were leaping on top of the Mega-dome and sliding off. Their nails were digging into the barrier and creating a high-pitched screeching sound.

The red-haired woman didn't move. She was breathing and puffs of ashes were blowing to the north of the island. I couldn't figure out why she was calm. The rest of us were running around frantic and she couldn't be bothered. It was hard to figure out if she was a friend or foe.

The Imps around the Mega-dome were slowly lit up. A bright light was shining from their stomachs and showing their skeletal systems. Many of the Imps backed away from the Mega-dome and tried to react to the pain inside them. They were lying on the ground with their arms flailing.

Bardock said, "We run on three. Ready! One..."

The lights inside the Imps were going off inside. Their chests were exploding outward and causing harm to the other Imps. The explosions were attacking the side of the Mega-dome. Aoi had a harder time keeping the Mega-dome up. The barrier was the only thing keeping us alive. I wanted to help Aoi, but didn't know how.

The explosions going off caused a lot of heat, blood, and flesh from the Imps. In a matter of a few seconds, it flew everywhere. Even though the explosions hurt them, it didn't kill them. Their skin was coming back together. Which was probably why Bardock didn't wait until three to start running. He knew that his flesh would withstand some of the heat and went for the entrance.

I didn't want to miss my chance to escape either. I yelled to Aoi, "Come on!"

Aoi yelled, "Wait!"

Before anything else could be said. Bardock was already at the entrance to the room. His axe in his right hand was carried like a baton. He kept running at his fastest speed, which wasn't much since he was a Barbarian. They have little brains, lots of muscles and strength, but not very fast. Its why people refer to them as a tank class.

I ran toward the entrance and looked down. There in plain sight were Flea's knives. I reached down and scooped them up. I was excited because I thought they might have been lost forever. I ran faster to escape the Imps and got right up beside Bardock. This was a crazy plan, but it was the only one we had. If we got back, we could turn this into an H class mission.

Aoi wasn't very fast. He let down the Mega-dome and tried to run up to us. He realized that there was no way to escape. I looked back at him. He was yelling, "Smite, Smite, Smite, SSSMMMMIIITTTTTEEEE!" The room was shining with white light. He did everything that he could to kill as many as possible.

Aoi died a valiant death. The Imps snuck up behind him and scratched his back. He fell forward and got off one more Smite before a Licatung came up behind him and rammed its tongue through the back of his head. The tongue wrapped around his head and spun him around before slowly dropping his head into its mouth. It crunched down and bit the head off.

Aoi's body fell to the ground. The Imps ran at the rest of his body and devoured him. There was no way to save him. I just kept running alongside Bardock. We were halfway through the cave. All we could see was darkness. Without the Mega-dome bright white light or Sparky's flames lighting the cave, there was nothing but darkness inside. Our only hope was to reach the light at the end.

I did my best to stay with Bardock. At the time, I figured the only way to finish the mission was to work together. I was wrong. This was a lesson in trust. You work together as a team but never trust the team. Just pray that everyone will do the right thing and not try to kill you to claim a bigger bounty or save their own ass.

Bardock took his axe and swung it at me. The ax got stuck in the wall and continued to run. I ran up next to him and asked, "What the fuck was that?!"

Bardock replied, "I don't have to outrun the Imps. I just have to outrun you."

Bardock paused for a moment. He appeared to be out of breath. He dropped to his knees and reached out to me. His eyes were wide. His left hand was holding his chest like he was having a heart attack. He was groaning and hoping that I was foolish enough to help him to the end of the cave.

I looked him straight in the eyes and said, "I just have to be faster than you right."

I ran to the end of the cave. The Imps had plenty of flesh to eat. I turned around and watched. He screamed at the top of his lungs. The flesh kept growing back. There was no relief for him. He had to endure until he was fully consumed by the demons. I smiled watching him die. You could call it cruel, but it gave me a taste of surviving. I was the last remaining member of the team.

When I said, I didn't care about the bounty. That was true. I will tell you this. I was the last surviving member of the group, and I did it without hurting a single party member. That feeling of being on the edge of death was quite a rush. A feeling I try to replicate. Every time I get into battle. It's why over half the world sees me as a monster.

I ran through the forest to the village. The red lights were shining brightly. They filled the streets with light. Even though, the sun was out. I ran to the inn, but the doors were locked. I slammed on the door. I wanted to get to my room. I wanted to rest and see if I had anything to help me battle the Imps that were coming toward the town.

The Innkeeper said, "Who is there?"

I responded, "I'm one of the heroes brought to the town."

The Innkeeper asked, "Where are the others?"

I responded, "Their dead. I need to get my things. I need help to take them on. I don't think I can do it alone."

The Innkeeper opened the door and said, "You don't have the ability to kill them. The reason you are here is to feed them. They must be fed to save our town from destruction. Now get lost."

The mission had changed. Why did they want to feed the demons? Everyone in this fucking town had turned crazy. The door to the Inn was slammed in my face. All I had was this extra leather strap filled with knives from the Rogue. I took off my holster and placed them in my hands. I put the Rogue's six knives holster over my shoulders.

The Rogue's holster smelled burnt. It was probably from the flames Sparky made. I walked out into the middle of the street. The red lights were surrounding me. I could feel it glowing on my face. I'm not sure why but when I was getting mad. The lights were helping me feel stronger.

The sound of the Imps was coming this way. I could hear their steps and screeching through the forest. My blades were ready. I walked toward the entrance to the town. There was no escape this time. I just had to figure out a way to fight them or I would be doomed. I had to find my inner strength. I denied for so many years.

The Imps made their way to the entrance of the village. These people hated me and wanted me to turn into Imp food. That didn't mean the children didn't deserve to be saved. I was getting nervous. The knives were clanging against my body. I couldn't charge in yet. I needed to find the most opportune timing. Turning on my Overdrive came at a price.

The first Imp made it to the village. He saw me and ignored everything else around me. It leaped in my direction. The red lights changed to white and dropped the Imp to the ground. The flow of Holy energy coursed through my veins. I could hear my ancestors singing to me. My body glowed a white light in my chest. My Angorian roots were bringing a swell of power throughout my body.

I knew the only way out of this was to embrace who I really was. I dropped to my knees. I leaned forward and placed my hands on the ground. My knives were underneath my palms. I felt a burning in my back. I had spent years trying to hide who I really was, but this was the moment I had to use it. I had to let loose.

The back of my shirt was torn. A pair of white wings were coming out from underneath the strap holding up the holsters. The wings shot out fast and spread white feathers all over the ground. My hair was trying to turn golden but couldn't because of the black dyes in my hair. It didn't matter. I had to survive against the Imps.

The Imp that came in was burning on the ground. I could have just waited here until a bunch committed suicide to get to me but there would be no experience in that. There was also the red-haired woman that was waiting for me to save her. If she was my enemy, I would find out. If she was my friend, I would take her back to the village and reunite her with her family. Either way, I needed to go back.

I stood up with my white wings spread out. They were large enough to cover the area of the road. My knives were in my hand. I walked over to the injured Imp on the ground and stabbed a knife into its head. The blade was twisted to make sure I got it good. I pulled out the blade. The body was twitching.

The Imp did not heal. The truth is that I'm only half human. Just like you. I came from a race that is angelic in nature. As I mentioned before, I have Angorian ancestors. Every weapon that I touch can absorb enough Holy energy to slice and kill any demon in existence. This same gift was given to my children, and your father has given the gift to you.

Once I realized the Imps could die from my blade. I turned on my Overdrive. Overdrive is a skill that makes me faster than the speed of sound. Most Fury Warriors can attack much faster and stronger while in Overdrive. Since I have the speed of my ancestors, I accelerate faster than anyone else. Well, everyone else except for Marcus. I'm not sure how but he exceeds all possibilities.

My eyes turned bright red. My heart sounded like it was being beaten to death. Red sparks of lightning were surrounding my body. I let loose into the crowd of Imps. I ran straight in. The first Imp was almost to the light. I slid and rammed a knife under its chin. I pulled it right out. He was dead before he realized I was there.

I swung around and stabbed the next Imp and the next Imp. Purple blood was flying everywhere. I was covered in it. I wanted more. I needed more. I leaped upward and threw my knives into the head of my next Imp. My legs were in the air like I was doing a split while dropping the blades between my legs. When I came down, I sat on its head and pulled the blades out of the top.

I reached behind and decapitated a few. I felt invincible. I was so busy trying to make sure nobody knew that I wasn't human that I forgot to be who I truly was. My smile went from ear to ear. I still remember the taste of demon blood. It has a sour and sweet taste to it. Most humans would never get to taste.

I got to the entrance of the cave. The red-haired girl was probably sleeping in the ashes. I needed to find a way to her in the darkness of the cave. I ran forward, attacking everything in my path. I felt like a god. I couldn't be touched by anything. After a while, there was nothing but darkness. I did the only thing someone like me could do. I swung my knives around violently hoping to kill everything until I reached the island in the center of the room.

I ran for a while until I got to the room's island. When I touched it, giant rocks were shot at the ceiling. I felt the debris flying around me. I took a trip and flew to the center of the island in the room. My Overdrive shut off for a minute. I felt around for her body. When I reached around, If felt her soft, smooth waist. When my grip was good, I bolted for the entrance. The light from the entrance was so small that I could cover it with my pinky finger.

I turned on my Overdrive and rushed her to the front entrance. The floor was much more slippery from all the exploding bodies. When I sliced the demons up, they exploded, and body parts went everywhere. The slippery floors were terrifying because if I were to fall. It would have been like a high-speed crash, and she would have surely died.

The entrance was now covered in Imps. I ran up the wall and across everything. The village was the only safe place for her. When I got to the very edge of the entrance, I leaped over top and landed on the back of an Imp. I leaped from Imp to Imp in hopes of getting to the village where the lights would keep her alive.

The trees were getting in the way I had a difficult time maneuvering around them. My speed the first time passing through apparently knocked the tree almost bare of its leaves. I jumped up and bounced from tree to tree. My feet never touched the ground until I got right in front of the village.

I ran forward and sat her in front of the Inn. I figured the Innkeeper might know what to do with one of their own. I ran back to where the Imps were attacking. I still had a lot of Chi left. My speed kept increasing the longer I was in the battle. That is the best Blessing of all to someone like me. Increased speeds and endless stamina were perfect for a man that likes too... I'll leave that part alone. You're just a kid still.

I walked over to an Imp. When I tried to stab it, my wings decapitated the two Imps next to me. That was when I realized the wings could be used as Holy weapons. I ran out there and sliced up a lot of demons with my wings. I swung around and danced to a tune in my mind. It was fucking glorious. The smell, the taste, the feeling of battle, it was all too natural. It felt like a part of me that needed to get out. It was a part of me I would still have to hide from the world unfortunately.

I killed a total of twenty-seven Licatung and I lost count of how many Imps I killed. I still find it hard to believe that there were that many demons within the cave and nobody said a word. I mean there had to be at least one person that would have escaped from this place. I couldn't possibly be the first. That's when it occurred to me. The flesh and blood on the ceiling. The people of the town had been killing anybody that survived and tried to get help.

I rushed back to the village to make sure the red-haired woman was okay. I was covered in so much purple blood and demon flesh. I looked like a monster myself. I turned off my Overdrive and noticed her still sitting in front of the Inn. It was hard to see with all darkness in the cave, but she was the most beautiful woman I had ever seen.

I sat down next to her. My white, blood-covered wings were still out. She appeared to be frightened of me. She gulped loudly and stared into my eyes. Her eyes were green and seemed to be staring into my soul. She was the one that was afraid. I was the one that had my breath taken away by her beauty.

I smiled and said with a crack in my voice, "I'm Draco."

Chapter 26

I asked, "What is your name?"

The red-haired girl didn't speak. She stared at my blood covered wings. She appeared to be afraid of my white wings. I can't blame her. I did just use them to kill a lot of demons. Upon this realization, I put them back into my shoulders. They went in slowly not to scare the poor girl. The sound of slurping happened while entering back into my body.

I looked into her eyes and asked again, "What is your name?"

The red-haired girl's voice was shaky. She replied, "Miranda."

I said, "That's a pretty name."

Miranda asked, "Can I kiss you?"

I replied, "Why?"

Miranda said, "I just need to know the man who took me from the cave."

Miranda was slow about kissing me. She got up on her knees. Her hands reached out and massaged the back of my ears. I had never met a woman with such soft hands before. It was weird because she appeared to be a hero and was stuck in the cave for a while. The ashes on her head fell between us. She waited until the dust settled.

The kiss was magical. Her lips were soft and tasted like apples. Her tongue was soft and worked around the inside of my mouth. Every good emotion that I ever had come to the surface. I wanted to reach out and grab her but couldn't. My body felt so wonderful. I was too weak to hold her.

Miranda pulled back. A drop of drool dripped from her lower lip. She licked her lips and stared into my eyes. There was a smile on her face that seemed creepy at first but grew on me over time. I wanted to forget about the kiss but couldn't. I reached up and tapped my lips to see if this was real.

Miranda said, "I was right. You are the one for me."

I responded, "The one?"

Miranda asked, "Would you be willing to marry me?"

I replied, "We barely know each other."

Miranda said, "I got all I needed from today. You saved my life and your kiss. I just needed to make sure your kiss was wonderful."

There was a saying that only fools rush in when it came to marriage. When marriages were arranged, it was because the parents found use in it. Even at that age, I knew something wasn't right with rushing in. The strange thing is. I wouldn't change a damn thing. She was everything that I would want in a wife.

I said, "Just don't regret it. I accept your proposal."

I stood up and dusted myself off. She was getting ashes all over me. I walked out to the center of the street. My hands were raised upward. I clapped while laughing in the middle of the village. Everyone in the town needed to give me their attention. Since I got back, they had ignored me. The dead Imp bodies could be seen from their homes.

The old man from earlier opened the door to the Inn and walked out. His hands were behind his back. The back looked straighter than before. The whole thing was an act. He wanted to appear weak and feeble to all travelers coming through. The belt on his waist was new. It was the same type of belt that Flea used.

I said, "I have completed the task. I just need to make sure that you confirm I completed to gain my bounty back home."

The old man's left eye twitched. He responded, "Give me the girl."

I said, "She has chosen to give her life to me. I will not."

The old man responded, "Give me the girl now. You don't know what you're doing. If you do not give me the girl, you will not get your bounty."

I asked, "What is she to you?"

The old man replied, "She is an important member of this community. Give her to me or I will be forced to take action."

I asked, "Do you know who I am?"

The old man replied, "You are a worthless demi-human. A being that knows nothing about the world. She is far too valuable for the likes of you."

I said, "Well, I will tell you who I am. I am the Legionnaire's son. A royal soldier being groomed to be the next Legionnaire for the great Alexander Varguss, the ruler of these lands and the champion to all mankind. In other words, you tried to kill a member of royalty. The penalty for trying to kill a royal is death. How do you plead?"

The old man looked at Miranda. He had an angry look on his face. He said, "You two deserve one another. May you and your children be Hellbound."

I didn't like that. I went into Overdrive and stabbed the old man in the stomach. I lifted upward and dropped his chin over my shoulder. The knife was sharp and allowed me to cut upward into his rib cage. I pulled out the knife want ran back to my spot. The blood from the pull was too slow and didn't touch my body.

When I pulled the knife from the old man, his body got launched across the street. His intestines flew out of his chest and wrapped around his body up to his neck. He lay there staring up at the sky. His eyes wide open but nobody was home. I killed the leader of the town. The people were hiding.

The biggest problem I had was the people of the town. They knew who I was, and the leader called me out as a demi-human. If even one person in this town came forward with the accusations. My life would have been over. I couldn't trust anyone. The only person I could trust with my secret was Miranda in the town. That was because she chose to be my bride. It would have come out eventually.

I looked up at the villagers' homes. They were peeking through the windows hoping that I wouldn't notice. I walked over to Miranda and held out my hand to pick her up. She grabbed my hand and flew up into my arms. I caught her. Her face went into my chest. She looked up at me so adorably.

Miranda said, "Go get em' tiger."

I went over to the red lanterns and jumped up. I pulled the lantern down and yelled up to the people, "I will give you all to the count of ten before I burn this town to the ground. I suggest you vacate the premises."

The people didn't waste any time. They ran out of the buildings to escape being burned alive. The sound of steps pounding echoed through the streets. I was holding onto the lantern tightly. I kept asking myself. What would my father do in this situation? The answer was simple. He would have killed them all anyway.

I yelled, "One, two, ten."

I threw the lantern at a house across the street from the Inn. The flames were slow but spread, giving enough time for the people to get out. A man up top stared at me from his burning home. He refused to leave. He put up both his middle fingers and let the flames come over him. He wasn't so strong when the flames engulfed him. The fire made him scream loudly. The sound of the air popping in his lungs could be heard outside.

The sun was going down and the sky was getting darker. The flames were looking brighter and more beautiful. The mothers of the town were covering their children in hopes of saving their lives. The men of the town hid behind the women and children in hopes that they would be spared.

Miranda asked, "Are we burning it all down or just that one."

I replied, "The whole town will be burned to ashes. Just be..."

I didn't have enough time to tell her to be patient. Miranda was a Fire Mage. A gifted Fire Mage that could easily make blue flames. She shot off Fireballs at every building in the village. The flames were wild, and the forest was catching fire. She even attacked the Inn I was staying in.

As the town was burning, and it dawned on me. Shit, my stuff was in there. The backpack filled with all the survival stuff was in the Inn and burning up. I had to pretend that nothing was bothering me but not knowing where to sleep or eat that night took a toll on my psyche. I just looked away.

Miranda was dancing around and laughing. The sight of all the flames burning everything made her happier than any human being could achieve. It turned out she was crazy. Her red hair was lighting up with each cast around the town. Everyone was burning hot from the heat except her. She just kept yelling, "It's beautiful. It's beautiful."

The flames were covering the sky. I wondered if the kingdom could see the flames. The yellows and blues. It really was quite beautiful. The shadows were flashing across the ground. With the fires coming from so many directions. The shadows kept moving around and looking lighter. The best part was watching Miranda dance around trying to stomp on her shadow.

The crackling of the flames made it hard to hear most things. I did hear people screaming in pain in their homes. They tried to hide and took the chances that I was bluffing about setting their homes on fire. I wasn't planning on doing it to the extent of Miranda, but did plan to lure them out this way.

I walked toward the crowd of people. They kept huddling up to protect each other. At least, that was the appearance. The truth was that they didn't care about each other at all. I could tell the difference. My empathy was getting lower the more time I spent on missions. When you think with your mind instead of your heart, the frauds are easier to spot.

I walked toward the crowd and asked, "What do you have to say for yourselves? There were eleven groups of five people. You lured them into an ambush and killed them. Why did you have these heroes murdered?!"

A woman in the front replied, "We had no choice. It was the words of Beelzebub. If we didn't do as he said, the whole village would have died."

I said, "That is unfortunate because your about to die anyway."

I went into over Overdrive and ran at the woman. The knife sliced through her neck. The force was strong enough to launch her head toward the entrance and almost rolled all the way out of the village. Her blood flew everywhere but didn't hit me because I was faster than the blood splatter.

The men in the back were cowards. They were the next. I took the knife and skinned the top of their heads. There is nothing more traumatizing than a good old fashion scalping. I ripped off the hair and threw it into the fire. The force from scalping them was fast and strong. It whipped their heads back and broke their necks.

When I left Overdrive, all the men were laying on the ground suffocating to death. They were all foaming at the mouth. The foam would probably have been white, but it had a blue and yellow tint to it from the flames flashing against it. The sound of gargling was loud enough to drown out some of the crackling from the fire.

I looked at all the mothers in the crowd. I said, "Let your children go. Let them find their own safety. None of your mothers will survive this day."

The mothers were staring at me and refusing to leave their kids. They held on as if it would change anything. They figured that I wouldn't kill them if a child was in their arms. Unfortunately for them, they were sadly mistaken. I turned on my Overdrive and rushed through the crowd. I stabbed each mother in the head and ripped backward. The blade pulled blood and brain matter from their heads.

The blood squirted all over the children. The mothers were tossed around by the force. Some of the children ended up with broken bones because their mothers landed on them. I could hear the blood spurts and the crackling of bones from the attack. I did my best to warn them. It wasn't my fault that the people didn't listen.

I went over to Miranda and said, "Let's go home."

Miranda responded, "You're kidding right. There are still people alive."

I said, "They are children."

Miranda responded, "That is even more reason to kill them. There is no safe place for them to be. The area is filled with wild animals. Even if they did survive in the area, slavers might pick them up and cause more damage than we ever could. With them witnessing what we did to their parents. Do you think they will be mentally okay?"

I said, "That might be true, but they are still children. We have to set limits on what we do."

Miranda responded, "They know you're a demi-human. What if they tell the people who pick them up for a scrap of food. You don't want any loose ends. Do you?"

I looked over at the children. They were sobbing. It wasn't their fault that their parents were awful. Unfortunately, I realized the hard truth. I couldn't let them live. They could grow old and try to kill me later. They knew who I was. This night would be seared into their brains for the rest of their lives and would probably hold a grudge to destroy me at all costs.

I slowly walked toward the children. They were huddled up into a giant ball. The children knew there was no chance of escaping. I was too fast. I had tears running down my face. My bottom lip was quivering. I didn't want to do it, but it had to be done. I went into Overdrive and decapitated all the children in less than a second. I prayed that none of them felt a thing during their last moments.

I was stuck watching all the children's heads roll around the streets. My heart was sinking. It made me feel like a monster. This had to be the reason most people fear demi-humans. My arms were shaking, and my teeth were chattering. I could hardly breathe from all the pressure on my chest.

Miranda came up to me from behind. She wrapped her arms around my waist and said, "You did what you had to do. I support you one hundred percent."

I responded, "I killed children."

Miranda spun me around. I looked into her eyes. They sparkled brightly from the fire surrounding us. She said, "One hundred percent."

Miranda came in and kissed me again. In my harshest of moments, it was wonderful to know that someone had my back. That was the moment that I knew I loved her. The best way to know if it's love. If that special person is in your life, she will be by your side when the world is burning around you. We call those people soul mates.

Chapter 27

The flames glowed across Miranda's skin. She looked deeply into my eyes. I felt like prey. A part of me thought she might have been evil The other part of me felt like this woman will give me the rush of my life. I grabbed her from behind the ears and pulled her in for a kiss. She fought me at first but gave in shortly after.

I wanted to taste the apples on Miranda's lips. I wanted to feel the chaos that caused my heart to beat hard with each passing second. We refused to let each other go. The heat from the flames only made the passion more intense. Her lips were warm and when she finally pulled away. I had a chill run down my spine.

Miranda bit her bottom lip and asked, "What are we doing about the bodies?"

I replied, "I thought we would let them lie there. The streets are covered in their blood."

Miranda said, "The flames are high. People know that you were here. Even as a royal, it could become problematic. Wiping out an entire town, even if justified, would scare the neighboring towns."

I asked, "What do you suggest?"

Miranda replied, "The bodies should be thrown into the burning buildings. Nobody will know who belongs where."

Miranda had a point. There might be some questions about how the town burned down. I was the only person alive on record. Everything that happened could easily be blamed on bandits. It was gross to do. I grabbed all the body parts and tossed them into the burning buildings.

The village had so many bodies. The burning flesh turned my stomach. It didn't seem to bother Miranda. She was my pyromaniac. My psychotic red head that loved the heat. She would use her magic to stoke the flames and make sure nothing was recognizable. The flames grew higher and flickered across her devilish grin.

Miranda watched the flames all night. Nobody came to the village's aid. The trees around the village burned down but didn't spread too far. The only safe place around was the center of the village. We appeared to be trapped like wild animals, but she was right where she wanted to be.

After many hours, the fires dimmed and all that was left over was smoke. The wood on the buildings was broken down and brittle. The second floor of many of the buildings still existed. They weren't safe to walk on. The sound of wood crackling could still be heard. Some of the wood was making noises like it was ready to collapse.

Miranda said, "I'm tired. I need a place to sleep."

Miranda's eyes were red from staring at the flames all night. More than anything, I think her eyes were dry. There were dark circles around her eyes. There were red veins coursing through the white of her eyes.

I didn't know what to tell Miranda. We were in the middle of nowhere. There was no place close to go. The closest town was a two-hour walk. The only place I could guarantee was in the city and that was at least a twelve-hour walk.

I said, "My home is far away, and you burned up my camping gear."

Miranda responded, "Oops, well, how far away are we talking."

I said, "A twelve-hour walk."

Miranda responded, "How long is that flying?"

I asked, "What do you mean by flying?"

Miranda replied, "I fly. We can fly there. I can probably fly an hour or two."

I said, "I guess a while. I'm not sure how much of a speed difference that would be."

Back then, I had no idea that Fire Mages could fly. I knew Ground and Water Mages could glide thanks to their elements. Also, I never met an Air or Lightning Mage. Those were rare and still are rare. The Fire Mages in the city that I met never really fought and did a lot of cooking. They were always quiet and listened more than they spoke. Everything I needed to know about Fire Mages. I learned from my wife.

Miranda walked up behind me and placed her left cheek on my back. She reached around and felt up my pecks. She slowly pulled her arms back. I think she was aroused from feeling up my muscles. I don't know why, but she kept sniffing me. I smelled of smoke from being around the fire all night. She seemed to be addicted to the smell of my sweat and the smoke.

Miranda's arms reached under my armpits and lifted me off the ground. I wasn't used to being off the ground and freaked out. She flew above all the treetops. The height caused me to stiffen up. The air was blowing in my face and causing me to freeze. I gulped and couldn't bring myself to close my eyes.

Miranda asked, "Which direction are we going?"

I was petrified and couldn't seem to get the words out. I raised my right arm and said, "ai wal."

Miranda ignored my incoherent words and moved in the direction I pointed in. Fire was coming out the bottom of her feet and shot up in that direction. The cheeks on my face rippled and I couldn't close my eyes from the pressure. My eyes dried out and got sore. The wind blew into my mouth drying it out.

The city was within sight after only a few minutes. I still have no idea how fast she could fly. I just knew that the journey was short.

When we got close, she flew down to the road in front of the city. At least she had enough common sense not to fly over the wall. That would have ended badly with all the Archers and Hunters trying to shoot her down.

Miranda's landings weren't the most desirable. She got me six feet above the ground and dropped me. It wouldn't have been so bad if she wasn't going fast when dropping me off. It was like getting tossed from a high-speed running carriage. I had to duck and roll to take less damage. It still hurt with my flesh scrapping across the stones on the road below.

The dirt flew up and created a dust cloud. Miranda's speed caused most of it. She slowly sat herself down on the ground. When coming down, she stumbled a few times and waved her arms around. She dropped her feet down and slid a bit. When she came to a complete stop, she wiped around and looked at me.

Miranda was breathing heavily and asked, "How was that?"

I smiled and replied, "It was definitely much faster than walking."

Miranda smiled at me and grabbed my right arm. She pulled me in closely. She leaned in and placed the left side of her head on me. All we had to do was walk to the city gates. With us being at the city already, there was no way people would suspect that we killed the village. I just needed to make my way to the guild hall.

Miranda and I walked to the gate, The guards saw her on my arm and asked, "Who is the lovely lady?"

I replied, "She is my fiancée."

The guard said, "I had no idea. Everyone thought you were a lifelong bachelor. Congratulations."

The guard let us through the gate. The first stop was the guildhall to get the bounty. With the village dead, if the mission was complete, I would be paid. My body was shaking. I was afraid of getting caught. I opened the door to the guild hall and let Miranda come in first.

I came in after looking around. It was morning for most of the members. All the people inside were trying to get breakfast and work off their hangover.

I said, "Morning Henry."

Henry responded, "Morning Draco. How did the mission go?"

I said, "It's complete."

Henry responded, "That's good. Where are the others?"

I said, "They didn't make it. The force was stronger than we realized."

Henry responded, "Well, at least you're okay. I wasn't sure the way the other four were talking about you. I don't think your dad would forgive me if you died."

I asked, "Why aren't you concerned about the others?"

Henry replied, "We are the highest paid guild in the nation. The reason is that we take on the most dangerous missions. People dying is part of the job. Otherwise, anyone would do them."

I grabbed Miranda and kissed her on the top of her head. She looked at me with those beautiful eyes of hers and smiled. I didn't understand what was happening and the reason why. I just knew that I was in love. It wasn't just love. It was an infatuation. I never wanted to leave her side.

I asked, "Can I have the bounty? I want to get use some of it."

Henry replied, "I can give you access to your account. We need to confirm the threat was eliminated."

I said, "That will have to do."

Henry responded, "Let me give you a wedding gift. I have something. I created. The problem is that people aren't strong enough to handle it."

Henry gave me a small bag. It seemed common and made of brown leather. There was a brown leather string wrapped around the outside. I opened the pouch and inside was a black swirling portal. I, to this day, have no idea where the portal leads. All I know is that I seem to have an endless supply of gold. Over the years, nobody has ever questioned it because I'm a royal. It's really funny.

Miranda and I went to church. The Priest was hesitant to marry us. He seemed to fear Miranda. His hands were shaking. His voice cracked while talking to us. He could barely breathe, and a few tears were coming down his face. He looked over toward a door to his left. A few Priests were standing there. They went and got the High Priest.

The High Priest showed up and looked at the two of us. He said, "The two of you are here to be married. I have to ask. Why the rush?"

I responded, "No time like the present. I just know she is the one for me."

The High Priest said, "This will come at a price. The price for a quick service and a price to keep this marriage to myself."

I responded, "I don't know what that means but okay. How much?"

The High Pries said, "Twenty gold."

The High Priest was always a man that had no morals. His only god was money itself. The only reason Priests were in the church was because the class signified Holiness and a connection to God. This was not the case. These people might have the class but nothing about them is Holy.

Miranda and I got married right there. It wasn't a special event like most weddings. It was small and just an intimate thing between us. Our witnesses were several Priests that watched over the ceremony. Sometimes, that's all you need. It was enough for me anyway. I had no suit and was scuffed up. She was covered in ashes. It was the perfect way for two flawed people to get married.

After the ceremony, I told my father that I was a married man. There was rage in his voice. He seemed to have something against her. I won't tell you all that was said. I will just say this. I will never degrade you for marrying the woman you love. Having my father rip me apart for getting married, was one of the worst days of my life. I always looked up to him until that day. He just didn't understand. The truth is that we just didn't understand each other.

Shortly after my father flipped out on me. Marcus, your grandfather, came and talked to my father for a bit. They walked outside the house and spoke for a long period of time. My father's hair kept getting blonder and his fist was clenched. Above all, he believed in something called the Sacred Timeline. It's apparently the timeline where Lucifer loses at the end, but certain events must happen to get there.

My father came inside after cooling down. He looked at the two of us and said, "It appears this was destined to happen. I had no idea what to say. I would like to do something for the two of you. I would like to help you two build a house in town. There is no reason the two of you need to stay here."

I responded, "I would love this offer. I just want a change. I don't want Miranda to live in a place that doesn't accept her. Everyone seems to be showing hostility towards her. I think we should build a house on land right outside the city. I always planned to build a house out there. The land right next to James. It would also be better for our future kids."

My father said, "That is fine. It's your land anyway."

Within a few days, a group of builders erected our house. I took three weeks to build because he paid top dollar for the best builders. They all worked day and night to make us a home. I felt indebted to them. Until the house was done, Miranda and I shared a bed that was designed for only one person.

There was one good thing about having a smaller bed. There was less room to sleep and when you can't sleep. You can't help but come up with fun activities all night. I mean the sex was amazing. The best that I could have ever asked for. The first night we were unsure of one another but after that. She was feral.

Miranda had claws. Every night she dug her nails into my back and scratched me good. She would bite into my shoulders and draw blood. The raw intensity at certain points made me feel like my life was in peril. I had to palm a blade in my left hand and hold my body up with my right. There were times when I would use Overdrive to give myself some strength. She would always take it and ask for more.

I probably shouldn't have told you that part. I was just remembering her. All nine of my kids with her would have been something special. Don't get me wrong. I love my daughters. I just know with her. The girls would have been so much more. It's probably why I'm the most protective of Matilda. Even if she spent most of her childhood with other people raising her.

The house was built, and ten months later Matilda was born. She was my beautiful little angel. When she was born, there was a connection between Miranda and I that seemed unbreakable. I can't believe I let that happen to her. It was all my fault. It was all my fucking fault. My angel isn't here today. I should have done the right thing.

Miranda died saving Isabella's mom a few years later. My hatred of men is too strong. The hatred of anything that people don't understand will slowly destroy the world. The worst part is Matilda watched her mother die. She couldn't have been more than two years old and lost her mother.

In case you're wondering, I'm overly protective of my daughters. For me to say you can marry a daughter is something. I have faith in you boy. I also understand what you are. Even if you don't know what you are yet. The only thing that I ask will be that you treat my daughter the way she needs to be treated.

Chapter 28

I sat in the bath across from Draco trying to think about the story he just told. He kept puffing on his Jun Jun cigar and taking swigs of scotch out of the glass. He kept filling the glass during the story. I had no idea if the story came from a drunken mindset or a high mindset. I just knew that at nine years of age. I didn't trust it.

I said, "Let me get this straight. You met your wife in a dark cave filled with demons. You committed mass genocide to a group of people that's only flaw was hiring people for missions. You sprout wings like a bird. You are faster than the speed of sound. Against what everyone told you about your wife, you still married her. Am I getting this all, correct?"

Draco responded, "Yeah."

I asked, "How much Jun Jun have you smoked?"

Draco replied, "More than I think and less than you think."

I said, "I don't believe you."

Draco responded, "I wouldn't believe me either. In your life, stranger things and more deadlier people will be in it. Your father didn't show you the world for nine years. After today, you're about to be in for a culture shock."

The waterfall was flowing. I walked over and gave myself one last rinse. I closed my eyes and held my breath for a second before I got out. I walked over to the steps leading to the outside of the bath. Once I got out, a cold chill came across my body. I looked up and realized that we were outside. I thought this place was imaginary. A place created by a powerful portal master. Everything around Draco and I was real. I still have no idea where this bath was.

I walked over to the rack next to the exit. It was covered in towels. I put one around my waist and was walking into the changing room, when I heard a sigh behind me. The water was moving around. I looked back and realized Draco was getting out of the bath. He seemed a little unsteady from all the alcohol he drank.

Draco said, "Wait up. I want to see how the uniform turned out. I gave Wong specific instructions."

Draco got out of the water. He stumbled a bit from left to right. His eyes were blinking fast. He looked over to me and stood up straight fast. His back cracked loudly. It sounded like every vertebra in his body snapped. He walked over to the door and put his left arm around me. He didn't think to put on a towel. I was small and didn't like the view.

I said, "There is a towel rack over there."

Draco responded, "I'm more a drip-dry kind of guy. Let's see if the clothes are here."

Draco and I walked into the changing room. On the closest bench was a set of new clothes. I looked back at Draco. I didn't understand his choice of clothes. It was a light blue suit. I grabbed the pants and started to put them on. Draco looked at me and shook his head as if I did something wrong.

Draco asked, "Boy, are you forgetting something?"

I replied, "Not that I'm aware of."

Draco said, "You have to put your underwear on first."

I stared at Draco. I didn't remember the last world and never wore underwear a day in my life. The closest would be when I was a baby and cloth diapers were used on me. I couldn't figure out what he was talking about. I continued to put the pants on when Draco grabbed my hand. I wasn't sure what his problem was.

Draco handed me my first pair of underwear. He said, "You're not going to the enlightenment ceremony while freeballing. You're such a strange child."

I put the rest of the clothes on and looked in the mirror. There was a white shirt with frills around the neck and cufflinks. I looked ridiculous. It was puffed out and made me look fat. I wanted to rip it off and put my old clothes on. I didn't want to be rude, and the clothes did look expensive.

Draco said, "You look incredible."

I smiled and pretended to like it. I felt like a giant ball of cotton candy. There was a pair of white socks and black shoes to go with the outfit. I put them on. The shoes were bigger than my feet. When I walked forward, the front of the shoes clopped down. I didn't know how to describe it back then, but I do now. I felt like I was wearing clown shoes.

Draco wrapped his left arm across my shoulder and said, "Let's see if Isabella is ready."

Draco's steps were longer. I was pushed out of the changing room. I stumbled a bit and almost hit the bamboo wall separating the changing room from the waiting room. He gave me one last push to the waiting room. I got hit in the face with a weird smell. It smelled good but wasn't something that a farm boy was used to.

I looked over toward the girls' bath. There was a bench next to it where Isabella was sitting. She had a nasty look on her face. She looked up at me and stood up. She pointed at me and started to laugh. It was infectious. Jasmine was standing next to her and tried to control her laughter. We both looked ridiculous. It was the way of the royals.

Isabella was clean for once. I could see the freckles on her nose. Her skin looked smooth as silk. Her hair was pulled back into a pony tail. I could see her ears. They were kind of cute with little points on them. She had eyes green as grass and sparkled like something powerful was behind them.

Draco did the unthinkable to her. He bought a giant pink dress with layers underneath. The dress almost touched the ground. I thought I looked like cotton candy. She was definition of cotton candy. The bottom of the pink dress had ruffles and was six times the size of her legs. No human being should be able to move around in it.

The top of the dress forced her to suck in her stomach. The puffiness of the top part made her chest puff out more. For a second, I thought she might have some boobs. I was clearly wrong. It was nothing more than an illusion. Kind of like when a girl stuffs her bra to deceive boys. It doesn't work because when we kind out. All the boys are disappointed.

Isabella kept pulling the strap on the dress up. It fell to the side. The clothes weren't perfect, but we wore them. I'm not sure the reason why. She gave in to her father on this. She seemed way too stubborn to just accept what her father wanted from her. The whole time we were together that day. She only thought of herself. What a difference a day makes!

Isabella said in a snarky voice, "What the fuck are you looking at loser?"

Isabella's eyes were looking harshly. It felt like a knife had just entered my chest. I couldn't get any words out. I didn't understand what was happening. My chest was hurting and all I wanted to do was give her a proper comeback. While trying to speak, my voice cracked and nothing, but noise came out.

Draco responded, "I'm sorry my little princess. You just look so damn beautiful in that dress. You for once look like a proper lady."

Isabella yelled, "Go to Hell!"

Draco said, "But you do look beautiful, I just wish that I had a way to capture this moment forever."

Isabella asked, "When can I take this thing off?"

Draco replied, "After the ceremony, if we are lucky, the dress won't fit you anymore."

I asked, "What do you mean she won't fit in the dress anymore?"

Draco replied, "You too. If you get blessed, the muscles in the body tend to expand. Barbarians are over eight feet tall because of the amount of Chi in their bodies. We all grow larger. As for you, you might grow to be almost five feet tall if you get Blessed."

The idea of being almost five feet tall sounded incredible. I always felt weak and small. All the cubs were getting bigger than me after a few months. Even Isabella, a freaking girl, was far taller than me. I finally found some inspiration to do this stupid ceremony. If I could grow just one foot, I would be happier than any other child in the world.

Isabella asked, "Now what?"

Darco replied, "Now we go to the ceremony. James should be done making sales by now. He might be saving me a seat in the church as we speak."

Isabella asked, "Do we go back the way we came?"

I replied, "Probably not."

Isabella said, "What do you know! I was asking my father anyway."

Draco responded, "The boy is right."

Isabella said, "Well, tell me where we are going."

I pointed behind Isabella. She didn't see the giant sign that said "Exit" above a bamboo door. There is a joke about this later when you see what kind of person she becomes. She had so many blonde moments and yet always allowed her fiery temper to get the better of her. It was something that took time for the group to deal with.

Draco walked over to the door. He opened it. There was a rainbow portal like the one we went through to get there. The wind was trying to pull us in. My eyes were closing from the pressure. I put my right hand up to cover my face. My feet were scraping against the ground trying to hold on.

Isabella didn't fight it. She flicked off Draco and me. She dove into the portal. Her hair was raised over her head and the dress flew up past her face. I finally saw the purpose of underwear. She was trying to swat the dress down but wasn't successful. I finally saw her skinny pale legs and the ruby colored shoes. The shoes sparkled and shined from the light reflecting off them.

I said, "You can go."

Draco smiled at me and responded, "Ladies first."

That jackass pushed me into the portal I swirled around in circles and felt sick to my stomach. I wasn't laughing when the white shirt under the blue suit's frilly parts were flying up and tickling my face. My eyes slowly worked into the back of my head until finally. I fell onto a bunch of pillows below me.

I was getting up. I should have moved faster because Draco cannonballed through the portal again. This ass was flying through the portal at incredible speeds. I didn't have time to move. The last thing I saw was the crease in his pants flying onto my face. When it hit me, the only thing I could think was "Mother of Fuck, he is heavy."

Draco kept moving back and forth. He was having a difficult time getting up. One thing I figured out from that experience. If you ever want to get something from someone, never go for the head. It makes their head fuzzy and lose control of all their other faculties. Or at least, don't suffocate them to near death.

Draco finally got up. He turned around and put his hand out to get me up. My hair was a mess. I couldn't move. I was traumatized from having his ass in my face. This was something I believed would haunt me for the rest of my life. Realizing I wasn't grabbing his arm, he grabbed mine and got me on my feet without my help.

My clothes were getting brushed off by Draco. I was getting patted down hard. The dust was coming off me, but bruises might have been forming. I know he at least left behind handprints on my legs, back, chest, and butt. He got behind me holding my shoulders still. I stood there in shock.

Draco said, "Your good. Sorry bud. It's time to leave for the ceremony."

Isabella was standing there with her arms crossed and tapping her...right foot, I think. I could just hear the shoe tapping against the floor. The dress swayed every time she lifted her leg. I'm not sure what happened when she took a bath, but for some reason. She got meaner.

Isabella said, "Let's go. The sooner we get this over with. The sooner I can get this damn thing off."

Isabella stormed off down the hall. It appeared to be the same hall as before. The portal locations just changed in the bath. There appeared to be a powerful force in control of everything happening inside the house. The only explanation would be Wong had total control of the house and could kill anything within it. I wouldn't want to piss him off. He could easily entomb any person that crossed him.

I walked through the hall and went up the steps. I looked to the right and there was Wong waiting for us. He had a smile on his face. His eyes looked almost closed from smiling so hard. He laughed a little. The pitch in his laugh went from high to low gradually. It creeped me out. I think it creeped out Isabella too. I noticed her face was scrunched up.

Draco walked over to Wong and held out his fist. He was waiting for Wong to pound it. When Wong hit the fist with his little hands, Draco said, "We'll see you later, my brother from another mother."

Wong laughed at a high pitch and kept it high this time, he responded in a very deep voice, "Good luck children. I believe in you. Come see me when the time comes. I will give you gifts."

Wong's eyes spun in their own directions. I didn't know if he could see nothing or everything. His sharp teeth were showing while he smiled more. The layers of teeth that had were freaking me out. I thought that if he wanted to. He could easily bite my head off. I was weak and short. I wouldn't stand a chance.

Draco opened the door and walked into the street. He closed his eyes and breathed in the air. He exhaled hard and looked back at us. I don't know why anyone would want to breathe in the air outside after being in the bath. It smelled like shit from the backed up sewer system no matter where we were in town.

Draco said, "Come children. We need to get to the church. The sun is coming down and might be in the back of the line at this rate. If we're lucky, maybe I can pay your way to the front. I doubt it though. Priests can be superstitious about the ceremony."

I walked outside and looked at the sky. There was darkness forming on the horizon. Within the darkness, there were two moons. One large White Moon and another moon that was red. The Red Moon reminded me of blood. I didn't understand what they were important until later. The moons were what determined the ceremony. At least, in this city it mattered.

Chapter 29

Reginald was waiting outside the door still. He was taking a brush to the horse's mane. When he realized that we were done inside Wong's, he set the brush up on his seat. He walked over to the door to the carriage and twisted the handle to open it. He kept the door open and waited for us to jump inside.

Reginald didn't appear to be a being with a lot to say. His eyes were halfway always halfway closed and watched me closely. I didn't get the feeling he liked me very much. He saw me walk over to the carriage. I couldn't get up to the door because of my height. He didn't try to help. Instead, he scoffed at me for not being able to get up by myself. It was a slight personality shift when my father wasn't around.

Draco came behind me and lifted me up the steps. The suit was thick on me. I grabbed the inside of the doorway to pull myself in. The shoes weren't giving me a good grip on the steps. I pulled myself forward. I couldn't believe how heavy the suit was on my body. No wonder my father stayed away from the royals. This life was a pain.

Isabella was the next to get into the carriage. She jumped up the steps. The red shoes couldn't land well. She almost fell backwards and onto the stone ground. Draco got behind her and pushed her into the carriage. Her dress was way worse for getting inside. The outside of her dress was getting caught on the door.

Draco took his left hand and pushed on parts of the dress. His right hand remained on her back to keep her upright. Isabella was holding onto the inside of the carriage to prevent herself from falling to the ground. The dress was way too much. I'm not sure why Draco thought that this would be a good idea.

Isabella went inside and sat down across from me. She scowled at her father. He was trying to get inside. He raised his right leg and got in all on his own. The light above us turned on when he sat down. He stared at me while waiting for the door to close. I couldn't figure out what he wanted and began to shake.

Reginald closed the door to the carriage. He pulled the handle locking the door. The handle made a high-pitched squeaking sound that caused me to squint. My hands dug into the seat. I couldn't stop myself from violently shaking. My chest was hurting from the anxiety. I wasn't used to high stress situations.

The lantern was flickering across Draco's face. He wasn't moving a muscle. He kept staring at me. The carriage started to move causing the lantern to sway from forward to back. When the carriage moved, he tapped his foot on the ground. It had a beat to it like he was thinking of a song.

Draco said, "When we get there, there will be three actions that are required. The first will be that you buy a parchment. It's not a necessity but the church is keen on it. As much as I hate the church, if we don't buy one, they will hold it against us for all future transactions. At least, the first Blessing requires it."

I asked, "What does the parchments do?"

Draco replied, "It's a basic printing of your stats, your skills, and at times your class. It is all determined by what the Angels write. The parchments themselves are useless but because of the podium they are on. They seem to recognize everything else. A Creationist made the podium many years ago."

I said, "Okay, I won't argue. I mean the Priests are giving them away."

Draco responded, "They are five silver pieces."

I said, "You said it's just regular parchment paper. That is robbery."

Draco responded, "It raises money for the church and most people don't realize that its regular paper."

I said, "I don't have any money."

Draco responded, "I will provide you with one. That is nothing to me."

I asked, "If that is the case, why not just ask for donations? I'm sure people like you would likely give more money than ripping off the poor."

Draco replied, "Because knowledge is power, they pick up the parchments and read them off. They see how strong someone is and can even see if they are valuable to the church. It makes things easier to spot demons because only certain classes are demonic."

I wanted to ask what classes would be demonic. The problem was that I knew of a class. The Hell Spawn was considered a demonic class. It was my grandfather's class and the bane of my father's existence. He moved so fast that some revered him to be god-like. Others, like my father, felt he was nothing more than a demon that would one day destroy the world.

I asked, "What are the other two?"

Draco replied, "Pay attention to what the other children do at the podium. I know you have never seen the ceremony before. The children coming to this have practiced the rituals a hundred times. If you don't do it right, the church might scold you in front of everyone. This becomes even worse when the people don't get their Blessings."

I asked, "Can you show me what I need to do?"

Draco replied, "No, just watch the others. You'll get this done."

I asked, "Okay, what about the third thing?"

Draco replied, "Do not be afraid of death. If you are chosen, you will enter a world that has never been seen before. There might be incredible amounts of pain. Some suffer and some are Blessed with a Holy glow. If you receive pain, you might be powerful. If you are suffering a fate worse than death, that means you are destined to be more in this world. Your soul will feel like it is being ripped to shreds from the pure force of the Angel.

I don't know what will happen to you. I just want to prepare you for any situation. It may sound queer, but I hope you suffer greatly."

I said, "Thanks for the encouragement. I wasn't this fearful before. I kind of am now."

Draco responded, "I'm glad to have helped."

A few minutes later, the carriage came to a stop. I could hear Reginald sliding across his seat upfront. A clicking sound went off from him locking the horses in place. The horses made a noise and stomped their feet onto the ground. The metal from their shoes had a small ringing from hitting the stones in the street.

Reginald opened the door and said, "I got you as close as I could."

Draco jumped out of the carriage and looked to the right. He said, "Let's go kids."

Draco turned around and looked up in our direction. Isabella walked over to the door and tried to push her way through. The dress kept getting caught on the door. He grabbed her by the waist and tugged on her dress to get her through. I still think it's funny because she hated that dress and complained about it for years.

It was my turn to leave the carriage. I walked over to the door. I held my arms out and leaped in Draco's direction. He stepped to the side and let me fall on my own. I dropped onto the cold, wet, hard street. My blue suit was now covered in water, mud, and stones. I got up and tried to wipe away the dirt.

Draco said, "Never trust anyone and walked toward the church."

Isabella came over to me and asked, "Why would you jump?"

I replied, "I trusted him."

Isabella said, "You never trust him. That will only get you killed. He will see it as a sign of weakness and use it against you. There is only one person that can depend on him and that is James. He cares for James more than his own kids."

I responded, "Good to know."

Isabella asked, "Do you trust me?"

I replied, "You haven't done anything to make me think I shouldn't."

Isabella said, "Don't trust me either. You will only get hurt. I belong with the trees and no human will ever change that."

I replied, "Why did that come up then? I thought you were looking for a friend."

Isabella said, "The world was not made for naïve people like you. Give it time, your parents will set you to the side like an unwanted toy when things become too much. My own mother abandoned me, and my father only cares about how I can benefit him in the future."

Isabella walked away and went to the back of the line to the church. Her head whipped around, and her hair flung violently in my direction. I was almost hit by her hair in the face. The girl had some problems. I wasn't mean to her at all. At first, I thought it might be because she was a royal. It turns out. There was clearly more trauma there than I could ever handle.

I ran over to Isabella in line. I stood behind her and looked in the direction of the church. There were lights flashing across the sky. The steeple appeared to be missing from the top of the church. I had never seen anything like it before. The only churches I had seen were drawn ones in the books my father had around the house.

Draco was walking back to see us in line with the parchments. He bought three parchments. I wondered why he grabbed so many of them. He looked at a boy and handed him one. The boy stepped out of line for a second to receive the parchment. I recognized the boy. It was the same boy with the large man in black and what looked to be a Priestess at the market buying apples. He stared at me Isabella and myself. The boy freaked me out a little. Small world.

Draco came back to Isabella and me. He handed Isabella a parchment. I was handed the other. He said, "I haven't seen your father yet. I'm keeping a lookout. I know he won't want to miss this.

I know you two are anxious. I know the line looks long. Just keep in mind, the line looks to be going fast tonight. I'll see you two there shortly. I counted only twenty-seven kids in front of you."

I nodded at Draco. He wasn't wrong. The Priests were flying through the number of kids. We got there just in time. The number of kids behind us grew every second. There had to be over a hundred kids that I could see. I looked straight ahead. I didn't want to lose my spot. If I left for even a second, the line would move forward, and I would be stuck there all night.

The Priests were walking up the line trying to sucker people out of their hard-earned money. Each Priest had a hand full of parchments. They walked the line trying to convince people to buy them. Most of the poor kids' parents gave them money to buy a one copper sheet of paper.

The line moved forward and got me closer to the church. Draco was standing at the door. He appeared to be waiting for something. He looked back at Isabella and me. There was a sinister smile on his face. I wasn't sure what he was planning. All I know is that he couldn't sit still. He tried to accomplish a bunch of things that had nothing to do with the two of us.

I finally got closer to the church to see the outside. The windows were flashing images. The images were moving around like the windows came to life. The window closest to us was the images of a man being hung on the cross. A spear came up and stabbed him in the ribs causing him to bleed everywhere and die. The images kept repeating over and over again in thirty second cycles.

Isabella and I went to the door. Draco said, "Good luck kids. I'm visiting a friend."

Draco was keeping a watchful eye on Isabella and me while in line. I think he was afraid something might happen to us. He tended to be overly cautious about things. He was a Legionnaire. Being cautious might have been part of the job. It could have also been that he had a reason to be cautious. The church was a wild evil place from what my father told me.

I looked in the door and saw Draco walking over to large dark man with a hood over his head. I didn't recognize him at first but the woman next to him was the same person who was buying apples. I wondered why, if they knew one another, the dark man didn't come over to say hello when we showed up at **Wong's**.

The dark man exclaimed, "Fuck off Draco. Keep your fucking daughter away from me today."

Draco looked around and tried to avoid any more of a scene. He walked up to the front pew where my father was. He sat down next to him. The church was mostly silent so the slightest noise could be heard throughout the church. He sat down next to my father. He whispered something in his ear. I couldn't make it out.

I looked at the ceiling and saw three chandeliers. Each chandelier had twelve candles lit to make the church bright. They were so high that I wouldn't know how to get a ladder up there. They rotated in circles and flickered. Alone the candles wouldn't have done much to light up the room. Together, the place looked bright as day.

I looked to the right and saw more window images moving. The images were of angels with swords swinging. I could see them battling a dark figure within them. They would glow brightly, and the dark figures would disappear. Again, these would restart every thirty seconds.

The closer we were to the church podium. The more that I wanted to leave. I was getting scared from what Draco said earlier.

Who in their right mind would want to be in pain. He wished me a painful Blessing. The guy had to be crazy. My body was shaking, and I was looking for any reason not to do it.

A boy behind me asked, "If I give you three gold, can I cut in front of you."

There was my reasoning. I could make money by holding off the Blessing. When a few of the rich kids heard that I was selling a spot in front of me, the parents gave each of them coins to pay me. I made twenty gold coins by doing this. Twenty gold is twenty gold. The line was fast anyway. The people behind me weren't pleased and the only reason I got away with it was the Priests didn't notice.

Isabella looked back and saw a strange boy next to her. She looked back at me and wondered why we were separated. I waved at her. She rolled her eyes and looked forward. She thought I got taken advantage of. The truth was that I took advantage of the situation. It didn't matter when I got up there despite what the Priests said. It just mattered that I was there that day.

The boy I saw earlier was next to go up. I thought he would be nervous. There was something about him seemed eager but he knew what he was doing. I looked up and the White Moon was perfectly over the steeple. I wondered if he was about to be Blessed. He smiled and walked forward under the light of the White Moon. I saw a quick shift and the Red Moon crossed paths with the White Moon above him. I didn't know what it meant but this guy looked like he would be the first to get Blessed tonight.

Chapter 30

The boy had blonde hair and blue eyes. He appeared to be physically stronger than most kids but with his baggy shirt and pants. It was hard to see his definite size. He was taller than me. I guessed he was almost five foot tall. His feet were bare. The dirt stuck to his feet and looked filthy. He left off a small odor like I did when I first got to the city.

The boy had the parchment Draco gave him. His chin was tilted downward and refused to look into the High Priests eyes. His head tilted downward while handing the parchment to the High Priest. The High Priest reached out and grabbed the paper. The parchment was set on the podium created by the Creationist.

Everything felt so slow. The boy's steps were almost dragging on the ground while walking up to the podium. His hands were open and centered on his body. The right was on top, and the left was on the bottom. They were shaped like he was carrying a large ball. When he got to the podium, he dropped to his knees.

The boy whipped his head upward. He stared into the sky. The Red Moon was perfectly aligned with the white and shined down a golden light. The boy's eyes rolled back into his head. His body turned limp causing his arms to drop. His body was being lifted into the air. The boy's arms were spread out and raised to his side. His back was arched and floating around in a circle.

The feet were dangling while the boy floated. I had never seen anything like this before. I thought it was the coolest thing until

I noticed something happening to him. His flesh was pierced and drops of blood were coming out. His nose flared up and blood was dripping out. He floated up through the area where the steeple was.

The golden light was disappearing. The boy was falling slowly. His feet were the first thing to touch. He flung his body forward. A loud crackling came from his back. He whipped his head forward and puked up blood in front of everyone in the church. He was trying to recover. The boy could not speak. He could barely breathe from whatever happened to him."

The High Priest looked down at the boy. He said, "Get up you little fucker."

The boy looked up with evil eyes. He wanted to kill the High Priest. There was a smile on his face. His teeth were stained red from the blood. I thought the kid was awesome. I watched every movement he made just like Draco said. A part of me wanted to be just like him. The other part of me wasn't sure if I wanted to go through this. He looked like he was suffering from whatever happened.

The boy struggled to stand up. When he did, the High Priest turned him around and pointed him toward the church. He smiled because he thought the benefits of the child would suit him. This was until he picked up the parchment. He saw something in the parchment that caused him to squeeze the shoulder of the boy.

The High Priest said, "This is a boy from our very own orphanage. He came to us almost the same day as his birth. Today, he has made proud to be called a Paladin. The boy is now up for sale to a family that will take him in. His status is low now but there is room for great growth. I shall read off the skills of the young man."

The High Priest looked pass the people in the front and stared at the dark man from earlier. It appears they weren't his parents. The Priestess did look to young to have a child and even though the dark man looked rough. He was probably young too. It was hard to tell since he was over six feet tall and had scars all over his face.

The High Priest said, "The first skill the boy has is called Holy Roar. This is a tanking skill that can lure many foes to them. It shatters the senses of all who oppose. This disorienting skill causes many people and beasts to go after the source and can be the determining factor of protecting your loved ones.

The second skill is Resurrection. Resurrection is a skill that can be used to revive the dead if done within a certain period. Not only does he save those around him from being injured but he makes sure the group can't die as long as he lives. Look upon this young man and see him as a valuable resource.

The third skill is Blood Healing. Everyone knows that Paladins have a natural ability to heal those around them. The healing in their blood is a constant to those around them. Blood Healing allows for an extra layer of protection for the party. It removes all the poisons and other elements from the blood.

The last skill is Internal Healing. The most basic of all Paladin gifts. Natural healing from the blood always causes a healing area of effect. The blood builds up healing to Holy Armor and anyone within a certain range will receive a small heal from this young man.

Can I get a starting bid at one hundred gold?"

The crowd was talking. The church was trying to take someone for a fool. The fact that he was a tank discouraged many. There was something else that bothered the people in the church. The rich and educated knew something else about him. Nobody raised their hand to bid on the boy.

Draco said, "That's not what Blood Healing does. If you are to sell the boy, at least be honest."

The High Priest responded, "Shut up! You know nothing of the boy."

Draco said, "I do know something of the boy."

The High Priest scoffed at Draco and looked over the crowd. Nobody was willing to bid on the boy. That was a lot of money to throw away. The average slave was a few silvers for the high end. People wouldn't buy the boy for slavery. They would use him to increase their family name. Giving him their name would mean he would need to accomplish great things. They didn't see that in him.

The boy looked pissed off at the crowd. He seemed to believe he was worth more than the rest of the church. He looked around and realized he needed to appear likeable. He smiled at the group of people. His teeth seemed to have changed shape. It looked like he had two giant fangs in his mouth. When he saw people getting scared from his smile, the long fangs shrunk, and he looked like a normal kid again.

The High Priest asked, "Will anyone take him for eighty gold?"

Draco looked at my father. He had a smirk on his face. He said, "The boy appears to be special. When I say special, you know what I mean. I know his brother quite well. I'm thinking of put in a bid."

My father responded, "Are you crazy? He has Blood Healing. We both know what that means."

Draco said, "The truth is. He is also a Paladin. A mixed being like that is rare. I mean. You and I would be the best fit for someone like him. He is also your son's age."

My father responded, "I don't know why you're asking me for advice. You're going to do whatever you want anyway."

Draco said, "I know. I just want you on board because you're the tank in this relationship. I might need your help."

My responded, "What would I get out of this situation?"

Draco said, "Isn't it obvious. You will let me teach your son if he is a non-Protection Warrior. I will laugh if he is a Mage of some kind. I will need Bizul to train him then."

The High Priest asked, "Will anyone take the boy for sixty gold?"

My father asked Draco, "Are you going to bid?"

Draco replied, "I will bid when I think it's low enough. If someone bids an amount before twenty, I will just bid upward."

The boy appeared to be strong, but a tear was starting to fall from his left eye. He had a look of someone hoping to escape. I wasn't sure what he was trying to escape from, but it must have been awful. I saw nothing but fear and sadness through his eyes. He appeared to have lived a hard life.

The High Priest asked, "How about forty for the boy?"

The High Priest was getting angry. They only cared about the profit from the boy. His teeth were grinding while seeing the crowd deny the boy. He looked over toward the man in black. There appeared to be a feud between them. I didn't think he wanted the man in black to get a chance to have the boy. The truth was. There was so much happening behind the scenes. I didn't understand.

The High Priest asked, "How about twenty gold?"

Draco raised his hand. Twenty was low for a hero to be bought. The High Priest didn't seem to like Draco and ignored his hand. He looked around the room and saw that nobody else was raising their hand. Draco was the only person in that church who wanted to adopt the boy. The value was low but going lower would come at a cost.

Draco said, "Hey fucktard, my hand is up. I am willing to pay twenty gold for the boy."

The High Priest responded, "Very well then."

The High Priest snapped his fingers and a Priest right behind him brought out a parchment for him to sign. It was an agreement to pay for the boy and give him the family name. Before the Priest would let him sign, he held out his hand for the gold. His hand kept opening and closing waiting for the payment.

Draco pulled out the twenty gold coins from his pouch. He handed them to the Priest. The parchment was signed. The boy belonged to Draco. It didn't seem like a welcoming set of events. The

High Priest pushed the boy in the direction of Draco. His nose was twitching while staring him down.

My father caught the boy and prevented him from falling over. The night continued with the people of the church watching their children go up to the podium. There were six kids in front of Isabella. She seemed to be getting impatient watching them all walk up to the podium. To her, it seemed like a waste of time because they were clearly not hero material.

Draco looked at a fat woman that was sitting closely to him. She had a fan in her hand blowing air in her face. I don't know much about the woman, but Draco did. He slapped his hand down on the pew to get the boy to sit next to him. There wasn't enough room for him to sit there. He didn't want to appear rude and just stood there.

Draco asked, "Can you move down a little? There is plenty of space and my new son needs a place to sit."

The woman replied, "I paid good money to see my son from this very spot. It's not my fault you didn't plan ahead."

Draco seemed to have a disdain for rich people. They always looked down on those around them. I think he could have handled her saying no if it wasn't so condescending. He reached down by her ass and gabbed a handful. He made sure to freak the woman out. She left out a yelping sound. Clearly, she didn't plan ahead.

The seat opened and the boy sat down next to Draco. He slid closer to Draco to stay clear of the fat woman's wrath. He gulped and looked up at Draco. He wasn't quite sure what Draco would want with him. The status of his power was lower than most. He knew what he was, which was weird for someone to want him at all.

Draco asked, "What is your name, boy?"

The boy replied, "My name is Lucas, as in the disciple of Christ."

Draco said, "From this day on, you will be named Lucas Simpson of the Simpson clan. I plan to treat you as my one and only son."

Lucas responded, "How many sons you actually got?"

Draco said, "I have none. God had a sense of humor and gave me nine daughters. I live in a house so feminine that this was my only shot to gain a little testosterone in the home."

Lucas smiled at Draco. He was starting to warm up to the idea of Draco being his new father. His heart was pounding from still being nervous. I don't blame him though. He spent every day with his friends within the church. Well, sort of, he adapted to the church and accustomed to their rituals.

Draco wanted to put Lucas at ease. He said, "Watch this."

Draco spun around and looked at the pew behind him. The pew was filled with a group of people. The only pews in the place you had to pay for were the ones in the front. The ones upfront were special because you felt most of the Blessings while they were happening to the children.

Draco looked at a red-haired woman with freckles. He still had a thing for the red-haired freckled women. He said, "You are looking good tonight. How about you come home with me and be my mistress."

The red-haired woman scoffed at Draco. A man to the right of the woman said, "That is my wife."

Draco responded, "I wasn't trying to marry her. I was just trying to see if she wanted to jump into my bed tonight. Thus, the term mistress."

The man pulled back his right fist and was getting ready to punch Draco. It would have been well deserved if he had punched him. The red-haired woman put out her hand and stopped him from punching. The way he was riled up. I think he might have punched his wife by accident while trying to attack Draco.

The red-haired woman said, "I think he is a royal. Put away your fist."

The man sat down and crossed his arms. His anger was getting the best of him anyway. He didn't realize it, but his foot kept coming up and kicking the back of the pew. The fat woman was right in front of him and kept getting kicked. The sound of his foot could be heard at the back of the church.

The High Priest called up the next kid which was two away from Isabella's turn. The poor kid was trying to focus on his walking to the podium. He ended up turning his head when the fat woman stood up from her seat. She turned around and took her leather purse filled with gold coins and started to beat the husband.

The fat woman yelled, "I have fucking had it! You people need to grow up and stop disturbing me while I watch the fucking ceremony!"

Draco looked at Lucas and shrugged his shoulders. This was all a game for him. Everything he ever did was a game in a way. He would plan out things. The plans were always interesting because you didn't know the results until the very end. I still don't know if he was trying to fuck the red headed woman, or he knew that the fat woman who disrespected him earlier would get hers. Either way, things always seemed to end up in his favor. It was almost like that was his true Blessing.

The room watched the whole thing unfold. It was entertaining for Draco until he noticed the next person up was Isabella. He wanted to watch her closely. That was his little girl. There were no games to be played this time.

Chapter 31

Isabella was pushing through the aisle. The dress was so wide it grazed across the legs of many people in the pews. Her feet were stomping down hard. It sounded worse than the horses clomping down the street. She grabbed ahold of the dress and hiked it up a few inches to help her walk down the aisle.

The High Priest looked down upon Isabella. He knew who she was. There was a look in his eyes of absolute hatred. I didn't think Isabella had anything to do with his anger. It turned out. The High Priest had a grudge against the whole family, and it wasn't even Draco's fault. It had to do with the family's lineage.

The High Priest said, "Parchment."

Isabella handed him the parchment with the left hand and when the High Priest turned around to set it down. She flicked him off with both hands. Her eyes looked like they were squinting and downright evil. She smiled and quickly put them away when the High Priest was turning back around.

The High Priest said, "You can come to the podium now you little bitch."

Isabella skipped up to the podium just to piss the High Priest off even more. She adjusted her dress to sit down on her feet. She looked up through the steeple area and saw a White Moon. I was curious if she would get the Blessing because I noticed a pattern earlier. There was a Red Moon directly over Lucas he was Blessed.

Isabella raised her arms and stared at the sky. The light didn't come down. She closed her eyes. The High Priest was about to kick her out of the church went glow surrounded her body. The inner glow pushed out what looked like were two butterflies flying out from the back of her neck.

The High Priest was getting ready to kick her in the face. The butterflies flew up to his face. They flashed a bright light in his face knocking the High Priest onto his butt. A bright light shined down from the sky and picked her up. Her arms were sprawled out. It was just like Lucas floating through the air.

The light was forming images of tree branches spanning in all directions. Weird symbols and green energy were flowing around her. White feathers were falling from the sky around her. Her eyes turned green. Her mouth opened and a gold light spewed from her mouth. Her red hair was lit up with strands of hair having a golden red glow causing it to sparkle.

Isabella's body was growing. The dress didn't fit her anymore. The straps were now tight against her skin. The shoes broke and fell to the ground. The power of the light was shredding parts of the dress. Her waist was tearing through the material. The church could see her lower back and her belly button while she floated around.

The light stopped shining down. The two butterflies flew up to Isabella's body and entered her mouth. She was slowly being lowered down to the ground. There was no blood this time. All Blessings appeared to be different in their origins. She knelt in front of the High Priest. Her body was adjusting to the change.

Isabella whipped back her red hair. She watched. The two Priests went out of their way to grab the arms of the High Priest and help him up. His robes were so heavy. It was difficult to stand up. There had to be over ten layers to his outfit for the ceremony. The back of the robe was now dirty, and he kept blinking to adjust his eyes to the light blast.

The High Priest finally got up and walked over to Isabella hoping to take control. He said, "Arise little one and claim your birthright."

Isabella responded, "Don't you talk to me you piece of shit. You aren't him. You aren't the man I am to give my life too. I will not obey anyone but him."

The High Priest said, "Feisty aren't we. That will end over time when you know your true place in this world."

Isabella looked around the church and yelled, "Where is he?! I can smell him! I can sense him! Where are you? Where are you, my love?!"

Isabella looked lost. She went from a person who hated all boys and only thought about herself to confessing her love for a man that didn't exist in this world. She was lost. The church felt sorry for her. She gained her memories from the past life but couldn't connect with this one. She yearned for someone, and nobody knew how to help.

Isabella's head kept twitching trying to look for someone. Her eyes grew large while scanning the crowd. She didn't find anything. She was disoriented and looked at her hands. She didn't seem to recognize who she really was. She had to cope with her past and her new life at the same time to determine who she really was. Both lives were very different.

Draco walked up to Isabella. He hoped to calm her down in her time of need. Tears were rolling down her face. This was the first time I saw her hug Draco. Her head leaned on his left shoulder. Snot was running from her nose and soiling the shoulder. I couldn't seem to grasp everything that was happening. I just knew this was a solid father/daughter moment.

The High Priest went back to the podium and lifted the parchment. All we understood from the status was that she had a descent level of stamina and dexterity. It made sense since she was known for climbing trees her whole life and not doing much more. She was destined to have this type of Blessing.

Darco stared at the High Priest while he was going over the parchment. He wanted to grab onto every word. The parchment would tell him how to guide his daughter. There were many clues about what she would become, but he didn't know what skills she would gain from the Blessing.

The High Priest said, "The class appears to be Hunter. A well-known class used for a balance of support and attack. Their long-range capabilities allow them to guide a group to victory along far terrains. May your skills guide your future little one.

Her first skill is Arrow Manipulation. This skill is used amongst the Star Piercer classes of Hunter. They have a keen eye and shoot from afar to always hit their target. Using their spiritual power, they can slow down and speed up any arrow while being able to pierce any adversary. May your arrows be blessed and your skills increase from the days.

The second skill is Passive Scan. Scan is the ability to find traps and weaknesses. This skill is used upon the Trapper class of Hunters. This is the most important skill to those entering dungeons. When lost, this ability will always be the best bet to find our way out. May this ability be used to save lives and push the depths of your knowledge in the world.

The third and final skill is Beast Tamer."

Draco yelled, "YES!"

Isabella got startled by the yelling in her ear. She pushed back her father and used her arm to wipe away the tears and snot from her face. She didn't want to hear anymore and ran through the aisles. The children in her path were being pushed away. I knew better and got out of her way.

I almost fell into the pew but the woman in the pew pushed on my face. My face looked like it was pressed against glass. I got back in line after stumbling a bit. The woman scoffed at me and folded her arm. She wasn't sure how far to go with it after seeing the type of clothes I was wearing. The bright blue was apparently a sign of nobility.

The kid who in front of me I sold my spot to asked, "What was her problem?"

I replied, "You know girls."

I didn't know girls at all. I should have said it with more of a question behind it. Besides my mother, she was the first human woman that I truly got to know. The crying and change in personality were something that my mother did sometimes. I just kind of accepted it as a girl thing to do.

Draco said, "Sorry, please continue. I'll get her soon."

The High Priest scowled at Draco and continued, "The third skill is Beast Tamer. Like the class suggests, Beast Tamer allows a Hunter to gain control of the animals around them. They create a bond with a spirit that directly controls them. These animals can be used to gain intelligence and in certain instances, dependent on the owner. The animals can work side by side with Rogues to take down Kaiju.

May she have many Blessings in her future and create a better world."

Draco bowed toward the High Priest. He turned around and walked up the aisle leaving Lucas up front with my father. He stayed to the right and used his right hand to touch each pew on the way out. He needed to find his daughter and understand what was happening. The road ahead was about to be a difficult one. He needed to train not one but two children at the same time. To a man that lacks real emotions, this was reason he needed my father and mother.

My father reached over and grabbed Lucas's head with one hand. He yanked him closer. It appeared to be aggressive to the people of the church, but that was just the way he was. It didn't hurt. My father probably did the same thing to me a thousand times in my life. Especially when we sat in front of the fire.

With Draco not there to scold my father for being too relaxed, he popped out his feet and leaned back into the pew. His right arm lay on his stomach with his butt almost falling off the pew. If anyone tried to walk by, they would have been tripped by his legs. He was a large man in every sense of the word.

The boy in front of me was shaking. He kept looking down at the thin red carpet that touched the front of the podium. He acted like he was cold and kept trying to hug himself. His teeth chattered. He didn't seem like the hero type. The truth was. I wasn't the hero type either. I just came to make people happy.

I asked the boy, "Are you okay?"

The boy replied, "I was excited about this. The longer I think about it, the less I want to be here. I want to go home."

I said, "This is your opportunity to be great. You will make your family proud and be able to help the weak."

The boy responded, "Take a good look at me. I am weak. I do my best to look strong. I must look strong for my family. I must remain strong for the staff."

I said, "My father once told me that overcoming fear is weakness leaving the body. He used to say the same about pain. Walking up there is literally the minimum."

The boy responded, "The first kid ended up with blood all over him and the other might have turned insane. They both looked to be suffering from their Blessings. I live a good life. Why would I want to make myself suffer like them."

I said, "That is a good question. Why would you want to suffer? The only thing I can say is that without suffering. How can we grow as beings?"

The boy responded, "You mean humans."

I said, "No."

The boy looked at me strangely. He was like me except with humans. The idea of a demi-human being a hero was beyond his comprehension. He probably had a bunch working for him but none of them had Blessings. Most of them didn't even get the chance because in Tryanon. It is forbidden to let a demi-human into the Enlightenment Ceremony.

The next turn was the boy in front of me. He could barely move. His feet would barely leave the ground while walking up to the podium. His arms were shaking violently while handing off the parchment. He dropped down to his knees and raised his hands. His head was looking upward at the White Moon.

The moon dimmed a bit from earlier. He waited all that time to get nothing. He didn't want to be a hero because expectations and pain would come from it. When he realized that the light was not coming for him, his eyes were watering. It was from relief. All that anxiety about the ceremony was for nothing.

The boy dropped his arms and could barely move. His body was still calming down from going up. He closed his eyes and looked at the High Priest. The High Priest wanted him to leave the stage, but he knew the boy's parents. They were high stakes donators of the church. He didn't wish to piss them off.

The boy on his way out of the church stopped at me and said, "What a relief? Good luck to you. I hope you get whatever you were after."

The boy skipped the rest of the way out of the church. It would be an easy life for him. There would be no turmoil. People would probably wait on him hand and foot. Every day would be easy. He might even have a few vacations a year and never accomplish anything in life. In a way, I'm happy for him. I also pity the guy.

It was now my turn. I slowly walked up to the podium. My feet sliding against the carpet. It caused certain sections to ride up. The

High Priest looked at me being worried. He crossed his arms and tapped his foot. I didn't want to do this. I was frail and always had my father protect me.

Draco wished me a lot of pain. The words of wishing me a lot of pain from the Blessing bothered me greatly. I couldn't figure out why someone would wish that upon a child. Those words were repeating in my head. My arms were shaking. I was worse than the boy in front of me. I too wanted to leave without a Blessing just like him.

I got up to the front pew. My father leaned forward in the pew. He noticed it was my turn. He smiled and gave me a thumb up. Realizing that my father had my back made things a little easier. I put my head down and walked up the High Priest. I handed him the parchment and dropped to my knees.

While the High Priest was placing the paper on the podium, the voice that plagued me spoke. It said, "You fucking coward. Straighten up. A whole room full of people are watching. If you get Blessed, the way you're acting. Nobody will respect you anyway."

I tried to ignore the voice. I wouldn't let him bother me anymore. I needed to be strong in front of my father. He raised me to be strong. I plowed the fields with the wolf people and built up my own stamina. I knew that I could do this. I raised my head and looked at the Priest. I didn't feel anything happening.

My father yelled, "Raise your arms boy!"

I knew I forgot something. I raised my arms and pointed my face at the sky. I looked up realizing something was different. I couldn't believe it. The White Moon was bright and directly over me. That wasn't all. I had the Red Moon over me as well. The same moon that caused Lucas to bleed and suffer. I felt fear come over me. I knew this was about to hurt.

Chapter 32

I stared at the Red Moon. My heart felt like it was seizing up. That tight pinch in my chest blurred my vision. Something was happening to my body. My muscles were flexing on their own. They were rippling like waves across my arms. My body started to violently shake from something changing me.

My fingers were stretched out and trying to touch the sky above. It was like an iron rod was stuck inside my fingers. It felt like something was preventing me from clasping my fingers. A small bolt of purple lightning came down and touched my middle fingers. I could only watch as everything around me slowed down to almost nothing.

The purple lightning created an arc that rolled down my arms. The arcs were small and didn't cause any damage. Instead, they tickled the top of my skin and left tiny burns that would immediately heal up. The lightning all seemed to end up going up my nose and into my mouth. My teeth glowed purple and shined bright toward the High Priest.

A bright light shined down from the sky. There were little red beams of light mixed within the bright light. The red lights were shooting through my body. When the light went through, purple light was coming out the other side. After a few moments, the bright light blinded me. My eyes turned into a pure white color with no veins, pupils, or irises. They were just two glowing white orbs.

I was stunned by the event. My body felt like it was in a completely different place. I could no longer feel the rug that was below me. The smell of stone and blood filled the air. I could taste the air. The air tasted like burnt flesh. I was starting to believe that I was in Hell. It seemed like a myth for so long. I didn't believe it existed until that very moment.

I heard a voice say, "Wake up."

It wasn't just a normal voice. It was the voice that had insulted me all my youthful life. My eyes were still adjusting, and I couldn't see the being that called for me to wake up. My eyelids appeared to be slightly glued shut. I struggled to open them. My eyes rolled back into my head while trying to open them.

The voice said, "Wake up you fucking pussy."

I felt a punch in the face. The being didn't hold back. I felt him repeatedly punch me with his rough hands. My eyes were trying to open and focus on what was coming. I wanted to dodge the punch. I just needed to recover from being transported to the new world. It wasn't easy with what felt like a million pounds on my chest. I could barely breathe.

I blindly swung my right arm at whatever was on top of me. I hit nothing but it was enough to scare whatever was there. I heard the clanging of a chain moving around me. The sound got louder and pulled on my left arm. I felt handcuffed to whatever was punching me in the face.

I asked, "Would you stop moving? It's hurting my wrists."

The voice replied, "Open your eyes fool. We need to get to the next area. Maybe a meeting with Gabriel will change you. I'm so sick of seeing you be so fucking weak."

I took my right hand and rubbed my fingers across my eyes. They were still blurry, but I was able to finally see what the voice was. It was a gray being with what looked like incredibly large eyes. The eyes looked like they were about to pop out of the being's head. I realized that I was looking at a stone creature.

I sat up and used my arm to wipe my eyes again. I finally got my sight back. I kind of wished at the time that I lost my sight again. The area around me was the stuff of nightmares. I couldn't catch my breath. The smell of blood was intoxicating. I could barely remain conscious from all the sights and smell in the environment.

I tilted my head to the right. There was a skull with flesh still attached to the eye socks. An oozing green material was seeping through its teeth. It kept making a popping sound like the inside of the skull was cooking. I couldn't stand the sight of it anymore and took my right arm to smash the skull. My hand was now covered in a thick red slime that might have been melted brain matter.

The gargoyle said, "That was smart."

I responded, "I just didn't like the sight of it."

The gargoyle said, "Whatever, just get your ass up."

I sat up and looked around. The room was blocked off in all directions except a set of stairs. The stairs had blood streaming down them. I could hear it slowly flooding the area we were in. If I stayed in my spot for too long, I would surely drown in the blood. The blood on the stairs were pouring down like a million little waterfalls

There was a tug on my left wrist. I realized there was a cuff on there. A chain was connected to the gargoyle. The gargoyle had a collar around its neck that connected the chain to me. Against his will, he was stuck with me. No wonder he was angry about me not moving fast enough. He wanted to escape this place but couldn't without me.

I stood up and looked down upon my body. The blood was up to my ankles and bleaching my skin red. My feet could seem to lift out of the blood due to its thickness. I could only slide my way through the blood to the stairs. When I reached the stairs, I heard noises crunching underneath my feet.

My foot was in pain. Something jabbed the bottom of my foot. The pieces of a baby skull started to float to the surface. My stomach was having a difficult time dealing with all the death and decay in this place. My eyes were watering from the smell that made me feel like I was eroding from the inside out.

My left hand reached out to what appeared to be a railing. The railing appeared to be hundreds of orbs with six legs on each side. The legs were fighting to get free. The shape reminded me of a millipede that was being held up by stacks of bones and skulls. The outer layer lined at the bottom of the railing was made of rib cages.

The gargoyle ran up the steps dragging me along. His neck was solid and didn't appear to be affected by the strain from the collar. He pulled forward and forced my hand on the railing to remain standing. The legs on the railing were sticking to my arms. They were rubbing against my flesh in hopes of sticking to me and removing my flesh.

The stairs were spiraling around while going up. A floor remained at the top of the stairs. I couldn't see past that point. The only thing I could do was climb the stairs and hope that the gargoyle wouldn't lead me to my doom. He appeared to be my only guide. He was unfortunately my only hope of survival.

My hands were sliding across the railing, and I was doing my best not to slip down the blood covered stairs. I grabbed the slots in between each orb and held on. I was slowing down and the gargoyle looked back at me. He saw nothing but weakness in me. I was young and frail. My body was still growing. At least, that's what my father told me.

The gargoyle said, "You need to hurry up. The longer we stay here. The worse things will...Oh shit!"

I could hear something coming from the top floor. It had the sound of an ocean crashing against the rocks. I really hoped it was water. I would never be so lucky. The gargoyle heard the crashing sound and jumped up on the railing. It dug its claws in and waited for the blood to come crashing down the steps.

The blood struck me hard. My frail body held on for only a few seconds. I was ripped off the railing and tossed into a sea of blood on a staircase. My chain was still attached to the gargoyle. The only reason I didn't float away was the gargoyle's neck was strong. The chain tightened and choked the gargoyle. He didn't stop and pulled himself up the railing. I was slowly dragged to the top of the steps.

When we got to the top of the steps, there were about two feet between the top floor and the blood. My body moved off the steps enough to lay on top. I kept coughing up blood. Dry blood was stuck inside my nose and made the back of my throat sore. I kept coughing in hopes of getting all the bad taste out of my mouth. I kept spitting any fluid that was in my body. I couldn't get the taste and smell to disappear.

The gargoyle was on the steps. It wrapped its claws around the chain and slowly pulled me to the steps. When I got to the steps, he jammed his claws under my chin and dragged me up the steps. My back was getting sliced up while scraping against the edges of each stair. My back was swelling, and the cuts were bleeding everywhere. It couldn't be noticed because of how much blood was already on the steps.

The gargoyle took me to the top floor. It dug deep into my chin and punctured holes. The holes went to the bottom of my tongue. I could taste the stone stroking the bottom of my tongue. It was set and seemed to almost be nourishing in a way. I swear at times, it felt like I was drinking a glass of water and others tasted like pennies.

The claws were removed from my chin. The holes in my face almost immediately closed. Very little blood came out of my face. I sat up and put my right hand on my chin. I could feel the healing taking place. I used my hand to adjust my jaw because it had popped out of place. The sound of my chin crackling echoed through the room.

I said, "Looks like we made it."

The gargoyle responded, "No thanks to you."

I asked, "What is your name?"

The gargoyle replied, "You don't need to know my name. When this is over, the chain will be released, and we will be free of one another."

I asked, "What happens if we are bound together...forever?"

The gargoyle replied, "The madness will ensue both of us."

I said, "I don't think this is over after we reach our destination. Your voice has been in my head for my whole life. You really think it will end just because we finish one objective."

The gargoyle responded, "I watched you in your prior life and now this life. You play innocent. You think of yourself as a man. The truth is. You're more of a demon than I am. Once you gain your memories. The pain will start, and you will start to remember your past life. This Blessing is nothing more than an entrance into madness that will destroy the world."

I asked, "What do you mean by past life?"

The gargoyle gritted his stone teeth. He replied, "I do not need to explain a thing. You will learn it all in due time."

I looked to my left and upward. There was a giant window in the room peering to the outside. Every inch of the window was showing a giant red moon. The bright red light of the moon was the only light inside the room. I felt the warm glow of the light on my skin. It gave me a feeling of a second wind across my naked flesh.

I stood up. My legs were wobbling still. I leaned forward and braced myself on my knees. It felt as if my whole body was preparing for something. I could feel the warmth inside. I looked at my arms and saw ripples and red spots across my flesh. I was changing on the inside.

The gargoyle yanked on the chain and pulled me forward. I lost my balance and fell face first into the ground. It took its foot and placed it onto my head. The pressure was immense. My head felt like it was about to pop. His claws were digging into my neck. I could feel my warm blood trickling down my neck onto the floor.

The gargoyle said, "I'm in control. If you don't start doing what I say, you will suffer. I haven't been telling you how worthless you are for no reason. It's a reality check. You are fucking worthless. You are nothing compared to me. Unfortunately, I'm stuck with you. Now get your ass up and let's finish this."

The gargoyle removed its foot off my head. His foot touched against the cold steel of the floor. I felt the vibrations and heard the clanging of his feet. I needed a minute to get up. I wanted to do what he said. It was just difficult to move my body. There was something about this place that made it hard to move. It became increasingly more difficult to even want to stand up and do normal things like walking.

A loud siren went off in the distance. The siren was making the ground shake. I covered my ears because the sound was making my eardrums shake. I curled up in a ball and lay there waiting for it to be over. My teeth were biting down and almost cut my tongue. My head was shaking violently. I wanted to escape from this place, but I didn't know how.

The room was moving. The gargoyle was reaching for the floor. He felt a shift in the room. His claws dug into the floor. The gravity took over and the floor was grinding and falling apart from his claws. The siren stopped but the room continued to move. The only sound I could hear was metal grinding from its claws digging into the floor.

I didn't even try to grab anything. My body flew straight to the wall. I hit the wall hard. A little blood spit up. My teeth were stained red. I spit out the blood onto the ground. My right hand pushed into it spread against the wall while I tried to climb to the window. I couldn't see the moon anymore from this position.

The window had a giant metal piece that I had to crawl over. I got to the metal piece but couldn't move forward to see, because the gargoyle was still clinging to life. My arm was pulling backward. This time, he was preventing me from moving forward. It was like an anchor for a ship. An anchor that was fighting to stay below the ocean.

I pulled on the chain. I hoped that the gargoyle would easily fall with me. He appeared to be afraid to fall. The claws dug deeper. The grinding sound was echoing through the room. The pulling on the chain was causing his neck to crack. The collar was grinding against his stone exterior. It was smoothing out his neck and making him more brittle.

The gargoyle closed his bulbous eyes and said, "If you want to see what is down there so bad, you fucking got it."

The gargoyle leaped from its spot and aimed for the window. Its teeth were bearing while it straightened its body. It aimed at the center of the window. This was not the plan. My body was still feeling weak and only wanted to see what was there. I didn't want to be forced to go down there. The glass shattered into millions of little pieces.

My hand was still connected to the chain. I took my feet and slammed them against the metal frame around the window. My legs were still weak but straightened to hold myself in place. My right arm wrapped around the chain and pulled. I made sure to hold not only my weight, but the weight of the gargoyle. He was made of stone which was far heavier than me.

My arms were bending. I struggled to stay up. It was just a matter of time before I gave in. I hoped the gargoyle would stop moving. It seemed to be getting a kick out of watching me struggle. It used its momentum to swing around the area below. It made this more difficult. I did my best to stretch my legs upward and have my feet touch the metal in front of me. My feet touched for only a second. My feet lost their grip on the edge.

I put out my hands to catch myself. My hands were the only thing preventing me from falling. I looked down and saw a stone bowl thousand feet below. The bowl was filled with more blood than the world had ever seen. The blood bubbled in certain spots. There was black smoke coming from certain areas of the bowl. The bowl of blood had to be hundreds of miles long.

The blood was boiling. It was almost like it was cooking. It left an aroma that filled the air and kept the ravens in the sky at bay. The sky was dark because of all the black some and clouds in the sky.

The area I came from was filled with blood poured out a hole. It was replenishing the millions of gallons that were syphoned into the room. It was an endless cycle in what could only be described as one thing. I was in HELL!

Chapter 33

Blood was falling from the room like a waterfall. I had to hold on just long enough to have the building tilt upward again. My fingers were on the edge. I was so little and frail. I don't know where the strength in my hands was coming from. I just knew that I could have never done this in the old world.

The gargoyle realized the swinging wasn't enough. Its claws went up the chain and held on. The closer it got. The harder it was to hold on. It climbed halfway and tugged onto the chain. It would thrust its weight downward sliding a few inches with all its grip strength. The damn thing kept laughing at me while trying to get me to fall.

I couldn't hold on anymore. The gargoyle went down one last time. I lost my grip and fell into the waterfall of blood below. The blood pushed me down faster and harder. I was drowning in blood before I even hit the surface. There was no chance of me being able to escape this painful fate.

My arms were flailing while falling to the pool of blood below. I tried to spin around but my body couldn't move. The gargoyle was preventing movements with his neck. It wasn't falling at the same speed. It kept pulling upward keeping my arm up. This lasted until I hit the pool of blood below.

I looked around and saw nothing but red. The blood entered my nostrils and went down the back of my throat. I was getting used to the taste and smell. I felt sick in the beginning but now. I felt freedom to swim in it. The blood was being absorbed into my skin and giving me a new feeling of power.

The gargoyle stood on the surface of the blood. It grabbed the chain and started to pull me to the surface. When I fell from that height, I could have sworn that I was about to die. In this world, I barely felt sore. In fact, I felt invigorated by the fall. The blood was making me feel something powerful. I was feeling more human than human.

When the gargoyle got my head to the surface, it grabbed under my chin and pulled me the rest of the way. It laid me on the surface and looked around. I spit up blood stuck in my lungs. The blood covered my chest and dripped from the right side of my mouth. I gasped for air. I coughed a few times before taking my right arm and wiping away the blood from my eyes.

The blood was sticky and stuck my eyelids together. I could see a little bit but couldn't get my eyelids fully open. I could see the gargoyle looking around through the small holes left in my eyes. Most of the sight was now blocked my thickened eyelashes. The gargoyle appeared to be scared. There was a nervousness in its face like we were about to be killed.

The gargoyle said, "Wake up. We need to find a way out of here."

I responded, "I can't see. Give me a minute."

The gargoyle took its fingers and wiped away the blood from my eyes. The stone on its fingers rubbed my eyes raw. There were red bumps on my eyes. Its ugly ass face was inches from me. I was horrified. The gnarly teeth, the bulbous eyes, and the horns that could kill a man were within inches of me.

The gargoyle said, "We don't have time. Look around you, fool."

I looked around. The bowl was cracked with orange and red lava material in the cracks of the rocks. The lava was shooting off red sparks and smoke. There appeared to be no place to go except outside the bowl. Even if I ran to the edge of the bowl, it had to be over a thirty miles to the edge. I was stuck.

I responded, "Where do we go?"

The gargoyle said, "I'm not sure, but I can sense my brethren."

I didn't see it at first. On the edge of the walls around us, there were little stone men. Gargoyles just like the one I was stuck to. Each one was unique and more horrifying than the last. Some of the gargoyles stony exterior glowed with lava between the cracks in their skin. Others were smooth and well kempt. They were beating against the edge of the bowl.

The gargoyle said, "It's too late. The Gargoyle King is coming."

I looked in the distance. A large being with lava running down its chest was walking in my direction. The blood was bending to its will while walking. The blood parted away from its feet and a stone path formed underneath. The moment the being walked past the built stones placed in front of it. The stones were destroyed by the blood around them.

The being got within a few feet of the gargoyle and myself. The gargoyle said, "My lord, I have this under control."

The being responded, "This isn't about your Maduk. This is about the boy. I am here under the orders of Gabriel."

Maduk was the name of the entity that haunted me. I wanted to reach over and beat the hell out of it. It made me drop out of the room because it lunged out the window. My self confidence was shot because of this prick. I now had his name and that made me feel powerful.

I looked at Maduk. It was deeply afraid of the Gargoyle King. When I saw blood shift from under its feet. I wasn't sure if I should be thanking it. It saved me from drowning a few times but taunted me my whole life. I still feel the malice of it in my head. I felt indifferent because some of the things it did make me stronger. There other parts put me into a deep depression.

I got a good look at the Gargoyle King. I was terrified. Its whole body was made of a black stone. Its chest and abdominals were carved out with red lava. Its head looked like a skull with spikes coming out of the chin. The biceps were larger than its own head. Above each eye were red markers carved out in lava shaped like lightning bolts. Its eyes were missing with a red glow deep inside its skull. The light flowed through the back of the eyes and down through its mouth.

The Gargoyle King had steel gauntlets that had chains wrapped around them. The chains were bound to its belt that had three skulls on it. The skulls were made of black iron. The chains rattled with every small movement it made. The belt was holding up a long brown cloth that looked like a dress. The cloth glowed and flickered from the flames underneath.

In the right hand of the Gargoyle King was a large axe. The axe was held with one hand but required at least two for most men. One side of the blade was sharp enough to carve stone and the other side was flat like a hammer. The top of the axe had six spikes that could be used as a secondary weapon. The blackness of the weapon had a shine that reflected the light off the blood.

A bright light appeared a few feet from where I was lying. I used all my strength in an attempt to slowly stand up. The bright light could only be one being. I rolled over and did a push up. I rose to my feet and turned around. The light was always beautiful when he appeared. The light gateway closed and there stood Gabriel. I figured he would save me from what was happening to me.

I smiled and said, "Gabriel, I need help."

Gabriel responded, "I'm not here to help you. I'm here to make sure you get your Blessing."

The Gargoyle King asked, "Are you sure? Did God truly say to do this?"

Gabriel replied, "Who are you to question me, demon.?! You need to do what your told."

The Gargoyle King said, "As you wish."

Gabriel said to me, "This will hurt you more than it will hurt me. Control yourself and stay strong."

Gabriel took his middle and his pointer finger. He pushed them into my head as hard as he could. A bright light blasted my forehead. I was in shock from the blast and fell backwards. I lay on top of the blood and stared up at the sky. I was in a catatonic state. Gabriel decided that it was necessary to put me in a paralyzed state. Unfortunately for me, I could feel everything that would happen next.

The Gargoyle King took his axe and raised it over his head. He took a few steps toward me and slammed the chain that held Maduk and myself together. The chain chimed and echoed throughout the sky. Purple sparks flew off the chain when it was smashed. I felt a little relief thinking that I finally got rid of Maduk.

Maduk pulled the chain in his direction. The chain was wrapped around its arm. It scurried a few feet behind the Gargoyle King and made a bunch of growling noises. It took me way too long to realize that Maduk was a very weak gargoyle. He hid and schemed but didn't seem to have much value on its own.

The Gargoyle King said, "If you think your free, you are not."

The Gargoyle King raised its arms into the air. Purple lightning was flashing off the gauntlets. It screamed loudly into the sky. Flames came out of its mouth and eyes. I couldn't believe the amount of intimidation. My heart stopped for a second because the stress was too much. This was what a true monster was.

I neglected my surroundings. Five chains came up from the blood. There were purple melted spots in the chains causing them to glow. One chain wrapped around my neck and pulled upward.

It tried to strangle me. The other four chains were wrapped around each wrist and ankles.

I was being pulled in five different directions. The chains moved around my arms and got a better grip. It felt like a snake was crawling across my body. The hot steel from the chains caused a burning sensation and rubbed my limbs raw. It got tighter and slowly lifted my body three inches off the top of the blood.

My muscles felt like they were tearing from being pulled. I tried to just focus on the sky. The clouds were black. The only place where the light was shining was the Red Moon to the left of me. I could hear the blood bubbling behind my back. Small bubbles of blood were consistently splattering against my back and slowly dripping back to where it came from.

The black ravens with purple eyes were screeching through the sky. I watched them fly in circles around my body. They seemed to act like vultures while watching my body almost ripped apart. I pulled with everything I had to get free, but it was no use. The Gargoyle Kings chains were stronger than the chain between Maduk and me. There was no way to escape my fate and the ravens knew this.

I asked, "What do you plan to do to me?"

The Gargoyle King replied, "I plan to split your soul open to allow demons inside."

I said, "This is a joke right."

Gabriel responded, "This is no joke. Your Blessing will be to control demons and use them to become stronger."

The gargoyles on the edge of the bowl jumped off and walked on the top of the blood in my direction. It sounded like a million stone grinding against each other. They started to clap while walking toward me. Dust and dirt were tossed up from each clap. The rhythm of the claps matched and created a perfect drumming sound.

I yelled, "Fuck you! I don't want this! Let me GOOOOOOO!"

The Gargoyle King didn't say a word. He raised his axe into the air. The wind was blowing violently. The black clouds were forming purple lights within them. It clenched its mouth. The fire in its mouth could no longer be seen. Its arm was shaking. It was waiting for something. I gulped and looked up at the sky.

The clouds were shooting off purple lightning all around them. They were slowly coming together to form one giant cloud. The lightning crashed across the sky. Each bolt of lightning was getting longer. It was aimed in the direction of the Gargoyle King's axe. I knew I had time to escape. I fought with every bit of my strength. My movement only made the chains pull tighter.

The purple lightning came down from the sky and finally touched the spikes on the top of the axe. The lightning flowed across the gauntlet and wrapped around its arm. It dropped the axe down and carved through my chest. The power from the axe slammed me hard and got stuck inside my chest. The blood underneath me parted for a few seconds before going back to normal.

The purple lightning was surrounding my body. I could feel the tingling sensation as it crawled across my body. The lightning was covering my body until it found no other place to enter. It came back to the carved-out area and crawled in my chest like a worm. It made my heart race. The sound of my heart was all I could hear. Everything around me was turning deaf. Even the claps from the gargoyles.

The Gargoyle King pulled on his axe to pull it out. It was stuck in there good. It required it to pull up with both hands. Each yank was spilling out a few drops of blood and raising my flesh upward. It screamed while pulling up again. The axe was stuck within my chest and refused to move. I was spitting up blood through my mouth after a while.

Gabriel asked, "You need help?"

The Gargoyle King replied, "I am the fucking Gargoyle King. I do not need the assistance of some angel."

Gabriel said, "Suit yourself. I don't usually offer my assistance to demons like you."

The Gargoyle King replied, "It would be like you to belittle my kind. I hope my gargoyles destroy every last bit of this kid's humanity. I hope they make you and your cause suffer."

The Gargoyle King pulled one last time. He finally got his axe out of my chest. A bright white light shined from my chest. It shot upward and blinded the King temporarily. It took a few steps back and shook its head. The fire in its eyes glowed brighter while trying to adjust. It looked up at the sky and the light was strong enough to shine through the black clouds above.

A giant white orb was poking its way toward the surface of my chest. It had its own heartbeat. The Gargoyle King said, "That looks strong. How many do you think will fit in that soul?"

Gabriel responded, "Every demon in existence can fit in there. That is why he was chosen. Your job is to split it open. We need to make it easier for the demons to get inside his soul."

The Gargoyle King said, "I've never seen an angel go through this much trouble to corrupt a human before."

Gabriel responded, "He's not a human. He's a demon."

The Gargoyle King said, "If you say so."

The Gargoyle King raised his axe toward the sky. It was to gather the purple lightning again. It took its left hand and squeezed it shut. I could feel the chains pulling tighter. My chest was opening, and my rib cage was poking through my skin. The rib cage was separated. The white orb in my chest could be hit more easily.

I screamed out in pain but not much noise came out. My neck was cracking while all my vertebrae were stretched out. I could hardly breathe with the chain pulling and squeezing my neck. I tried to reach up and remove the chain from my neck, but the chains wouldn't let me move an inch. I just coughed while choking out.

The purple lightning came down. It was an easy shot to attack what Gabriel called my soul. The black axe lit up and slowly changed to a purple color. The purple lightning transformed the color and gave it a bright glowing power designed to shred my soul. He dropped the axe downward with all his might.

My soul was fighting back. It didn't want to be cut. The power of the purple lightning flashed brightly against the outside of the soul. Sparks were flying while the Gargoyle King pushed into my soul even harder. It grunted and realized that it needed to use two hands. It slid up its right hand and dropped all its weight on the left arm.

The axe started to break through. I felt a pinch in my chest. It was the same feeling someone had when they are about to have a heart attack. My soul was cracking under pressure. The purple power found its way in. My soul was sucking in the power that the axe gave to me. All it took was a small hole on the outside of the orb for it to enter. There was now a way for demons to enter inside me.

The Gargoyle King asked, "Will that be good enough?"

Gabriel replied, "It only takes a little opening to let the demons in. I would say this is good enough, but this is merely the beginning."

Gabriel whipped his wings out. The feathers were falling upon the blood below. The white and the black feathers were soaked up by the blood and disappearing. He flew up into the sky. A lit-up portal opened, and he flew through it. That was the last time I saw Gabriel this time around. I can't say I wanted to ever see him again. Unfortunately, it was part of being Blessed.

The ravens with purple eyes were coming closer to my body. I couldn't move. They circled around me and made screeching noises. I couldn't close my eyes. The chain around my neck pushed up my jaw and made it almost impossible to close my eyes. I watched as the birds got closer to me. They were getting ready to feed.

Chapter 34

The ravens flew over me. They flocked in a circle. The first raven flew down to my chest. Its talons grabbed ahold of a flappy piece of flesh on my rib cage. It looked up and shook its head rapidly. The beak tapped my skin a few times. It hurt a little, but no damage was done. When it realized it was safe to eat, it pecked at my flesh. My flesh was ripped of my body. The pain was getting worse. Tears were trying to form around my dry eyes.

The ravens watched longer to see if anyone would attack the lone bird. They realized that nothing would save me. A few more birds flew down from the sky and pecked at my arms and legs. I wished my body would heal like before. I didn't understand why I wasn't healing this time.

The Gargoyle King walked over to Maduk and said, "You will be the first. Grab your brethren and strengthen him. He will be the best line of defense against Lucifer."

Maduk responded, "I was in his head for nine years. Can we find someone else my lord?"

The Gargoyle King didn't respond. Instead, it took its left hand and grabbed the broken chain connected to Maduk's collar. It lifted the chain up. The chain clanged against its gauntlet. Its enormous size was four times the size of Maduk. It lifted upward and stared straight into Maduk's eyes with intensity. It didn't have to say a word. Everyone knew there was no way to counter such a being.

Maduk was clawing away at the collar to escape. The chain swayed back and forth while Maduk was fighting for its life. Maduk choked and suffocated like it was being swung from the gallows. It tried to claw the Gargoyle King but was too weak. It finally swung high enough to wrap its arms and legs around the King's arms.

The ravens were covering my body. I couldn't see anything after seeing Maduk crawl up the arm. The ravens covered my face. They were eating me alive. The ravens on my face were trying to eat my eyes. The pecking ripped out my eyes and left only sockets. All I saw was darkness.

Maduk yelled, "STOP! SSSSSSSTTTOOOOP!"

The Gargoyle King said, "See you on the other side."

I felt the ravens leaving my body. The pain hit a threshold. I couldn't seem to feel much. I was left with a tingling sensation that paralyzed my body. The chains were loosening. It made the sound of jangling keys. My body slowly lowered to the surface of the blood. Once my body hit the surface, I felt a sense of calm. My heart was feeling either dead or glad things were almost over.

The blood I was lying gained a life of its own. It turned purple when touching my skin. I could feel the blood creeping up my cheeks. It targeted my eyes and filled the hallow holes up with purple blood. A tingling sensation was making the inside of my eye socket have an uncontrollable itch.

The blood was slowly healing my eyes. My vision was coming back. A little bit of light was entering my eyes. I was feeling restored. I took a deep breath and realized. My arms and face were gaining the flesh back where the ravens had eaten me. I no longer felt like I was about to die for the first time since entering this place.

The first thing I saw was the Gargoyle King dangling Maduk over my chest. A bright White light shined upward from my chest and grabbed its body. I felt a sharp pinch. The light was pulling Maduk into my soul. Maduk's body was dissolving in front of me. Every piece of its body was crumbling. I could feel the dark force being sucked into my soul.

My soul closed and a piece of chain was left outside. The sound of the chain breaking pinging sound. The link flew into the blood next to me. A few bubbles sprang from the blood. I fell to the deepest parts of the bowl of blood. It hit the bottom and created a tremendous amount of weight. The bowl was shaking and the look on the face of the gargoyle was that of fear.

The Gargoyle King yelled, "Brace yourselves!"

The blood was turning purple. It gained a life of its own and created waves. The blood waves were blasting against the side. The bowl was losing control. The lava in the cracks of the bowl were changing to purple. The cracks were crumbling under pressure. Dust was shooting off into the air. Nothing was keeping the bowl together anymore.

My body was still feeling paralyzed. My eyes watched the birds in the sky fly away into the dark clouds above. They were slowly disappearing at the slightest moments of danger. I watched the gargoyle run across the blood in a panic. When the blood was moving too violently, they flew into the sky like the birds. They hovered over me and watched me suffer.

The sky was turning purple. The clouds were making thunderous noises while charging up for one final lightning bolt. The sky lit up brightly and the Red Moon could no longer be seen. The bolt from clouds shot down from the sky. My body was seizing up. It knew that the bolt was aimed for it. The purple bolt struck my soul and caused my eyes to turn pure white. The pain was immense. My mouth opened and nothing could come out. The bolt caused me to arch my back. The lightning burned my body. When things settled, my back fell to the surface of the purple blood.

My soul now had a purple tint to it. It was flashing purple inside just like the clouds. I grunted after it closed. I was breathing heavily.

My body was twitching while I stared at the sky. After all I went through, I hoped Draco was right. I hoped this would make me one of the strongest beings on the planet.

Purple blood began to rain from the sky. My body was soaking up the blood rain, I believe the blood rain was slowly repairing my chest. It was filling my chest cavity up and pushing the blood throughout my body. I wanted to pass out, but this world wouldn't let me get any rest.

The ribs were moving back into my body. They made a snap, crackle, and pop sound while shifting in my body. I felt the ribs pinching me. After a few more seconds, my chest finally closed and looked normal again.

My body completely healed. I was able to sit up now. I sat up. My body felt weird. A big change occurred. I looked at my reflection in the blood. My face had changed, and I looked very strong. My hair had changed too. I couldn't tell if it was because of the blood. It seemed much shorter than before.

I stood up and stared at all the gargoyles in the sky. They laughed and cheered. It was interesting watching them all dance in the blood rain. They opened their mouths and tried to take in and absorb as much as possible. The blood was smoothing the stones on their frames. It made each of the gargoyles appear younger.

The bowl hit its breaking point. It shook more violently than ever before. I tried to stay stable. I looked around and noticed that the cracks were breaking the bowl to the center. The blood was draining from the bowl. I couldn't stabilize myself and dropped to my knees. Blood was wrapping around my legs. It was pulling me under. I reached up hoping that maybe I could fly like he gargoyles. After all, Maduk was inside me. Apparently, he couldn't shit for me in this world.

I lost my legs in the blood below my feet. My legs sunk in like it was quicksand. I did my best to swim. I couldn't swim because the blood was too thick. I went under and couldn't see anything. The darkness of the blood was too much. My right hand was the last thing to go under. I was trying to reach the surface and pull myself up. My hand kept splashing the top and eventually forced me several feet under.

A whirlpool formed within the blood. My body went around in a circle. I felt myself being thrashed through the blood. My limbs were on the verge of being broken. I couldn't breathe. The force was causing me to lose all my air. I was passing out. My eyes were shutting while floating into what appeared to be an endless abyss.

My head slammed against the bottom of the bowl. I was alert again. A little light was shining. There was a powerful force pulling me toward it. That was when I realized there was a hole in the bottom of the bowl. All the blood was pouring out of it. I got dragged fast against the bottom having every part of my body slam against the bowl. The edge of the hole was close by. I reached for the edge.

My hands grabbed the edge of the hole. The power of the blood rushing against my body while trying to stay up was difficult. The strain was causing the veins to pop out of my arms. The purple veins were glowing and shooting off little lightning bolts that tickled the top of my skin.

I couldn't hold on any longer. My fingertips were eventually the only thing keeping me in the bowl. My hands let go. I was falling. The blood was covering my body and making me fall faster. I turned around and did my best to spit out all the blood in my mouth. I was puking it up and swallowing it again because of gravity. Blood was pouring out my nose while falling through a set of clouds.

The drop seemed endless until I saw a bunch of black mountains below. The black was because they were made of a very hard mineral. It would have been worth billions of golds in the world. The air was starting to change. It smelled like a coal mine. I did my best to enjoy the air before falling to my doom.

My body slammed across the mountain. I tried to grab anything but kept slamming different body parts against the mineral mountain. My body was covered in black soot that clung to my flesh. The soot made my skin smoother and made it easier to slide down the mountain. My body was scrapped up badly. I brushed against the rocks enough to rub my arms, back, and legs raw.

I couldn't see well because my head was pounding against the rocks many times. I was feeling a little fuzzy while falling down the mountain. Up appeared to be down. I couldn't figure out where my arms were to grab anything around the slick mountain. The stones were coming down and attacking me while I was rolling down.

The blood from the bowl sprayed the area. It was raining across the land and flooded a path at the base between the mountains. Blood was falling on and across the mountain from where I was. The blood was smooth and flowing down the path to the left side of my current mountain. That direction appeared to be going downhill.

I finally reached the bottom of the mountain. My body was frail. My wounds were healing from all the damage the mountain did to me on the way down. A river of blood was close by. I did my best to crawl to blood. I noticed it healed me very fast earlier. My nails were digging into the ground and pulling me inch by inch to the blood. I slammed my head into the blood and drank from it. I didn't care that it was tainted. I just need to feel some relief from the pain.

The purple rain was pouring down hard. My face was under the blood, and I was trying to soak in whatever I could. I couldn't lift my head. I spent the whole time drowning in the blood in hopes of healing my wounds. I was in luck for once. The pain was subsiding enough to let me roll over in the stream of blood.

I sat up and realized. I had to figure a way out of this world of madness. I could either go up the stream or down. Downstream seemed easier for the time being. I walked in the direction to see what was down there. I didn't get far before realizing that the stream was creating a waterfall into a lake of blood. That was clearly not the way to go. I turned around and walked upstream.

The ravens were flying above me again. They were waiting for me to die. My feet were sore from no shoes. The constant number of times a stone had stabbed the bottom of my foot was getting out of hand. I kept tripping while walking up the stream until the purple blood rain stopped. The blood on my skin was drying. I was feeling sticky and could hardly see. The blood was sealing my eyes shut.

I walked further to see a hill. At the top of the hill was an old run-down church. The grass around it was dead and most of the land was black dirt and weeds. There was a lone black tree in the yard with not a single leaf on it. The branches were breaking from the slight wind that blew across the land. The church sounded like it was about to fall over.

I walked up to the church and saw the wood was gray. There was nothing fortifying or protecting the church. At least the churches back home were colorful and properly maintained on the outside. This church was clearly abandoned for a reason. The slightest touch to the pillars could make the whole thing crash down.

I walked over to the door. I didn't even have to twist the knob. It came open all on its own. The door creaked and almost fell off the hinges. The inside of the church was nothing but darkness at first. The windows were smashed out on the sides and glass covered the floor. The inside of the church looked like a battle took place.

My right foot crossed a threshold. The inside started to light up. The pews were filled with ghosts. At least it appeared to be ghosts. The aisle appeared to have tiny ghosts with white and black orbs in them. In fact, the ghosts in the pews had black and white orbs as well. This place reminded me of the church that I was in before coming here. I even recognized all the Priests that were standing behind the High Priest. It was strange that all the Priests had black orbs.

The High Priest had the darkest orb of anyone in the place. It was blacker than a moonless night. When I realized that all the orbs were the souls of the people in the church. I looked up to the front and noticed that my soul was white. I wondered what the colors could mean. The man dedicated his life to God. There was no way he was bad. At least, that's what I told myself back then.

I walked around all the souls in the aisle and looked at the location I was supposed to be. The orb was shining brightly, and the ghost looked small. In this place, I appeared to be over a foot taller than my body normally was. I walked around the ghost where I was. My eyes stared at the ghost version of me. A chill ran down my spine.

My body was raised five feet in the air still. My right hand reached up. It touched the orb in my body. A bright light shined. I couldn't see a damn thing. My body felt like it was dissolving. I became lighter than air and rose up. My soul from the ghost was crying out to me. I needed to reconnect with myself. My mind went blank and let the soul of my body be taken over. I merged with my ghost self.

I opened my eyes and there was the High Priest in front of me. My body was lying on the ground. I couldn't seem to move. I felt exhausted. There was a little blood in the back of my throat trying to come out. While trying to throw up, I smelled the air from the blood tickling the back of my nose. I smelled it. My blood smelled different. This time. It smelled like apples.

I turned my body over and looked at the church. The man in black was standing over my body. He was sweating and hyperventilating. Blood was rolling down his arms. He looked intense. I couldn't figure out why he appeared angry. His nose was twitching, and his teeth were grinding. His arms healed almost instantly in front of me.

My father was grunting. His shirt and pants were ripped to shreds. His skin was burned. I had never seen my father with burnt skin before. He was able to take on anything. I witnessed him grabbing hot pans with one hand all the time. My head was too fuzzy to figure out what happened yet. All I knew was everyone in the church was in shock.

The carpet below my body was burned. I could smell the stench of the carpet burns. The pews in the front weren't just shifted around. They had burn marks on them. The floor was covered in broken wood from the pews. Everything around me appeared to be destroyed. Even the podium that held my parchment looked broken.

The High Priest yelled, "Get him out of here and take your fucking parchment."

The High Priest threw the parchment on my body. I reached for it and realized my new suit was destroyed. My arms and legs ripped through the suit. I was practically naked on the floor in front of a bunch of children. I closed my eyes. My body was too weak to do anything. I felt the parchment pulled off my chest.

I heard Draco asked, "What happened here?"

My father replied, "There was an explosion. Give me a minute. I got this."

Draco said, "I'll get Lucas. You pick up your son. The carriage is waiting out front."

I felt my father take his arm and scoop me up. My legs were hitting against the pews while walking past all the children. He was holding onto me by my stomach and nothing else. My arms drooped down and touched the floor. I wanted to wake up, but the change was too much. That night, I became something else.

To be Continued... The Third Gate Saga Part 2

Photo created by Rapture

Curtis Yost Publishing 2025
All rights reserved